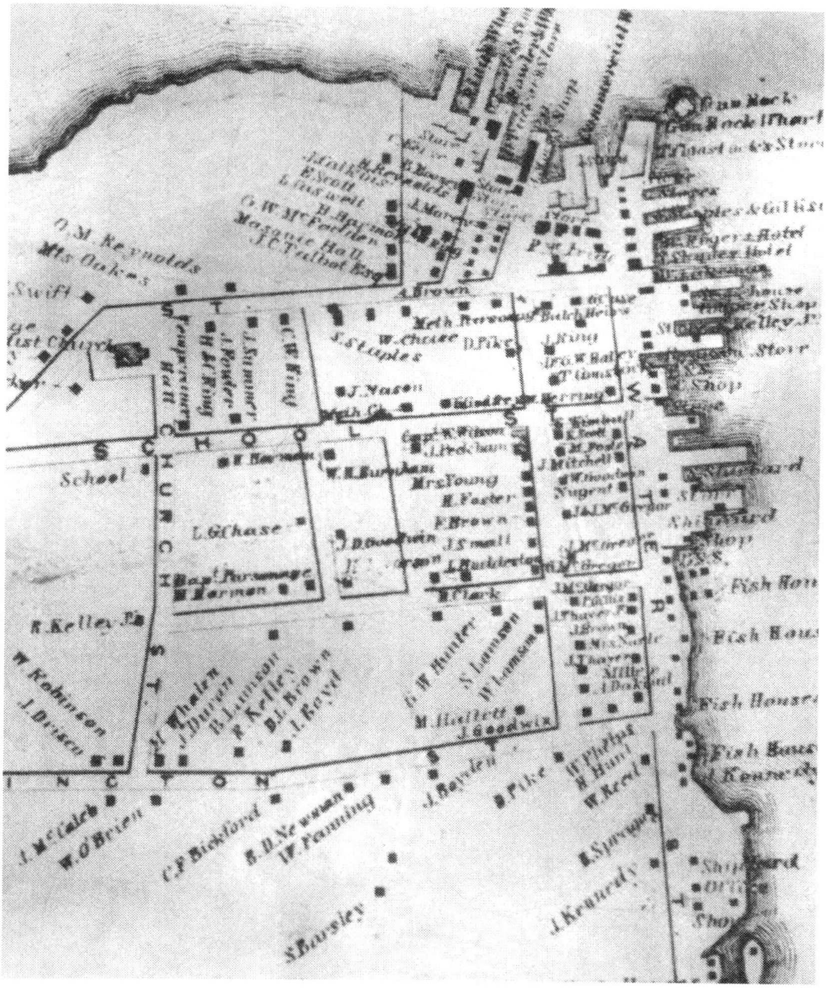

O. M. Reynolds
Mrs Oakes
Swift
Masonic Hall
J.C. Talbot Esq
G.W. McFadden
E. Scott
A. Brown
S. Staples
W. Chase
D. Pike
J. Nason
J. King
C.W. King
J. Sumner
School
L.G.Chase
Bapt Parsonage
H. Harmon
W.H. Burnham
Mrs Young
E. Foster
F. Brown
J. Small
J. Mitchell
Nugent
R. Kelley Jr
W. Robinson
S. Lamson
W. Lamson
M. Hallett
J. Goodwin
C.F. Bickford
W. Fanning
W. O'Brien
W. Reed
H. Hunt
J. Kennedy
S. Barsley
Fish House
Shipyard
Shop
Staples Hotel

COLD HARBOR

Copyright © 2017 by JD Rule

Published by South Bay Associates, Lubec Maine
jdrule@lubecscribbler.com
ISBN-13 978-1543119091

Cold Harbor is a blend of fiction and fact. Modern-day characters are entirely fictional and any resemblance to a real person is strictly coincidental. Modern-day places are real and the reader is invited to visit them. Of the historical characters, those based in Lubec are also mostly fictional however places and events are real. The Civil War travels and battles of the 6th Maine Volunteer Regiment have been carefully researched; they are real and documented and are as seen through the eyes – hopefully – of one who was there. The historical characters Freeman Lawton, Isaac Cooper, James Gaultier, and Elias Sheehan are fictional however all other regimental characters are real and every effort has been made to portray them faithfully.

Acknowledgements

The author wishes to express gratitude to those who have helped on this journey. The Peavey Memorial Library in Eastport, and particularly Dana Chevalier, patiently tolerated my lengthy reading of their microfilmed copies of the *Eastport Sentinel* and other materials, without which this project would not have been possible. Kathy Upton of the Cherryfield Free Public Library provided valuable material that helped bring to life Brigadier General Hiram Burnham. Davis Pike, of Lubec, provided maps that helped ensure that the Lubec of 1861 was correctly portrayed. Historians Kenneth Ross, Ivan Kossak, Bonnie Healy, and Lisa Rude Ph.D. provided their insights into particular aspects of the story and kept me straight. The Campobello Library and Lubec Memorial Library put up with my pestering insistence for details, and both the Montville Writer's Group and the writer's group meeting at CCLC helped keep my prose honest. More resources have been accessed than can be listed here, however many are listed in the bibliography. I owe in particular a debt of thanks to the people of Lubec, who have graciously endured my intrusive research.

Cover art by Sherry Ashby, Lubec Maine

Other works by JD Rule

<u>The Delsey Trilogy</u>
Bridge to Someday
Delsey
Johnson Canyon

Murphy's Revisited
Neap Tide
Monument Lot
Mowry Beach
Orion's Belt and Alnilam
Voices of the American Muse

<u>Due out shortly</u>
Buster Loman

Cold Harbor

Table of Contents

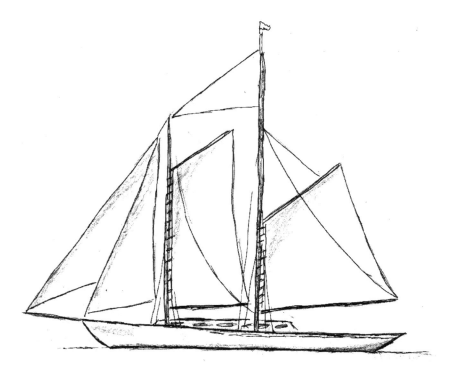

Chapter 1
The Journey Begins

The memory of the just is blessed: but the name of the wicked shall rot.

Proverbs 10:7

* * * * *

My Dearest Alma   *June 21, 1861*

    I am only to Portland and I already miss you some thing wicked. Last I seen you was on the pier waving your big yellow scarf over your head like it was a rainbow. I know it was me you was waving to but Alma do not worry I will be back soon. When the steamship rounded Flaggs Point and steered at the Narrows I knew I was waving good bye to you but this adventshure will only be for a short time. Col Knowles says it may even be over before we get to Washington.

    The trip down here was some thing special. I never been on a steamship before and the Eastern City[1] is a marvel. I remember when I helped build Gray Feather[2] in the yard in Eastport how tall them masts were like it was a wonder the moon could get by. Maybe that is why they called it a clipper ship on account of it clipping the sky. They call this here vessel a ship too but there aint enough canvas on them masts to make a boy a decent pair of britches just that thumping noise from below and that black smoke that sometimes comes down and makes ever thing stink of sulfur like it was the Divvuls breath blowing down on us with all them coals. I know what a ship is I have helped bild enuff of them but this is not like any ship I have bilt. If it is the Divvul making this ship go then he did make the trip to windward seem short. I never before seen the coast beyond that new light they put at Bass Harbor Head. I wish you could of seen it too.

It is good that Isaac Cooper and James Gaultier both signed up same time I did so now the three of us is together with the other Cobscook boys in Cmpny K. I know James misses Katherine but I be ready to bet a meal ration the girls back home are already wishing Isaac had not signed too. If they seen how fine he looks in that uniform with that big smile he has got I bet none would let go.

They finely gave me a uniform my size. I am sorry that when you kissed me good by my uniform made me look like I was wearing somebody else clothes the way my arms and legs all stuck out. I know I am the tallest in my company by a good two inches and may be that was why they did not have one in my size. James thought it quite funny said the Army would make me pay when I split the seams

Them parades in Eastport was something grand to see I am sure. The way they showed us to wheel in formashun and turn and keep in step with the sergents was sure different from working in the yard. When the Rebs see how we can do that and see our flags and heer our drummers they is going to turn tail and run and we will be right back home before the snow comes. They say they are going to learn us how to do these drills whilst carrying our muskets some time next week.

There is seventy four privates in Co K along with three officers and thirteen sergents and corprals. Menny is frum Trescott and Pembroke and Perry but we have a few from the British Colonies all the way up to Moncton. We elected Theodore Carey of Eastport to be our Captain[3]and Charles Witherell[4] is one of our sergents. All of our officers and sergents is frum Eastport none are frum Lubec.

Alma I hope you can understand why I felt cumpelled to join up. Growing up an hearing all the stories abowt my great grandpap Hiram and his brother my great uncle Hosiah fighting in the Revolution and being in the fray at Yorktown it was just some thing I feel I must do like may be it is in my blood. To me it was just the right thing to do to answer Father Abrahams call to save the Union. Be sides we are all ankshus that the boys from New York and Massachusetts do not get there first and end it before we can earn our share of the glory.

The 6 Maine is a three year regiment meaning ever one of us has agreed to serve for three years not like the 1 Maine that signed up for only 90 days. We all know that this war will not last that long and our officers tell us that we will be home long before this time next year.

I know tomorrow will be your birthday and I will not be around to help you selebrate being twenty. At least we know next year I will be with you and we can bake a cake together and do it all up just fine. I was rite sorry to give up my share of Achenars catch this year but Zadoc will understand and next May I will be out on Cape Sable with him at least you will be paid my share this year for the vessel.[5]

They are calling for mail so I must end right now. I will write again real soon.

Your Loving Husband
Pvt. Freeman Lawton
Company K, Eastern Battalion, Sixth Maine Volunteer Regiment

Practice had been good. A few strong hitters and a promising infield but the pitchers were going to need some work. This year's team might prove a winner, but probably not dominating like last year's. That day Herbie showed up on the diamond, even his own father thought him a hopeless klutz. Hidden talent like his doesn't come your way very often.

Richard paused momentarily in Clancy's little park, just to think about things. Those women, the ones who had glared at him from the sidelines like he'd committed some kind of mortal sin, it had only been a few seasons since he'd seen that but the vision still hurt. It was never his players' mothers, they were fine. The dagger-stares came from a handful of grandmothers and occasional great-grandmothers, those who bragged about family trees with Revolutionary roots.

3

Those women had made him feel as if he bore some kind of curse. If that were so, he'd thought all along, it would've been damned considerate if they'd clue him in as to what *that* was all about. They acted like they were sure he knew.

Six doors away, Amanda waited for him. Below, down on Water Street, balls clashed on Annie's pool table, punctuating the laughter and music from the nearby village tavern. Shreds of dirty snow and half-melted ice lurked beneath the shrubbery, stubborn reminders of a particularly brutal winter, but the monumental drifts had at long last followed the tides out to sea, flowing with the current under the bridge into the Bay of Fundy.

Richard Lawton, son of one of the older families in town, always enjoyed the sounds of springtime, the way they lifted the village out of the doldrums of a long Downeast winter. Two centuries of life in Lubec, the small town clinging precariously to the easternmost patch of rock in the United States had not always been idyllic but maybe tonight it was. Although the weight of the town's past was quite familiar, he'd learned to pay it no heed.

He had known from the start that Amanda Bellingham, the daughter of another of the town's older families, was one of the smartest people he'd ever meet, anywhere. But there was even more. That first Christmas morning after the foggy April day when they'd swapped rings and vows, the way she'd surprised him by lying concealed under the tree, wearing only a few strategically placed ribbons. It was like Mandy knew he would find her there, and that soft little giggle when he did...

So what was this nagging feeling that something was not right? It wasn't as if he'd awoken one bright sunny morning, peered into the tall narrow mirror with the bugle on top and declared to himself, *Shit! Now here we have a jolly fine mess!* There had never been such an epiphany, and he was at a loss to explain how he had come to that point. Perhaps whatever it was had been there all along, lurking in the darkened corners of the ancient mirror. They had often entertained each other by making up stories about what that glass may have witnessed, but so far it had proven reluctant to disclose its secrets.

"It seems odd," she had said one of those times they had lain awake, just talking, late into a hot July night, "How you have so much fun with other people's kids, but..." Maybe it was last summer, or perhaps the one before, just at the close of softball season.

It was the way she said it, not argumentative or anything, just a simple statement of fact – that was why he remembered it. "There are things," she'd said that night, "I cannot change." The way she pursed her lips, it was as if she swallowed the part that remained unspoken but clearly heard: "I am not getting any younger."

He recalled staring off into the darkness over their bed, trying to think how to answer, wondering whether he was merely being selfish, reluctant to share her affections, or if there was something else, perhaps dark and sinister. Not even his Aunt Elizabeth had ever said anything specific, beyond broad hints that *she knew things*.

5

"Mandy," he'd said. "We're not going to wait forever." He clenched his jaw, knowing that she recognized the waffle. It had never been her style to demand the last word – that was only one of the many reasons he loved her. Even though she made no reply, there was no doubt in his mind: *Amanda has not forgotten that conversation.*

My Loving Freeman   *July 1, 1861*

Saying good bye was the hardest thing I ever done. Only thing made it tolerable is I am so proud of what you are doing. Deacon Fowler says that you and the others are doing Gods work by ending slavery and releasing the negroes frum unholy bondage. I can not walk a block down Water Street without folks stopping me to ask if I heard from you and to say how proud you boys have made our town. Only Mrs Cooper keeps to herself like she is not happy her only son has gone off to fight and now Bernadette is all she has left.

You probly did not see James brother Michael. He was with Katherine when she waved good bye and wisht he could go but sense he just turned eleven they would not even talk to him. Michael was some wicked upset he could not be part of this but I do hope that he does not have the chance to be in another war when he is older.

The papers and speshully the Sentinel[6] they all have big articles about how you boys answered Father Abrahams call and took on the job of ending what Jefferson Davis started. They are going to be right sorry they started shooting at Fort Sumter back in April. By the time our boys have finished with them they will wish they had not done that.

The Deacon says it just is not right to say you own another person like they was a cow or a chicken. As far as I know the only negro in Lubec[7] is that man out Bassett Creek[8]. He mostly just keeps to himself on that farm but I never heard any body say nothing bad about him.

The town has got real hushed since the steamboat left with all the boys from Lubec and Eastport and Perry and Pembroke. It is like there is more than just the three[9] of you gone off from Lubec. But when it gets quietest is when I lay my head down and you are not here. Hurry up and get this over so I can hold you and hug you again.

Your loving and faithful wife
Alma

He lay in bed, listening to the wind pick at the loose clapboard up near the eaves. Amanda snored softly beside him, all soft and warm. It had been the cold, wet nose of Bonkers insistently poking its way under the blanket that first warned him that the night had ended.

At least with the wind blowing like that there'd probably be no fog. It wasn't so bad when it followed the tide in later in the day, like it does so often in Lubec, because then at least you know why it's there. Those days he'd wake up to the grey nothingness outside his window were just so damned depressing. But despite the fog he still had his work and the never-ending parade of requests from his clients. What would really be depressing? If that parade of requests were to end.

Leave it to the dog to be the one to awaken him.

On clear days he liked to just lie quietly for a few minutes and let his eyes wander around the Narrows and Campobello Island and wonder where the cars on the Roosevelt Bridge were going. April mornings were perfect for that, because it meant March had finally come to an end.

The worst thing about March was the way it teased with promises of spring but still let winter hang around. The best thing about March was that it meant softball season was beginning and he'd soon be heading out to the field with a duffle of gear and an armload of bats to coach the current crop of schoolkids. The *crack* of a well-swung bat against a hard-thrown ball – that was a sound he cherished. That, and the sweet leather smell of the mitt.

When the alarm sounded he reached over to silence it. "Good morning," she yawned, stretching her arms out like a cat on a sunny window ledge.

He made no reply. It seemed like none was needed, even when she reached over and stroked the side of his face. They lay in silence for a minute or so.

"Do you think," she asked quietly, "we need to get up right away?"

"Busy day today," he mumbled. "Have to get online with Detroit, gotta finish wrapping up this module today."

"You better get going." He recognized that she'd used her best matter-of-fact voice. If she was disappointed, he couldn't tell it from the way she kissed him before tossing back the blanket.

By the time he got showered and downstairs she had breakfast out. Scrambled eggs and toast, with black coffee and one of the muffins from the chocolate shop down the street. Just like he liked. While he poured himself a cup, he felt her arms surrounding his chest.

"You do know I love you," she murmured in his ear. "Right?"

"I know that," he said, trying to stifle a sigh. "I love you too. Always have."

"Just checking." She turned back toward the sink. He took his plate and wandered out to the deck, high over the harbor. He pulled out two chairs and wiped the night's dust off the table, sitting off to one side to make room for her.

Amanda sat down on the opposite side and picked up her fork. "So what's the deal with Detroit? Something due today?"

"It's the new behavioral module for their customer database. I uploaded it last night and they're testing it today. This morning I'm leading their owner service supervisor through the interface so her people can get up to speed."

"What time is that?"

"I'll meet her online at ten." He swallowed hard when he realized that she knew what that meant. His client didn't expect him online for nearly two hours, yet he still didn't have a half-hour to share with his wife.

"So where are you off to today?" he asked.

"This afternoon I'm in Meddybemps," she replied with a shrug. "Forty-five minute drive. Back for dinner. Don't forget tonight I'm calling Beano down the nursing home."

"Bonkers needs to go out," he said, gazing over the railing at the fishing boats in the harbor. "I'll take him around the block."

"Fine." She scooped up the empty plates and headed for the kitchen.

Richard followed the playful mutt towards the corner of Main and Pleasant where he would pass, as he did most days, the small park with the Civil War monument. Every town in Maine, or at least so it seemed, had a statue exactly like this one, or else one of the fellow's cousin. The statue in Lubec even had a name, "Clancy," but nobody seemed to know – or care – where that name had come from.

He remembered the hot July day when the big memorial plaque had been dedicated. When was that? He and Amanda were both going into the eighth grade, so it must have been 1996. By that time Clancy had been protecting the town for most of a century, watchfully surveying the harbor for intruders.

That steamy day, they were just a year from the point when their classes would be moved to the other side of those big doors, to the western end of the school where they'd join the other high-schoolers. Best part about that would be that the two of them would be largely out of sight of his Aunt Elizabeth. *Dizzy Miss Lizzie*, as all of the students called her except to her face, taught fifth-grade. Even in kindergarten he had this irksome feeling that she seemed to be trying to keep Amanda Bellingham out of his sandbox.

Anyway, that had been one of the rare Fourth of July speeches that he actually listened to. A state legislator, in town for the photo op with the head of the town's Board of Selectmen, pointed out that Maine had sent a greater proportion of its men to fight in the *War Between The States* than had any other state in the Union, and that many of the older families in town had their surname inscribed on the shiny black stone back in the rear of Clancy's little park.

After the crowd thinned out a bit, together they'd wandered back to where that particular list was displayed alongside other wars from other times, all engraved on the big rectangular granite slab installed a week or so earlier by the Historical Society. Sure enough, there was a Lawton on that list but Mandy searched in vain for any Bellinghams. There were also many more where the family name was currently listed in the phone book, including a few he knew as close friends. All in all, 187 names and this from a town that totaled a mere 1290 male residents at the time.[10]

Ever since that fleeting moment, he couldn't escape the feeling that Clancy was more than just carved stone, that there was a soul in there that had some kinship with his own.

"Morning, Richard." When he looked up, he spotted Silas Gaultier kneeling down to pat the dog. Bonkers seemed to turn himself inside out for the older man with his handlebar moustache, ready smile, and booming laugh. "How's the missus this morning?"

"Silas, you know how it is, she's just…"

"She's peachy keen, that's what you were going to say." He glanced up for a second but continued scratching behind the dog's ear. "Right?"

"What, have I said that before?"

"I hope you know you caught yourself the prettiest woman in town," Silas chuckled. "But that's all you ever say about her."

Richard smiled and turned to leave. "Hey!" Silas called out. When he turned back, Silas continued. "That was quite a team you turned out last year. Think you can do *that* again?"

Following Bonkers back to the house, Silas' words kept rolling around his head. 'Did I catch Amanda, or did she catch me? Time was, we were playmates and – what were we, six? – that time Aunt Elizabeth caught us 'playing doctor?' *What a hissy fit she threw!* Our first time wasn't until ten years later, when we were both headed off to college. And now we've been married eight years.'

My Dearest Alma   *July 4, 1861*

We marched in the Fourth of July parade in Portland today. I think I druther watched the parade from under a shade tree with a cup of cold water or maybe a cider. They were so happy to see us here they forgot that even tough soldiers like us need some thing to drink[11]from time to time.

Hearing all the fine speeches for our countrys birthday put me in mind to think of what my Great Grandpap Hiram and Uncle Hosiah went through to make our grate country what it is and how sad it makes me feel to see it breaking apart like this. I can do no less then what they done.

I wish you could see some of the Old Town boys from Bangor Batallion I Company. Ever body says I am tall and I is the tallest in K Company but these boys all stand above me. They calls them the Jam Brakers because they are all lumberjacks and they go out on the river to brake up log jams in the spring. The tallest man in the Regiment is Lt Reuel Furlong[12]a schoolteacher from Calais of D Company.

My company and most of the Eastern Batallion is mostly shipyard workers like me and fishermen and a little of ever thing else like tanners and spar makers. But we is all one regiment the 6 Maine and we shall fight as one.

A lot of the boys wanted Hiram Burnham[13] to be the Colonel but Governor Washburn give that to Abner Knowles[14] instead. Sergent Witherell told me Burnham had militia experience from 1839 when he took a company to Calais[15] becawse ever body thot the British were going to invade. Sense that was the year before I was born I do not know abowt that but he is older then most here has gray hair but knows how to get boys to want to do what they need to do.

I met Mister Burnham once before but many of the boys thet worked for him in the woods sed god things abowt him. He owns a lumber business out Cherryfield and we bought a lot of his wood for all the barques and brigs we bilt the last few years. The boys who worked with him thought he should be Colonel but instead the Governor made him Lieutenant Colonel. The boys call him Old Grizzly[16]on account of his whiskers make him look like a bear.

Colonel Knowles says we will learn to march just like it says in the Hardees[17]book.

Charles Witherell[18]from Eastport got in a tussle with Isaac and clearly come out the better so may be he is the right one to be Sergent.

Let me tell you abowt the boys in my company. There is none from rich families but we comes mostly from near salt water.[19] We has got a number of woodsmen and a few joiners like me. There is some from up Moncton and other parts of the British country an even a Irishman. You should hear how he talks hardly no body can understand what he says. There is a few worked as clerks and a couple of drovers and a bunch of sailors. Why they did not sign up Navy I do not know. A right scrappy group as you might ever come acrost an most wearing rough shoes and homespun. There is other companies in the 6 Maine come from other places but still there is nobody cepting folks like us. If you draw a line from Bangor to Ellsworth ever man in the regiment come from east of that line.

Yesterday they gived us our muskets and we started learning how to march the right way with them. They say they weigh fourteen pounds but if you ask me it is a bunch more then that. Smoothbore with percussion caps[20] and longer then the squirrel gun Pops always had hanging on the wall. Sergent says that these muskets are all converted from old flintlocks. It has got a big bayonet a pointed spike that you can fix on the end of the barrel that the boys call a pig sticker. But now when we march we carry the musket. The way they have us marching our left elbow touches the musket carried by the man to our left and the man on our right is touching our own musket.[21] I heer we be learning to shoot these pretty soon. I hope so. Do not see no purpose in toting it round if I can not learn to shoot it.

We have been getting instrukshun in bayonet and swords frum Sgt Isaac Ambler[22]who come from the British Army. He is not a member of the Regiment but Col Knowles asked him to help teach us how to use those weapons. Looks like we will be here in Portland for a little while marching in big circles out on that dusty parade field.

Your Loving Freeman, Private, Sixth Maine Volunteer Reg'mnt

My Dearest Freeman   *July 8, 1861*

     Yesterday Reverend Smith had a special prayer service for the boys who have gone off to fight. I did not want to go but Mum said it would be disrespectful to the new Pastor[23] if I did not so I did. I do not want to pray for you. I want to hold your hand and walk down the street with you and let everbody see you is mine.

     You remember Elias Sheehan. Being a fisherman he did not spend much time in town but now he is gone off and joined the Navy. When they heerd how much time he had spent working on the Ellie Mae and the other schooners way out on the Grand Banks they made him Able Bodied Seaman right away and put him on a Navy sloop called Cumberland. When he left several of the girls was really mad but the maddest of all was Gwyneth Josephine. She put up such a row so now people are saying may be the two of them got together quiet like and done something and now he is running off. I do not know. I can see Gwyneth doing something like that but it do not seem like Elias to run off if that is what he done with her.

     Freeman I do worry about you when you are off with the Army like this. It is my job to tend to your soul and keep you thinking good thots and away frum the playthings of the Divvul. When we are together you protek me from one kind of harm and I protek you from an other kind. That is a womans right full job and I take my task serious. Pleeze do not think I do not trust you I do trust you but I do not trust the Army to look after you like I would do.

     At the Post Office they tell me I have to be payshunt because getting your letters here might take some time. I do not want to be payshunt. I know you have signed up for three years but we all know this thing will be over before this year ends. I want you to hurry home.

Your loving wife,
Alma

Please do not pay attention to my clumsy writing. I never rode on a train before so I also never before wrote a letter whilst riding on a train.

It was starting to look like we would never get out of Portland and that the war would be over before we got to be part of it and we would spend it all on the parade field marching in circles for the Colonel. I think Grizzly Burnham is bored with all the drilling but he has to do what Colonel Knowles says. So we march in circles.

At least I got to practice with the musket and the bayonet. Sergeant Witherell says we have to learn to load aim and fire at least three times per minute[24]but I do not see how that is possible. You have to bite the end off the paper cartridge wif your teeth pour the powder down the muzzle put the ball in the barrel ram it down hard pull the hammer back to the second click then put a cap on the nipple. Then you can aim and shoot and start all over again. After five shots your face is all black from the powder. They say if you are not careful you might think it fired but it did not then you put in a second charge and may be even a third.[25]

Riding on a train is lots better then riding on a buggy. You can get up and walk around and look out the windows on both sides. Them windows can be open but then some times all the smoke from the engine comes pouring in just lak on that steamship and some times cinders fly in so most of the time we keep them closed. The noise makes it hard to talk but you get used to the shaking and some times if you are lucky you can sleep.

There is even a toilet on each car. If you look down it you see the wooden parts of the track passing by.

I do not know how fast a train goes. Some of the boys said they thought it was so fast it was at least twenty knots. Do not seem right to me that some thing this big could akshully go that fast but I guess I just do not know. Some day I will take you some where on a train so you can see one of these things too for yourself. We are going to stop for the night in some place called Philadelphia. I know I spelled that right because Sergeant told me how.

James showed me a pocket knife Katherine gived him as a going away present. It is a beautiful Barlow with bone handles and a sharp blade. He is right proud of that because she gived it to him and sometimes I catch him just holding it and staring at it. I know that James misses Katherine some thing awful just like I miss you.

I will write again soon.

Your loving husband, Private Lawton

The on-line conference had gone well. The supervisor was a good study and she picked up the entry process quickly, just like he expected. It helped that all of the edits and cross-checks were programmed in, so it would be tough for one of her clerks to enter incorrect data.

Before the call started Amanda headed down the street to visit Nana Bellingham at the nursing home, a seven-minute walk, and would soon be taking off for her appointment at a town so small it made Lubec look like a big city. Didn't matter, she worked for the county and they wanted her to stay in touch with even the smallest municipality.

Every now and then Richard went along on her visits with "Nana Bell," as she liked to be called. "Nobody wants to say my whole name," she would often say, "and that's fine with me." Until the time she'd fallen she'd been rather nimble, but now was pretty much bedridden. Her hips were a problem but there wasn't anything wrong with her ninety-three-year-old head. Nothing, that is, beyond her penchant for remembering things from long ago as though they had just happened.

"I don't want to live in the past," he'd protested once to Amanda, begging off on one of her nearly-daily trips.

"She's the only one from that generation either of us have left," she'd replied. In that she was right. Both of his grandparents had passed on, years ago, as had her grandfather. Still, with both sets of parents scattered between Pembroke and Steinhatchee, holiday meals were always a big deal.

A little after five Amanda returned, lugging a bag of groceries. "How'd your call go?"

"It went well," he replied. "Already started my next project."

Amanda didn't reply, just started putting away the groceries. He pulled down a couple of wine glasses and poured each a comfortable three fingers of a nice Malbec.

"I'll have to go and sit with the client for a couple days before I get too far into this one."

"Oh?" She continued with the groceries. "Which client is this?" When he motioned towards the deck she put the ice cream in the freezer then followed him out. The harbor spread below their feet, sparkling like a bowl of gemstones in the afternoon breeze, and the crew of a fishing boat noisily negotiated their catch with the wholesale buyer on the nearby commercial pier. He spotted the big blue tote perched on the scale on the back of a refrigerated truck, loaded with early-season lobster destined for some place downcoast.

She sat down and leaned back. "I'm meeting with Aladdin Research," he replied.

"So you're off to Atlanta."

"It's only a couple days."

"Got it." She may have intended to conceal her resigned sigh, but he still heard it. "When're you going?"

17

"Next week. I'll be back Thursday. Friday's our first game, find out who's really playing ball this year."

"Remember," she said, turning back toward the harbor, "That's the day I'm volunteering at the Food Pantry."

My Dearest Freeman   *July 15, 1861*

It will be good when you boys put an end to all this nonsense and come home. All the papers say it will be over before Christmas. If you ask me that is already too long but if it has to be then we will make the best of it.

Things have been very quiet here in Lubec specially with you and the others gone. There is no more parades but Reverend Smith and the other Pastors preach every Sunday about the evils of slavery. I still do not know what a Negro looks like but that does not matter soon enuf they will be free and maybe some might want to come live here.

It made me feel good that you saw me with the yellow scarf. It means so much to me because it was the first birthday present you gave me after we were married. I know you paid more for that then you could afford but sense you got it from one of the ship owners you done some work for it meens no body else in Lubec or any where else has one just like it.

Mister Watkins came over the other day said he wanted to talk to me. He said that he missed having you work for him and wondered if I need a job. I told him I am not a joiner like you. I would not be much good in the yard and do not know an adze from a bit brace but he said he hoped I would come work for him in his office. Said he needed a woman to keep figures and talk to visitors and thought I would do it just fine. He told me he used to do this work but now with so many men going off to fight he does not have enuff time to spend in the office he needs in stead to be in the yard. I told him I wud think about it and let him no.

Even with the boat building business being slack like it is right now he has work to do. They laid up the keel for a new schooner just last week. Seventy footer displacing almost seventy ton. With you off to the war I am thinking about doing this I need the money but also I need to be busy.

Yesterday a new kind of vessel came into Eastport. They call it a barkentine. It is like a bark except it has two fore-and-aft sails like a schooner but also a single square rig forward like a ship. It is bigger than a schooner maybe three hundred fifty ton and can carry cargo acrost to England. They say it handles with a smaller crew than a ship. This one is called Artemis. I will see if I can get you the name of the builder. I wish you were here to see it.

I wish you were here.

Your loving Alma

"Rack 'em up sweetheart." Richard turned from the noisy bar towards the front of the room. "Your break."

"Must you insist on compelling me to take candy from a baby?" Dana Cooper looked back at Richard while he continued dropping the balls into the frame.

"I love how foolish you look when you scratch." Richard rotated the cube of chalk against the cue stick, attempting to produce an irritating squawk.

"Yeah yeah yeah." Dana pulled back on his own stick, preparing to fire the cue ball into the triangle of colored balls. "You stand back. We'll see who plays the clown."

Richard turned toward the bar to retrieve the two beers waiting for him and his childhood chum. He knew it'd be a few

19

minutes before he had his chance at the table. He paused mometarily to scan the license plates on the wall behind the bar and wondered if there was one from Georgia.

Dana Cooper and his wife Claire had both graduated from Lubec High the year after Richard and Amanda, in a class of twenty-one students. By that time he had already acquired that rarity – a brand new lobster license – having been able, thanks to his uncle, to take the student route. Richard and Amanda were two out of seventeen; he was the standout pitcher who had gone on to study computers and psychology while she became a social worker. Richard and Dana often argued over which one had done better. It was always a friendly argument, because both had fine homes and spectacular wives. The small class sizes led the town, not so many years later, to close the high school but the memories all remained intact.

"Six in the corner." Dana cheerfully pointed his cue stick at the far end of the table, towards the left corner.

"So how're you and Claire making out with the little one?" asked Richard, hoping to break his friend's concentration and interrupt the parade of balls dropping off the table, each one properly announced in advance. It was like they were following secret orders, the annoying way Dana went about mopping up the table. "It's been two months, right?"

"Hank, he's gonna be a big one," replied Dana. "Three in the side." He lined up for a cross-table shot and loudly sank it. "He's up to fourteen pounds. Already got him signed up as my new sternman."

"Fourteen pounds!"

"She's having trouble keeping up with him, says he sucks her dry." Dana moved to the other side of the table and glanced up. "So when're you guys gonna start. You waiting for me and the old lady to pop out our third?" The way he laughed made Richard wince, knowing that more was coming. "Let me guess. You're sending Mandy off to all those town committees to keep her from asking."

"Nine in the corner," Dana continued. "I got it. You're still practicing, right?"

"Go to hell, pest."

"Sure thing." Dana pointed at the pocket below his elbow. "Eight ball in the side. I just hope you're keeping up with business. Lotsa guys would love to help you out." Just friendly banter, Richard reminded himself. He knew Mandy too well to take his friend's taunt as any kind of warning.

Dana pulled back the stick and dropped the last ball remaining on the table. The cue ball, responding to the backspin, gracefully retreated to the center of the table. "You still in this?"

Richard pulled another twenty out of his pocket. "Just you wait."

"You got me on pins and needles." Dana racked them up again. "But I'm sure beholden to you for helping out like this so's baby can get them new shoes."

"Glad to oblige, asshole."

"I just knew it." Dana lined up for the break. "Claire and Amanda, you know Wednesday's girl's night out. That's when you're away, right? My turn to mind the kids."

"Yeah," replied Richard. Since none of the balls had dropped, it was finally his turn and he stepped up to the table. "I'll be in Atlanta."

"Atlanta!" Dana looked up with a grin. "Sounds like an old WC Fields line."

"What are you going on about?" mumbled Richard, lining up for his first shot.

Dana forced a theatrical monotone. "First prize was a week in Atlanta."

"Two in the corner," replied Richard, scowling at the table.

"Second prize," rumbled Dana, "was *two* weeks in Atlanta."

"Damn!" Richard looked at the table in disbelief as the purple four-ball dropped into the side, leaving the blue two-ball abandoned in the middle of the table.

"Golly gee," Dana smirked. "How could *that* happen?" As he lined up to take the next shot he added, "Off our game a bit today, are we?"

To My Loving Wife   *July 23, 1861*

So much to tell this time. We are in Washington right acrost the river from Virginia and have heerd the cannons in the distance.

We got into Philadelphia at midnight but still they had to give speeches.[26] Along with the speeches they gived us coffee so hot it makes you feel lak you just had a good night sleep. The coffee was real good and the officers thought the speeches were mighty fine but the boys was all ready falling asleep.

Next morning we was on to Washington and in a big hurry. They were not telling us much but it did sound like some thing was going on. When we stopped at a place some where in Maryland called Haver de Grace a turrible thing heppened. Man from New Brunswick in Company C got shot[27]whilst sitting in his seat in the

22

train car. He walked off but bleeding. I heard somebody was wrassling over a musket outside the car it fired and the ball went through the side of the car an hit him. The train left without him and a couple days later we were told he was dead. This got me to thinking that may be this might not be just abowt waving flags and marching in circles.

We got into Washington late at night and marched through the city to our encampment. Our route took us past a big white house that they said was where the President lives. When we went marching down the drive he come out and stood on the steps watching as we went past.[28] That was the first time I ever laid eyes on a President. Father Abraham is very tall and even in the dark I saw sadness in his eyes like he fears this thing might not end like Colonel Knowles tells us it will.

Next morning we were sent to guard a bridge over the Potomac called Chain Bridge. Off in the distance we heerd cannon fire and ever body said it was our boys beating up on the Rebs so we all cheered and wisht we cud join the fray.

They moved us acrost the bridge into the woods on each side of the road because they said that way we cud surprise the Rebs if they tried to come acrost. We stayed in those woods the rest of the day and all night too.

Alma I wish I did not have to tell you what I seen from them woods. In the middle of the afternoon crowds started coming our way from Virginia. They was all disorganized and confused and many were running scared like. Some of them wore uniforms but was not carrying muskets[29] and there were even some fancy folks that did not look at all like soldiers headed towards our bridge riding in carriages pulled by fine horses. The cannon fire did not seem to be coming any closer.

One fancy coach went by so close I cud have reached out and teched it. I never seen one like that before all painted and gay. It had a man and a woman and two young children all dressed in finery like we never seen in Lubec. The man had a fancy coat with all kinds of buttons but no hat but the woman did and she was waving a fancy little ombrella and the children was crying. Up in front I seen a black man he must have been a Negro and he was driving the coach some hard. He had on a fancy green coat with the back hanging down below the seat and he had on a tall black hat. His seat was covered in some kind of red cloth but he was pushing them two horses like the very Divvul was chasing them all.

We was ordered to hold our positions on both sides of the road on the Virginia side and to prepare to defend the bridge from the Rebs and keep them frum crossing but none of them come near just crowds of people running towards the city behind us. There was a few companies marching and carrying muskets and quite a few who were wounded. Some of the wounded were walking and some were in carts with their arms hanging over the side. I saw a couple of men with blood all over.

We never fired one shot that day but we was sure ready to. Later we heerd a couple of the officers talking abowt a place called Manassas and a battle they was calling Bull Run.[30]From the look of things I do not think we was the winner in that battle. I heerd the 2 Maine had a hard time of it lost a lot of men.

Maybe this war will not be over as fast as we hoped. You may not think it is so but I am still looking forward to my first fight. I did not come all this way to just turn around and go home.

Just now they handed me over your letter of July 8. I am not surprised Elias done signed up with the Navy. Long as I knowed him he wanted seawater under his shoes just like his Pap and this would be just like him. Gwyneth always had her eye on him since we was all young uns. If they done something they may be should not have done it would not be a surprise.

Keep them letters coming because it is what keeps me going. I see you in my dreams waving that yellow scarf and want to feel you in my arms.

Your Loving Freeman

He stared out of the airplane window, watching as Bangor fell beneath the wing, wondering how things had gotten so mixed up. *Sure I love my wife, and Silas is right.* Lubec has its share of lookers, but she is by far the tops. What is it that's happening to me, I won't give her what she wants, deserves? I know it's not an equipment

24

problem. It can only be in my own head. Sunday morning she told me she was satisfied, but her eyes said otherwise. *Never in my life have I as much as kissed another woman.*

The flight rumbled on. The one-thirty departure had been simple enough to make, in fact was easy given the two-hour plus ride to the airport. The connection was tight, but it would get him in at six-thirty so this way he'd be fresh in the morning. He knew he could get away with looking, shall we say, sub-optimal when doing his coding, falling through the screen and haunting the magic caves where the *lingua franca* is based on arcane computer tongues denied the layman. But not when sitting in the client's marble-table conference room surrounded by managers, each demanding to know how he would actually justify the big bucks each one had to carve out of an already tight budget. To pull that off, a good night's sleep and a fresh shave is critical.

He let his mind move on. Last year's season, that was something special, the way it turned out. Nobody could recall the last time a local team made it to the championship, and to lose the big game in a squeaker was still something to be proud of. Who'd a guessed Herbie had an arm like a cannon? Certainly not his own parents. The disparaging comments the kid's father made about him the day he simply dropped him off were disappointing, to say the least, but with a bit of encouragement the loser became the winner. *It wasn't me did that, it took the entire team.* But look what we did! If he plays his cards right, maybe even a scholarship is in the offing.

The plane touched down in Philadelphia. He'd have to make a mad dash to get to the next gate, and hope that his checked luggage would find its way through the system somehow.

He settled back as the jet accelerated down the tarmac, waiting for that point when the overhead compartments stopped rattling and the plane lurched skyward.

When he closed his eyes, Nana Bell's words came back to him, from one of his infrequent visits. Maybe it was half a year ago; he'd sat on one side of her bed and Amanda sat on the other. "You know," she'd said, with a note of triumph in her voice and reaching for Amanda's hand, "this is the first time *ever*, a Lawton has taken a Bellingham's hand in marriage. In fact," she'd added with a flash in her eyes, "time was, no Lawton would even *speak* to the likes of us."

Was there some connection here, to what his meddlesome Aunt Elizabeth had said that one time? She wasn't even truly his aunt – only his mother's second cousin, older than her by eleven years. Despite marrying fisherman Lucas Willett, Elizabeth never let anyone forget she had Lawton blood coursing through her veins. The morning after the tenth-grade dance she'd confronted him.

"You and *Miss* Bellingham," she'd said, leveling the kind of knuckle-busting stare that schoolteachers must stay up at night practicing, "I *do* hope the two of you had a good time last night."

He'd stammered through assuring her that they did, hoping that as chaperone she hadn't noticed they'd quietly slipped off into the night an hour before the event ended. But why else would she have tracked him down, dragging him out of second period math class like that? She must know. *She had to.*

"You might want to stop in and talk to your grandmother," she had said that morning. The way she faced him down in the hallway he was sure the sheriff was waiting out front. It wasn't so much what she *said*, it was how she said it. Richard decided right then that he had deeper feelings for Amanda than for Grandma Lawton. He'd assured *Miss Lizzie* he'd do just that, but somehow the time was never right. Not once had his mother said anything that suggested she was aware of that conversation or, for that matter, that Grandma Lawton had any kind of privileged information he'd think important.

My Dearest Husband   *July 24, 1861*

I hear that Philadelphia is a lot bigger place than Lubec. You are seeing things I have only read a little about. After this is all over we can take a trip and you can show me these places.

I started my new job at the yard a few days ago. What I do is get work hours and lists of supplies used and invoices from the various different parts of the yard then enter them in a big book according to what vessel they are working on. Once a week I do my sums then Mister Watkins pays the men and the lumberyard. It is interesting work because I am in the office most of the day and talk to so many people from drovers up to ship masters and owners. They all ask about you. You have many friends here.

It did not make me happy that Rodman Bellingham has also been hired here but may be it will work out all right. I do not need to be his friend to do what I am expected to do.

Mister Watkins gets newspapers from all over and he lets me take them home after he is done. I read the Eastport Sentinel regular and also the Saint John Morning Freeman and some times others like from Moncton and Calais. They talk a lot about the war and what is going on and do not all ways say the same thing about what has happened. Some times I read the Machias Union but it does not look like they support the war like the Sentinel.

Mister Jeffers a lawyer from New York with the group having the new schooner bilt come up to see Mister Watkins. He told us about a speech given by one of the top Rebels in Georgia. In that speech he said that slavery is the cornerstone[31]of the Confederate sosiety. Mister Jeffers said Corner Stone was the word he used and said if that is how they see it then the only right way to end the war is either for the Union to win or the Rebels to give up slavery. I hope this is not right because if it is this thing may not be over so soon.

I see Katherine Gaultier in church and also at the church library. Sometimes she shows me the letters that James has sent. Sometimes I show her your letters too. Isaac sends letters to his mum but she does not share them with any body. I think she is real sad her only boy has gone off to fight. Bernadette some times talks about her brother but she more often wants to talk about how demon rum is luring people to the Devil.

27

Mum is worried about the First Christian Church because Elder George Garraty has left and many parishoners went with him to start a new church they call The Disciples of Christ[32] right acrost the street from Big White. They took over the old Temperance Hall that the Masons got from the Sons of Temperance but never used.[33] I hear that building was not very nice but may be the Disciples cleaned it up because that is where they are meeting.

Some say the Elder was preaching heresy[34] but I do not know about that. I think Pastor Smith is satisfied that Brother Garraty has departed with those who chose to follow him even though it was half the congregation.

There is maps at the church library so I can look to see where you might be. Maybe when you get to Baltimore you will have more news. It means so much to me when I hear from you.

Your Loving Alma

Chapter 2
Cyprians

"… its foundations are laid, its corner-stone rests, upon the great truth that the negro is not equal to the white man; that slavery subordination to the superior race is his natural and normal condition. This, our new government, is the first, in the history of the world, based upon this great physical, philosophical, and moral truth…"[35]

Alexander H. Stephens, CSA
Vice-Presidential Inaugural Speech, March 21, 1861

* * * * *

My Loving Husband   *August 3, 1861*

Maybe I should not say anything yet. They say it brings bad luck to talk about things before you know you are right. But this news I can not keep back from you.

I think I am going to have your baby. Please do not say anything to your friends yet not until I know. I have not said any thing to Mum yet about this but I know what the signs are and I am seeing them. It is exciting to think that you and me might bring another Lawton into this world.

The papers are full of that battle you wrote to me about. They call it Bull Run and one paper said it was The Great Skedaddle the way some of the Army just turned and ran. If the Six Maine was in the fray I am sure it would have been the Rebs to run. Here is what the Sentinel said I will write it just as it was printed.

This is but the beginning of the end. The feeling of every man is that the war must be prosecuted to a successful issue, let the time, the loss of life, the sacrifice of property be what it may, without a government all these things are of little value.[36]

Mum says that it is a trying time at the church right now. So menny of the members followed Rev Garrity to his new church that they are not sure if they can carry on like before. I do not know what the difference is sence I do not belong to the church like Mum does but she is quite upset by what has happened. The building that they moved into the old Temperance Hall[37]*was in such sorry shape the Masons would not use it.*[38]

Rev Charles Smith is in the First Christian pulpit right now at Big White and Deacon Fowler says he is a good man and not a heretic like Brother Garrity. Reverend Smith says we all should pray for the soldiers because maybe you will not be home for Christmas like we all figured when you left. I miss having you with me specially now.

Your Alma

Richard's reverie was interrupted when the flight attendant brought him the glass of ginger ale he had forgotten asking for. The ice rattled in the plastic cup but he resisted the urge to suck on it. Far beneath the wing Washington slipped by while the pilot skirted a nearby thunderhead.

"No Lawton would ever speak to the likes of us." What the hell did Nana Bell mean by that? Sure she was an old woman given to rambling about bygone years, sometimes well gone by, as if they were just yesterday. But if I went back to ask her about that now she'd just hike up her left eyebrow and say how *absolutely* pleased she was that I'd found her words worthy of consideration, specially after so much time had passed.

30

Maybe I have. But I don't want Nana Bell to know that, or Amanda either, as far as that goes. When she and her grandmother put their heads together I have no idea where such a question might go, only that the two of them are certainly going to be cooking up some kind of hash.

How about that comment from – what was it? – twelve, thirteen years ago... Could it possibly have anything to do with the way my own grandmother reacted when Amanda and I stopped by, early the same day as the Senior Prom? Some memories last longer than others, and some are indelible.

It was well understood at the time that there were only a few blank pages left in Grandma Lawton's diary, so we were all taking turns visiting her and this happened to be my day. I had rather hoped that bringing Amanda, at that point my steady girlfriend, would have made the visit less dreary, maybe even sparked some interest instead of my grandmother's normally caustic outlook.

Not that anything would make it a pleasant task, mind you, since she had long ago determined to defend the role of family curmudgeon, but she was still family, so you did what you needed to do. When it was your turn, you hiked up your pants and went in with a smile.

"Is this the one your Aunt Elizabeth told me about?" she'd asked in her most imperious manner, leveling a bony finger at Amanda. "She's one of those Bellinghams, *right*?"

As far as Richard knew, Grandma Lawton had never attempted getting to know Amanda or even spoken of her family, and therefore had no call to be so dismissive. Amanda simply smiled gracefully at the interrogation but he knew from the color of her ears that she was seething.

When he'd confirmed that this beautiful young woman by his side was indeed Amanda Bellingham, Grandma Lawton simply turned her head and refused to speak. The two of them stood alongside her bed like a couple of imbeciles for what seemed like hours then quietly left, another word not having been spoken by any. He was determined not to let his grandmother's nameless grudge cheat them out of what was supposed to be a grand day that would culminate in a long-planned celebration.

Who could blame Amanda for her obvious dismay when they walked together out of the nursing home? She'd been warned that Grandma Lawton often became cantankerous, but this did seem a bit excessive. Richard had no answer for the obvious question.

A few days after the funeral he'd asked his mother what his grandmother had against Amanda. "I have no idea," she'd replied. "Probably something to do with long ago."

"Long ago?" he'd asked, puzzled. "How long ago?"

"Years before her own time," she had replied, "from the precious little I've heard. Silly superstition, some kind of a curse." He had never gotten any farther than that but the question still called out for some kind of answer. It had been a long time since the matter had been raised... Why was it still festering, and what did it have to do with Amanda?

"Those of you seated on the left side," intoned the captain in a soft southern drawl and interrupting his reverie. "If you look off just a bit you'll see Fredericksburg. Some of the bloodiest days of the Civil War happened right down there at the base of that hill."

Richard glanced down, slightly irritated at the intrusion. From five and a half miles up the place looked no different than any other medium-sized town. "Why is that interesting?" he asked himself. "That was a long time ago." His eyes followed the nearby river as far to the east as he could see. He wondered where it went and if it meant anything, before closing his eyes again.

Everybody in town knew the story of how, as a sixth-grader, Amanda Bellingham had taken top honors in the state Spelling Bee, making her way to the finals in Washington before being eliminated in the last round. On her return home the Lubec Fire Department met her at the Whiting Corner and proceeded, with flashing lights and wailing siren and accompanied by a parade of honking cars, to escort her back the final ten miles – an honor normally reserved for athletic tournament victors.

"I wasn't even sure what the word meant," she'd confided to Richard years later. "Standing up there in front of that huge audience and those cameras and lights, the way they groaned when I put down the fourth letter as 'i,' it was clear I'd missed it. I mean, what normal person would ever say '*antediluvian*'?"

But the worst part, the way she told the story, was when the bespectacled boy from Akron with the unpronounceable Indian name got "*nonpareil*" and then the blue-eyed girl out of Salt Lake City with the blonde pony tail got "*vexillate*" she thought she'd been sandbagged. "Those words I knew," she laughed. At any rate, the episode was neither resented nor forgotten, and she'd vowed to get it right when the next opportunity to use her special word came around.

Far below, the rolling hills of the western Virginia piedmont slipped under the wing and the plane continued its rumble deeper into the South.

My Dearest Alma   *August 8, 1861*

It made me feel right good getting your letter seeing the marks on the paper I know was done by your hand. Some of the boys have not heerd from nobody and they is some wicked unhappy when they see ever body else getting mail but not them. When I gets a letter from you I feel good for a week.

They say a soldiers life is supposed to be excitement but do not ask me because I would say different. Since that big battle we have been in Washington not doing much except marching. They say there is no big battles going on so may be we are not missing any thing but it still is not so much to keep us busy.

I never seen so many women walking around with nothing to do. Some of the boys call them Cyprians[39] but I do not know where that name come from. What I heered was that for money they will do anything a man wants them to do. Isaac tole me that he paid one and then he said he went for a ride with a Dutch gal. Maybe you should not tell Missus Cooper that part. Maybe he will. Probly not. Them gals is all over the place and they make it hard to stay away. If a boy just looks at one of them she will put her arm in his and try to pull him aside. Do not you worry none abowt me. I will not do that.

Let me tell you abowt Washington. You know I have not spent much time in cities but this is not what I thot I would see. Pennsylvania Avenue is the biggest road through the city and it is a muddy ditch that we do not want to march in.[40] In Philadelphia we saw streets that were paved but here may be they forgot to do that. James and me went looking around yesterday and saw the Capitol building. There is a big crane sticking out of the middle and it looks like someday there will be a dome but right now is only walls that go part way up but no body is working on them. We got to talking with a boy from a different unit and he pointed acrost the street to a big building that he called Willards Hotel. All the fancy people go there and we heer that the business of our government is done at the bar. I do not think they would want to see soldiers like us at that bar.

One thing I did do I hope you will see soon. In Washington they have these places they call Tempel of Art where you can go have your likeness taken. They call it a Dagger-o-tipe. I know I spelled that right because I wrote it down to make sure I got it right. Anyway you sit in a chair and they got this kintrapshun that holds the back of your head perfeckly still. Then the man takes a cover off a round glass thing like an eye and you hold real still for a long time till he says you can breathe agin. Then he takes a little piece of silvery metal out of the back of his machine and goes into a little room. What you get is like a little painting on a mirror with your own likeness on it. I will send it to you and I hope you get it because if we move out I do not know when I can get another. I never seen anything like this back home but here in Washington they are common.

My Uncle Samuel sent a man around and we got paid yesterday for the first time. Thirteen dollars a month.[41] They said they would pay us ever other month but I do not know because it did seem to be a bit longer then that. I told them to send ten dollars each month to you. They said it will be delivered to the Town Treasurer[42] a nd they should bring it direkly to you. I need the other three to pay the sutlers[43] for warm socks and mebbe sum terbacco. Let me know if that money do not find its way to your pocket. Do not you worry none becuz I will not lose it at any of the card games the boys is always playin.

It maks no sense to me how we can end this before the snow come if all we do is march in big circles. Sence that one battle looks like nothing is heppening. The Rebs is probly digging in deeper ever day and getting more ready for us to come at them but still all we do is march in circles. I heard tell it is General McClellen holding off so I just have to figger he knows what is right.

Thet new schooner Mister Watkins started building does it have a name yet? Who is the foreman watching how it goes together? Is it one of the new three mast kind?

The bugler just tooted assembly so it is time to go start marching agin.

Your loving Freeman

The plane started to drop slightly, announcing the beginning of the descent into Hartsfield-Jackson. That meant that he'd be searching for his luggage in just a few minutes. At least so far it had actually been the best kind of flight – boring and uneventful. With a window on one side and a vacant seat on the other, it was just perfect for daydreaming.

He watched as the fields of Georgia grew closer and closer, then the plane's shadow appeared on the ground beneath and the aircraft and its shade were reunited.

Fortunately, his luggage was not delayed and there were cabs lined up in front. "Where to, pal?" asked the cabbie, with that note of condescending familiarity that Richard always found irritating.

"Omni."

"Right-e-o, matey." The little window behind the cabbie slid shut and they took off. The seven-mile ride didn't take very long. The hotel was a little more expensive than he needed but it was close to Aladdin's offices. He'd stayed in a less costly place last time and Johnson had invited him over for drinks in the evening, high up in the Omni's South Tower where the windows of the Latitude Bistro look down across the city.

The big city lights were so different from Water Street, where late at night there were few that remained on. Problems and questions from home were a long way off.

Before he could say 'No' the bellhop had his bag and was heading through the big glass doors. He paid the cabbie but waited outside just long enough to savor the balmy Georgia evening. The air was warm and humid and just barely scented with Magnolia, so different from back home where there was still a salt-tinged chill. He already missed Amanda, and thought for a moment how it would feel to stroll around the grounds with her, maybe visit the nearby Olympic Park and share a kiss on the Quilt of Dreams. Maybe next time.

He put on his party face and headed into the lobby. While the desk clerk checked him in he listened to a musician playing on the grand piano.

My Dearest Freeman   *August 10, 1861*

I am still holding my breath about what I told you before but there is nothing new to say. Mum asks me nearly ever day but I have not said a word to nobody else yet. Just you.

The boys in the yard ask about you nearly ever day. A couple of them came over to the house on Sunday to help Mum and me clean up the yard after the storm we had last week. Nothing much just some branches down and a broken window. Jake Dubois and Elmer Monclef fixed the window and cleaned up the yard for us but would not let me pay them any thing. I gave them some cider pressed fresh from our tree and some others on Green Street. Jake told me he would have gone off with you boys ceptin they would not let him join on account of him being nearly fifty. Elmer did not say much but I happen to know he be older than Jake.

Zadoc says your share of the profits from Achenar will be about two hundred but then some will haf to go for refit costs before he starts hauling lumber in September. I trust him to treat you right effen though you are not here. If you think I should I can get Mister Watkins to look at the books like you would do if you was here.

You should not be too upset about Bull Run. According to the paper[44] some of the Rebs took that battle pretty hard because they lost two generals and a number of men. Some of them think it was a draw. Mister Nutt[45] wrote in the Sentinel the general feeling was that it was virtually a drawn battle.

Your faithful Alma

My Loving Freeman   *August 19, 1861*

I been puking in the morning for about two weeks. Mum says that is a sure sign I am with child. She says if I eat watermelon it will make me feel better and mebbe it does. Elmer brought me some and he says he got more coming on the vine. Mrs. Ballard[46]come over today and we talked about what it is like to have a baby.

Maybe it is too early to ask this but what do you think we should call our baby? I got lots of ideas but hope you can make a good one.

I know you are hoping to be in a fight but I be just as happy if you do not. Far as I am concerned long as you complain about marching in circles there is not any body shooting at you. I do hope you do not start playing cards even if others are doing that. They are the plaything of the divvul and will not do you enny good just lead your heart to places it should not be.

We got news that a mob destroyed the offices of the Bangor Democrat a week ago becuz their editor M. Emery was writing things in support of the confederate cause. I do not like what the paper was saying but I also do not beleeve that destroying a newspaper was why your Grandfather fought along side of Gen'l Washington. Hope fully this war will not make us forget who we are.

Lubec is always nice in the late summer but it is not the same without you. The town is very quiet with you and the others gone away. After Elias joined up the Navy some of the other fishermen did the same and now I hear the masters is having a hard time getting a full crew to go fishing. They say there is so many cod out on the Banks you can walk across them in the water and do not even need boots only now there is nobody to catch them.

The new schooner is starting to get big. It will have three masts and a gaff-topsail rig and I hear they will call it the Bessie Watkins after Mister Watkins mother. That is what I hear them calling it but until the name is on the transom in gold letters nobody knows.

Your loving wife

My Dearest Alma   *August 22, 1861*

I got your letter of August 3 just yesteddy. That is sum kind of great news but it kind of mekes me sad too. The idea us having a baby I think is grand but me not being there to help you get ready and to be there on the big day makes me wish I did not sign up and stayed with you instead. Soon as you are sure we needs to make up some names. Mebbe if it is a boy we call him Luther after my Grandpap and if it be a girl we call her Esther like your Mum. We gots time.

It is very hot here in Washington. In Lubec we get the breeze come up ever afternoon and sometimes them fogs that roll down the street makes it get cold. Not here. Here it is hot before we gets up then it just gets hotter. Sometimes we have to stand guard at these big bildings they have here and that means we stand in the sun. Two of the boys fainted clear away just yesteddy. We had to haul them into shade and splash water on them.

Today we marched around in circles some more. This time we have new muskets to use and better ones then before. The First Maine Volunteers went home because they only signed up for ninety days so we got there muskets.[47]These are the new Springfield 1855 58 caliper model. They be lighter[48]then the old ones and do not effen hafta have perkussion caps. Sergent says this musket can put a Minie ball through a Reb at a thousand feet. I sort of hopes I do not have to kill a Reb that we can end this before any body else gets hurt.

The Thirty-First New York regiment arrived here yesteddy and do they look something fancy. Way they march and way the sun shines off there muskets and shoes makes us look wicked bad. Colonel Knowles he did not look so happy way they marched past us. Specially after there colonel saluted him whilst sitting way up high on a big mare.

Isaac told me abowt going to a place called Madame Wiltons Private Residence For Ladies.[49] I know he did not go there to drink tea in there pahlor. He said the place is fancier then any place he seen back home with walls that look like schooner cabins and books lined up nice and neat and fancy looking women walking round like they were searching for sum speshull man. He sed many of the women did not wear much clothes except for the woman who was in charge she was older and wore fine rich clothes and much jewelry.

He said he had to stand in line to get in and there was a bunch of officers a waitin in that line too. He did not tell us whut it looked like up the staires. Me and James we told him to spend his money on as many of them Cyprians he wanted but neither of us wanted any of that tea. Sounds like he been going there regular like.

We been hearing rumors that we will not be staying in Washington much longer. First one man comes in tells us we be goin to Baltimore then another one says he got it on good athorty we going towards Richmond. Then same day an officer tells us we be going no where for a while.

You ask me it is not time to move to winter quarters yet but nobody is talking abowt going off to fight. I do not think I be home to help you with Christmas selebrations but I sure do miss you. Please tell me ever thing abowt my baby I want to know it all.

Your Loving Freeman

My Dearest Freeman   *August 26, 1861*

I am feeling better in the mornings now just like Mum said I would. Can not see any other signs things happening. Mum says I worry too much I just have to let nature be.

You asked who was the foreman on the new schooner Bessie Watkins. Mister Watkins give that job to Rodman Bellingham. I know you remember him. He was the one promised to marry Adela Wulf but insted did not even show up at the church to tell her he done thought differint. Her family will not ever forget the way her father stood by her at the altar but Rodman went off huntin instead. Mister Watkins says Rodman knows how to loft a hull better than anybody else that is still here an that is why he gived him that job. May be that is so but still I do not trust him. Mum would say that is not Christian but she does not know him like I do.

Zadoc has not brought Achenar back to Lubec yet but he is expected soon and then I will tell you how they did. The price of cod has been down lately to three dollars a quintal^{50} but the catch is up even for a handliner so may be your share will be good as long as the price of salt does not get too much higher.

Jake comes over here pretty regular fixin little things for Mum an me after he does a whole day over at the yard cutting out ribs an knees. Mister Watkins says they is nobody never made a better lock-scarf keel joint then Jake and will not let nobody else do it. Maybe when you get back Jake can learn you how to do that. When you get back I will be one happy gal. Can not be soon enough.

You take care now and do not let any Rebs get too close.

Your Loving Alma

There had been so many sleepless nights lately that they all kind of ran together. On waking, most mornings, there was a lingering sense of uneasiness that things were not right, but never any real explanation. This sensation was often mingled with a feeling of relief that the night was over and he could get on with his day.

He had married a spectacular woman who was his intellectual equal, created a successful business from scratch, and even paid off his credit cards at the end of each month. Yet there was something that was not right.

At least this time he knew his tossing and turning would not alarm Amanda. She always seemed to sleep well, but still he worried. What was it she would soon be doing to prepare for her day, besides walking Bonkers up past Clancy's statue? Was today her visit to Meddybemps, or had that been yesterday? Her position with the county had her traveling around a bit, but seldom so far that she'd not be home at night except for those infrequent meetings in Bangor or Augusta when the county and state social workers all got together to talk about what ever it was they did. He never worried about what she might do during those occasional nights out. She'd never given him the least cause for suspicion and he could not imagine her playing the role of stray cat.

And this evening? Probably volunteering for something around the town. Yesterday was the food bank, so this evening must be the town's Fourth of July Committee, working to entice vendors to the big street fair when they'd close Water Street for the day. She always had time for things that were important to him and for others too. That was just how she was.

So what was happening? It wasn't sex. Amanda was a great lover, at least so far as he could tell, never having experienced another. She certainly kept herself well and had not gained as much as a single pound since the day they had gone to the Senior Prom. Later that evening was the first time they had sampled each other's delights, but it was hardly the last. He knew she still turned heads, particularly in the summer when all the out-of-towners were in. Watching how those guys, and not a few women, looked her over always made him feel good but he never once spotted her looking back. She appeared oblivious to envious stares, except for those times she'd caught him admiring her in the big mirror on the closet door in their bedroom. Some of those times events quickly turned, well, memorable…

So what *was* happening? Had his ardor *really* cooled? He closed his eyes and returned to one of his favorite scenes. Prom night in the back of his father's car, parked under the moon twenty minutes out of town in a secluded spot on a farm access road a quarter mile off of Wilcox Settlement Road. It was a plan they'd worked out in advance, knowing that his older relatives would think it worse than scandalous, and so would hers. He didn't care, it was Amanda he cared about and it was her plan too.

He rolled back over and pulled the blanket tight. The alarm would announce the new day in just a few hours.

My Darling Alma   *August 29, 1861*

The papers today here in Washington gived us our first really great news. Our Navy took two forts from the Rebs down North Carolina. I do not really understand why they are so important but smarter men then me say it makes a big difference specially to shipping. For me I think it is good that we won some thing specially after Bull Run. Fort Hatteras and Fort Clark somewhere down North Carolina was captured.[51] One of the ships that done it was the Cumberland. Did you tell me that was the ship that Elias joined up with? It makes me excited to think a Lubec boy had some thing to do with that.

So much has been going on but so little of it is important. I do not think you wanted me to complain abowt marching around in circles any more. Some of the boys have been grumbling abowt Colonel Knowles becuz he do not seem to be interested in how we are doing. Lieutenant Colonel Burnham is always asking questions abowt how we are doing and trying to make things better. I know

43

Old Grizzly said some thing quiet like to Isaac abowt all the time and money he was spending with them Cyprians.

I want to hear more abowt how you are doing with my baby. Are you sure yet? I want to tell the boys but not until you say so.

Tell me how the apple crop is doing this year. I all ways look forward to your apple pies and now all I can do is brag abowt them. That new schooner. They got the garboard rebated in yet? That should have been my job. I want to know how is things at home.

We still hear rumors abowt moving but no orders yet.

Your loving Freeman

My Darling Freeman   *August 29, 1861*

Earlier today I got your package with your likeness in it the Daguerreotype you had made. I nearly fainted when I saw your face looking out at me like that becuz it made me wish I could hold you instead of just looking at you on that little mirror. You look so handsome in your uniform and holding your musket and looking so stern. The Rebs see someone like you coming there way I am sure they are going to give up post haste.

Jake promised to make a little frame for it with a piece of glass so we can put it on the hutch and let ever body see it. When Mum looked at it she did not say any thing for a long time but I saw the tears in her eyes. If we can not have you here then now at least we has your likeness. I think Mum is getting sweet on Jake.

You probly remember that my friend Rhoda Joy was planning to get married to Sam Lawrence. The wedding was yesterday[52] and it was done by the Deacon in the sanctuary at Big White and most ever body was there. I think you know Sam his family lives up on North Road near Cap't Huckins place.[53]

Mum went with me and we both cried because Rhoda and Sam looked so good standin together like that in the front of the whole town. The bells must have rang for an hour afterwards. Least that is how long seemed to be.

When I woke up this morning I felt like I had too much to eat even tho I had not eaten yet. And sometimes I just want to cry but I am sure that is because you are not here. When I told Mum how I was feeling she just smiled and patted me on the belly.

I am glad your likeness arrived today because tomorrow Mister Watkins is having a big party to celebrate getting another order. He wants the whole company there on Friday to here the good news so I will be in Eastport all day. Mister Watkins has made speshul arrangements to have a boat bring me and a few others back to Lubec after the party.

Tonight I am going to put your likeness on the dinner table so it will be like you are having supper with me and Mum.

Your Faithful Alma

My Dearest Alma   *September 2, 1861*

This letter will hef to be a short one becuz we is packing to move out in the morning. We got orders today to Virginia Fort Ethan Allen[54] in some place called Arlington. Can not say I am unhappy abowt this because there was nothing for us boys to do in Washington except march in circles and do things we ought not do.

Seems funny. Just as I start getting your letters regular we move. I hope the post office knows how to find me. Please excuz my bad writing. You was all ways the writer and here I can not even hardly find a smooth place to write.

I hope Virginia not be as hot as Washington. Sometimes in the evening it cools down just a little but then the fog comes up from the Potomac and ever thing gets feeling soggy. Not like in Lubec when the fog sometimes follows the tide up the narrows because then it is cool. Here it is not cool only soggy. I do not like Washington and am very glad to be going any where else.

I wish I could walk down Water Street an hold your hand an tell the whole town you are going to give me a baby. Soon this thing will end and I can do that but it will not be soon enuff.

Your Loving Freeman

The meeting had gone well enough and he was confident that all the loose ends would be wrapped up when they got back together the next morning. Plenty of time to get done what was needed before presenting an action plan based on today's discussions. It did seem a little odd that Johnson showed no interest in getting together that evening for a drink or two, as he always had before, but that's just the way things go. Perhaps his wife had gotten them show tickets or something.

Richard dropped back on the bed, kicked his shoes to the floor, and dozed off for a few minutes. Spending the day on your feet, dealing with a group of managers who do not always, shall we say, display the finer points of southern hospitality, was rather exhausting. He considered the fact that not one of his family had made it to the south, at least as far back as he knew. His father often spoke of his travels in Germany and France, but when he went to those places he wore a khaki uniform and carried a rifle. *If one of the Aladdin guys were to show up in Lubec, it'd be my opportunity to show off old fashioned New England hospitality.*

The statistical analysis of program results that Johnson asked him to pull together was quite doable, although the data was in his computer back at home so that part of the task would have to wait.

"I thought," one of the managers had mumbled, "that was what we had come here to review." It may have even been a smirk that flashed across Johnson's face at that instant.

46

He awoke to a noise in the hallway and realized it was nearly seven. Too late to call Amanda. Her committee meeting started promptly at six and would last until pretty late. He called anyway, just to leave a message on the machine so she wouldn't be worrying.

Richard pulled his shoes back on, pocketed his room key, and headed for the bar. At least he could take in the view. For a Wednesday evening, the place was doing a brisk business but it was still easy to find a seat at the bar where he could sit and think. A finger or two of good whiskey would help him plan the next morning.

As soon as he came through the door, he spotted the woman down at the far end of the bar, conspicuously one of the few sitting alone. She looked to be perhaps early thirties, dressed as a professional, and seemed to be comfortable sitting alone.The way she showed off a neat pair of legs reminded him of an old pin-up he'd seen once. Betty Grable, perhaps. But there was work to be done, and a distraction would be just that.

My Dearest Freeman   *September 14, 1861*

The days is getting cooler now an we sleep with blankets at night. I do not like sleeping alone but I know you will be back soon. Ever body tells me you will be home before the snow but I do not know it will be that soon. I can hope.

I have not puked in a while now and feel hungry pretty often. Mum says I am now eating for two but it feels more like I am eating for twenty. Mrs. Ballard come over today and teched me in a few places. She says ever thing looks fine.

The Bessie Watkins is looking more like a real schooner now and not just a pile of lumber. They got most of the planking on and some of the deck is done. The joiner work looks real good but not as good as if you was doing it. She has nice lines with high sheer and low freeboard amidships will be a fine lady when under sail.

Ever day somebody in town gives me or Mum some preserves or bread so we can set some aside for winter. Sure wish I had a big strong man here help with the fire at night.

I do not like to hear you talk about killing but I know that may be some thing they expect you to do some time. Why does this war mean people must get hurt? I expect if you could sit down and talk regular like with a Reb you would find him a good family man maybe with a girl or a boy who wants him come home an tuck them into bed at night. Some of the papers say Rebs is like monsters but I do not think they know what they are talking about.

The apple crop is good this year. Some of the trees out West Lubec like in Split Hill have so many the branches nearly tech the ground. If I cud make you Apple Pie I would sit and watch you eat the whole thing and be so happy just to watch you.

Governor Washburn was elected agin last week. The Republicans say they promise to uphold our constitution[55]which I guess means they is behind the war effort. There is just a few Copperheads around and Mister Nutt is pretty quick to put things in his paper the Sentinel they maybe do not want to hear. Anyway it do not look like the election was any thing like close.

If I do not get this to the post office I will not get it mailed and you will not see it.

Your loving Alma

My Darling Alma   *September 14, 1861*

At last we have sum honest work to labor at. Fort Ethan Allen is not so much a fort as it is a hill. We boys are working at turning it into a fort by digging bankments and bilding roads.[56] We send a crew off each day to cut down forest so the gunners can have a clear field. From morning to night we labor then we can sit back and smoke our pipes and see what we have done.

James likes to sit at the fire and whittle with his Barlow knife. Some times he gets bloody fingers from trying to carve out things. I told him he needs smaller blade for some of what he is trying to do but he pays no heed just keeps poking his knife into his fingers.

We is working with some Vermonters but they do not no how to handle the ax like our boys do. It seem like for every tree felled by a Vermonter ax there is four by one of ours.[57]

Sometimes we adds to our supper by going out into the cornfields[58] and hepping oursefs. I do not know how far out we get but I know we is outside the picket line. Mebbe we be in Rebel country but have not seen no Reb yet. Mebbe they is pickin corn too. Sesech[59] do grow some mitey fine corn.

Ever day it looks more like a fort like a place where the Rebs might ought to take cawshun before attacking. It feels good to go to sleep each night feeling like an honest days work been done and not just standing in front of some big door.

The weather has got better. It is still hot under the sun but then it cools off at night. And they is feeding us better then they did when we was in Washington.[60]

I do remember Rodman Bellingham but not for what you reminded me. He probly do not want you to remember this but he was in my class in school. One day I think we was in the fifth grade he said something bad to me right in front of the class. I do not even remember what it was he said except it made me mad. After teacher let us go for the day I said to him I was mad and he said he did not care. When I put up my fists he turned and ran. He would not fight me. After that I just laughed when he said some thing becuz I knowed what kind of man he was. But I guess he did turn out be a good carpenter.

I am glad you like the likeness I sent. The places that do that are in Washington but there are none in Arlington least as I can see. I wish I could sit at that table with you and your Mum and not just a little piece of metal thet kind of looks lak me.

There is a new Sergeant in the brigade over in Company A.[61] His name is Charlie Clark[62] and he seems like a pretty desent kind. Even though he is one of the few who did not labor before the war he

49

was a student at Foxcroft Academy[63] he still acts like the boys in Company K are his boys too. He joined up early but until now was a private like me.

Pat your belly for me and for my baby. I must hurry because the bugler is blowing assembly.

Your loving Freeman

My Dearest Freeman   *September 23, 1861*

I have not tole Mum this yet but I think my belly is starting to get big. Maybe next week I will let her look an see whut she says. I feel good now in the mornings no more puking. I like your suggestions for names. Luther or Esther. Now I am getting ankshus to see which one it will be.

Bessie is starting to look like a real lady now. All the hull planking is done and they is hammerin away with the oakum. The rudder is hung and most of the deck is done and they started the deckhouse. Jake did such a good job with the keel and deadwood they got it faired real easy so you kin run your hand acrost it and not even feel the joint almost like you had done it.

The masts is all most ready to be stepped in. Rodman told Mister Watkins he exspects to have the topsides painted in a week and then they can launch. Wish you was here to see her go into the water. They still have a lot of work to get done but they wants to have her in the water before the frost.

Mum and I got eight cords wood delivered last week and I am paying young Charlie from next door fifty cent to stow it in the shed. Did I give him too much? Seems lak a big pile and it will probly take him two days put it all away.

Yestiddy I saw Mrs Cooper. She told me she had been heering regular from Isaac and that he said you and James was doing fine. She did not say anything about Cyprians but probly if she knowed about them she still would not say. That can be our seecret.

The town is awful quiet right now with all you boys gone off.
Reverend Smith asks the town to pray you will all be home soon. I do
not know if that will help and I do not think he knows any more then
anybody else. I do not want to pray. I just want you back.

Your loving Alma

My Dearest Alma   *September 26, 1861*

   I is getting ankshus to hear abowt our baby. Are you sure yet
so I can tell the boys? It makes me feel better thinking that if may be
I somehow do not get past this thing that I left you with someone to
help you carry on.
   It has been four months and two weeks sence I signed up.
Some times it seems lot longer then that and other times seems like
just yestiddy. The last time I seen you was waving your yellow scarf
on the pier and I was on the deck of the Eastern City. I see you in my
dreams most ever night but that do not really count.
   We is still working on bilding the fort. They say we will be
moving off to winter quarters soon but may be that is just another
rumor. Ever day another rumor comes through and the one sayin it
always swears that it be Gospel.
   Heer in camp there is no whiskey but we do get our coffee.
Ever day the company gets a ration ten pounds of green coffee for all
of us to share. You take the beans and put them in the bottom of a pot
or even your cup and cook them until they is a light brown. Then you
crush them a bayonet works good or some thing that you make them
like fine gravel. You can put cold water in then boil it or else put in
scalding water and let them soak for a few minutes. Once the water
turns dark brown you put in just a little cold water so the grounds
sink then some sugar. When you are done you have a drink that is
worth the work. Some times some body will make a bigger pot and
we can all share but either way it is sweet and makes you feel good.
We all know who here can make decent coffee and will not share our

beans with some one else. When I come home I will make you some like we do here and I know you will like it.

Several of the boys come down with Measles[64]some thing bad. They is keeping them apart from the rest of us so may be we will not all get it. I heerd there was quite a few sick.

They are calling for mail so I will end now and write again real soon.

Your Faithful Freeman

My Dearest Freeman   *October 1, 1861*

Mum says there is no question now from the way my belly has started to swell. She sez it is too early to tell if I am carrying high or low so she will not guess whether it is Luther or Esther in there right now. Mrs. Ballard also will not say what she thinks. When I ask her if it be a boy or a girl all she says is only God knows and he does not go telling no tales.

But if you want to tell the boys you can. Tell me what they say because I think that would be fun to know. Now that I told you the good news I will tell Deacon Fowler. Soon as I tell him ever body in town will know.

We had a spring tide yesterday and they launched the Bessie Watkins. Halfway down the ways she stopped and they had to get out the jacks and then wait until all most midnight when the next high water come. I saw the look on Mister Watkins face speshully since the vessel has his mothers name right there on the transom in big gilt letters. I did not see Rodman but I am sure he knows sence he was the one built it the curse is on him.

Tomorrow they will pull her round to the crane and step the masts but right now she looks happy enuff to be moving to the current. Mister Watkins said there was no leaks at all even after what they had to get her moving down the ways. They is still working on the crew quarters and the deckhouse.

I do remember the story you told about Rodman now that you reminded me. You forgot I was there when it happen. I do *remember he was bigger than you but would not stand his ground aginst you.*

This fort you and the boys is building sounds grand. Will it have a church and stores where you can buy warm cloths and the other things you need for the winter?

Last nite was cold but still no frost. Mum keeped the fire going in the stove warm up the house a bit. This morning we was comfy enough but would have been better you was here. Last Sunday Reverend Smith preached about how you and the boys was freeing the Negroes and he looked strait at me when he said that. Made me feel real proud of you the way ever body looked at me.

Your Loving Alma

Richard pulled up a stool, dropped his elbows onto the polished surface of the bar, and commenced scrutinizing the bottles lined up along the mirrored wall. Four Roses sounded pretty good right about now, straight up. *When in the South, can't miss with a good Bourbon, right?* The bartender poured out a double finger of single mash and opened a tab. The first sip tasted wonderful, trickling off the side of his tongue. He started rummaging through the events of the day and planning the work he needed to do to prepare for tomorrow.

Johnson already knew that the statistical analysis he asked for would have to wait until he got back to Lubec, but there were still some things he needed to prepare for. A good couple hours should do it, he just needed to concentrate.

He cast his eye casually down the bar. The woman still sat alone, setting her apart from the rest of the bar's patrons. His mind went back to the questions Johnson's team had posed. With all of the data in hand he would need maybe four hours to compile, analyze, and build the tables with the expected graphs. He was confident the results would justify both his work and the money they paid him. Aladdin may not be his biggest client, but they were still important.

Two strangers sitting apart in a place where most everybody else had a companion… Perhaps she'd enjoy some conversation. What would be the harm in hearing a friendly voice, if just for a few minutes? *Can't spare much more than that.*

He carried his drink down to the far end of the bar. *Maybe I'll try a business traveler's ice breaker…*

"Are you a Turtle?"

She sat back and looked him over. Her slight smile suggested that she was familiar with the opening gambit and was considering whether to provide the correct response to the coded question. He must have passed muster, because she chuckled softly before replying, "You bet your sweet ass I am."

"Can't be, two Turtles drinking alone. Can it?"

"Looks like until now." Her voice was soft and carried a note of authenticity. She took her purse off the empty seat and pointed at it. He noted that she had sparse makeup, modest jewelry, and wore a simple business suit like maybe she did training. Unlike him, she wore no wedding ring.

"Being alone in a place like this can only mean one thing," he said as he sat down. "You are here on business."

"Can there be any other reason?" She gestured around the room. Most of the males in the room sported ties and most of the females wore tailored suits and all seemed to be closely engaged in their own affairs. "Not really first choice for a pick-up joint."

When she smiled at him it was like her entire face glowed with some inner heat. He felt its warmth down his spine and wondered if she smiled like that for everybody, or if maybe there had been something in his approach that had triggered it.

"By the way, I'm Dolores."

"And I'm Richard."

"And Richard is in Atlanta, all by himself?"

"Exactly as you see him."

My Dearest Alma   *October 4, 1861*

I hope you have enough wood to make it thru to spring. It gets some wicked cold when that wind blows off Johnson Bay and I worry that you can stay warm enuff specially in your condition. That harbor be some nasty cold in a few weeks and you know how the drifts pile up on the bluffs along Main Street them folk can be trapped for a week if there be a blizzard. Flaggs Point is not a good place to be alone in the winter you be better off staying with some body up Sewards Neck maybe your grandfather or Zeke.

We are hearing rumors again abowt going to winter quarters soon but no orders yet. Sergeant Witherell says Grizzly told him it is time to finish some of the jobs we started so I think something is coming.

Did the papers say any thing abowt a fight a bit west of here at a place called Cheat Mountain? We are heering that three hundred of our boys held off three thousand Rebs.[65] What we heerd was that the Rebs captured our picket line but then our boys told them our officers knew all abowt there plans and that there was a big force waitin for them. Guess there Genl RE Lee must have believed them because they let them go and withdrew.[66] But in the skirmish there were boys killed both ours and theres. That part made me sad. I wish there were sum way we could end this and nobody more get killed.

That new schooner sounds like a marvel. Wish I was part of the building of it. I would have carved my name and yours in some place they would never see just to know they was there.

We lost two boys to the measles yestiddy and I hear there is more that mightent not come thru. They are trying hard to keep the rest of us from going near there tent. I did not know the two who died they was from another company. Some other Regiments have a lot of sickness. Colera and typus they say. So far I am fine and so is James and Isaac. You can be sured that I will do my best to keep it that way. Sometimes it is hard speshully when we are out on the picket line for two days. Way we do that there is three of us to a post an one has to keep lookout for two hours close enough to the Reb line we some times hear them talking. The others wait until it is there turn. They can sleep or do what ever they want but they has to stay there[67]and be ready to go if shooting starts. If the weather is nice it is not so bad but I know it is going to snow soon enough. Even worse then the cold is that cold rain some times falls.

The bugler will be tooting assembly soon so I must end this letter. Write me soon because hearing from you is what makes it all bearable.

Your Loving Freeman

My Dearest Freeman   *October 15, 1861*

You know how autumn in Lubec is always lovely with the coolness in the air and the warm sun and all the maple and oak leafs ablaze. Two nights ago we had the first frost but today it is warm. Mum and me we got the tomatoes in before the frost and the potatoes was dug up couple weeks ago. The vines are dying so we can find all those hard squashes and the punkins are in. When I am done writing this letter I am going to make punkin pie like I know you like and

Mum and Jake and me we will eat it in your honor. I will put your likeness on the table so you can be with us too.

Member I told you what folks was sayin about Gwyneth Josephine and what they thought may be she and Elias Sheehan had got done? I bet maybe they did not because if they done that I know she would be showing now just like I is. I know where that little bump come from. It come from you. Luther or Esther be growing a bit but Gwyneth has no bump.

When I told Deacon I was with your baby he got so proud it was like he was gonna proclaim it be his own. Now folks I am just barely knowing are wanting to give me hug and good wishes.

I showed Mum what you wrote about coffee and now we both want to try it like you make it. Mum said any thing that comes out of a fire must be okay it is what comes out of a bottle that she worries about.

It is good I got the job at the yard working for Mister Watkins. Sum days ago Randy from the town office brung around your pay allotment thirty dollars just like you said. It will last us for a while but you know how winters are here. If they pay you regular we will be all right but if they do not then it might be kind of not so easy. But we will be okay you do not worry none. I still do not know what your share is from Achenar but the reckoning should come soon.

You be some kind of careful around them Measles. I want you back just the way you was when you left.

Your Faithful Alma

It didn't take very long to get past the basics. Dolores was an RN, employed by a hospital supply outfit, in from Hauppauge to train the staff over at Fulton-Dekalb on a new piece of equipment, and would be heading back in two days. Divorced four years ago and now living with her mother. She was easy to talk to and seemed genuine in her interest in what he was doing. The conversation was relaxed and comfortable, even for two strangers in a business-traveler bar.

"Tell me about your town." She crossed her legs and leaned up against the bar on her left elbow. The way she looked at him, he felt the pressure of her gaze. "It must be wonderful living so close to the ocean."

"Really should be, I guess." He shrugged. "Lived there all my life, born and raised. Maybe it's too easy to take things for granted."

"We've got Fire Island but that's too touristy for me."

"We're more a fishing village but the last few years a lot of artists have been moving in."

"Can you hear the surf?"

Richard laughed. "If we start hearing the surf, we've got a problem." She gave him a quizzical expression. "We're in a sheltered harbor, not exposed to the open water. The town is partly protected by a Canadian island." He paused and gestured to the bartender to refill both of their glasses. "We get sea-smoke, Fundy Bay twenty-four-foot tides, killer currents, but no surf."

My Dearest Alma   *October 15, 1861*

We got our orders today and tomorrow we head out for our winter quarters. Some place called Lewinsville. I think that is what it is called. Not sure where it is but we will march there.
I hope that in winter quarters we will have regular cooks in stead of the way we cook our own meals right now. I have a tin plate and a ladle and I cook and eat from both. Uncle Samuel gives us

58

each some salt pork may be once a week other wise a little beef and some flour. I can cook the flour in my drinking cup then cook the pork on the plate and eat right off of the plate.[68] *Then I use my cup to boil my coffee.*

In thet regard I am no better or worst off then any body else because that is how we all do it. So I am hoping that in our winter quarters they have a regular cook to do it for us. Please do not send me a pot becuz then I would have to carry it when we march or else leave it behind.

I do not know what will become of Fort Ethan Allen after we go. From the rifle pits and the gun placements there is a clear view where there used to be forest. If the Rebs want to take this and there is a company or two of our boys here there will be a real good fight.

You should be hearing soon from Zadoc Dubois abowt my share of the Achenar profits. My twenty five percent should get you may be thirty five dollars clear for the fishing season.

The boys got all kind of excited when I told them you was with my child. James tried to borrow a cigar from one of the officers but there was none to be had. We have not seen either a cigar or a woman since we left Washington.

You take good care of my baby now let your Mum do any heavy lifting. I wish I could be there do that for you. It should be my job but for now my job is here and I have to see it to the end.

Your Loving Freeman

My Dearest Freeman   *October 21, 1861*

It has been very quiet here lately. We had frost on the ground last three mornings but today it is warm and sunny. We have laid in two quintals of salt cod and got the potatoes packed up in sand. The squash harvest was good so we traded for some beans. Mum and me should be okay until at least the end of February and then we will buy some more. By then you should be home.

The riggers are at work on the Bessie Watkins right now and the sail loft is busy too. With those masts rising above the docks she looks like she is ankshus to go to sea. Mister Watkins pays me each week so with the money you are sending home we should be as okay as we can without ackshully having you here. Ever body still asks about you and how you and the other boys is doing.

Jake comes around almost ever day now. He and Mum sit in the kitchen by the fire and talk. He has taken to sitting next to her in church Sunday mornings and some times I see them holding hands. It is okay with me because she still some times goes down to visit Father's grave. Does not feel like it has been ten years since he was swept off the Ellie Mae and I am sure she is lonesome at least I have you.

We got word a few days ago that Cap't James Foster was lost off the brig Union on a passage from Machiasport to New York.[69] I did not know him but Mister Watkins did and he is quite upset about it. He was not even thirty and the vessel was in fine shape.

Do not ask me why but I think your child will be Esther. I just think so. No reason. On warm days when I do not have my coat on when I walk down Water Street a lot of people want to rub my belly. I do not really like that but since you are not here then that is close as they can get to you so I let them. Pretty soon I will not be able go out without my coat so then they will not do that. I guess I can let them do it for a little longer.

You take good care now and do not get Measles or any of them other Reb sickness either.

Your Loving Alma

My Dearest Alma   *October 22, 1861*

We have moved to a place called Lewinsville.[70] It is in Virginia a little to the north and west of Fort Ethan Allen not even a long days march. There has been some action here a small battle and a skirmish so I guess Gen Baldy Smith[71] figures that if we is here then the sesech will not come back. It is not much different from what we had before except there is a farm house where some of the officers stay. You can tell there used to be farm animals here but they must have all ready filled a hungry boy because there is no thing to be seen of them excepting a manure pit.

Where we are right now is just a few miles south of the Potomac River and may be six miles from Chain Bridge where we were stashuned when Bull Run heppened. That was may be ten miles west of Lewinsville.

Please take good care of my baby. The boys some times ask abowt how you are doing and I read to them what you have written. Do not let yoursef get a chill or be hungry and when winter comes you be extra careful on any ice so you do not take a spill. Listen good to what your Mum tells you because she raised a pretty good chicken herself.

Your loving Freeman

My Darling Freeman   *November 9, 1861*

Esther has started to move a little. At night when all is quiet I can feel her moving just a bit so I know she is okay. Mrs. Ballard laughed at me when I said it was Esther and not Luther. She said I was being a silly goose.

I want to hear all about Lewinsville. Is it a nicer place than the fort you and the other boys built? Is there places there you can get things so you can be more comfortable? There is none of them Cyprians in Lewinsville is there? Mum read some thing in the papers about all them women and she wants you to warn the others they is doing the Devils work for him.

An anouncement in the paper called for women to help provide for the soldiers. They are asking for women to make blankets quilts socks and warm undershirts to be sent to the men at the front. Mum said we should see what we can do and I say she is right. I am not the only one here thinks we women can do more to help our men we are part of this fight too. After Esther is born I might not have as much time but then I will have a very important job. Working with others to help all our boys at the front can not fail to be of service but it also might make it easier to have others to talk to speshully with you not home.

I miss you so much. Please say hello to Isaac and James. Tell James I see Katherine pretty often and she always tells me he says you are doing well. Do not see so much of Mrs Cooper.

I want you to come home soon.

Your Loving Alma

"Sheltered by a Canadian island!" Her eyebrows went way up. "You must be way out there. Sounds like a romantic village."

"Campobello Island," he replied, taking a sip of Four Roses. "They're our closest relatives, just over the bridge."

"Sounds nice to me." When she put her hand on his arm it felt soft and warm. It was just a gesture, didn't mean anything, but it still felt nice.

"Dolores," he said, looking up at her face. "Is that what your friends call you?"

"You know," she said with the trace of a giggle, "there are a few nicknames that go with the name my parents laid on me."

"Let me guess," he chuckled. "I'm sure nobody calls you Lola."

"Actually, a few do." She paused and looked across at him. "When I was in college there were some that called me Lolita."

"I'm not going to ask."

"It's okay," she laughed. "I never was like that. Only in my mother's head. She didn't like it when my boyfriend called me that."

He spotted her reaction when he let the corners of his mouth twist up, like she knew that something was coming. "As I recall," he said, "In that story, she was the instigator."

It felt good, listening to the inflections in her voice, the way the sound complemented her smile. "Well," she replied with a smile, "It was better for me that Mom never got that part."

Richard could imagine, minus a few pounds and a few years, Dolores playing that role. "She didn't trust you?"

"Hell, I'm thirty-two and she still doesn't trust me." She lifted the glass to her lips and took a small sip, dropping her voice down a bit. "Times like right now," she said in a soft voice, "Only chance I have to let my hair down."

My Dearest Alma   *November 8, 1861*

So you have decided that I will be the lucky man to have a daughter. Long as she is smart and pretty as her Mum then that will be fine with me. Sounds to me like you should listen close what Mrs. Ballard says.

We here is settling down and it looks like this is where we will be for the winter. Even though this used to be a farm there is nothing for a boy to put in his dish to eat excepting what the Army gives us or we buy frum the sutlers.

I tent with James so I know how much he is missing Katherine. Isaac is tenting with a boy frum Pembroke used to work in the Iron Works.[72] *Can not handle an axe for beans but you should*

63

see what he can do you give him an old piece of metal. There is some busted farm machines here and he takes pieces off heats them up and makes fancy hooks to hang coats and things on.

For a man who would be much more happy sleeping with his woman I do pretty all right. Theres lots of pine trees here so I made myself a bed of bows and laid a piece of old tent atop. I put one blanket down on the canvas and roll myself up in my other blankets. Sometimes in the night James gets to missing Katherine and forgets who he be with but I know what is in his head so it be okay. He do not bother me none when he gets his sweet dreams but he all ways acts kind of sheepish if he wakes up

Yesterday a woman from the sanitary commission[73] come by. First woman any of us seen in the camp. She give us some wool socks and new undershirts and asked a lot of questions.

I like the idea your Mum and Jake getting to no each other better. Jake is a good man. I have known him long time never a cross word. I know she not be asking my permisshun but I give it any way.

The bugle just tooted for parade so I must finish.

Your loving Freeman

My Dearest Freeman   *November 13, 1861*

All is quiet here we are just waiting for winter to start to set in. Mum and me pretty much got things set least as well as we can without a strong man with us. Jake comes around mostly ever day to check on things. Some times he stays late after I gone off to bed and the two of them just talk.

Governor Washburn proclaimed yesterday to be Thanksgiving Day.[74] Mum cooked up her best dish including your favorit punkin pies. Jake and Elmer came over and took supper with us and it was a grand feast. The next special day is your birthday only we will have to celebrate it with your likeness instead of with you. December third will not be the same with you not here.

The Saint John paper is full of news about the Union Navy capturing two Rebs frum a British mail ship near an island called Havana.[75] The ship was called the Trent and the two Rebs was trying

64

to go to Englund to talk to the government. *Now the Saint John paper is saying that was an act of war and that probly we are going to invade British territory up north and annex it. I do not really know what all that means. If you see any newspapers look for the story because ever body here is talking of it. Specially people from Campobello. Some of them think differnt about the war*[76]*like they is hoping the Rebs win.*

They are starting to bend the sails onto the Bessie Watkins so she will be heading out to sea real soon. I got to go on board yesterday and it looks real nice. Mister Watkins told me she is set up to haul lumber but could carry other cargo maybe even from the iron works. I asked him about what I have been reading about Reb pirates[77] *capturing boats. He told me the new owners were worried about that too so they might fly a British flag insted of our own.*

Zadoc come by a few days ago and gived me your share from the Achenar forty three dollars and twenty seven cents. He sed they will be laying her up for the winter soon at one of the docks up the Pennamaquan.

The schooner Mary Louise from Machiasport went down in a storm with all hands save one. Zadoc found the cook drifting at sea near the banks and hauled him aboard nearly dead. He said the rest of the crew told him they seen mermaids swimming and calling and knowed that something terrible would soon befall.[78]*A big wave over the bow stove in the main hatch and she went down fast. He was the only one to get out. I hope Michael never sees a mermaid.*

Esther is moving about pretty regular now. I know if she could speak she would say she wants her daddy home. Her mommy does too. So does her grandma.

Your Faithful Alma

My Darling Alma   *November 24, 1861*
You do not need worry none abowt Cyprians hanging around our camp. Them that I saw in Washington would not want be around here all this mud and cold and frosty nights and no place to get warm. But may be there is something that the officers know abowt. I do not know how many women it takes to do the Colonels[79]

65

lawndry but he got a bunch of them to do it. May be I do not no what a washerwoman is supposed to look like may be they are supposed to look fancy.

Yesterday I saw the durndest thing. Remember I told you abowt the Sergeant in Cmpny A Charlie Clark? Everbody thinks highest of him except may be Colonel Vinton from the 43 New York Regmnt. Story I heard was that Charlie went to deliver some papers to Colonel Vinton but refused to remove his hat. Colonel Vinton got some wicked mad and swore at him but he said that he was an American citizen soldier and was not abowt take his hat off to nobody especially outdoors. Colonel Vinton said he was insubordinate and had him court marshaled and then stript him of his stripes right front of the whole 6 Maine.[80] Made him private soldier again. Old Grizzly did not say much but from the look in his eyes he was not happy but Colonel Knowles looked like he was going along with Colonel Vinton. Some how I do not think we have heerd the last of Charlie Clark.

My health is good except for a bit of a cold. If I can get a good nights sleep I can probly get rid of it. The bugler is tooting tattoo so I has to blow out my candle. Take good care of my little girl and give your Mum a big hug for me. Please tell her I am looking for her to make some of her special Timbale for me when I come home.

Your Loving Freeman

My Dearest Freeman   November 24, 1861

If any body did not think I am with child they would not think that now. My belly is getting so big it feels like I am following it around like it goes through the door and then a little later I do. Mum put her ear to it yesterday and said she could hear Esther reciting the Lords Prayer. I do not know where she could have come up with that becuz I only go to church when I feels like it which as you know is not very offen. Mum some times tries to get me to go with her but most offen I do not.

We get frost ever night now and today it stayed freezing until lunch time. Hezekiah Case brought me some scallops this afternoon said he got a good catch and wanted to share some with me. Mum

66

cooked them up with bread crombs and they was some wicked good. Only thing would have made them better would be for you to be here share them with us.

Sleepin on them pine bows sounds like it might be kind of nice especially if they smell good enough. I seen Katherine two days ago and told her what you told me about James and his dreams. Maybe I should not have told her because she just put her hand on my belly and started to cry. I know she misses him some thing terrible and I got Esther to keep me company.

Last week Miss Ursula Penniman[81] from Machias came to town to hold a meeting with as many women as would come. She wants us to work to help make supplies to help the boys things like knitting socks and mittens and sewing shirts. I went and so did Mum and Katherine and several other women from town. Miss Penniman is part of the Sanitary Society.

Please give my regards to James and Isaac and especially give my love to my darling husband.

Your Loving Alma

My Dearest Alma   *December 12, 1861*

Things here is all in an up roar. Yesterday Colonel Knowles[82] resigned his commishun and left. Right now Old Grizzly is in charge but only for now. Mebbe I should call him by his real name but his nick name is how we all know him. It sounds funny to call him Lieutenant Colonel Hiram Burnham but that is his real name.

They do not tell us how these things heppen but we got more eyes to watch with then the officers gots things to hide. Couple weeks ago we had a big fancy dress parade where each regmnt was to show off how they could march in formation. You might guess the 43 New York looked some kind of sharp. But we did not. Some how Colonel Knowles was not there so Old Grizzly got the job of leading us through the manoouvers and we ended up doing some things that was not in the Hardees book. Apparently General[83] Baldy Smith was not impressed and Colonel Knowles heered abowt it later. Rumors say there was other things too but I do not know abowt that. I think may be Genl Smith knew what he was doing and wanted to see if Colonel Knowles made sure Grizzly knowed how to make us march right.

I wish I could have been there with you for Harvest Festival dinner. With all kind of respect for your cookin your Mum makes some kind of grand pies and I would be the happiest boy in Lubec to have some of that pie whilst sitting with my wife and daughter. May be next year. I sure hope so.

There are not so many papers that come out to where we are. I have not heard but a bit abowt that Trent Affair as you are calling it. I do not know just being a private the smart men do not ask me what I think but what I do think is that we have our hands full dealing with the Rebs and do not have much stomake for invading the British territories. What would Lubec want with Campobello? They are nice peeple and all that do not get me wrong but with no bridge and not even a decent town to go on Satidday night I would say let them be. Saving the Union and releasing the negroes be enough for me.

The cmpny received a nice present from the ladies of Eastport a box containing 103 pairs of mittens.[84] I hope the ladies of Lubec helped with this because there will be some warm hands this winter and if you were part of it I wud be prowd.

You take good care my child and save some love for yourself.

Your Faithful Freeman

"So," he asked, looking at the way her hair was pulled back into a thick rope hanging halfway down her back. "Do you let your hair down often?"

"Hah!" She sat back with a big smile and a bigger laugh. "First sign of a pick-up line."

68

This time it was Richard's turn to laugh. "Those were your words," he said, taking another sip of the whiskey and enjoying again the warmth of her smile. "Do you always shoot the messenger?"

"No," she replied, peering at him over the top of her glass. There was something in her eyes that he didn't quite understand. "Only if they're a Turtle."

"Lucky me, I hope." This was getting to be fun. "So what's the second sign?"

"I don't know," she replied, speaking softly with her head down, looking up at him. This time when she put her hand on his arm he decided maybe it did mean something. "Maybe you can tell me."

Richard looked into Dolores' eyes. He wondered how long she'd been there before he arrived.

"Tell me something," she asked. "You ever live with your mother?"

"Me?" Where'd this come from? "Not since I went off to college."

"I don't get to go out all that often," she said, looking away and twisting her napkin into a knot. "It's been a long, cold winter."

"Should I guess?" He glanced around and swallowed hard. The bartender was at the opposite end of the big copper top and appeared to be paying no attention to the two of them. "Sounds like you're maybe looking for a chance to warm it up a bit."

"I don't know." The way she said it, it sounded like a simple statement of fact, like she knew where she was going even if he didn't. "Could be."

"Your mother… You can't go out when you feel like it?"

When Dolores looked into his eyes, he saw a different expression than the one he'd previously seen. "You have no idea."

"I think you're trying to tell me something."

"You think?" Before she turned away, he thought he caught a brief sadness in her eyes.

"Maybe." He didn't know what to think, or how he would respond to what he thought she was thinking.

"Maybe…" she repeated with a sigh. "You should use your imagination."

"My imagination?" He ignored the buzzing in his ears. "How many things do I need to imagine?"

"Tell me just one."

Chapter 3
Right Man For The Job

*Warfare is the greatest affair of state, the basis of
life and death, the Way to survival or extinction.
It must be thoroughly pondered and analyzed.*

Sun Tzu
Art of War

My Dearest Freeman   *December 10, 1861*

*It is hard to believe that Christmas is in just two weeks. This
will be the very first Christmas since we met that we was not
together. You will be off fighting and I will be here with Mum and all
I can do is think about you.*

*Last night we got snow maybe six inch. The first snow of the
season ever thing looks nice but I know that by February we will see
things differnt.*

*I knitted Mum a nice hat for Christmas but can not afford
more. Hopefully the package I sent to you will arrive in time. Will
not tell you what is in it but wanted you to know you should be
looking for it.*

*I am glad to hear that the lady from the Christian
Commission[85] stopped by to see you and the boys. Mum has been
writing to a group in Bangor that is part of that. She was some kind
of worried to hear about them Cyprians. Said she read about them
and how they was corrupting some of the camps and hoped they was
not coming near the Six. The group that she is writing to is worried
that even men who are not wounded in battle may come home hurt
even worse on the inside.[86]*

*Esther is getting bigger now and so am I. I can feel other
things too. Last week I got new shoes because the old ones was
getting so tight made my feet hurt. Mum says that is way suposed to*

71

be but I am not sure I like it. Mrs. Ballard looked my belly over and said it was just right for some time in March. I do not know if I can wait that long.

All I wants for Christmas is to have you back with me and soon.

Your Loving Alma and Your Daughter Esther

My Darling Alma   *December 23, 1861*

I know Christmas is just two day away an I will not be there to give you a Christmas kiss and pat your belly where my little girl is waitin. I will be thinking abowt you but for now that is all I can do.

Since Colonel Knowles left things is a little diffrent. Old Grizzly may be put in charge and most of us hope for that but it is not up to us. Any way he is acting in charge and now the boys is paying more atenshun to whut the officers say. I do not know what made the difference but there is one.

One thing heppen that surprised all of us. Remember I told you abowt Sergeant Charlie Clark getting stript of his stripes? Less then three weeks later they made him Second Lieutenant Clark.[87] I do not know what Colonel Vinton would say but he is from the 43 New York not the 6 Maine. I heerd this come from General Baldy Smith him self. It would be interesting to hear what Gen'l Baldy might say to Colonel Vinton.

We buried three men yesterday from being sick. No Reb bullets has come our way but Reb disease is doing it in stead. I heard that these boys was killed by diptheerea. I hope you are not worrying abowt me catching a Reb disease. I can take care myself good since I been here had a cold a few days but that was all.

Do not know when we might be in a fight with the Rebs. We been here since summer and have not been in a fight yet. That is probly fine by you because I know you do not want me to be in a battle but I know it is coming. Probably in the Spring because it is just as hard for them to move round as it is for us. Some times when we are on picket duty we can hear Rebs and I bet that means they can hear us too but there has not been any shooting.

I think Zadoc gave you abowt the right amount for my share of the Achenar. Ask him if may be there is someone who wants to buy my twenty five percent. When I bought my share the schooner cost twenty two hundred dollars but I do not know what it would be worth now. A forty two ton schooner that is fourteen years old must still be worth some thing.

Please let Missus Cooper know that Isaac is doing fine and so is James. The Barlow knife that Katherine gave James keeps him busy after his fatigues is done.

I wish I could see you even for just little time especially with Christmas coming.

Your Loving Freeman

Richard paid the tab in cash, dropped down an over-generous tip, and ignored the knowing glance from the bartender. He turned to follow Dolores towards the hallway. She walked with a confident stride, without looking to the right or the left.

After the elevator door rolled shut, she put her arms around his waist and nuzzled her nose into the crook of his neck. When she squeezed him tightly, it gave him a warm and comfortable feeling. Her perfume was unfamiliar; it was unlike anything Amanda ever wore.

He well knew what arousal felt like – Amanda could bring him to that point with just a glance, and often did. This time the feeling was different and in his mind he saw a bridge looming in the fog. It was a narrow bridge and the far end was lost to the gloom, and it only went one way. When he drew a deep breath, he realized the feeling was that of fear, that he would soon take one step then another onto that bridge, and that he wasn't even sure he could give Dolores what he knew she sought.

When the light over the elevator door showed six, it rolled open. Fear turned to panic and his knees started to shake. He fumbled with the card before getting his room open, but when the door closed behind them the sound of the latch echoed in his head, like a gunshot.

Dolores set her shoes off to the side, then walked over to the bed and pulled back the covers. Without further ado, she started to unbutton her blouse. He watched in disbelief then kicked off his shoes. By the time he reached for his belt his hands too were shaking, and he turned away to catch his breath.

Glancing up in the mirror he swallowed hard when she stepped out of her dress and casually draped it across the chair. He watched while she reached behind to unhook her bra. The way she tossed it onto the chair looked practiced, like she'd done it like that more often than she'd let on. The fog cleared a bit and the bridge became more distinct, and now he knew for sure it only went one way. If he crossed it, he'd never be able to come back.

My Dearest Freeman   *December 24, 1861*

It is Christmas Eve and you are not here. For me that is not much of a Christmas. You been gone from here six months and five days. The closest I can get to you is knowing that you will be holding this paper and reading my words.

Esther is getting big now and moves a lot. My back hurts a bit and so do my legs but Mum says that is the way it is sposed to be. She says it will not be too much longer maybe three more months. I

74

feel fat and my feet are swollen look like loafs of bread. Mister Watkins asks me ever day if it is okay for me to keep working but I do not want to stop and Mrs. Ballard says I do not need to stop long as I do not do heavy liftin or get a chill.

We got a big snow storm yesterday.[88] I hear up Saint John they got nearly two feet but here it was less. May be fourteen inches but that was still enough.

Papers here still full of talk about the Trent Affair. Some of the British newspapers say the US Army will be invading any time. I tell folks what you said about that and if they be from Campobello or Saint John they say you are wrong but if they is from Moncton or Bangor they say you is right. People are some nervous hearing that the pirate vessel Sumter[89] has been seen near Machiasport we think it has some thing to do with the Trent.

There was a mentshun in the Sentinel that said Private W. H. Johnson of the Lincoln Cavalry has been shot for desertion.[90] The paper said this was the first execution in the Army of the Potomac.

The Bessie Watkins is almost ready to go. They is working on some of the trimwork and a few last things in the rigging. She went out into the bay two days ago and the new owners are right pleased how she goes to weather. I think Bessie will be a fast lady.

Last week they brought a brigantine in for some repairs. They said it had outrun a Reb pirate may be the Sumter but had been hit by one of their guns. Nobody was hurt but there was a piece of the wheelhouse shot away and also the starbord side coaming. They was pretty shook up but the pirate did not chase them into the bay. The brigantine flew American colors and so did the pirate until it got in close and ready to fire then it showed Rebel colors.

Not long ago the Sentinel included some thing that might make you laugh. The paper said that the Machias Union printed that the editor of the Sentinel declared that he recently saw a curious cabbage head. The Sentinel added Just so, the editor of the Union has been in town recently.[91]

A few days ago I put your likeness up on the shelf where we can see it all ways. Funny thing but I am sure that when I move around the room your eyes is following me where ever I go. That makes me feel real good because it is like you is right here watching me. I know it can not be real but it sure do feel real.

75

I hope the army at least gives you decent dinner for Christmas. If I can not hold your hand I would like to know you did not go to bed hungry.

Your Loving Wife and Daughter, Alma and Esther

My Dearest Alma   *December 28, 1861*

Life in camp is pretty slow these days. We had four more boys to bury from Rebel disease and still no Rebel bullets. Do not know which is worse. The hospital tent is off limits because they do not want any of us to catch what ever is in there.

Christmas was not much of a holiday. Some of the officers got furloughs to see their wives. When they come back they were all smiles and I know why.

There is something coming because there is all kind of fancy folk coming to see Old Grizzly. Nobody is telling the boys what is coming just that we must keep marching and practicing. I did hear that we are doing lots better at marching. I know there is more to being soldier then marching and think we soon will be finding out what that is. They did not bring us down here just to march and practice listening to what officers tell us and learn what all the bugle toots mean.

I am glad Mrs. Ballard is helping you with my daughter. I remember hearing how she helped other girls become mothers she all ways knows the right thing to do. I do not want to hear that you do not listen to what she says. I can not afford to pay her much but will do what I can.

Is my allotment being delivered to you regular like? Uncle Samuel does not send his moneybags man around here to pay us as often as they said they would but they was here a week back. You have not said lately and if we actually go on campaign I will not be

76

able do much to help. At least right now I can write letters and may be get help from our regimnt officers.

The bugle just tooted us to parade review so I has to go.

Your Loving Freeman

My Dearest Freeman   *December 31, 1861*

Here we are at New Years Eve and you and the boys are still not home. When you left we all figured on this being over before now and it do not look like it is any where near over. I miss you and so do Esther and Mum too.

The papers are saying the Trent Affair is over.[92] Father Abraham decided to let the two Rebs Mason and Slidell that our Navy captured down Havana go on there way. He let them board a British ship and leave. Apparently he figured it was not a good idea to keep them especially since the British was pretty mad over the whole thing and the French were agreeing with the British. One visitor here said the Rebels were upset that they were allowed to go they hoped that the British would recognize the Confederates because we kept those men but in stead they will stay neutral.

The Sentinel said one British paper said there is no reason why Mason and Slidell should not be restored to the quarter-deck of a British Admiral in the face of 12 British Men of War.[93] Some how I do not think that will happen.

Papers still say the British Army is coming to keep the US Army from heading up to take their lands to the north. They say they are scared they can not keep us from taking over the western territories and the prairie lands especially because some of the people there might welcome us doing that.[94]

They brought another vessel into the yard for repairs that outrunned a Reb pirate. This time it was a schooner and they lost part of the for'sl gaff but was able to get away in a fog bank and come up the Lubec narrows. With the broken spar they was not able to point as high as they should but they knowed the bottom better and

77

may be the pirate was skeered of running aground. Next one may be will not be so lucky but if a Reb does run aground in the narrows it might be fun to see what happens especially on falling water. They say the Rebs use Nova Scotia for base and some times come in to Saint John for supplies but not showing the Rebel flag.

Mum asked me to wish you Happy New Year. She knowed I was writing this letter but she and Jake went off to church. Mrs. Ballard was by and says that Esther is doing fine but she still do not believe it be Esther and not Luther. I will show her and soon I hope.

There is a lot of snow on the ground now and it did not go above freezing in the last week. Looks like it might be a cold winter. Paper said temperature went to zero the other day and it was the first real cold of the winter.[95] With you not here I know it is going be a long winter. Nearly ever morning now when the current comes in thru the narrows it brings the sea smoke. I remember when you and I went up to the cliff above the wharf to see the way the fog lays on the water like that. You called it Gods Camp Fire and I think that is right.

I hear Mum and Jake coming in now so I will end this letter. Hurry home.

Your Faithful Alma

The phone by the bed... His heart sank at the insistent blinking of the message lamp. There was only one person in the entire world who would be calling him in his hotel room. Amanda's voice awaited him in that little box. Dolores lowered her panties, leaving her with nothing and undoubtedly wondering why he was still fully clothed.

When he pushed the button, the cheery voice popped out of the box. *"Hi sweety!"* It sounded far away and tinny, but it still sounded like Amanda. As muffled as it was, her voice saturated the room and he heard Bonkers barking in the background. *"Just wanted to tell you I love you, give you a good-night kiss. Hope you sleep well. Bonkers and I, we both miss you."*

The icy feeling started in the middle of his back and quickly spread downward. He turned away from the phone with a shudder. "I… I can't do this."

"What?" Dolores looked at him with a question mark in her face, holding her panties in her hand and shaking her head.

"No way I can go through with this." He turned away and buried his face in his hands.

"But…" The incredulous tone to her voice was obvious, unmasked. "But I thought you…"

"It's got nothing to do with you," he said, trying not to cry out and squeezing his ring tight, making sure it was still right where Amanda had put it, right where it had been all along. He had never attempted to conceal the gold band, or its symbolic meaning. "It's me. I can't do this." He turned away. "I can't cheat on my wife like this."

"You never told me you were married."

"You have to go." Richard retreated toward the sanctity of the bathroom. "This is not your fault." When he pulled the door closed behind him the swirling fog closed in, shrouding the bridge in the gloom.

My Dearest Alma   *January 6, 1862*

     It was a great surprise to get the package you sent me. Did you knit the socks yourself? They fit perfect and really keep my feet warm. I could not ask for some thing more perfect. And the cookies were so special since I knowed it was you made them and put some love in the batter. I shared them with Isaac and James and we all three sat by the fire and cried like babies from being homesick. In two weeks we will be seven months gone. Some days it seems like just yesterday an other days it seems like it has been years. James misses Katherine and Isaac misses his mother and sister and I miss you something awful.

     Not too much is hapning here right now. We still do not know who will be our new Colonel but Old Grizzly is acting like it will be him. There is a lot of us boys who want it be him in fact I do not know no body who thinks otherwise. But until Baldy Smith says it is so then it is not so. Pretty boring being down here with no thing to do but practice marching and following orders.

     Reb sicknesses got two more boys yesterday. We have not lost a single one to Reb bullets but now there is a lot we has buried because of Reb sicknesses. So far none are from Company K but I do not know how long until that changes. The sanitary lady come by again this morning and wanted to know if we got our Christmas packages on time.

     They are tooting the tattoo so it is time to blow out my candle. I will mail this in the morning and wish I could go home with it. I will dream of you with your yellow scarf.

Your Loving Freeman

My Darling Freeman   *January 7, 1862*

     Esther was busy last night I think she is as unpatient as her daddy. Mrs. Ballard says it is not time yet so there is no thing I can do but wait. Mister Watkins told me I should start staying home now because he is worried about having me around as big as I is on account of I can not fit down the companionway into the new schooner. He said he would have some body bring some work home for me if I want but he do not want me to come back until I is carrying Esther in a basket. The money he pays me comes in real handy and I like working around the other people and hearing what the visitors tell us about the war.

Katherine was here yesterday and last week Gwyneth come around. Gwyneth told me she got a letter from Elias last month but only three since he been gone. When she seen how many I had from you she got all kind of sad but then said that if she had married him like he had asked she knowed he would have written more regular. Katherine gets letters from James ever week and some times we share. She read one to me where he told her about his dreams made me miss you even more. I do not know how many letters Mrs Cooper gets because she does not share them with any body.

We have been meeting one or two times each week downstares at Big White to work together knitting socks and things that Miss Penniman takes to be sent to the army. It is much nicer to work together because then we can talk makes the time go much better. Gwyneth has joined the group so now there is eight of us.

Tomorrow I will go down to the narrows so I can see the Bessie Watkins head out. The new owners will take her out around Grand Manan just to check ever thing out. Mister Watkins says he is not worried they might find some thing because she is a fine boat. Hope she is fast enough outrun Reb pirates may be hiding out in Seal Cove where they could come out real easy.

I would have gone except they say they do not want women on board especially on the maiden trip. I think they was more worried about Esther than they was having me on board because Jake told me Mister Watkins is taking his wife. I know I am not supposed to know that so please do not say no thing about it when you get back.

Hurry Home to Your Loving Alma

He must have remained perched on the toilet seat for an hour, shivering. However long it was, it was well after he'd heard the door click shut and knew that Dolores had left him to himself. *But had she really?* Had he already passed beyond some sacred threshold, betraying the promise he'd made that April morning? If he told Amanda about this, what would she think? He knew what she'd *say,* but what would she *think*?

However long it was, it felt like a lifetime. The promises they'd made, were they still valid? Had he walked away from the only thing in his life that really mattered?

Mandy is so beautiful, so dedicated, so wonderful to be with. How could I have been tempted by such a tramp? Dolores was nothing, nothing at all, compared to the one I love.

When he finally opened the bathroom door and looked out, the open bed was the only evidence Dolores had been there. That, and the two drinks they had brought with them. She could have rummaged through his possessions or even taken his wallet, but she had not touched anything. She had simply left, presumably after putting her clothes back in order.

He flushed the remnants of their drinks down the toilet and put the glasses in the hall where the hotel staff would find them. Just thinking of things was bad enough, even a Turtle didn't need any more reminders.

Had he cheated, or had he not? Did backing away from that dismal bridge at the very last instant, denying only the final consummation, provide absolution? He pushed the button on the phone again, just to hear Amanda's voice.

My Darling Freeman   *January 19, 1862*

This morning I ackshully went to church. Reverend Smith preached a sermon about how you boys are doing the right thing and how we all should be proud of what you are doing. I felt like asking him why he did not go down and tell you that hisself but Mum told me not to. Do not ask me why I went because I do not know except may be it was the snow last night made me think of it. You know how pretty Lubec looks when there is a layer of white covering every thing. Mum likes all the singing and praying and amens but you know how I feel about that.

Mister Watkins stopped by few minits ago said he just wanted to know how you was doing and how I was making out. I told him ever thing was doing fine by me and that you was healthy or at least you tell me you is healthy. He left me some of the papers from Saint John. He told me he often gets papers from Boston and New York but because of the snow the stage could not travel the Airline Road from Bangor so may be he would send over some to read later.

The Morning Freeman says England is sending troops to Saint John and Quebec and other places[96] because they is sure you boys will be done soon and then Father Abraham will send you north to annex the British colonies. I hear folks here saying that is what is going to happen but I say I just do not know.

I also do not know how much longer Esther will make me wait. I am ready but it seems she is not in any kind of hurry. Mrs. Ballard just keeps saying I must be patient and that Esther will let me know when the time be right. I am tired of being patient. I want to hold my daughter and hold my husband to. Hurry home please.

The Sentinel said that the brigantine Alice Maude went aground down Bass Harbor. It was a new vessel on its first voyage.[97] Paper did not say who was the captain but may be he will find a job ashore now.

With Kisses A Plenty, Your Alma

My Dearest Alma   *January 24, 1862*

We still do not have our Colonel. Old Grizzly is doing every thing the Colonel is supposed to do except he still is wearing silver leafs insted of a bird on his sholder. I guess they must just be waiting for Guvner Washburn to make up his mind. If we are actually going in to a battle then it would be good to have some body we can trust leading the way. I seen the way he treets Lieut Clark and it makes me feel like he would do the same for all the rest of us.

Since my last to you we buried three more boys for Rebel sickness. I heerd this time it was diptheerea. You can trust me to keep my distance from that hospital tent. Regimnt nearby buried several for the colera last week.

You did not tell me how your Mum liked the hat you made for her for Christmas. Bet she was suprised. I sure do like the socks you made for me.

I did not know that Gwyneth give Elias the mitten he never said nothing to me abowt that. Seems funny she was so mad abowt him going to the Cumberland if she had all ready refused him but you never knows what is in some one else head.

James is not the only one who has sweet dreams abowt the woman he left at home. I see you some times wearing your yellow scarf and it makes me miss you even more. I do not think James knows that I dream of you may be as much as he does of Katherine. May be I do not like to rite abowt that becuz it makes me miss being home and that might not be a good thing for a soldier.

Take good care Esther for me now. Listen to what Mrs. Ballard tells you because I know she knows what she is talking abowt.

Your Loving Freeman

This time he knew why he woke up. It had been hard enough, going to bed knowing whose hand it was that had pulled the covers back, that it had not been Amanda's but someone else's, someone who had no rightful place in his life. That was not the prescription for a good night's sleep.

The way the faces emerged from the fog, one by one, their reproachful silence speaking louder than words, he was certain it was real. First it was Amanda's, tear streaked but silent, her chest heaving and eyes closed. Then his mother's, with a quizzical expression like she was asking what else he was willing to walk away from. Aunt Elizabeth was in the parade, her schoolteacher's wagging finger coupled with the sneer of disdain. But when Amanda reappeared, this time with her face buried against Bonkers furry chest - that was when he sat bolt-upright in the strange bed.

Another favorite image formed up out of the fog, of Amanda brushing out her hair after they shared intimacy. Standing in their bedroom in front of the darkened antique mirror, tall and narrow with the gilded bugle carved into the top of the frame, it was one of the few things left behind from his uncle's time in the house. He loved to come up behind her at such moments and draw her into his arms, feeling the bareness of her backside pressed into his groin and her shoulders on his chest, savoring their love and her heat. Was this too, something he wanted to give up? They had often laughed about the spirits in that mirror – what would *they* think?

He stepped over to the window to look down into the sleeping city. Traffic moved slowly below and a lone ambulance worked its way along the avenue, its flashing lights reflecting off of the mirrored buildings. The upcoming discussion in the Aladdin offices had the potential to lead to the loss of a client. But instead of spending the evening preparing an airtight presentation, like he had planned on doing when he left their office, he had allowed himself to be distracted. He hadn't planned on inviting a strange woman into his room, and planned even less for how *that* turned out.

It would *not* be a good idea, stepping back out before some of those managers, for him to pretend they were simply picking up where they'd left off the day before. The message was incandescently clear, the way Johnson sat back and let them sharpshoot his presentation. Failing to heed would not be a sound strategy except for an ostrich. However, three a.m. was not the right time to go to work on it, but if he got up at five he could get at least two hours in.

He knew it was not Dolores' fault. He had asked her to his room, and then changed his mind. Richard understood, well before they left the bar, exactly what it was she was expecting, and that he had willingly offered to provide it. He had turned back from that bridge at the last moment, but if Amanda's voice had not been in the room too?

To My Loving Alma   *January 29, 1862*

We are still in winter quarters and trying keep warm. I can tell you winter in Virginia does not feel any warmer then winter in Lubec. We get snow and then we get mud. Then we get more snow. No wonder boys are getting the Rebel sicknesses all around. I had a touch of the diarhoe for a few days but the doctor gived me laudanum and it got better. So far I have dodged the sicknesses and have not had to dodge the bullets.

Did Gwyneth tell you anything abowt what Elias told her? I do not know where he is except what you have told me so I guess he is still on the Cumberland. I see James all day long most days so I pretty much know what he is telling Katherine. Seems he is the healthiest man on earth.

I know it is not what you want but I hope we see some action some day soon. Ever now an then we heer cannonading off in the distance but can not tell whether it is our boys firing on the Rebs or the Rebs doing it to our boys or some big wig showing up some where and getting a salute.

I am eating just fine because I got used to this hard bread and salt pork. A week back they gived us some potatoes and onions and it was like a feast. Some times we get together and cook our rations together and make a big stew. Compared to what we can do for our selves it is quite good.

I would rather be eating at the table with you and your Mum and a bowl of her Batter Pudding.

Your Faithful Freeman

There were no terrors in the hotel when he checked out in the morning. He'd dreaded the possibility of having to face down Dolores' scorn had their paths crossed in the lobby, but that didn't happen. When he checked out he was sure the clerk wore a smirk, like maybe the staff knew more than they let on and would share a good laugh in the back room after the guests had departed.

Richard breathed a sigh of relief when he flagged down the cab for the short ride to the Aladdin offices, where the second challenge of the day awaited him. Two hasty hours to prepare for a five hour meeting may not have been what he wanted to do, but it was all he had left for himself. The sleepless night didn't make things any better.

When the cab pulled up to the sidewalk, he swallowed hard before climbing out. The day was not promising to be a good one.

My Dearest Alma   *February 1, 1862*

I know I wrote to you just two days back but we got the news we have been hoping for. You may see this in the papers before my letter reaches you but we now have a Colonel. Early this morning the brigade was called to review by General Smith. We all knowed some thing was abowt to heppen when the regimemtal musicians started playing and the color sergeant had all the flags brought forward.

Old Grizzly stepped in front and read off the governors orders that he was now our Colonel. He now has a bird on his sholder instead of leafs and that made us all very happy and from the look on his face he was very prowd of being selected to lead the 6 Maine. Then he had Charles Chandler[98]read his orders too and he is now our Lieutenant Colonel. After that General Smith told us the new Major is Benjamin Harris. Chandler[99] may not be so easy when he talks to the boys but he knows what he wants to get done. Everybody likes Benjamin Harris.

There is not so much more for me to write abowt having just done so. Please take good care of my daughter Esther

Your Loving Freeman

Airline schedules are often a figment of someone's imagination: a fantasy. They are what is *supposed* to be but not necessarily what *will* be. The flight from Atlanta was not the problem; the challenges came from the connecting flight he had to catch in Philadelphia. Difficulties in Timbuktu, the airline had said. Or maybe it was Tuscaloosa or Tallahassee. Didn't matter, it was still nearly two when Richard and his fellow road-warriors staggered out of the plane in Bangor, found their way down the escalator, and headed off into the Maine night.

After retrieving his bag, there was still that little two-hour ride back, navigating the Airline Road in the dark then the twisting narrow 192 down to Machias followed by Routes 1 and 189 out to Lubec. As many times as he'd traveled these roads, this time of night it was still white-knuckle driving. A collision with a deer could wreck the car, but a moose could wipe out a lot more. And they owned the night.

After last night, and particularly today in front of the Aladdin staff, he wanted nothing more than to be home. He'd called Amanda from Philly and told her not to wait up, but she still left a few lights on for him. After kneeling to greet Bonkers at the door, he quietly deposited his clothes on the couch then tiptoed up the stairs, the dog padding along silently.

When Amanda rubbed the sleep out of her eyes, he realized she was lying awake, awaiting his return. "You really want it right now?" She seemed surprised by his request but rolled over to face him when he asked. "At four-thirty?"

"I do," he replied, one by one opening the buttons on her nightgown and kissing her tenderly. "I've missed you."

"I've missed you too," she murmured a few minutes later, cuddling up by his side. "A lot."

Chapter 4
Quaker Guns

"And Dear, Iv been put on another duty that I don't like much, but my motto is to do the best I can under any and all circumstances: go ahead and do my duty. I am now in command of the First Battalion of Sharpshooters composed of the detail from the 12th and 4th Reg., about 70 men. It is a post of honor, not one of ease."

S. G. Pryor, Capt., CSA[100]
May 22, 1863
Fredericksburg, VA

* * * * *

My Dearest Freeman   *February 2, 1862*

There is not so much to write about from here, other then the snow and the cold. Mum has a path dug through the dooryard to the barn where Charlie stacked the wood and every day Jake comes by and helps her bring in enough for the next day. I am not much help with that because Esther gets in the way no matter which way I turn. Seems like every time one of them shovels out that path then the wind brings the snow back and they have to shovel it again. I know the days are getting longer but so far it is not easy to see because it is still dark early. With you not here the days are too long any how.

Mum has been working with the Ladies Aid Society in the downstairs at Big White to help make knitted socks and scarfs for the soldiers. I do not know if the Sanitary Society will send them to the 6 Maine but I hope that is where some go. I know some is going to the 20 Maine. They say that regiment has no home[101]so the Society is careful that they take good care of them. Miss Penniman sent word that she will be here again when the roads clear just a little. For us it is easy we just have to climb School Street not even two blocks.

Do not worry yourself about James and his dreams. Katherine shared one of his letters with me and he says you are the one that has those dreams reglar like and not him. Some times I have those dreams too and I like to think you are having the same one at the same time. When that happens I wrap your yellow scarf around my neck and that makes me sleep better.

Deacon Fowler tells me I need to be more patient but that is not what I want. My husband back and my daughter borned that is what I want. The paper says that there is three officers from 6 Maine in town last week on furlow.[102] Do they ever let the men go home too?

I am not sure how to understand some thing that is in the latest paper here it says that Rev Henry C Leonard of the 3 Maine was put under arrest[103] for reproving one of the officers for swearing. Maybe there is more to the story then what Mister Nutt wrote in the paper.

Your loving Alma

My Dearest Freeman　　　　　　　*March 5, 1862*

When I read this in today's paper I just had to write to you to tell you how it made me feel. The Eastport paper printed this in the issue that come out today and I will copy it down just as they printed it.

The Army correspondent of the Boston Journal relates the following:

A word for the Maine Sixth. At a recent brigade drill – for it has been dry enough to drill once, since I wrote last, many months ago – General Smith, in command of the division, rode up to Colonel Burnham, and said: "I would not be doing my duty, Colonel, if I did not express an opinion I have long entertained; I think your regiment the best drilled in my command and one of the best this side of the Potomac."[104]

*When I read those words and knew he was talking about you
it just made me feel so proud of my soldier and what he is doing for
our country.*

*Mum sed she remembers your Hiram Burnham from when
she was my age. He led a militia from Cherryfield in the Pork and
Beans War[105] in 1839 as Captain. This was up near where the Saint
Croix and Aroostook Rivers come together. They did not ackshully
do any fighting but was ready to they woud have fought the British
because they was coming acrost the border to try to claim our land
was theres.*

*Esther is kicking something wicked and I know it is because
she wants out as much as I want her out. Mrs. Ballard says it should
not be too long now.*

*There was a report in the paper a week ago[106] that said there
was a riot in Virginia on February 4 and they had established
martial law. May be not every body in Virginia thinks the war is a
good thing.*

Your Faithful Alma

My Freeman   *March 7, 1862*

*Jake was here yesterday. He showed me some thing in the
paper he thought to be quite funny. It said that a man in New
Brunswick received a contract from the British Govt to transport
their soldiers and they would pay him sixty four dollars each. He
payed another man twenty four dollars to do the work and put the
difference in his pocket. Since he was transporting fifteen British
soldiers every day he was putting six hundred dollars in his pocket
every day.[107]Mister Watkins told Jake that just proved there was fat
contracts in New Brunswick too. I do not think he ever got any thing
like that from our government.*

*The papers from New Brunswick say that those soldiers are
coming this way because the British Govt believes that the war will*

be over soon and then we will invade their colonies. I am skeptical that would happen but that is what they are saying.

Here is another thing from the paper might make you and the boys feel better. Paper said it was from a Confederate Lady to her lover. I will copy it for you just as it is written. Here is what it says.

You did not bring on all this trouble and it is nothing but a nigger war, and if I were you I would have nothing to do with it. [108]

Sounds to me like she misses her man too. Any way Esther is kicking crazy like today and I think she wants out as much as I want you back.

Your faithful Alma

On Friday evenings the tavern was always crowded, and not just because they usually had live music. This was particularly true on those days in April when the good folks of Lubec have grown truly weary of winter and any excuse to get out will do just fine.

Richard slid into the seat with his back to the window to let Amanda watch the dusk settle over the harbor. From where she sat, she'd be able to catch the last glinting rays of the sun reflecting off of the windows of Eastport, forty-five miles away by car but just a few across the water.

"So how'd you make out in Atlanta," she asked absently while scanning the menu. "The Aladdin boys okay?"

He looked back across the table at her. "*My god, she's beautiful,*" he thought to himself, not wanting to immediately address her question. The musicians, one with a laughing clean-shaven face and the other with a ZZ Top beard, belted out the opening lines of

Barbara Ann. For an instant all conversation ceased while the crowd roared out the first stanza.

Baah-Baah-Baah!

He saw her glance out of the window and turned just in time to see an orange-hulled lobsterman crossing into the anchorage, its deck crowded with blue bait barrels. "Milt's out late," he remarked absently as the boat swung into the current and a crewman snagged the mooring line.

Baah-Baah-Ber-Annnn

Silas passed the bottle of wine Richard had ordered across the bar to the waitress and the music died down momentarily.

"I think Aladdin's going to be okay," he mumbled half-heartedly, pouring her a glass then one for himself. "Johnson's got a few questions I need to work on." He held his glass up to the light. "Good dago-red," he said, tipping it towards Amanda.

Glancing across the room, he spotted Dana and Claire. Both Coopers were deep in discussion with the local newspaper reporter, likely trying to pester the fellow into writing another article about the woefully low boat price for lobster. He wondered where the two children were, since he seldom saw the two out together without the kids.

"Hey, Richard," he heard from across the floor. "Rambling Man has come home to Mama." A lanky fellow wearing a Red Sox cap and a Patriot tee-shirt slouched across the floor towards their table.

"Hi Billy," he replied. The man came up behind Amanda and placed his hands on her shoulders. She turned toward him, smiled, and reached up to pat his left hand with her right. "What's new in your world?"

94

"We're putting her back in tomorrow morning," Billy replied. "I didn't figger on springin' for a new wheel but hey, what're you gonna do?"

"So you got off easy," said Richard. "Go running stuff down like that you never know what you're gonna bust. Lucky you didn't twist your shaft." A blonde woman approached, touched Billy on the arm and the pair went off to watch the musicians.

"Hello Mary-Lou,"

the smiling face warbled, with the bearded-one filling in the rhythm and the crowd stamping its feet.

"Good-Bye Heart!"

The crowd surged back and forth, sometimes responding to the music and sometimes swirling around a new arrival. Even though all of the seats were long-filled, those standing showed no inclination to stay in one place.

"Mandy," the woman said. "You survived the winter."

"Just barely," replied Amanda. "How 'bout you, Lilian?" Richard looked up at the statuesque redhead. She had materialized from the depths of the crowd where she seemed content to circulate, chatting up people she likely hadn't seen since the town's Christmas Parade.

"We did okay," Lilian shrugged. "As okay as six and a half cords'll get you. Kept Ricky busy all winter humping that stuff cross the dooryard."

"You run out?"

"Damn near."

"Hah!" laughed a much shorter and rounder man standing nearby. "That'll learn you guys," he snickered, "moving out Coffins Neck Road. You lucky you ain't still under a drift with the other two people dumb enuff ta' hide out in them woods."

"Louie," Lilian replied, glancing across at Amanda. Richard spotted the glint appearing in the corner of her eye. "Just for that I'm going to make you buy me a drink."

Louie stood up straight, threw back his shoulders, and sucked in his belly. "Sure thing, babe," he replied, pointing towards the bar. As the two moved off, Lilian towering over Louie, the waitress brought their dinner over and the musicians launched into *Little Deuce Coupe* with the smiling-faced singer somehow reaching up to the high notes.

You don't know what I got!

Richard spotted Claire whispering something into Dana's ear while looking across the floor at Amanda. Dana smiled and then worked his way across the floor to the musicians. When the song ended he leaned over and whispered into the bearded-one's ear. The musician grinned and nodded in assent to something unheard beyond the small circle. Dana found his way back to Claire's side and the two laughed.

"Seems we have a bit of a celebration here tonight," the beard announced. When the crowd quieted down momentarily he continued. "Wouldn't 'cha know it, a couple of lovebirds thought they could sneak in here, celebrate their eighth anniversary on the QT." The crowd roared out then hushed again. "Richard and Amanda Lawton," he called out, "you guys owe us this dance!"

The parting of the Red Sea had nothing on this crowd, the way they pulled back, urging them forward. It was obvious there was to be no escape. While Richard led Amanda to the tiny clearing, the two musicians conferred and the clean shaven one broke into a huge grin. The sudden quiet stood in stark contrast to the usual full-throated roar of the place, with all waiting for the singer to begin.

Midnight at the Oasis,
Send your camel to bed

Whether the singer was able to carry the song to its conclusion nobody could tell, the bedlam had resumed. Richard didn't mind, however. Feeling her pressed against his chest was a celebration in itself.

My Dearest Alma   *February 16, 1862*

Deacon Fowler is right. You need to be payshunt even if you do not have a say in the matter. Esther will let you know when the time be right and there is no thing you can do abowt it.

Ever day we hear more rumors abowt when we will be moving and where it is that we will go but each time we hear some thing diffrnt. I guess that means I must be payshunt too.

The last few days I have had a little bit of a cold but I am pretty much over it now. I am still tenting with James and he seems to be the healthiest man alive. May be it is his dreams makes him that way. Or else it is his Acadian blood. Isaac had a touch of a cold too but I think he has gotten better. All this cold and mud makes me miss Lubec even more. Up home we have an honest winter with snow and ice and not all ways mud. It is no surprise boys catching Rebel sickness down here.

At least we are eating okay. I hope that do not change when we get orders to move out.

I think your Mum is doing good work by getting hitched to those sanitary ladies. They are the only women we see in camp now no more washerwomen for the officers. The sanitary ladies spend more time with the enlisted men then with the officers. They keep asking questions abowt the camp and our health and when they find some thing wrong they go directly to Old Grizzly and he lissens.

The bugler is tootin the tattoo so I have to blow out my candle and go to sleep.

Your loving Freeman

Heading back up the hill after dinner, Amanda steered Richard into the little park. His belly was full, the wine had been wonderful, and the evening was still warm. Clancy loomed overhead in the moonlight, maintaining his vigilance over the sleepy village. The big memorial plaque listing the town's veterans gleamed, but there was no noise except for an occasional burst of music and laughter escaping from the tavern or the crash of balls from Annie's pool table.

Amanda started laughing.

"What?" he asked.

"You really think we could have gone in there," she said, pulling him close, "without that happening?"

"Didn't even think about it," he replied sheepishly, "not until it was too late."

"That part was pure Lubec," she said, now speaking softly. "But I'll forgive you."

"For?"

"Forgetting our anniversary." The way she spoke, he was sure she was concealing her disappointment, that she had looked forward to at least a spoken acknowledgment. It was like the town had just celebrated something that he had overlooked.

"Madam, you are accusing me of a *most* serious offense," he replied, standing back with a severe look. "Am I not entitled to a fair hearing?" He paused for a moment, enjoying the confused look in her eyes before digging into his pocket.

The necklace looked great hanging down, the small emerald glistening in the glow from the distant streetlight. Better yet was listening to her try to stammer something out when, for once, it was clear she didn't know what to say. Even Clancy appeared to be enjoying the scene.

He reached over to stroke the side of her face. "Did I get the right size?"

"Right size?" she sputtered, before throwing her arms around his neck. They stood in silence, leaning up against the base of Clancy's stand, each breathing deeply. "You can tell me later," she whispered, "whether you think it fits right."

They stood momentarily in the shadow of the monument, for now sharing the little park with the soldier, standing high above, proudly erect with his weapon by his side.

"You think he's really been up there since 1904," Richard asked, "Like it says right here?"

Amanda giggled softly. "You think I would really know different?" That little giggle – it rarely escaped her lips in public, but when she did it in private it always made his knees quiver. He wrapped his arms around her waist and pulled her close, feeling her squeezed up against his chest.

When she pressed her lips against his, the vision of Dolores standing unclothed in his hotel room suddenly flashed across his mind, along with the dismay painted on her face at the instant she realized what had just happened. It was the same moment that he realized what nearly did happen. He closed his eyes and hoped the vision would fade. *"How could I have been such a fool,"* he silently asked himself, hoping that the darkness would keep Amanda from spotting the change in his face.

They crossed the street and headed home, where Bonkers would still be expecting his evening constitutional.

Approachng the porch, Amanda broke the silence. "You know what I've been thinking?" He glanced over with one raised eyebrow. "We haven't had your parents over for dinner in a long time."

"I suppose that's so." Pembroke was only a half-hour drive but it had been months since the last time they'd sat together at the dinner table. Since her parents had escaped to Steinhatchee, all the way down on the Gulf of Mexico shoreline, it was only on special occasions they got together, but at least his were nearby. "You think maybe it's time?"

My Dear Alma   *March 9, 1862*

I hope this letter finds you promptly and do not get lost. We have been ordered to break camp and get ready to move on campaign. They have not told us where we will be but I have only heard rumors abowt heading tords Richmond. Tomorrow morn we will be heading out and not a moment too soon.

If you ask me this place is pestefferous we have lost many men to Rebel sickness. We will be leaving behind a city of the dead where over seventy good[109]men have been laid to rest and not one of them from Rebel lead. I am truly sorry to leave those men behind but

100

am real glad to get away from this place because I do not know how many more would join them if we stayed here.

I got rid of my cold but then had a mild bout of the diarhoe. I do not know but may be it is the water here that we get that from because I am not the only one has that.

You asked abowt me coming home on furlough. Some of the boys from Maryland an Pennsylvania do that but we haf to pay our way home. I send most of my pay to you and the train and boat wud cost most of what I make in a munth. It is better I stay here do my duty an make sure you haf what you need. Hopefully this thing will not go on to much longer I can come home to stay.

Since we will be moving I do not know when I will be able to write again but soon I promise. I must end this one because they say all hands is to help with the packing. Take good care of my Esther she probly be ready soon.

Your Faithful Freeman

The data were all there. The operational reports had been updated regularly on the website, so they were already in the client's hands. There were no flaws in the system, and his servers had been reading Aladdin's transactional records without any interruption. Everything was working as he had intended. Except, apparently, the process itself.

Richard paced the floor, alternating between peering out at the fishing boats and the scatterplot filling in on his monitor. In just a few minutes it would be complete, the trend line computed, and the truth told. His other clients enjoyed profitable results from his efforts. Why not Aladdin?

He dropped back in his chair, shaded his eyes, and waited. Whatever the results were, Johnson was awaiting the outcome. That one pesky manager, the one who'd asked all the questions while

Johnson sat back - he had already called twice. There'd be no shading of the truth, not if he'd avoid a lawsuit.

Point by point, the chart filled in and the line formed up. The confidence interval at the 95% point started to narrow, but the line remained stubbornly level. Every other client showed a strong and rising curve, but not Aladdin.

He stared out of the window, down at the fishing fleet, and watched for a minute as a crew labored over a deck winch. Hammer blows against a recalcitrant bolt echoed across the water – sounds of an honest day's labor. Richard returned to his desk, stared at the phone for another minute, then dialed Johnson's number.

My Darling Freeman   *March 15, 1862*

You are a father. Yesterday Luther was born. When we knew it was not going to be Esther both Mum and Mrs. Ballard thought it a huge joke that I had told myself and was wrong but I am happy because Luther is a healthy baby and ever thing went just as Mrs. Ballard said it would. I will call him Luther Freeman Lawton unless you think different. I am fine too just a little bit sore. Maybe more than a little bit. Mum and Luther and me will go to church tomorrow so Deacon can see your little boy. Wish you could sit with us.

The papers are full of a story about a big Navy fight in a place they call Hampton Roads that sounds kind of like where you are going. Mister Watkins says what he heard was the Rebels took a steam-powered screw frigate called the Merrimack that our Navy had burned because they could not get it out before the Rebels took over the Navy yard. He said he heard it only burnt to the water line then sank. They hauled it out built an iron fort on top of the hull named it Virginia and then used it to attack our ships that was blockading the harbor. Cannon balls from our ships just bounced off the iron plates so we could not touch it. Then they used a big ram to poke a hole below the water line so our ships sank.

One of the ships they sunk was the Cumberland and Elias is among the missing. They say there was a hundred twenty two of our sailors killed in that battle and he was one of them. Next day one of our ships the Monitor showed up and stopped the Rebel floating iron-fort from sinking another of our ships. They say the Monitor and the Rebel floating-fort fought for four hours but neither could get any advantage over the other. When the Rebel tried to use the ram on the Monitor it did not work the same and actually damaged the Virginia.[110]

Gwyneth has gone into seclusion for mourning the loss of Elias and Reverend Smith said a special prayer for him. I am sorry I had to deliver this news to you. The papers said the Cumberland kept firing on the Rebels even when it was going down so Elias died a hero. Lubec lost a good man but yesterday another one arrived.

The weather is still cold we have big piles of snow and ice but today it is warm and sunny. All the streams are choked up with ice flows. Pretty soon all will be mud.

The town office delivered your pay here on Tuesday thirty dollars. So far we are doing okay but it will be a long time until we get anything from the garden.

Time for me to go nurse your little boy. I will show him your likeness so he can see what his Daddy looks like.

Your Loving Family Alma and Luther

As usual, they arrived right on time. His mother elbowed past him and headed into the kitchen with a huge bowl of salad. His father wandered out onto the deck, dropped his elbows onto the rail, and gazed out over the harbor. Richard poured four glasses of wine and carried two out into the evening air.

103

The elder Lawton had never been one to mince words. "How's business?"

Richard chuckled. "All things considered," he replied, taking a sip of wine, "it's still pretty good."

"*Still* pretty good?"

"I think…" He wished his father had brought up their shared passion, baseball, instead of landing on this. "I'm going to have to go into promotion mode pretty soon."

"Do I know what that means?"

"You might."

"Last I heard…" William Lawton leaned back, sipped his glass of wine, and continued staring out over the harbor. Two boats lazily motored from the commercial pier back out towards their moorings. A few puffy clouds decorated the sky and a contrail announced a new arrival boring its way in from Europe, the plane's altitude suggesting a New York destination. "Last I heard you had six clients. And you served them all without any help." He paused for a few seconds. "That not still the case?"

Richard closed his eyes for a few seconds and swallowed hard. "I think I'm about to lose Aladdin."

William said nothing for maybe a minute. "I'm sure you're doing what you can to salvage that." He took another sip of wine. "How much of your business are they?"

"About twenty-three percent."

"What happened?"

"To be sure, I'll probably never know. But their numbers don't pan out like the others." This, he thought to himself, is the

104

vendor's fate. Sometimes terminating an employee brings in all kinds of legal issues, and vendors are often brought in to sidestep that challenge. Even if he thought he had grounds, his contract specifically prohibited acting on them. "I think one of the managers had it in for me, for what I was doing for them."

"He had a better idea?"

"S'pose maybe." He hated it when his father cut to the chase like that, but that was where he himself had learned to do it. "I think the guy thought he could identify defecting customers more efficiently than my system does."

"Sounds like you're suggesting sabotage."

William dropped his elbows onto the railing and resumed looking out across the harbor. Richard followed his gaze out over the contour of Dudley Island, directly out in front, and the larger Treat Island close behind. The sun hung low over Seward Neck and a fisherman motored across, heading for the Globe Cove anchorage. *On the scale of things that really matter, just how high did a business loss rank?*

It was his father that broke his reverie. "Somebody did a nice job refurbishing the old clock."

"Mandy came up with the company that did that," Richard replied. "Came back from Boston maybe a month ago. Cost a bit but it seems it was worth it."

"Oh?" William took a sip of wine. "How so?"

"They told us it dates to 1842, made by a London firm called E.J. Dent, same outfit that made Big Ben. The guys in Boston say it's rather valuable. It's actually a chronometer, probably came here on a sailing ship."

"Keeps good time?"

"Perfect time. Never saw a mechanical clock as accurate as that one." He paused to refill their glasses. "They told us the case was made later." He took a sip of wine and added, "There's names carved inside."

"Names?" William looked up in surprise. "Whose names?"

Richard stepped inside to retrieve the invoice. "Jake and Esther Dubois. Also, 1863. I have no idea who they were."

"Me neither," shrugged William. "Right in the middle of the Civil War. Looks great on your mantle. Better than squirreled away up in the attic."

"It *was* rather a surprise, finding it up there. It looked like whoever cleaned out the place overlooked it."

"There was nothing else there?"

"Nary a scrap."

"Funny," said William. "Your uncle lived here nearly fifty years. For a bachelor pack rat to leave nothing behind..."

"*Somebody* went in and cleared it all out. Likely whatever was there is all in the landfill."

"Depend on this," chuckled William. "It wasn't Oscar did that. My brother never threw a thing away in his entire life. Elizabeth probably convinced your grandmother it needed doing. Anyway, the clock is a nice find."

"The shop said it probably hadn't been wound in eighty years, maybe more."

The elder Lawton turned towards the kitchen and the sound of rattling dishes. "Never heard that name before, Dubois. Sounds Acadian, maybe someone from Campobello."

To My Freeman   *March 19, 1862*

Luther will grow up to be a fine man. Mrs Ballard says he is very alert and shows good promise. When he takes my finger he squeezes very tight. I am proud of our son and know he will do his Pappy proud.

It finally stopped snowing early this morning but it will be a while before we have got dug out.[111]We can get to Eastport but not to Trescott because the roads is all full of snow drifts and they say out by Split Hill the mounds are as high as a horse. It started Saturday and went to Sunday and piled deep blowing a gale the whole time. Mum will not let me help dig the path to bring in wood and Jake has not been able to get over here.

I am feeling fine and Luther is taking all I have to give him so I guess that is about all the work I can do right now. Mister Watkins sends some work over for me regular like but I do miss going to the office.

Ever body is upset about losing Elias not just Gwyneth. I can still see him walking down the street with Gwyneth but now she walks alone. I am sure that this snow makes it even harder for her because now no one can go visit her she can only look out at the drifts and the icicles. She does not even have a likeness like you sent me.

Hurry up and make this war end we want you to come home.

Your Loving Alma

My Dearest Alma   *March 28, 1862*

I received yours of March 15 and had to write right away to tell you how happy you have made me. Luther Freeman Lawton is a fine name and I am sure that he will be a fine man because he has a mother like you. I read your letter to Isaac and James and they were all most as prowd as me. Charley Clark heerd James cheering and come over to see why then just after he left Old Grizzly him self was over wanting to shake my hand. Please write me and tell me ever thing my son does because I want to know.

We will be marching off again tomorrow morning heading south. I do not know exactly where we are right now some place in Virginia near the water. It is easier to be on the march then to sit in camp all day so I am glad we are at last moving. I hope my mail to you is not delayed because your letters mean so much to me and guess that mine to you mean as much.

Please write soon and tell me how Luther is doing. My diarhoe is all gone for now.

Your loving Freeman and Luthers Pap.

The dinner was great. Amanda and his mother had worked out the details and he had exchanged kitchen duties for a dishwashing pledge. Maybe the conversation with his father had been cut short, but that too was okay. Anyway, the tiramisu was a complete surprise even though Amanda refused to reveal where she'd come up with the recipe. "Girl's gotta have some secrets," she said, flashing a demure smile.

He retrieved the bottle of Redbreast. "Time for the private stash," he said pulling the cork and setting out four glasses.

"As long as we're talking secrets..." Arlene rose and pulled a small package from her purse. "Maybe that's what this is." She laid it on the table in front of Richard. He looked up at his mother with a quizzical expression.

"Go ahead," she said. "Not nice of you, keeping Amanda in suspense."

When he peeled back the wrapping paper, he found a small and worn wooden case with a tiny image staring out from behind a piece of wavy glass. "What's this?"

"It surfaced when I cleaned out your grandmother's place. It was buried away in her bureau drawer."

He peered into the glass. "Do you know who this is?"

"No. I never saw it before that day. It obviously meant something to her. It was the only one she had."

"Only one she had? What's that mean?"

"Some people," Arlene said, "collect dagguerotypes and other kinds of early photographs." She paused for a bite of tiramisu. "I kind of figure that if there was only this one, it was not coincidental that she hung on to it. Specially where she was keeping it."

"Dad," Richard asked, "you know anything about this?"

"Only that I remember seeing it once, many years ago. Never heard her speak of it."

Richard peered through the glass at the face in the image. "Whoever it is, looks like a Civil War uniform."

"That was near the end of the time those things were popular," said Arlene. "As far as I've ever heard, there was never a studio anywhere near here. If that's so, when it came here it was likely quite a novelty."

"If the uniform was Spanish-American war vintage, it might have been your great-great-grandfather," said William. "I think that's the right number of 'greats'. But then it wouldn't have been this kind of photograph."

"This is definitely Civil War." Richard tapped on the glass like maybe he could wake up the man behind the glass. "Just look at the hat."

"But who this is…" William took another sip of wine, "is as much mystery to me as you."

"Grams never mentioned anything else?"

"Not of any significance. There was a box, I do remember hearing about that. I must have been all of nine."

"What kind of box?"

"They described it as an old sardine crate. Admiral Brand."

"Admiral Brand?"

"Don't ask why I remember that detail. There was a bunch of newspapers, maybe a few old letters. Sat in a closet for a long time before the whole mess got hauled off to the Historical Society."

Richard looked closely at the little image. The man was tall and maybe gaunt, and held a long weapon with a vicious looking bayonet. There was nothing familiar about the face, at least as far as he could tell. The box had been carefully constructed by someone who knew how to work with wood, and the glass had started to purple from age. The back was covered with a thin plank that bore the marks of a large diameter blade, but there was no inscription, no pencil marks, and no carved-in name to suggest why his grandmother had held on to this one solitary image. The side of the case was worn and stained like someone had, at some distant time, held it in their hands for perhaps a great many hours, maybe weeping over it. Beyond that, the tiny image and its case kept its secrets.

To My Loving Husband   *April 3, 1862*

> *I hope you received my letter of March 15 but I have not heard back from you. In case that letter was lost I will tell you again about your son Luther Freeman Lawton who was born March 14. Ever body is fine and he is a healthy young lad looks just like his Pappy. Ever thing else I told you about I am sure you have read in the papers.*
>
> *The weather here is getting better because it looks like Old Man Winter has finally decided it is time to go. There are a few of the early spring flowers peeking up but the best part is going out for a walk with Luther and seeing all the people on the street. I do miss working in the yard and seeing all the different people every day. Some times when Luther is taking his nap I think of how busy the office must be and what I would be doing but there will be time for that soon I am sure.*
>
> *Two days ago we had a party for Mums birthday. Uncle Zeke brought Grandfather Willett down from North Lubec and we had a grand time must have been twenty people here they all asked about you and told me you will be home soon.*
>
> *It looks like Mum has set her cap for Jake but she has not said any thing to me I think she thinks I do not see but she does not hide it and I think it is good. Mister Watkins come by yesterday and asked how you was doing and then he asked if I was ready go back to work. I told him maybe in a couple more weeks.*
>
> *Miss Penniman stopped by at the church picked up a big pile of stockings we knitted and also a few things we sewed shirts and bandages. She sat and talked with Mum and the others but I was*

111

home taking care of your son Luther. I hope the 6 Maine gets some of the things we made.

Your Faithful Alma and Luther

My Dearest Alma   *April 21, 1862*

    I think I killed a man today and it does not make me happy. We have just had our first real fight it was a place called Lees Mills in Virginia. He was maybe a hundred yards off and when I fired I seen him fall and not get up. When I seen that heppen I puked but had to keep moving. I did not see him from up close even later so have no idea if he was dead but I do believe he was. I was hoping I would not have to shoot no body but Chaplain Thompson[112]tells me I did what I was supposed to do and that God knows I done right. I do hope he be right.
    They brung us here by steamboat to a peninsula not far from where Elias was lost with the Cumberland and come ashore at a place called Fort Monroe. I seen that ship the Monitor[113] from the steamer and it was the queerest thing I ever did see. It looked like a birthday cake atop a plank of wood laying low in the water with just this round iron house sticking up. The house had two cannon sticking out of iron doors on one side and its sides was dented some thing wicked probably from the battle. Did not look at all like any kind of vessel I ever seen before.
    Not too long after we started marching I saw some thing else. From far off we saw heavy cannon pointed our way from behind a steep embankment. When we got closer we saw that only a few was firing and our cannoneers was able to hit them and after that they was silent. Closer yet we saw that the ones that were not firing also were not real they was just trees carved up to look like cannon. Some body said they was called Quaker Guns because they will not shoot. It was some hot that day and some of the boys threw aside there warm clothes did not want to carry them. The road was littered with

coats blankets and boots and there was sutlers picking them up probly to sell back.

After a few hours march we come to a line of placements where the Rebs was waiting in a heavy pouring rain. Our company and also one from the 5 Wisconsin[114]was picked as skirmishers and we went tords the embankment.[115] This time the cannon was not of the Quaker perswashun. They was dug in deep on a hill so we could not see them but when they opened fire we knowed just where to find them. After the battle James told me he heered some one call it Fort Magruder.

We was told to move fast acrost the field so their gunners could not follow us. I never before heerd the sound of a shell going above my head kind of like a long whistle. First comes the report then you here the shell going by. Do not like that sound one bit but at least if the sound goes over your head it will not hit you. We had our first casualties when a rebel cannoneer was able to put a ball close to a group that included Old Grizzly.[116] A man from Company E lost his arm and another was hurt in the foot but Grizzly was not hurt.

The battle was over shortly and we mostly got back safe even had four Reb prisoners. One of them had been on a smoke stack waving a flag before we got close then he tried to run off. Adjutant McFarland was mounted and he chased the man down almost to the line brought him back at gunpoint.[117]

I saw later I had a hole in my sleeve from a Reb bullet. James an Isaac both are okay I do not think either had to kill no body.

Today was our first blood. We had a few with some hurt and a couple were sent to the hospital but most will be okay they tell us.

The next day we lost a man George Riley from Nova Scotia. He was the first of the Six Maine to be killed by a Rebel bullet and it took the poor fellow near a day before he died. We gived him a funeral best we could buried him in a little churchyard nearby in their cemetery next to a few other graves to keep him company. Same day we did that a letter come in from his mother.[118]

The officers are telling us we be setting up a siege because the Rebels have a big force defending the line with reinforcements coming in ever day. Genl McClellan has ordered some big guns brought up including some heavy mortars.

113

They say that Rebel floating fort you told me abowt is out on the James River some where so our Navy can not come up. I guess that ship if that is what you call it can not go to sea but can do real damage on the river long as it do not run agrownd. If what you heerd was right that it is built on top of a frigate then with all that iron it must draw at least twenty feet and I do not believe much of this river is that deep.

I had a dream last night my great grandpap Hiram come to me and said we should move against the Rebs right now. I never ackshully met him but I heerd all abowt how he and his brother Hosiah fought under Genl Washington just a few miles North of this very spot.

Be sure to take good care of my boy Luther. I will write soon.

Your Loving Freeman

"Next time you're over," William said on the phone a few days later, "There's a few things over here you might like to see."

Richard carried his phone out to the deck. "Lemme guess. You found your old catcher's mitt."

"That too, but there's more. Couple of old medals you might find interesting, from 1898. Just now remembered where we had them stashed away. Didn't mention'em the other night, wasn't sure I could find them. They belonged to Luther."

"Luther? Don't think I've heard that name before."

"He was your great-great-grandfather."

"What're they for?"

"Spanish American War."

Later that evening he sat on the deck with Amanda, sharing a glass of wine and the setting sun. "Luther?" she asked. "Is this a riddle?"

"Maybe so." Richard leaned back and put his feet up on the railing. "An ancestor I never heard of."

My Dearest Freeman   *April 13, 1862*

We have been hearing about events down on the peninsula in Virginia. The paper says the 6 Maine is in the fray and also the 7 Maine. I hope that does not mean that you have been out in front of Rebel guns. I hope to hear from you soon because Luther and me we worry about you.

Your boy is doing fine and growing fast. He eats so much I can hardly fill him even though I eat and drink more than I used to ever do. Ever body tells me how much he looks like you.

Mister Watkins came by again yesterday to see Luther and me. I told him I wud go back to work on Monday May 5 for half a day. Mum will look after Luther for me until he is big enough I can take him to the office. Mister Watkins told me the books are in a state of disarray since I been gone but I do not believe it can be all that bad. I am ankshus to see how they have gotten along with the new bark after the Bessie was done. Rodman is probably foreman on that job too.

Michael Gaultier is going out on Achenar this year ever body says he is big for eleven but he is a hard worker. Zadoc says if he does okay he can go out on the other three trips too but after that they are back to hauling lumber and do not need the extra hands like if they was fishing.

The weather is getting to be nice with sunny warm days and no frost at night. I wish you was here to keep me warm at night.

Your Loving Alma and Luther

Pembroke's Leighton Point Road leads off along the Pennamaquan River and the deeply tidal shores of Cobscook Bay. Normally Amanda would look forward to going along for the ride but today her work had her heading off into the Unorganized Territories. "Enjoy yourself," she said, pushing Richard and Bonkers out the door. He headed up Route 1 and where the sign pointed west to Meddybemps he turned east, heading past the Irving station and into the forest.

When he parked and opened the door, the dog bounded out to begin his explorations and Richard headed inside.

William pulled down the antique wooden box and lifted off the cover. "This ribbon is pretty faded," he said, lifting out the first of the two medals. "Looks like it was once blue and gold." On the front, the medal read 'War With Spain' and displayed what appeared to be a castle.

Richard took it and turned it over. "United States Army, For Service," he read off. "And the other?"

"No ribbon," said William. "Just a bar that says 'First U.S. Volunteer Cavalry'." He pointed out the pentagonal device in the center of the medal. It bore the letters 'RR' in fancy script. "I read somewhere that Teddy Roosevelt gave these to the men who helped him take San Juan Hill. 'Rough Riders,' he called them."

116

Richard looked into the box and spotted the scarf, carefully folded and lying on top of an old book. "What about this?" When laid out on the couch it was better than six feet long, maybe a foot and a half wide. The fabric was a vibrant yellow, tightly woven with no fraying or faded spots. He felt an odd tingling in his fingertips when the silk poured, almost like a stream of warm water, smoothly across his hands. *"Doubtlessly caused by static electricity,"* he told himself.

"Obviously some woman's treasure," William shrugged. "Don't know a thing about it."

When he fingered the edge he found it supple, almost creamy. "This'd be expensive today." He looked at the box. It was made of carefully fitted pieces of wood and had a cedar lining. The aroma had only partially dissipated; probably the box had remained closed since the medals were stored. The craftsmanship appeared to be similar to the little box on their mantle, the one that sheltered the image, but it too bore no inscriptions or carved-in names.

"That would look good on Amanda," William said, looking at the scarf spread out on the couch. "Think she'd like to have it?"

"I'm sure she would," Richard replied. "You really want to give it up?"

"It was put away with Luther's medals so it belongs in the family. You got that big empty attic, you should take it all." William carefully folded the scarf, returned all three to the box, and handed it over. "Your mother and I don't need to hang on to this stuff."

"But...?" asked Richard. "Do you know anything more about Luther?"

"His full name was Luther Freeman Lawton. Outside of that, all I know is that he was my grandfather Adam's father and he's buried in the town cemetery. According to his stone he died in 1947 at the age of 85. You remember hearing of Adam. He was wounded in World War I, at Amiens."

"That was before he became the town pharmacist, right?"

"That came later. My grandmother Alice told me he really wanted to be a fisherman but learned the pill business because he could do it with his one good arm. He was gone long before I came along. He's also in the town cemetery."

"After that, you served in World War II."

"Hah!" William paused and chuckled. "Eisenhower's little garden party. I was one of the lucky ones at Normandy." He heard his father pause for a second. "So how's your season going?"

"So far, pretty good. We're four and two. No championship for us this year."

"Still a winning season. Too bad you lost Herbie."

"Bad for us, good for him. He's on the Machias team, already made varsity. Bit tougher competition but depend on this, Herbie's going to be a winner. The Bulldog's love him."

"Good work," William said. "Hey, if I find it, you still want that catcher's mitt?"

Bonkers barked at the door, signaling his readiness to head for home.

Richard headed back out onto the highway, wondering whether, if he and Amanda were to have a son, would he be fetching medals too?

My Loving Husband Freeman　　　　　*May 4, 1862*

You may hear about this before this letter reaches you but Union forces have just had a major victory. The City of New Orleans has been taken back by Admiral Farragut which means that the Rebels can no longer ship their cotton down the Mississippi River. Any way it is exciting that we have been having some good fortune even if the 6 Maine is not part of it.

We keep hearing about how the British Army is coming over here in case Father Abraham decides to invade after finishing off the Rebels. The Saint John paper says that we are going to do that but the Eastport paper says different.

Mum has been going steady to the meetings down the church for the Sanitary Society. They are knitting more socks and putting up boxes of preserves to ship down to the boys fighting the war. Some times I go with her but most of the time not because I prefer to spend my time with Luther.

I will go back to the yard tomorrow Mister Watkins has been asking and I am ankshus to see what is happening. Mum says she wants to take care of Luther when I am at the yard she says she enjoys it. I know he keeps her busy.

Ever day for a few minutes I hold your likeness and just look at it like you were right here with me. I wish I could hold you but holding your likeness at least lets me think that is what I am doing. Some times I put your scarf around my neck and close my eyes and think it is you holding me tight.

Your Loving Alma and Luther

It was certainly spooky, the way the eyes inside that little case followed him around the room.

"I do think there is a significance here," Amanda had said a few days earlier, after clearing off a spot on the mantle to display the

119

little wooden case, right next to the old clock. "Don't ask me why." Not surprisingly, Amanda had never felt any affinity towards his grandmother, and only once had she spoken of her feelings about the contempt that formidable lady had shown towards her. "She's an important part of *your* past," she did say on that one occasion. When she said something like that, he'd learned long ago that any argument would be futile. Whatever the elusive reason was that Amanda remained suspect as 'one of those Bellinghams' had apparently followed his grandmother to the grave.

Aunt Elizabeth had never mentioned whatever it was that Grandma Lawton may have wanted to tell him, even the day he helped her and Lucas pack up the truck for their move to South Carolina after she retired from the school. Both said they wanted warmer winters, but they often returned to Lubec for several weeks each summer.

Some party that had been, too, just a few days after she'd closed her classroom door for the last time in thirty-seven years. Most of the town, including everyone who had ever been a selectman or school board member in the last three decades, was there swapping stories about life in her classroom. As big as it was, the school's 'Cafetorium' could not contain all of her well-wishers at once but fortunately it was a sunny day so when the crowd spilled out into the parking lot nobody cared. A few of the town's bolder citizens openly called her "Miss Lizzie," after first confirming they had an escape route.

But still, each time he walked past the face in the little wooden box, he was convinced he felt the weight of eyes on his back, just watching. Just watching.

One time when Amanda was out visiting Nana Bell he'd confronted the image. "Who are you," he'd said, maybe a little louder than he should have. Perhaps he'd had one glass of wine too many. But, of course, there was no answer. It was probably just his imagination that after that time, the eyes pressed a bit harder. Staring into them served no purpose. They never blinked or looked away, just peered back at him like they knew something about him that even he didn't know.

The one time he'd mentioned this to Amanda she'd laughed at him. Never before had he ever felt like she had laughed *at* him, but this time she did.

"You, my love, have heard too many campfire ghost stories," she'd hooted, before retrieving a photograph of her own grandmother. He watched as she placed it alongside the troubling image, right next to the clock in its wooden case. "Feel better?" She straightened out the two, with Nana Bell smiling at the face behind the glass. "Think they'll like keeping each other company?"

My Alma   *May 11, 1862*

I know you have not got as many from me last few days as I would druther. We haf been marching and fighting nearly ever day and that do not leave much time for writing. Yesterday we marched twenty eight miles[119]an today we are stopped so the baggage can catch up. At least we haf time now to boil our coffee we did not get to do that yesterday. We haf been very busy and lost some good men to both Rebel bullets and Chickahominy Fever.[120]
The country here is swampy and wet. We are between the James River and the York River and the Chickahominy wanders abowt in between. It rains all most all the time and that river rises very fast so if any boys are on the wrong side they can be trapped. Sometimes the moskitos come up in swarms but at least they bother the Rebels as much as they bother us.
It has not escaped my attention that tomorrow is the one year anniversary of my joining up. Back then we all thought this

121

thing would not last past the end of the year and now it looks like it may never get done. Maybe the boys that joined up with the First Maine were the smart ones because their brigade has already mustered out but probly some of them haf all ready joined back up agin.

One day we push the Rebels back and the next day they push us back. Some days the sun sets on a field covered with grey and the next day with blue. I expect that we will keep fighting until there is no more of us left behind to do the fighting on either side. We have heerd from some of our sesech prisoners that they lose as many to fever as we do.

If I do not survive this war I want you to be proud of what I have done and to be able to hold your head high when you tell Luther abowt his Pa. We haf lost so many good men that I can no longer say that what is heppening is Gods will. You know I hold no truck with praying but in the night I hear those abowt me calling up to Him asking that this war end. Then the next day we find them on the field so I do not think He is listening.

I told you abowt the big siege guns Genl McClellan ordered brought up. By the time they was set up and ready to go to work the Rebs had all left like maybe they had been watching and decided not to find out what those guns could ackshully do. Mebbe I shud haf told Grizzly abowt what Granpap Hiram tole me in that dream.

A few days ago we tangled with the 5 North Carolina in a wheat field near Williamsburg. Isaac and me was among the skirmishers sent forward along with some boys from the 5 Wisconsin whilst the rest stayed back expecting a cavaldry charge that did not heppen. When the 24 Virginia showed up we was ordered back but then the sesech started yelling abowt Bull Run and Balls Bluff and that got us some wicked mad. We wanted to teach them a lesson and probly did but we was ordered again to pull back. When we got back to the line we found Grizzly had the rest of our cmpny lying flat with bayonets out waiting to see if the Rebs would follow us. I think they was sorry they tried.[121]

My great granpap Hiram suffered through worse then me but he never strayed from supporting Genl Washington so I expect I can do the same for Father Abraham. This country means more to me then my life but that do not mean I do not want get back home and be with you and Luther. But I think you and Luther would prefer to live in the country Hiram fought to make and now it has fallen to me to help keep it that way.

Some nights when I am on picket duty I can hear sesech talking and sometimes we talk. We have kind of agreed that if each stays on his own side of the line we will not be the first to fire.[122] I think their boys want to go home ever bit as much as the next man.

They are calling me to go to work so I must close.

Your Loving Freeman

Bonkers sat by the front door with that expectant look that dogs get when they have a particular urgency. "Okay, okay." Richard reached with one hand for the leash and with the other for the stash of plastic bags. The two headed out into the dusk, striding up the road towards the little park.

Clancy stood in his normal place, gazing protectively out over the tranquil harbor. Richard looked up and wondered whether the face on the statue was the same face now perched on his mantle. The man in the little wooden case, he realized, was clean shaven while Clancy had the kind of moustache that many men would be proud of. They both had the same look of grim determination.

While the dog sniffed about, searching for the evidence of earlier visitors, Richard walked around the base of the statue, reading off the names of battles carved into the stone, just visible in the moonlight. On the front, the north side facing Eastport, he read off Antietam and Appomattox. The west side showed Marie's[123] Heights and New Orleans and on the back, facing south, he read Rappahannock Station and Fort Fisher. The east side, facing Campobello, said Gettysburg and Petersburg.

Some of these battles, he realized, he had heard about in school, on those days he wasn't sleeping in class. Others, he had never heard of. Everyone knew of Gettysburg and wasn't Appomattox the end of the war? Marie's Heights? Never heard of that one.

Rappahannock Station? Sounds like a railroad terminal. What would happen at a train station that would justify being listed on a statue?

"I wonder," he asked out loud speaking to nobody in particular, "the man behind the glass. Was he involved in any of these battles?"

While Bonkers continued his investigations Richard stepped to the rear of the marble slab where the Civil War names were inscribed. He ran his hand across the polished surface, feeling the names, but in the darkness could see nothing.

"Some other day," he said to Bonkers. The pair headed off towards home.

My Dearest Alma   *May 16, 1862*

We are in camp right now at the supply base at White House Landing on the Pamunkey River. I do not know why anybody would put a supply base here except maybe because it is easy to get riverboats here but large vessels cannot make it this far up the river. All the way in we went through mud and pestefferous swamps and I am quite sure that all the way out it will be the same. I am happy enough with the life of a soldier except for all this mud.

I have heerd that this is the same place where Genl Washington courted Martha Custis and that the wife of a Rebel Genl lived here until Genl McClellan decided this should be where the supply base is. There is supposed to be a number of Negro slaves living here but so far I have not seen any. May be if it would stop raining it might look like a nice place.

There are medical boats here for moving wounded boys out to hospitals. I saw that there were some women working on those boats I think they are helping the surgeons.[124] The boats are made for the river steam powered and flat bottomed maybe eighty feet long. One was called Wilson Small and it had two women looked like fancy ladies but their cloths were simple like they had come here to work.

We are heering that a few days ago the Rebels blowed up the floating iron fort that they call Virginia because our Navy was pushing them up the James River and since it draws twenty two feet it could not go further. That is one problem gone.

They tell us we will be heading out of here in two days so we should relax here but it is not easy relaxing where all we see is mud. At least we know our supply wagons are full.

Write me soon and tell me what my boy Luther is doing.

Your Loving Freeman

My Dearest Freeman   *June 5, 1862*

The weather here is finally the way we like to see it a fine June day. I am sitting in the office at the yard and taking a break to write to you.

Yesterday the paper[125] printed a letter said it was from an Eastport boy a member of your own Cmpny K. They did not say who wrote it but I am guessing it was your Sergent Witherell it was about how the 6 Maine helped win the battle at Williamsburg. The letter was long I will send it to you but I will write here just how it ended.

125

With yells such as were never before heard we charged on them through the smoke. – They broke and fled at once. We halted on the line that they had occupied when we charged and when the smoke lifted no enemy could be seen except small squads running here and there as fast as their legs would take them. Just as we finished them reinforcements came in to us. The field in front was covered with dead and wounded rebels. Two hundred were buried, and five hundred and thirty wounded and prisoners. Our loss altogether was ten killed and forty wounded. All this was done in the space of twenty-one minutes from the time the first shot was fired until we had them in full retreat.

He wrote that there Gen'l Early was heard telling his men that the battle would be won in twenty minutes. May be he was right except he got one part wrong.

Please write me real soon so I know you are okay. And also James and Isaac. When I look at your eyes in your likeness I can see how a Rebel might not want to come too close. Makes me feel good when your eyes follow me around like it is really you being right here.

Seems like ever week some body comes to town hoping to get more boys to sign up. Just a month or so ago they were here from the Sixteenth Regiment then right after that the Seventeenth showed up. A lot of Lubec boys have joined the Navy. They say they grew up on the water and want to stay there. Mister Watkins is complaining that all the young men are gone and he has got nobody to build or fix boats except men like Jake and Elmer. And Rodman. He has still got Rodman.

There was a terrible accident last week[126] up Calais. May be your Col Burnham knows about this becuz it was at a sawmill. There was five men working under the mill when the bulkhead broke dropped the whole head of water on there heads. The wheel started to turn and two men were dragged around and Sawyer Murphy was killed right away. A man named Dinsmore survived but died later. The others excaped and are all right. Mister Watkins often bought wood from this mill so the men here are pretty unhappy about this.

I can not believe Luther is all ready six weeks old but now he can tell when it is me or Mum come into the room. She says he has got your smile. I do not know about that I wish you was here so we could see if that is so.

126

James brother Michael turned twelve a few days ago an now he works for Mister Watkins except when he is fishing on Achenar. To keep his job he has to stay in school for the next three years but he comes over in the afternoons and week ends to sweep up and help move lumber for the men. Some times Rodman gives him a hard time but Jake and Elmer are good to him. He is a fine lad and will do well. Please let James know that his brother is a hard worker. Zadoc says he is welcome on Achenar and he will probably go out on the July trip. The payment for your quarter share of the profit come to over a hundred dollars but some of that will go to the refit next spring.

Jake was over for supper yesterday. He and Mum went out West Lubec and come back with a fine mess of rasp berries for a pie. I wish you could have been here to get your share because it was some good.

Your Faithful Alma

It was like the Aladdin logo jumped right off of the envelope lying on the top of the stack. He saw Amanda glance at it but she said nothing. Client correspondence was a regular thing, but this one had 'Legal Department' under the address. The last time he'd received a letter from the Aladdin lawyers, it was when the contract had been signed.

He paced the floor, trying to look nonchalant while struggling with the feeling of failure. It wasn't really his fault, was it? Was this the consequence of that evening with Dolores? Or was his father right, a simple case of sabotage. He could always blame the latter, but he still worried about the former. At least that night, the worst didn't happen, even though he couldn't take credit for *that*.

The letter was short and simple. No explanations, no contestable details, simply "we are exercising our right to terminate our business relationship, according to the terms of the contract." That was straightforward enough, but they didn't have to add the final kiss-off. "We wish you the best of success in your future endeavors."

'Yeah,' he thought to himself. 'That's lawyer-speak, it means "Drop Dead".'

My Dearest Freeman　　　　　　　*June 14, 1862*

Luther and I walked over to the town beach this morning the weather was warm and sunny a perfect Saturday. He layed on a blanket in the sun and thot it grand. Out on the rocks east of Campobello there was waves breaking but where we were was calm and quiet. The water was out and men was out on the flats digging clams they gived me some so we will have chowder for dinner.

It has been quiet heer lately. Michael Gaultier is off working on board Achenar this month out at Cape Sable handlining for cod. They carried a full fare to Belfast at the end of May and hop to do the same this month and next. Zadoc says he is a good worker and if he does as well next month he will invite him back next year with an eighth share. Zadoc got three cents a pound and with the bounty[127]it might be a good year if we do not have big repairs and salt do not get too expensive.

There was a brief mention in the paper[128]that I will write just as it was printed. It is reported that the French have been defeated in a considerable battle in Mexico and that they have retreated to Vera Cruz. It did not say any thing more than that and I do not know what it means but we expect a visitor from New York in two weeks and may be by then I can learn more.

Miss Penniman says we shud keep making stockings but not mittens becuz the summer is coming and even eff this war does not conclude there will be time to start making mittens agin.

Some thing I found at the yard I think is a little fishy. Rodman says becuz he is not good at sums he some times makes mistakes. What I found was that all of his mistakes were to his benefit they all put more money in his pocket he never once made a mistake that cost him. I showed this to Mister Watkins he did not say any thing but I no he under stood.

Luther and I am enjoying the fine spring weather but it wud be a lot better if you were heer with us. If you are still in that supply camp it meens that no body is shooting at you and that is how I like it.

Your Loving Alma

My Alma   *June 15, 1862*

I hope this letter finds you before your birthday. I know it is just a week away and some times mail takes longer then that but ever since we left White House Landing we either have been marching all day long or sitting in the mud some wicked soggy so writing was just not possible. We can not even boil our coffee when all around is mud. It has been raining steady and now the Chickahominy has climbed so high that all the bridges are out and any of our boys on the other side are trapped.

Any way I did not figure on selebrating your birthday by only wishing I could kiss you. I guess you got Luther to do that but may be it is not exactly the same thing. Last time I wrote you to wish you a happy birthday we all figured to be home for the next time but it looks like that is not Gods will. Ever time it looks like maybe we could end this thing some thing heppens and then it looks like it will never end.

We are heering about a big battle they call Fair Oaks Station. The Sixth was not in the fray but a lot of other units was. Gen'l McClellan is saying we won but I also hear that the sesech claim victory. Our boys say they was close enough to Richmond to hear church bells but could not get any closer. There Genl Jos

129

Johnston was injured by artillery so now they have RE Lee as there top genl.

Rebel cavalry I think it was Jeb Stuart raided White House Landing and forced our surgeons and the transport nurses to leave in a hurry.[129]I heer a lot of supplies were burned keep them from the sesech.

Please rite me real soon and tell me how my boy Luther is doing. The bugler is tooting for us to get ready to move again so I must close now.

Your loving Freeman

"I'm going down shoot a few balls with Dana."

"Cool." Amanda glanced up momentarily from her book. "Don't lose your shirt. *Again.*"

"Not to worry." He grabbed his jacket and headed for the door. "Even if I did, Annie'd make me keep it on."

The bar had maybe a dozen or so regulars and back by the rear window, where it looked down into the channel, a musician picked at a guitar. A couple of twenty-something women were finishing a game of eight-ball. He spotted Dana with his elbows planted on the bar, studiously poring over the local big-city newspaper.

"Hey, bro, you see this?"

"See what?" Richard slid in beside him and held up one finger to the woman behind the bar.

"You were just in Atlanta, right?"

"Few weeks ago, yeah."

"And you stayed at the Omni?"

"I did... What of it?"

"I dunno." Dana shoved the paper his way. "Prob'ly nothing."

Richard wrapped his hands around the beer and looked down at the page. "What am I looking at?"

"Right here." Dana jabbed an accusatory finger at a picture that looked like a mug shot. "They arrested this woman."

There was something very familiar about the unsmiling face. Dana continued. "Says her name is Virginia Epstein, comes from some place in Georgia, but was going by 'Dolores' out of New York."

"That's not an indictable offense, is it?" He felt the tightening in the pit of his stomach, recalling the way she'd touched his arm that night, and the sad but confident look in her eyes.

"S'pose not," shrugged Dana. "But it might be, making a guy dead."

"What?"

"Says here she went up to his room then put something in his drink. 'Attempted robbery gone bad,' they're calling it. Says they think she wanted to knock him out, didn't really mean to kill him."

Richard looked again at the picture, then scanned through the article. His intestinal tract continued doing flip-flops.

"Poor bastard didn't even get laid." Dana lifted his beer and drained it. "Only screwed."

"So she gave him something."

"So it seems." Dana glanced towards the pool table where the women appeared to be finishing up but Richard's eyes stayed glued to the picture. "Paper says hotel staff smelled a rat, cops nabbed her boarding a plane to Seattle." He gestured to the bartender for a refill. "You never saw anything like that, did you?"

"Not this boy," gulped Richard. "Never."

"Can't imagine how Claire would feel if that guy turned out to be me." Dana turned towards the table just as the two women returned the cue sticks to the rack. The bile burned in Richard's throat and he swallowed hard, hoping his trembling knees wouldn't betray him were he to step down off the stool too quickly.

Dana spun around and headed across to claim the felt. "Your turn to rack 'em up, Ricky-boy."

Richard slowly stepped toward the table. "Hey," continued Dana. "Think they'll put her in a jail like the old one below your bedroom window?" He didn't feel like responding to his friends attempt at humor but feared not answering.

"Nah," he forced out. "Too leaky."

"S'pose," guffawed Dana. "Last guy they locked in there just pulled out the bars and went home to bed. He went up your place, right?"

"You know better'n that." One by one, he dropped the balls into the frame, wishing he didn't have to. "It was old man Collins did that. He slept someplace over by the skinning shed."

"Oh, yeah," Dana laughed. "Forgot."

Later that night, while Amanda slumbered next to him, Richard lay awake, trying hard not to disturb her.

What was it I almost did? It was her call that kept that from happening to me too, nothing else. Without that, I'd a'gone through with it. What was I willing to put at risk that night? What would I have lost if she hadn't called? What would I have done to Amanda? Was it worth it? What Dana said, how would she have felt?

He put his arm around her and pulled her close, but sleep did not come easily.

Chapter 5
Chickahominy One-Step

---

*"Your name is on every lip and many prayers
and good wishes are hourly sent up for your
welfare – and McClellan & his slowness are
vehemently discussed...Many say, they would
almost worship you, if you would put a
fighting General in the place of McClellan –
This would be splendid weather, for an
engagement..."*

Mary Todd Lincoln,
writing to Abraham Lincoln,
November 2, 1862

* * * * *

To My Alma   June 21, 1862

    *I write to tell you that I am alive and well and still numbered
among the living. We do not usually fight at night but this time we
did. The moon was waning but still bright except for the smoke which
some times makes it darker then the darkest night.*

    *A Georgia company[130]come acrost a field of wheat right at
sundown and we fought in the dim light most of the night and lost a
number of good men but held the field. The sesech is some wicked
marksmen. We could not tell where any body was except by the
muzzle flash when they fired and that was how they knowed where
we was. If they or we moved without firing then nobody would know
it until we saw the moon shining on a bayonet. I think I was too*

134

scared to know I was scared but we had to keep them from advancing.

A surprising thing heppen during that fight that we can not stop talking abowt. Major Harris discovered Captain Frazier and his son Lieutenant Milton Frazier from the Ellsworth Company hiding behind a log.[131] The Major tole Old Grizzly abowt it and he found them just like the Major said. He kicked the Captain so hard it was a surprise he could walk but now both of them are gone. We is hearing that both resigned before a court marshull could be set up.

Do not get me wrong here. We have been hearing the boys in Company B cumplain abowt the two Fraziers for a long time but that night we had a number of heroes too. It is easy to follow men like Sergeant Lincoln from Dennysville because he never asks his boys to do some thing that he will not do. He is all ways right at the front. So is Charlie Clark. It makes me prowd to fight along side men like that. Also Reuel Furlong and Sergent Witherell.

The bugler is tooting tattoo so I must stop writing and blow out my candle. I will write again as soon as I can. Give my boy Luther a big hug and make sure he knows it come frum me.

Your Faithful Freeman

My Darling Freeman   June 22, 1862

It is not fun celabrating my birthday with out you but next year will be different I am sure. We are hearing about victories every day and that must mean the rebels are going to surrender soon. Not soon enough for me.

There is a story[132]we are hearing about a lady in Machias Mrs Murphy. She was the widow of Timothy Murphy and she was recently found dead in her bed. They have not said why she was dead but they found she had sewn four hundred dollars in gold into the dress she said she wanted to be buried in. The sheriff searched her home and found an other fourteen hundred dollars. She must have

135

thought that money would do her some good where she was going to go.

Your boy Luther is just three months and a few days old and he is all ready sleeping through the night. Some times I heer him wake up and fuss but then he goes back to sleep again until the sun comes up. I think your son will grow up to be a big man. Mum says he will be tall just like his Pappy.

We hope you can come home soon I need you to keep me warm at nite. I keep your favorite yellow scarf in a speshull place just waitin for you to come home be cause I know what it is you want. Specially sense I know what kind of dreams you is having.

Your Loving Alma

My Freeman   *July 1, 1862*

Recently I wrote you about the big battle in Mexico. A few days ago we were visited by a lawyer from New York who was looking after a damaged brig that the yard is repairing. I asked him if he had heard tell of that battle and he told me he did. He said that the Frenchman Napoleon III wants to set up an empire in Mexico and thought it wise to attempt it now because Father Abraham has his hands full with the rebels. He sent an army over but they did not know how strong the Mexican army is and lost a big battle on May 5 at a place called Puebla with many of there men killed and only a few Mexicans lost. He did say that he thought it highly unlikely that the Emperor would give up after losing just one battle.

The town is preparing for the big parade this Friday. There will be fine speeches I am sure and all the children will be in the parade. There are not so many men left in town they are all either fighting or fishing. Luther will be there but next year he might know what it is about. By then you can tell him the story and may be he

136

can march next to you in the parade and show ever body your uniform. That would make me very proud.

Your Loving Alma

My Dearest Alma   *July 2, 1862*

By the time this letter reaches you the town will have all ready sellebrated our nations birthday. I am sure there will be many fine speeches and flags and a parade with a marching band and cheering school children. All the fancy people will be there to say what a grand thing we is doing and that God is surely on our side.

Three days ago the Six fought at a place called White Oak Swamp before we got back to the main regiment at Glendale. We helped Baldy Smith stop Genl Stonewall Jackson from attacking the rear guard so our boys took the day at Glendale. The Six got back after the bigger battle was over so we helped with bringing in the wounded and burying the dead.

Alma it broke my hart what I found on that field. There was a young Rebel who died with a bullet in his chest. I saw his face he looked so peaceful like he had just been told he was going home.

When I went to pick him up so we could bury him some letters fell out of his brest pocket. I read one it was from his wife in South Carolina telling him abowt there young son. Best I could tell his boy was abowt same age as Luther and the dead Rebel was just abowt same age as me. I do not know how old his wife was but her name was Penelope and his was Luke and from what she wrote it was clear she loved him and only wanted him to come home to her and there boy Daniel. I seen in her letter where he called her Penny.

Her letter could have been written by you to me. I do not think it was my bullet that will keep Luke from seeing Penny again but it could have been. I did not know Luke but from Penelopes letter I think I should have found him to be a likable person and I have had a hard time forgetting that letter. I stood there reading her words

137

and wisht I could have read more but James come over and told me Captain wanted me to get back to the burying.

I do not know how many men I have killed so far but I do know that I do not want to know. Sence I had a job to get done I could not read the rest of Penelopes letters I had to help bury Luke. I put her letters back in his pocket and they was buried with him in a muddy hole in Virginia far away from his home and Penny will never know where Luke lies with her letter close to his hart.

Some of the boys take things from dead rebels but I could never do that. They tell you not to take any thing except there muskets and revolvers and swords but to leave ever thing else. I have seen some of our boys with watches and other fancy things but I do not like that. I took a memry from Luke and I will probly never gif it back.

I do hope the town did a grand job of sellebrating the Fourth of July. I bet none of the people giving grand speeches will ever know what war ackshully looks like. Those who would tell you that any one of us can whup six Rebels never seen how they can fight. Also they never read Penelopes letter to Luke.

Your Faithful Freeman

By mid-April the sun starts to climb over the hills of Campobello Island well before six o'clock, giving a welcome respite from the winter doldrums - those stark days when it seems to linger below the horizon until suppertime. The low-angle rays sneaking through the window warmed his face and the glare hurt his eyes. As he rolled away, he heard the toilet flush and realized that, at that very instant, he was alone. When Amanda emerged from the bathroom and started heading back to bed, he followed her across the floor with one sleepy eye.

As she passed through the ray of sunshine the light flooded through the flimsy fabric of her nightgown, brightly illuminating all

138

that was normally concealed. Both eyes now wide open, he watched in fascination as she approached the bed, mesmerized by the view. Despite being familiar with every square inch of that real estate, he never tired of admiring her high firm breasts, the way the brushy little tuft seemed to catch fire when caressed by the lambent light, and the drum-taut belly separating the two. He almost overlooked her demure smile, and the way her eyes were locked on his.

Amanda paused for a moment in the shaft of sunlight, reaching her arms high over her head and stretching back, closing her eyes and turning just a bit one way, then the other. She reached down, clasped her hands behind her back, and stretched forward. When he realized her eyes were open and locked on his he tried, but failed, to stifle his smile.

She sat back on the bed, lifted her feet, and lay down next to him. He rolled over and whispered in her ear. "Oooh... I tot I taw a puddy tat."

"You *did*, did you?" He wondered whether her scowl was real, or maybe the way the corners of her eyes glistened was more to the point.

"I *did* I taw a puddy tat."

"You're a nasty man."

"Why don't you come over *here* and say that."

A few minutes later he lay back and took a deep breath. '*Gawd, how much I love her*,' he thought to himself. He was never sure which he liked better; what it was she did to him, or watching her turn bright crimson before that little shudder confirmed that all was well in the Lawton household. Whichever, didn't matter. She still wore that enigmatic smile, like she was safeguarding a few more secrets.

Just as with every other day, he was quite sure there were things that she would think about, thoughts that would rumble around behind those hazel eyes he never tired of gazing into. Things that maybe she'd share at some time – or, more probably – not.

My Dearest Freeman   *July 19, 1862*

We did have a nice parade but for me it was not fun after reading your last letter. To think that we are losing so many good men and so are they does not make me feel good even if I am proud of you for doing your duty the way you are.

In the paper today[133]there was a letter from Guvner Washburn asking for more men to sign up. Here is part of what he said.

And if raised immediately it is believed by those who have the best means of knowing that the war will be brought to a speedy and glorious issue.

So may be if he is right then all we need to do is send more men to fight and then all of our boys and those that are fighting for the other side can go home. I would like that and so would Luther. I do hope we can have faith in men like Guvner Washburn.

Your boy has a mind of his own. Mostly he lissens to what Mum or I say to him but some times he does not. Yesterday he pulled a pot off the shelf and it hit him on the shoulder. He looked at the pot and then started to laff. I think it hurt and surprised him but he laffed at it. Ever body says he is his Pappys boy.

Miss Penniman was here last week she sed that the Sanitary Society is getting reports back from the front that the work we are doing is helping. I was there when she described how some of the hospital supplies are helping men who have had terrible wounds survive and some even have gone home.

I wish you were here but if you can not be then at least I can help do my share and that makes me feel a little better.

Your Loving Alma

I hope my last to you did not leave you feeling like I was not well. Out here in the mud with all the death and disease it is a daily chore to try to think on the better days that must be coming. At least it seems that as long as we are moving there is less sickness but then we lose more to Rebel bullets.

Let me tell you what heppen to us last night. We had supper and sat around the fire for a while watching James whittle big sticks into little ones. We heerd the Rebel bugler play tattoo. Since they was well outside our picket line and on the other side of the river we thought little of it and shortly later went into our own tents.

In the middle of the night I do not know what time it was we heerd such a clattering of hoofs and clanging of metal we thought the sesech had gotten past the pickets and was in our camp. Old Grizzly was louder then usual ordering us to prepare to meet a cavaldry charge.[134]

Our officers was up and running around and we went for our muskets where they had been stacked for the night. Since there was all most a full moon it was obvious most of us were not in uniform and also had no shoes specially Isaac who hopped acrost in front of the fire on one foot whilst trying to get his trousers up with one hand and reaching for his musket with the other. We was just abowt to form up in battle lines to meet our foe when we seen who they was.

The first one come charging into the middle of camp dragging some ropes that had twisted around one of his legs and trailing a tent behind him. He was followed by two more including one who had stuck a hoof into a coffee pot and was dancing abowt trying to free himself of the baggage. There must have been thirty of them and all were braying like the mules that they was.

Sevral of the teamsters joined the fray cussing like only they know how to do. One got behind one of the mules and was rewarded for his efforts by a solid kick that sent him flying. By the time he got back up there were more of his kempedres and they was starting to get the mules to listen.[135]

It took several minutes to get the beasts back under awthority but the Rebels must have figured out what we was up against because their bugler started playing Yankee Doodle and we heerd a lot of laffin from acrost the river.

141

Any way we did not lose any body in the fray but later on after the sun come up I did see the teamster who had been kicked. I do not think he was hurt bad but he was limping some thing wicked.

Later that morning we was ordered to pack up to move. The mules did not look to be any worse off for there little party. Ever body but Isaac lafffed when I asked him if he would tech us all dance the Chickahominy One Step. Charlie Clark had ever body laffing when he tried to claim the sword lost to the valiant enemy by another Lieutenant as a prize of war.

They are calling for mail so I will close now. Give my boy Luther a kiss for me and one for you also.

Your Loving Freeman

To My Freeman   *July 30, 1862*

I read your letter about the battle with the mules to Mums Ladies Auxiliary friends when we were all together last night in the church basement meeting room at Big White. They laughed about it all night long and the best part was that no body was hurt. We are reading about how many men is being lost and a story like that one makes us all feel better.

The paper is starting to print things about letting slaves fight. There are some Rebels who think the slaves would fight on there side but I do not know about that. But there are some who say they might make good soldiers for the Union side. Have you seen any slaves? Do you think they would fight?

We are having hot weather but some days when the tide starts to come in it brings the fog and the hot day suddenly becomes cold like it did yesterday. Luther and I was out walking and the fog came in and we had to go home to get warm cloths. The garden is growing well and we should have good potatos for this winter. Luther is helping Mum and me keep the weeds out.

142

There has been some people get mad about how an officer election was held for a new unit being formed up. Company B is mostly men frum Lubec but they was told to go over Trescott to vote for their officers. Most did not go out of town and now a letter has been sent to Gov Washburn signed by several of the Huckins and Comstock and Mahar men. They think the way the election was held was not fair and want it done over.[136]

The paper printed a letter said it was from a slave owner in Kentucky and was printed in the Cincinnati Gazette. Here is what they said the letter said. And now, at this late hour, our immaculate government is frittering away what little time it can spare from the nigger question in blabbering about volunteers. The writer said we have more than 700,000 men in the field and they have a little more than half that so they should draft both free and slave blacks to fight.[137] *I am not sure what that means it can probly be understood different ways.*

I think Jake is courting Mum. They sit and talk for hours and sometimes he helps her weed the garden. Somehow he knows when she might need help but I never see her asking for it. Yesterday Katherine asked me how I would feel if Mum became Mrs Dubois I told her Jake is a good man and he makes her happy so I would be happy too.

Luther and I want you to come home soon.

Your Loving Alma

To My Freeman   *August 7, 1862*

I do not know how much you get to read the news papers and I believe you do not see as much as I do. There is a lot in the paper this week[138] *and I will try to tell you as much as I can.*

Father Abraham has ordered the states to send three hundred thousand more men to fight in the army and we in Maine has to send our share. The message came over the telegraph.

At the Lubec Town Meeting the men voted to give a fifty dollar bonus to Lubec men who join up along with the money they get from the state and from Washington. In Perry they voted to give a hundred dollar bonus and eight men signed up and one was your friend Lucius Gibson. In Perry they also gave the bonus to the four men who all ready signed up.

The paper has a story about a mob attacking the Saint Croix Herald because they think the paper is supporting the Union in the war. Many people in New Brunswick see things different then we do and the Sentinel said the Herald was the only paper in New Brunswick to have what they called a moderate stance.

Your pay arrived here yesterday thirty dollars. Luther and I will use it to buy sum fire wood with that we can get five cord[139]whic h will help us keep warm this winter but it would be warmer if you were here. Some how the night is never cold when you are next to me in bed.

Your Loving Alma

My Dearest Alma   *September 17, 1862*

It is very hard for me to describe what I have just seen and I all most hope this letter does not find its way to you. The scene before me is dreadful and I fear my words can not describe them. This thing they is calling reckless courage comes with a terrible price.

We was ordered to move to Maryland to a place close to the town of Sharpsburg. Antietam Creek would probably be a beautiful place were it not for what has heppened here. The Six had four casualties but our losses were no thing compared to what has befallen others. The Rebels were trying to head north into Maryland and our boys turned them back so even if we did not win the battle we did not let them do what they wanted to do.

In one part of the battle the Rebels set up a rifle line in a bit of sunken roadway where wagons had left the road surface may be

144

four feet below the near by ground. Our boys could not get close and a great many died trying. Then a unit of boys from New York fought there way to high ground where they could see right down the road. When they opened fire the Rebels could not escape and only a few got away. They call it enfilading fire because it comes from the side where you have no protection and a ball that misses its first mark will probably find an other. We was held back from the fray in reserve most of the day but then after wards was ordered to help bring in the wounded and bury the dead.

In the sunken road I saw a pile of forty six dead Rebels including Colonels and Majors but was mostly just men like me and I am sure that each had a family back home may be even with there own Luther waiting for them. They was the 6 Alabama and they fought like demons.[140] Many were hit trying to climb the sides escape the roadway and fell right where they were with there hands stretched out like they was reaching for heaven.

A boy I found on the field a private like me was holding a likeness of three children. He was lying where he fell wounded and died looking in on there faces I do not even remember what color his uniform was I had to leave him and keep searching for wounded who might be saved.[141] I hope some body took the likeness be cause the children looked sweet like all they wanted was there father to come home.

In some places the ground felt muddy but it was not from rain. The fields all around was mowed down by the bullets just like farmers had come through with scythes and even small trees were cut off. Dead and dying horses and mules was all abowt and there was as many blue uniforms as gray.

Alma you no I am not a man of words and my words do paltry service to tell of what my eyes has felt. I do not wish that you understand what it is I have seen the horror of so much suffering both ours and theres. The dead lie abowt some thing terrible but there is no thing that can be done for them beyond a proper burial. It is the wounded that I shall never forget. Many of them will die but those that do not will be forever hurt and those of us who can do so little to help them will never be able to forget what we have seen. I fear for my dreams and for the man I am loath to become.

In the battle for the Bloody Lane we lost our Corps Commander Israel Richardson.[142] They carried him off the field

145

wounded so Winfield Scott Hancock was promoted to replace him and now we have Colonel Cobb of the 5 Wisconsin as our Brigadier.[143] I do not know Colonel Cobb but the 5 Wisconsin has fine soldiers so I am sure we will be okay.

Enough bad news. I am still among the living and so is James and Isaac. We is all healthy and even eating well enough. James spends time around the campfire at night whittling with the Barlow knife Katherine gived him. He makes all manner of nice looking things but mostly just throws them in the fire when the bugler plays tattoo. He was happy when I told him what you said abowt his brother.

Before the fight at Sharpsburg Isaac said he had a bout of the diarhoe but he is okay now. As long as we are on the move we do not seem to be bothered by Chickahominy Fever.

Tomorrow will be another day and I must find sleep. I love you.

Your Freeman

All three headed south on Water Street, with Bonkers leading them in the direction of the town beach. Like most Saturday mornings the street was busy, so the half-mile walk took forty-five minutes. After all, Bonkers needed to be properly greeted by all of his two and four legged friends, of which he had many. Once across Washington Street the going was easier, at least in terms of interruptions. The walk was Amanda's idea, but it had taken very little to convince Richard to take the morning off. The day was overcast and warm with a light breeze. Crossing the parking lot at the end of Pleasant Street, they took the short path down to the beach.

"Perfect," she said. "Low water." When she reached down and snapped off the catch on his leash Bonkers took off, bounding down the beach to break up a gathering of birds obviously conjuring up some deviltry, with Richard and Amanda following behind at a

146

more leisurely pace. To their left the glistening mud stretched out maybe a half mile, and out near the edge a group of clammers worked the flats. To their right the marsh grass waved in the breeze, and a few gulls shrieked overhead. As was often the case, they had the beach to themselves. The channel light, known locally as The Sparkplug, sat proudly in the center of what little open water was to be seen inside the outer harbor, and Grand Manan Island lay on the horizon like a distant fogbank. Across the channel, to the north, the forested southern coast of Campobello Island did not look to be nearly a mile away.

"I read something the other day," he said, looking out across the water. "When they built the light, the first keeper was a Lubec man, a Civil War veteran."

"Where'd you see that?"

"Not sure, probably the paper. He was in a regiment that formed up from around here, the Sixth Maine Volunteer Infantry. Name was Morang. Frederic Morang."[144]

"Like Morong Cove?"

"Up by Coffin's Neck? Yeah, prob'ly."

She squinted to see the structure better. "Not sure I'd want to live out there. Kind of tough to just go for a walk."

"It is rather isolated." He pointed across to the Campobello side. "Almost as close over there as it is to Quoddy Head."

"Think somebody could row a dory across?" She looked off towards the craggy Canadian shoreline. "Pull into one of those secluded coves?"

"Maybe," he replied, shading his eyes and following the shore. "Get busted doing that, you'll piss off the border guards big time."

"Think you could you do it without being seen?"

"Maybe at night, knew what you were doing with the current. If you don't…" He pointed out at the Grand Manan Channel, then looked across at Amanda. "There something you want to tell me?"

"No," she said, stooping to pick up a piece of beach glass. "Don't *think* I have any smugglers in my family tree." They continued along in silence; the far end of the beach was in sight but still a ways away. Bonkers ran back and forth, grabbing at bits of driftwood and shells and investigating spots that had been visited earlier by one or another of his friends.

When they reached the rocky outcropping that marked their usual turnaround spot, they paused for a minute or so to look out across the flats. A few more clammers had arrived and two pickup trucks had been driven out. "Maybe we'll have chowder for dinner," she mused.

Halfway back Bonkers spotted another large cluster of gulls conducting some kind of meeting out on the mud and took off to investigate. The flock rose up in noisy protest long before he got near, so he started to circle back. Apparently the mud was inviting, because soon all they saw were four legs pointing straight up and kicking. He waited until he was back next to Richard to shake the water out of his fur.

"Looks like *he's* heading for a bath." Richard attempted unsuccessfully to dodge the muddy spray.

"Oh?" she asked. "Maybe not just him."

To My Freeman   *September 12, 1862*

The weather here has been very nice warm days and cool nights just right for bringing in our potatoes and turnips. We should be okay this winter at least as okay as we can be with you not being here.

Recruiters have been here talking to every man they can find trying to get them to sign up. Trescott had its town meeting[145] two days ago and they voted to pay a bounty of $100 to every man who signed up for nine months and $200 for each one that volunteered for the duration. Then they voted to give the $200 to the 9 month volunteers too.[146] I do not know how many have signed up so far. The paper[147] printed the quotas for each town Eastport must send 41 and Lubec 40 but some people are complaining that Eastport got 11 officers and Lubec got none.

Your friend Lucius B Gibson was one of eight from Perry[148] that signed up after the town voted to give each volunteer a hundred dollars. I heard that he joined the 18 Maine Infantry but we do not know where they were going to be sent.

There was also a letter in the Sentinel frum Father Abraham to Horace Greeley of the New York Tribune. He said his intent is to save the Union and if he thought ending slavery would do that he would take that action but if not ending slavery would do that then that is what he would do but either way saving the Union is his objective.

We have lost so many men to the army Mister Watkins has been having trouble finding men to do the work of the yard. Jake and his friends do very good work but by the middle of the afternoon they are starting to slow down. The yard has plenty of work but not enough help to get the work done. Mister Watkins asked me if Luther was ready get a job but I told him three other yards was after him so may be he would have to pay too much to get your boy to start work now. Rodman Bellingham is still working for Mister Watkins but he does not do as good a job as a joiner as you did or as Jake can do.

149

Michael Gaultier is trying hard to learn and may be some day he will help build some big vessels and make James proud.

The paper printed a story about our Gen'l Howard. He lost his right arm at Chickahominy and when being carried off the field met Gen'l Kearny who lost his left arm in Mexico. Gen'l Howard said to Gen'l Kearny I want to make a bargain with you General that we should buy our gloves together.

We had a storm come through a few days ago. All the boats and docks are okay but a big branch come down in the back yard. Jake brought a saw over and cut it up but Greene Street does not look the same with that branch gone.

Luther and I we miss you and hope you come home soon.

Your Loving Alma

To My Freeman   *October 7, 1862*

I have sad news for you. Two men drowned in Cobscook Falls[149] two days ago. Isaac Leighton along with one of the Mahar boys[150] died in a fishing accident. I know you knew Isaac and also some of his brothers. Several of them have signed up to fight. He just celebrated his twenty fifth birthday. The newspaper did not provide any details.

The paper also had a story[151] about a man who sailed into Saint John and was murdered. They say a man named John Collins killed him because he refused to lower the American flag. We has been reading about much Sesech activity in New Brunswick[152] speshu lly in Saint John and Saint Stephen but not so much up to Moncton.

Your son has two teeth now and he is crawling all over the floor. Mrs. Ballard come over today to see how he is doing and she told me he is very strong for his age. Ever body tells me how much he looks like you and now he is getting to be strong like you.

We did read about the battle at Antietam that you told me about. I was very worried about you and James and Isaac until your

150

letter come and we knowed you were okay. I know you are doing your duty and I am very proud of you for what you are doing but I still worry. You are seeing things that no person should have to see and I do worry about how you will carry those memories after this is all over. I do know that things like you are living through will never be forgotten and I hope that they do not change you from the man you are. Please keep in mind that as your wife it is my place in life to be concerned with your well being and your soul.

Luther and I we both want you to come home safe an helthy.

Your Loving Alma

My Dearest Alma   *November 8, 1862*

I am sure you will read more abowt this then I will see. Father Abraham has remoofed Gen'l McClellan and replaced him with Gen'l Ambrose Burnside. I do not know all of the whys and hows but I do know that Gen'l Burnside led the 9 corps at Antietam Creek. He was ordered to take a bridge but did not get it done before a sesech unit come up from Harpers Ferry. We stopped the sesech from getting farther into Maryland but they got away acrost the Potomac.

I am still helthy and so is James and Isaac. We will probably be heading for winter quarters soon because the roads will be all mud and when that heppens boys cannot march and mules get stuck and no body can move not us and not them speshully the artillery.

The last three days I have had picket duty. That is some thing that we all do when it is our turn and it is actually better then just being in camp waiting for orders. Those days are long and the nights are even longer. I know how you can warm up a cold night and thinking of that helps me keep going. Better days are coming and then I will not miss you I will have you by my side in stead.

On picket duty we go out to the line in three man teams located close enough we can hear the next team on both sides and stand guard making what they calls a defensive perimeter around

151

our encampment. Each of us on the team does a two hour turn where we stand and watch whilst the other two can sleep or whatever we want as long as we stay close by. All most all of the time no thing heppens but it is our job to let ever body else know if some thing does heppen. Even the officers do picket duty and some times we can see the Rebel pickets doing the same thing. We take enough provisions so we can eat but most times we can not light a fire. Most of the time it is not so bad but some times when it is cold or wet it is not so nice. To night I am looking forward to a good night sleep in my own tent.

Please give my boy Luther a special hug for me and tell him I love him. Soon may be I can tell him that my self.

Your Loving Freeman

Claire came bustling across the porch, toting Henry's baby carrier and an assortment of bags. Heather bounded ahead in the manner of a three year old going on eight. "You guys sure picked the right time go up Calais." Richard held the door and peered out at the rain cascading off of the roof.

"What?" She passed over Henry, shook the water off her coat and stepped inside. "Something wrong with today?"

"Silly me." He turned and headed for the stairway to let Amanda know the kids were here and all hers for the next few hours. Half a minute later she was kneeling down and sharing a joke with Heather.

"Sure 'preciate you guys doing this for us." Claire gestured out at the car where Dana sat behind the slapping windshield wipers.

"I look forward to it," replied Amanda. "My only chance to play with the kids." Richard tried to pretend not seeing the glance

152

she shot in his direction. He knew what it was she was saying. "You guys need to enjoy a bit of grown-up time."

"Don't you go letting Heather talk you into something weird."

"Yeah yeah yeah." Richard waved dismissively as Claire pulled her rainhat tight and dashed back to the car.

He glanced over at the girl. She wore a pink dress with brown shoes and had a tiara perched precariously on the top of her head. Her face looked fresh-scrubbed and she appeared nowhere near ready to slow down. A small pink raincoat hung by the door, dripping into a spreading puddle.

"Sweety, I have a puzzle for you." Amanda pulled a box down from the hall closet and dumped it on the floor. Richard sat down on the couch to watch the two. Henry lay in his carrier next to him, clutching a stuffed monkey and gazing about the room. Bonkers sat next to Richard on the couch, studiously watching but carefully avoiding the children.

"A puzzle?" Heather gave her a quizzical look and sat down on the floor.

"Sure." She pulled out a board with the outline of the United States, complete with each of the states. "I bet you can figure this out."

The girl looked at the board and the pile of pieces. "Where," she demanded, "is the Princess?"

"There is no Princess here," replied Amanda. "Can you put each of the states where they belong?"

"I already know how to do this," Heather declared. She picked up Indiana and promptly put it down on the Pacific shore. "See?"

Richard watched while Heather and Amanda took turns putting the various states in random locations.

"Do you know where California goes?"

"Sure," replied Heather. "Right here," giving the Golden State Hudson Bay waterfront property.

They went back and forth with occasionally a piece actually fitting. It was not clear who was having more fun. Amanda looked up at Richard, her face beaming. "You gotta admit she's a cutie!"

"Sure thing," he replied, resisting the urge to be too agreeable.

Slowly he became aware of a bit of an aroma coming from where Henry lay in his carrier, now with a huge smile. "Why don't you go ahead and take care of that, honey?" Amanda spoke without looking up. "His things are in the bag by the door."

"Wait… What? You want *me* to…"

"It's not so tough." She continued to hand Heather additional pieces and pointing out opportunities for placement. "Besides," she added, "about time you picked up a new skill."

By the time he was done, Richard had gotten smudges of brown goo on his own pants, smears on his arms, and spread across the towel he had laid down on the floor as a work surface. Henry appeared to approve of his handiwork, and so did Amanda. Bonkers watched carefully, but from the safety of the couch.

A few hours later, after the Coopers had retrieved their children, Richard handed Amanda a glass of wine. He sat down next to her and took a deep breath.

"Are you going to tell me," he started, somewhat hesitantly, "just why I need 'a new skill'?"

She laughed and rolled over, laying her head on his lap. "No surprises," she said. "That's not how we work."

"But you're still trying to tell me something."

"I love how you can read my mind." She reached up to stroke the side of his face. "You think something has changed?"

"Do we have to talk about this right now?"

"M'love," she said, "you brought it up. And you know it's not long before I turn thirty." He realized she had stopped smiling. "Before we were married I agreed when you said you 'wanted to hold off for a bit.' I'm hoping you're not planning on making Henry your star first baseman before that day comes."

My Darling Freeman   *November 21, 1862*

I have received yours of November 8 about Gen'l McClellan being replaced by Gen'l Burnside. The newspaper has reported on what Father Abraham has done and seem to think it a good thing. Here is what Mister Nutt wrote about that.[153]
The Army of the Potomac has shown that it can fight desperately; that it lacks not courage, skill in the use of arms, nor ability to shed an unusual amount of fatigue.

But, as we have said, it has not done what the people have expected it would do – it has not driven the rebel army out of Virginia, and it has not taken Richmond; on the contrary our own capital has been for a considerable part of the time been beleaguered by the enemy.

He could hold an enemy in check, but that would never conquer them.

I do hope that Gen'l Burnside will be able to bring this war to an end. If you have to be there fighting it I do not like the idea that they are wasting your time. Luther and I would rather you were here spending your time with us.

Miss Penniman come over last night and met with us at the church. She said she did not know whether Gen'l Burnside could get the war done but some of the people in the society had wondered if Gen'l McClellan was the right one to do it.

Mum asked me to send you her best wishes and so does your son Luther. And speshully me.

Your loving Alma

My Dearest Alma   *December 14, 1862*

It pleases me grately to say that I am still amongst the living and so is Isaac and James. We are at a place in Virgina called Fredericksburg and you will probably read abowt the battle. The 6 did not get in to the fray very much except a couple of skirmishes. We are part of the Sixth Corps under Uncle John Sedgwick and some of the other brigades in the corps lost heavily attacking a hill where the Rebels have dug in deeply behind a stone wall at the base. I do not know how any body could take that hill but the generals are smarter then me so they ordered a number of charges not one of which worked. We lost a lot of men trying to take that hillside.

We nearly lost James in one of the skirmishes. We was proceeding acrost an open field towards the Rebel line when a group

156

came charging tords us. James was may be fifty yards to my left and a little ahead and I saw him fall like he tripped on a rock. He was trying to get back up when a Rebel came after him with his bayonet fixed. I dropped to one knee and leveled my musket. When I fired I saw the Rebel fall over tords James. When he put his hand up and pushed the bayonet aside the Rebel musket fired and put a hole in his sleeve but did no harm. James got a cut on his hand from the bayonet but is other wise fine.

The 17 Infantry had a miserble day today. They are a US Army unit not a state regmnt an they ended up flat on there faces in the mud eighty yards back frum the sunken road stayed like that all day until dark. If they lifted there head to fire the rebels got them first. There Capt McLanburg and two men died and nineteen wounded but they got no thing.

I do not no how much James will tell Katherine abowt today so may be it is better you do not. The bugler is playing tattoo so I must turn in.

December 15

Last night we slept on the battlefield be cause we did not know what the sesech might do. We has been ordered to retreat but crossing the Rappahannock will slow us down. All around us were dead and wounded but we could not help them but only listen to there cries. I slept on my musket and kept it loaded with the bayonet fixed.

The bugler has started playing a new piece of music that we have not heard before. They call it Taps[154] and it is the most mournful piece I have ever heard. They play it to honor the dead and also to tell us it is time to go to sleep. I do not know if the Rebel buglers play it too but it seems so much more peaceful then the Tattoo they used to play at night.

During last night we saw the most amazing sight in the sky it was like curtains of light falling from the heavens to the north of where we was. They was all different colors and shimmering when they moved and only appeared for a few minutes but many of the boys seen the same thing so I know I was not dreaming. One boy from Moncton said it was called Aurora Borealis[155] and was some times called Northern Lights but he never heerd abowt it being seen this far south.

157

After the close call yesterday James wanted to sleep close to me. We was both laying on our muskets to try to keep from the damp soil but I do think he slept quite well because I know he dreamed of Katherine. When he does that it is quite obvious what he is thinking of specially if the dream wakes him. This morning the surgeon looked at his hand and said it would heal fine in a couple days.

We are moving off so I must end this.

Your Loving Freeman

My Loving Freeman   *December 15, 1862*

This will be our second Christmas since you went off to fight this war and our first one with Luther. When you left we was all sure you would be back before last Christmas and now we are not sure you will be back by next Christmas.

The town will have a parade and the churches are all planning big ceremonies and there are parties. I have been invited to go to many of them but I do not feel like going without you. Luther will sellebrate his first Christmas with me and your likeness but it will not be the same. We have a little tree and Luther has a stocking to hang up and he will find a new pair of stockings to keep his feet warm this winter and a hat that Mum has knit for him.

Mum and Jake are going to have dinner with the Spencers and I have decided that they should go with out me.

This is truly a sad time not just for us but for our country. As much as Luther and I miss having you home with us for this special season when we are supposed to be sellabrating. I take solace in knowing that you are doing your part to make it a better world and will dream of having you home with us even if it is only a dream.

We have not gotten any snow yet but we do know it will soon be here. We have eight cords of wood in the barn so Luther and I will be warm. We hope you come back soon and help keep me warm. That would be the best Christmas present I could ask for.

Your Faithful Alma

I hope the New Year is better than the last year. Soon it will be here and we hope you will be too.

The paper gave a list[156] of all of the vessels bilt in the area during this year so I know that when you come home there will be plenty of work for you to do. They say there was a total of twenty two vessels bilt this year between the seven yards and only six were schooners. The yard in Pembroke did the most with four brigantines and three barques launched. Even the yard in Lubec got one done a brigantine of 211 tons. We do not know where the larger vessels are going to go but we hear that mostly they will stay away from here because the Rebels have privateer pirates looking to capture them. We have heard about several that was captured and taken to Saint John and also to Halifax and some that was burnt.

Zadoc says the insurance on Achenar has doubled because of the Rebel pirates even though they hardly ever go after fishing vessels.[157]

The weather has been very cold. The paper says on Sunday[158] it was twelve below zero and that from Saturday to Monday it never warmed above zero. I hope it is not as cold where you are. There was a letter in the paper that said the 28 Maine is having trouble with measles. I hope this does not mean the 6 Maine is too.

Luther and I hope that this next year 1863 will see this war ended so you can come home. We both miss you and so does Mum.

Your Loving Alma

Early May in Lubec might bring a day of glorious sunshine, and it might bring a day of gloomy clouds and rain. Often enough it brings both on the same day, but on this particular Sunday the forecast only mentioned sunshine.

Richard put his stocking feet on the rail and leaned back, took a big bite of blueberry muffin, and looked beyond the outbound current. "When was the last time we hiked that trail?"

The map was on the shelf in his office. "Right along the water," Amanda replied, looking over his shoulder. "Been too long." They quickly packed a lunch and took off for a visit to Campobello Island and the Herring Cove Provincial Park.

There was no traffic on the bridge and they cleared the Canadian border station without delay. He left the main road and turned south at the visitor information center, following the dirt road into the forest. They left the car where the road ends and followed the trail along Upper Duck Pond, with Bonkers scouting out before them.

The narrow path led through dank woods and across eroded gullies, along tidal marshes and into the shaggy depths of pine thickets. To the west, the Quoddy Narrows opened up while to the east the darkness of the deep woods released the fecund aroma of the primeval forest. They paused to watch a fishing boat pass by the Sparkplug, its rumbling engine barely audible.

"Our little town looks pretty nice from this angle." He wrapped his arms around Amanda and hugged her from behind. When she reached up to caress the side of his face, he nibbled her ear lobe.

"That's Dana out there, right?" She pointed at the white vessel with the blue trim and lettering. It approached West Quoddy Head, where it would turn south and disappear off to the west. If it turned the other way it would soon be in Canadian waters and be watched closely to see if any gear went over the side. If an American is caught fishing in Canadian territory it rapidly escalates to an International Incident, but innocent passage is okay.

160

Richard glanced at his watch. "That's him. He's got the whole eight hundred traps out, usually outa here before the sun's up." They continued down the trail, still heading south.

Forty-five minutes later they reached the low cliff looking out over Lower Duck Pond. The quiet reach reflected the sunlight and a few cormorants dove into the dappled surface. It appeared that under other circumstances it might be the perfect place to bring a dory ashore unseen and drag it into the woods, at least when the tide was right, but for now it was the perfect place to enjoy a lunch break.

When Amanda sat down on a rock to take in the view, Richard stepped behind and started massaging her shoulders. Feeling how she relaxed when he worked over the nape of her neck made him feel good too, so he kept at it for several minutes. In the quiet of the forest, with the shimmering expanse of water stretching out before them, neither felt the need to speak. A bald eagle cruised by, looking them over before heading out across the rippled water, apparently seeking more likely prey, and the salty-soft aroma of drying rockweed drifted past. Bonkers, bored with checking out empty shells, sat down and leaned up against her leg.

He was surprised when she suddenly tensed up. "What's this place called?" she asked, shivering. The map was quickly spread out on the ground.

"Mink Point," he said, kneeling in front of her to read it better. Glancing up, he was startled to see that she was ashen and trembling. "Mandy... You okay?"

"I'm... Not sure." She closed her eyes and shook her head. "I'll be fine. It's just something..."

He rose to take her hand. It had turned icy, despite the warm day and their exertions.

"There's something out there," she said with a shudder.

"What is it?" He scanned the trees and the undergrowth, but there was nothing he could see.

"I... I don't know." She turned to glance into the forest behind them, then shook her shoulders and stood up. "Yes. It's there. I can feel it."

Bonkers menacing growl was startling enough, but when Richard saw the hackles up on the back of the dog's neck he followed his eyes into the forest. Something on a branch maybe ten feet up had caught his attention but he still saw nothing. Not a squirrel or even a bird threatened the group; there was not the slightest motion in the trees. Bonkers continued to growl while leaning hard against Amanda's leg.

"You know what it is?" When he looked into her eyes he was sure he saw an unfamiliar fear. "I don't see anything here."

"It's not a what." She whispered, as though she were concerned about being overheard. "It's a who." She clutched her arms across her chest and turned her head toward the trees. Her eyes were closed and her lips pursed. "There's... Somebody out there." He again followed her gaze but saw only impenetrable forest – tangles of vines, moss-shrouded pines, and deep purple shadows. Not even a trail led into the gloom.

"Somebody?" They hadn't seen any people or even parked cars since the border station, and except for Dana's boat hadn't heard anything beyond the channel buoy and the noisy birds.

"Somebody who seems to know me. Somebody wants something from me."

"What are they after?"

The quavering in her voice terrified him. "Don't... Know."

"Let's go." Crumpling the map into a hasty wad, he shoved it into the knapsack together with their uneaten lunch. Twenty minutes later the broad rocky beach of Upper Duck Pond hove into view, and Bonkers resumed his investigation of random shells.

"Thank you," she said, pulling him close. "You're a good guy."

"That was something new..." She was no longer shaking and most of the color had returned to her face. The brief walk did not explain her deep breathing. "Feeling better?"

"I will be," she said with a sigh, reaching for the lunch. "Just need a little time." They ate their sandwiches in silence.

Amanda was the first to break the silence. "I never saw anything. But I felt it." She closed her eyes and shook her shoulders. "It was just like before."

"Before?" He reached for her hand. "You've had that feeling... Before?"

"I'm sure of it," she said, speaking softly. "A real long time ago, last time I was over there."

Richard remained silent, but kept his eyes looking deeply into hers.

"Remember when we did our third grade class picnic?"

"Vaguely," he said. "We were both, what? Nine?"

"Remember where the teachers had us set up our lunch?"

"Remind me."

"Mink Point." She looked across the water for a few seconds, then turned back to face him. "Whatever it was got to me that day…" The way she spoke, he had to strain to hear her. "It's still there."

Chapter 6
Marye's Heights

That on the first day of January, in the year of our Lord one thousand eight hundred and sixty-three, all persons held as slaves within any State or designated part of a State, the people whereof shall then be in rebellion against the United States, shall be then, thenceforward, and forever free; and the Executive Government of the United States, including the military and naval authority thereof, will recognize and maintain the freedom of such persons, and will do no act or acts to repress such persons, or any of them, in any efforts they may make for their actual freedom.

Abraham Lincoln

* * * * *

My Darling Freeman   *January 3, 1863*

    The holidays is over again and once more without you. This thing has gone on long enough and I am not the only one who thinks it is time for it to be over. I am sure Father Abraham thinks that too but it is up to Gen'l Burnside to do it.
    I have received your letter from December 14 and must say I was very happy to get it. The Sentinel printed a letter[159] from Gen'l Burnside he described the battle at Fredericksburg that you mentioned and the hill that you boys were not able to take. He said that 1152 men died and anuther 900 were wounded and that it was the fault of not being able to get across the Rappahannock for a day so the rebels was able to dig in deeper. I am very glad you were not on that list but it makes me sad that so many were. I can only hope that there was some thing gained from the loss of so many good men.
    The Avery family has received a letter from the Army says there son Albion was in the same battle but did not survive. He was a member of the 17 United States Infantry that mustered in Portland last year. I do not know of any other soldier from Lubec who has

died[160] so far. Albion was a friend of yours but I do not know if you have seen him the 17 was in the 5 Corps under Gen'l Butterfield and I know you are in the 6 Corps with Gen'l Smith.

There is also a letter in the paper frum a soldier in the 12 Maine at New Orleans about the freed slaves volunteering to become soldiers. He said that their units were composed of smart men and I will write just what he said after that.

Indeed, the only trouble with these Regiments will be, they will show the Rebels no quarter if they fall into their hands. They understand their position well, and know that if they are taken instant death will be their fate.

Luther has started to crawl all over the place and pick up ever thing I put down. He can all ready stand up by him self. He keeps Mum quite busy when I am at work and she is very happy when I get back. We both miss you and want you to come home soon.

Your Loving Alma

My Dearest Alma   *January 24, 1863*

I have seen rain like this before but only when the wind blows from the north east acrost the bay and over Flaggs Point. Four days past Genl Burnside ordered us prepare cross the Rappahannock and head tords Richmond but shortly after we started so did the rain. It has been very warm so the ground is soft and then when the rain started coming down the whole world turned to deep mud.

As long as I have lived I have never seen mud like this. In Lubec we get rain and mud but then it gets cold and the ground freezes and gets hard and we can move around. Not here it just gets deeper and thicker and ever thing stops moving. Ever step you are afeered you will lose your boot if you try to move too fast and if you do not move fast enough the men behind you crowd forwards like to march right over except they too gets stuck in the mud. It is like thick

166

pudding with no bottom an as soon as you pull your foot out the hole fills up agin.

We watched one battery moving their guns and the horses was up to their knees in mud so they could not move. I seen where one horse fell over in the mud and drowned. The rain just come down in a steady pour like God was sending us a message. We was ordered to keep going heading tords the river where the pontoon bridge was waiting but it took us six hours to travel what we should have taken less then two to do. We kept at it until late in the day when we was ordered to turn around go back to our old camp. I do not think it was Genl Burnsides best day.

Some of us was ordered help move a gun a Napoleon twelve pounder. One of the cannoneers told us the gun was eight hundred pounds with out the munitions and it was all we could do to move it at all. After they sent us back to camp they ordered us all extra rations of whiskey. I am proud that the 6 Maine did not get into the trouble[161] that some of the other units did that night.

We are back to winter quarters for now and that meens we will be doing a lot of no thing for a long time. The divvul finds work for idle hands and I am sure he will be very busy around here until Genl Burnside finds some thing for us to do. I do not think we will be going any where untill this rain stops and the roads become passable agin. It stops the sesech as much as it stops us so that means may be the cavaldry can get out but not the infantry and sartenly not the artillery. I do not think the sesech would attack an infantry camp with cavaldry but we still have to keep our picket lines out and so do they.

We hef heered the story of the loss of the Monitor the ship I seen that stopped the Rebel floating fort. I did not think that ship shud go to sea but smarter men then me thot difrunt and now it is sunk some where neer North Carolina. What I heered was that it went down in a storm on New Years Eve and some number of men went down with her.

James and Isaac and I am all well and not sick. If we stay in our tents and this rain keeps up the way it is right now we may not stay well but for now we is. Please give my boy Luther a kiss and a hug for me and also one for you too.

Your loving Freeman

My Dearest Alma   *January 28, 1863*

    We have just got the news that Genl Burnside has been replaced by Genl Joseph Hooker they call him Fighting Joe. The change came just two days after we got back from trying to cross the Rappahannock in the rain. They is calling that the Mud March but I do not know if that was what made Father Abraham decide put Genl Hooker in charge. We do not know what may be different but with Genl Burnside we did not do very many drills. Fighting Joe Hooker is very handsome and there are rumors that he is what they call a three bottle man and that he is also very popular with the ladies. I do not care if any of this is so if he can win this thing so we can go back to our familes and towns.

    We have settled back into winter quarters so do not think there will be much action for a couple months. Mostly we just try to make our quarters more pleasant and try to avoid the smoke frum the campfires.

    Now that we is not going to be moving for a while the Cyprians have come around again. Mostly the only other women we see are nurses and they are all like some bodys mother. Some of the officers have their wives here but the only women we see that are young are the Cyprians and some of them are nice to look at. I have heerd that the officers prefer to visit the negro women because they are not as likely to get sick from them but I do not know and do not care. I will wait until I can be with the woman I love I do not need what these women sell.

    James and Isaac are fine and so am I so far not even any diarhoe. Some of the other units have some sickness but we are okay and hope it stays that way. The officers do not let us get close to the hospital unless we need to go there I think they are afraid we will catch some thing if we get too close.

    I do remember Albion Avery he was a good man comed from North Lubec up by Lawrences. It seems strange that a friend was here but none of us knew it. We did here that the 17 Infantry lost two men and a Captain but I did not no that he was one of those lost.[162] I heered that they also had six wounded but were not able to do any thing to the rebels. Do you know why he joined the 17 in stead of becoming one of us?

168

How is the yard doing? Does Mister Watkins have any new boats he is starting? I am ankshus get back to work before I forget how to do my job and James brother Michael weel take over my job.

Please give my boy Luther a hug for me and also one for your Mum. And speshully one for you.

Your Faithful Freeman

My Dearest Alma   *February 23, 1863*

The 6 Maine just received a very big honor. Genl Hooker has set up what they call the Light Brigade and we are part of it. I know there are some folks back home who do not think the 6 Maine is very good but we are the only unit from Maine chosen be part of this. Some of the other units have the sons of rich men or fancy families but not the 6 Maine we are all common boys who have come here to fight. They could have picked the 7 Maine or the 20 Maine but they did not instead they chose the 6 Maine.

Our friends the 5 Wisconsin are also part so is the 61 Pennsylvania and 2 units from New York. We also have an artillery unit. Insted of our gear going in wagons we will use mules so we can move fast. We also have a special insignia on our kepi so every one knows what brigade we are part of. Genl Pratt is our leader. He was wounded in the face during the Peninsula campaign and we hope he can lead us because we are ankshus to show Genl Hooker that he made the right decision.

Fighting Joe has also made some other changes we have some new officers and some old ones are gone. Also the food is better and I hear talk that the hospital has been made more clean that he works better with the Sanitary ladies.

These winter nights when we are in camp and not on the moof are long and it gives me more time to think of how much I miss you. The last I seen of you was when you were waving your yellow scarf when the steamship was leaving the pier. I see you in my dreams more offen now that we are in winter quarters and I see the yellow scarf too. Some times the nights are cold and I think how you could make them warm.

Please give my boy Luther a hug for me.

Your loving Freeman

It's not every day the water flows over the top of the Lubec breakwater, but when it does it bears watching, if only for a few minutes, and it was still rising. Richard sat down on the bench and Bonkers sat on the grass next to him. The seals wouldn't arrive in town for two months but the cormorants preceded them so there was plenty of bird activity. Those guys don't mind the powerful current, as long as it brings fish along. Across the channel at the Mulholland Light a man noisily mowed the grass but out over the expanse of Johnson Bay and Friar Roads all was quiet.

Heading back to the office to open the mail would just have to wait a few minutes. Between the drowsiness brought on by the warm sun and the noise of the rushing water, Richard drifted into into a state of somnolence. An old song he'd heard somewhere, from the ancient days of the sixties by the British singer Donovan, resurrected itself. *Atlantis*, it was called, and it spoke of the antediluvian kings that ruled in days of yore, in a place that no longer is. *That's Mandy's word, from her Spelling Bee*, he reminded himself, but he still couldn't get it out of his head. Out in front, the current slowed as the flood drew nigh. Does that mean, he asked himself, that right now, this very instant, is *also* antediluvian, and will remain so only until the waters reverse and the flood begins to recede?

He didn't hear him come up from behind. "Does Miss Peachy-Keen know you're goofing off like this? Again?" The spell

170

evaporated and Richard turned to watch Silas scratching behind Bonker's ear.

"It's all right," he replied. "She gave me a note says it's okay." Turning back towards the water, he added, "been a while since we've seen it like this." Silas dropped down on the bench next to him but continued petting the dog.

Richard closed his eyes and breathed in the salt air. "Antedeluvian," he proclaimed.

"Ah-yuh," replied Silas. "Reckon 'tis."

They fell silent, just enjoying the warmth and the sounds of the harbor. He gazed out across the reach, at the waves and the birds and the boats. Four months earlier, he and Amanda had sat on this same bench, right in the middle of scallop season when the draggers were working. Sea smoke blew across the waves and the shrubbery was shrouded with frozen mist, giving it a ghostly look so different from now. Ice coated the boats and buyers huddled in the parking lot behind the big white trucks, their breath billowing about while they stamped their feet in the cold. Today it was different. Most of the fleet lay idly to, a few with crews working on repairs or changing rigs over for the upcoming lobster season.

The older man was the first to speak. "I remember the year they put the bridge in."

"When was that?"

"Sixty-two. I flew an airplane underneath just after they opened it." He laughed. "Moi itou, j'êtoins jeune pis innocent!"

"That was a bit before my day," Richard said, looking across the water at the span, gauging the vertical clearance.

"S'pec so," Silas replied, pointing across the narrows. "Been a few things happen in my ancestral home, over the years."

"You're gonna tell me something." Richard closed his eyes and sat back. "I feel it coming."

"I'm sure you know the story of the Fenians."

"I do, but you can tell it again."

"Bunch'a crazy Irishmen, thought they'd have themselves a little invasion." Richard waited for the story. He didn't have to wait long.

"1866 it was, just after the Civil War. Thought maybe they'd disrupt the British in Ireland, set up some kind of diversion over here. Tried to make it across from Eastport. British warship out'a Nova Scotia put the kibosh to that."

"So they didn't get very far."

"Nope. But some say that was the last straw, why the British Colonies decided to become Canada."

"I hadn't heard that part of the story."

"That's not all from them years," Silas continued. "There was a bunch of draft dodgers went up there, too. Folks called 'em 'skedaddlers'."

"Draft dodgers?"

"That's what they say. Guys that were conscripted during the Civil War but must'a had other ideas. Folks up there didn't much take to them, dubbed their camp 'Skedaddler's Reach[163]'. Din't stay very long, year or so."

172

"So…" Richard twisted around on the bench, trying to imagine where in Campobello such a group may have landed. "They all came back afterwards?"

"Some kind of amnesty deal got cut," Silas replied. "Heard tell, folks here weren't real happy with'em, either."

My Husband Freeman   *March 8, 1863*

We have been having good sleighing the last week or so because the snow has been good. It is a nice winter we have had but spring should be here soon and we are looking forward to that. Mum and Jake and I took Luther out on a sleigh today and he laughed and laughed at the ride. The only thing that would have made it better would be having you here. Your son loves to be outdoors I think he will be a hard one to keep down.

The Sentinel reported last week that Father Abraham will be calling for six hundred thousand more men to fight. They are calling it the Conscription Bill and that men who are called do not have a choice. All men between 20 and 35 may be called[164] and all men 35 to 45 with out a wife may be called. Men who are called can hire an other man to go for them and they can also buy what they are calling a commutation for $300. To me a man who is called is not the same as one who chose to go but I guess if we are going to end this thing then this is what we must do.

Another thing the paper said is that on the Mississippi River a side paddle ram called Queen of the West has been captured by the rebels. Mister Watkins said he heard this vessel had already stopped a number of rebel boats on the Mississippi but was run aground by a turncoat pilot. They got the crew off but the rebels took the vessel. The fight for Vicksburg continues but with out this vessel.

A sickness has been going arownd Lubec and Whiting this winter they say it is diptheeria.[165] We are okay but are staying away from places where people have it. Probly when we start getting warm days it will be over.

I do hope your winter quarters do not leave you too complacent. Gen'l Hooker and Col Burnham want you at your best. Next week is Luthers first birthday. He and I are proud of what you are doing but we want you to come home soon may be in time for his next birthday.

Your Faithful Alma

My Husband Freeman   *March 13, 1863*

The snow is still good for sleighing and your boy Luther is enjoying it. Spring can not be too far off but he can have fun with the snow while it is still here.

Reuel Furlong was home on furlough last week and he got married[166] in Saint Stephen. His new wife is Fannie B. Higgins of Eastport and Rev. Philbrook did the honors. I do not know how long your friend was able to enjoy his honeymoon because it sounds like you will be out of your winter quarters soon.

We are hearing that Gen Hooker is planning bold moves they call him Fighting Joe because of the battle at Williamsburg last year. I just hope he can end this thing so you can come home and be with Luther and me.

Mum asked to be remembered to you. She is doing well and has been spending a lot of time with Jake Dubois. Some of his family has come visiting from Wilsons Beach. Mum has been busy with the Ladies Aid Society meeting at the church two times each week and sitting in a circle where they talk and make things to send down. I hear they talk about a lot of things that are not supposed to concern ladies mens business like how to run the town.

This time of year it is quiet in Lubec we are all waiting for the spring. Hurry home.

Your Loving Alma

My Dearest Freeman   *April 2, 1863*

*The rain has taken away the snow so now we have the mud.
Ever year we get this mud and by now you would think we have
become used to it but mud is still mud. At least we do not have to
move heavy cannons through the mud in Lubec.*

*Here is a letter the Sentinel printed yesterday said it was
from a Captain in the 6 Maine[167] but they did not give his name.
Could it have been Reuel Furlong?*

*It is unquestionably true that at no previous time during this
war has the army, both officers and privates, been so united in
sentiment in carrying out the war policy of the government, as now.
To win we must strike the enemy in the weakest and most valuable
points.*

*I am proud of you and the 6 Maine for being part of the
Light Brigade but I do hope that it does not mean you will be taking
bigger chances than others have to do. When you come home you
can tell Luther all about what you have been doing. Some times when
I look at your likeness I can see your eyes it looks like they are
moving. It is not long before you will be away for two years we never
did think it would be this long.*

*Mum and I will be planting the garden soon but right now
there is still a chance of frost. We will be planting potatoes and beets
and some onions and hope that you will be back in time to help us
enjoy the eating.*

Your Faithful Alma and also Luther

My Dearest Alma   *April 29, 1863*

*I think we are soon going to be on the move we have been
ordered to get camp ready to break. Yesterday Gen'l Pratt resigned
may be because his wounds were not getting any better. They made
Old Grizzly our leader and we all think that is the most grand thing
that could ever have heppened. He was the first real leader the 6*

Maine had. When Col Knowles was in charge it was still Old Grizzly that led us then when he was made our Col we knowed we was ready for any thing. Now we have him back agin. It makes me a little sad that he was not our leader when Father Abraham reviewed us three weeks ago.[168]

When we move out we will be leaving behind some women who seem to hang around camp ever time we set still for more then a week. These are like the Cyprians I told you abowt when we were in Washington they do the same thing. You do not need to worry abowt me I just think of you on that dock with that yellow scarf and then these women do not seem so inviting. They seem to be selling there services to many of our men but not to me and I think James and Isaac do not visit them eether. I for one will be glad to leave them behind all though I am not sure where we are going.

All hands have been ordered to help packing so I must get to work will close this. Please give my boy Luther a big hug.

Your Faithful Freeman

The last of the furniture had been pulled out and the rug rolled up. Dents in the plaster had been filled in and the walls lightly sanded. Richard spread out the drop cloth while Amanda opened the paint and prepared the rollers.

He glanced around at the big expanse of clear wall space. "Didn't realize this room was so big."

"Funny how that works," she replied. "Take everything out and this's what you get."

When she set the lid aside he wrinkled his nose. "What's that called?"

"Catcher's Mitt Purple." She poured some into the tray and went to work on the edges. "Pretty nice, isn't it."

"No..." He looked again. "*Really?*"

"You don't like it?"

"Didn't say that." He swallowed hard. "It's a chick color, right?"

"Gimme a break," she laughed. "Guys can't pick paint. Left to you the whole place'd be Moldy Mushroom Gray. So I got us Peach Brandy instead."

"Humpf." He started on the back wall, not wanting to admit she was right. At least, not right away.

"Anyway," she continued, "this is the last room."

"You didn't like the color my uncle painted it?"

"I am quite sure," she said while working carefully to get the edge by the closet door sharp, "when your Uncle Oscar painted it Bilge Water Brown, it looked *fantastic*. He..." She paused for a second or two, humming softly to herself, "probably got Lizzie to help pick out the right shade."

"I hear what you're not saying."

"You are *so* smart." She stifled a giggle. "For a guy."

They worked in silence for a while. As the room started to change color, he knew he'd be forced, at some point, to admit that she had selected a good color.

"So tell me," he said, while carefully closing in the last open spot. "You've been pushing to get this room painted. There a reason?"

"Other than we've lived here since we were married, and this is the only room we *haven't* painted?"

"Sounds like maybe there's another."

"I'm not going to hand you a surprise," she said with a shrug. "If that's what you're getting at."

"You want this room for a nursery. Is that right?"

"In that case…" When she looked up she wasn't smiling. "Don't you think we should have painted it Baby Blue?"

My Dearest Freeman   *April 19, 1863*

We are starting to see the spring flowers coming up and we have probably seen the last of the snow and ice for a few months. The garden is planned but not planted and we will probly have frost some time in the next few weeks.

The paper recently wrote about two house fires in Eastport in one week.[169] Enoch Bishop's house on Cooper Hill lost most of its roof and they are blaming a snow storm for the loss. There was also a fire at Mrs HL Chadbournes place but they got it put out with out a lot of damage. In Lubec we have been lucky so far no fires in a while.

Another thing that may be will make some people unhappy was in the paper. Revenue officers seized ten casks of brandy from the steamer Iron Age[170] they were marked as being oil casks. I do not know how much of a party some one can have with four hundred gallons of brandy but it would probly be a big one.

You have not been writing about any battles and the paper has not said you were in any. May be that means I can hope that you will not be fighting for a while. I know you would rather be doing that but I would rather you were not.

Miss Penniman came here last week and introduced Mrs. Aaron Hayden[171] from Eastport. Mrs. Hayden is the daughter of Deacon Hayden and has been part of the Eastport Female Benevolent Society[172] for many years and is maybe fifteen years younger than Miss Penniman. They are both part of the Sanitary Society. She spoke to Mum and the Ladies Auxiliary group at the church and may be hoping to start some thing here in Lubec.[173]

Mister Watkins has got two schooners on the ways right now and he is keeping the yard busy as he can with the number of men working. Rodman is the youngest man in the yard and men like Jake do excellunt work but they can not move as fast as some of the boys who have gone off to fight. Also a lot of the lumbermen have left many to go with your Col Hiram Burnham. They worked for him before the war and they want to work for him now.

Luther wants to go outside to play and soon he will be able to. He is getting bigger every day and one day soon will be as tall as his Pappy. Hope fully this war will be over before that happens. We both miss you and want you home.

Your Loving Alma

To My Alma   *May 4, 1863*

I do not have the words to tell you what we have been thru the last two day but I will try. It is not what I thot I was going to see but now I can not make the visions go away.

Fredericksburg looks like it was a nice place to live before the war started. Any more I am not sure. We crossed the Rappahannock River on a wooden bridge that our engineers built for us then we moved close to the town where the same embankment we

179

could not take just a few months ago was defended by the sesech like they had never left. It has a sunken road at the bottom and two stone walls between us and the hill. Rebel infantry was lined up behind the stone wall in the roadway and all along the top of the embankment they had artillery. This is the same place where Albion Avery died and we all most lost James. Many men have died on this field and for no gain.

Near the road there was a small house. I heard tell it was called the Ennis House. It was all shot full of holes by musket fire but most ever thing else had been knocked down by our artillery. They call the embankment Maryes Heights becuz the Marye family has a big house up there called Brompton. I heared that secesh Genl Longstreet is using it as his head quarters.

Last time we was heer we saw the Northern Lights whilst we tried to sleep on the battlefield. It is not a big hill may be forty or fifty feet high but the way the muskets are set acrost the bottom with the guns above it is like the devvul himself wants to keep us out. The boys call the place at the bottom the Slaughter Pen.

Old Grizzly got orders to send the Light Brigade to take that hill. Boys he said to us I have a goverment order to fill a thousand rebels and we need them in five minits.[174] We all told him he could depend on us to fill the order.

They told us to fix bayonets and take the cap off the musket becuz they did not want us to stop and reload just keep going at a full run. Charlie Clark was one of the first to charge an we all followed him and our colors up a shallow swale toward the slope we was yelling and cheering loud as we could be like the noise wud keep away the minie balls and cannister. When we crossed the Slaughter Pen I saw Major Haycock frum Cmpny D fall.[175] I think he had a mortal wound but cud not do any thing had to keep going. Men was falling all around but if we was to stop we wud be the next to be hit we had to keep running as fast as we cud.

I do not know why but when the sesech seen us coming at them they fell back. First we went by the little house then started climbing the hill we went up a bit of a slope with the big white house on our right and there guns above on our left. We was ordered to double quick and trail arms but do not remember how long before we was using the bayonet

180

The batteries fired canister at us an I do not know why I survived but James and Isaac and me we all did. I think may be the cannoneers could not lower their guns down enough to where we was. We all was like men possessed by devils just following our flag carried by Sergent John Gray[176]and screaming as loud as we cud the hole way up.

I am all most afeared to speak of it but where we was climbing the hill there were dead from the December fray that were only part buried an we ran acrost them too. I did not have time to puke but it was like some of the dead was reaching up bony hands to us[177] but we kept going. Some had uniforms and looked like they was almost sitting up to warn us but I could not tell if they was blue or gray I guess to the dead it is all the same.

We captured the batteries and took many prisoners. The first one we got the cannoniers fought like devils and did not give up untel we had our bayonets at there throats. When we got them their officer sed Boys you have just captured the best battery in the Confederate service.[178] The others broke an ran for the woods before we got close but we took seven pieces.

Genl Hooker is a smart man else Father Abraham wud not hef made him Genl. But I do not know why the whole army did not follow us up that hill. We could have charged all the way to Chancellorsville and may be even Richmond. We made it far enough in that the Rebels closed up behind us and took back the artillery that we had taken. It was Charlie Clark who found the way back later that night[179] so we was able to get down that hillside and join up with the 6 Corps. I think the sesech was expecting to finish us off when the sun come up and was some wicked surprised to find we was not there. The moon was so bright I do not know why they did not attack us that night. When we got to the bottom of the hill and crossed over our lines our pickets was some surprised[180]to see us they had thought we was captured or dead. Grizzly watched us come in he was sitting on a rock crying[181] because he thot we had been lost and was some releeved to see us come back. We did not all come back menny was lost but menny more was not.

That night behind the lines I did not fear capture because that is some thing a man might have to deal with. I did not fear dying because some times that is what a soldier must do. What I did fear was if I was taken prisoner then I would never see my haversack agin

181

where all of your letters are wrapped in a piece of rubber blanket. If I can not have you by my side then having your letters close by is may be the best I can do and losing them would be a hurt beyond all others.

They do not ask me but I can still tell you that I think when Genl Hooker just let the Rebels take back Maryes Heights after so many good men died to take it was a moral failing on his part. It was more then unfair and makes me wonder whether he is loyal to Father Abraham and the Union or is may be some thing else. We had a duty to take that hill but he had a duty to do the right thing after that. We did our duty but he did not do his. I know there is no thing I can do but follow orders and so I shall but I can still tell you what I think.

This fight is not yet over and I fear where we will go next. If we head for Richmond then may be it is for the better we can end this thing but if we turn to the north then all of this is for no thing.

Even though the sun is up we are going to try to sleep having been fighting for nearly two days with no rest or even a chance to boil any coffee.

Alma I probly shud not tell you this but now I know how it feels to put a bayonet into the chest of a strong man. It do not feel good at all an I pray to God I never have to do that again. I have seen things that I do not wish to tell you abowt but I can not escape seeing them agin and agin.

I must sleep. Pleez tell my boy Luther that his pap will be okay and gif him a big hug for me.

Your Faithful Freeman

Annie's was quiet this evening. The pool table stood vacant and no audience applauded musicians picking at guitars. Annie herself had filled their order but then retreated to the sanctity of her kitchen, out of sight and beyond earshot. Since it was a warm evening the deck doors yawned open, but they had chosen one of the round tables near the big mural. Richard carried the drinks back to Amanda.

Sprawled across the wall, whimsical figures danced in celebration of ancient loves. "Dance like nobody is watching," the legend proclaimed. "Love like it is never going to hurt."

Amanda sat back in her chair, nursing her glass and watching the four-knot current bring the next tide in. A pair of lobstermen glided by, engines throttled back to near-silence, taking advantage of the opportunity to return to port without burning up expensive fuel.

He followed her gaze out across the waters. From where they sat, the Mulholland Light partially obscured the view of Friars Head, beyond which lay the western side of Campobello Island, Head Harbour Passage, and the Bay of Fundy, and then on to the busy port of Saint John. The entrance to Harbor De Lute, the island's more secluded cove, lay along that stretch, nestled behind Man of War Head and visible only to those approaching by water.

"You," he said softly, leaning back in the chair, "are somewhere else."

"I've been wondering," she said without turning back, "about Mink Point."

"Have you come to some further understanding?"

"No epiphany yet, if that's what you're asking."

"That spot is kind of like the woods out at Carrying Place Cove..." He reached across for her hand. "You haven't seen anything out there?"

"Only at Mink Point. Nowhere else have I actually felt anything."

'The way you say that…" He paused for a sip of wine. "Does that mean there's something more?"

"Maybe there is…"

He recoiled in surprise but held his tongue.

She turned back to face him. "I don't know what it is. But it's like whatever it is, it's over there, Harbor De Lute, maybe near Bunker Hill."

"Do you want to go over, look around?"

He saw the way she shuddered, knowing it was warm enough something else was happening. "No," she replied in a soft but firm voice. "I do not."

"So it's just a feeling?"

"That's all."

"But you do know more now than before."

When she made no reply, he too fell silent, gazing out over the narrows. *Dance like nobody is watching.* It hit him that he was glimpsing things about Amanda that had previously remained concealed – things that he feared he might never understand. He rose to freshen their drinks and then sat back down at the table, marveling at her steady gaze towards the hidden entrance of the island's western harbor.

Looking over at the bridge, he tried to imagine Silas Gaultier flying a small plane under the span. A few days after hearing the story he'd dragged out a chart to see what Silas was talking about.

The vertical clearance was less than forty-five feet, meaning possibly sixty-five at low water, and about a hundred on the horizontal. A Piper Cub, if that's what he was piloting, has a wingspan of nearly thirty-six feet. Not much room for error, particularly with the fickle winds, and that concrete looks hard.

Will I ever be able to do something that impulsive, he pondered silently. *So outrageous that people would wag their fingers half a century later?*

He took a sip of his drink and reached again for her hand. The question in his head hit him hard. *Have I become one of those people who are afraid to step out of the security of their own little box?*

My Dearest Alma   *May 5, 1863*

Things are just happning too fast. We have been either moofing or in battle constantly since we left our winter quarters. And now comes the worst news I could send to you.

We have lost one of my best friends. James died in my arms from a Rebel sharp shooter. I was the one found him on the field surrounded by dead and wounded and I knew forthwith that he would not make it so I just held him. There was bullets skreeching over our heads but where he fell we was both safe he was very weak but knowed it was me. James and Me have gone together to the cannons mouth but he never saw the rebel that took his life.

I was the one heered James last words. He said La prochaine fois que tu vois Katherine baille-lui mon Barlow. He smiled when I took the knife from his pocket then it was over. The world does not seem like the same place with out James. I will write Katherine a letter and I know the Army will tell her. As much as this makes me sad and angry I am sure that she feels much worse only there aint nothing I can do for her.

Isaac and me we buried James at a place called Salem Church where we was fighting. He survived going up Maryes Heights and the night that comed after that but now a sharp shooter has got him. In one more week we will be two years in and only one

185

more to go. I am not confedent that the war will be over by then but I signed up for three years and losing James will not make doing my duty that last year enny easier.

I do not know what is heppening here and may be the papers you read will explain it. We was able to take the heights but then the sesech took them back only hours later. It was like General Hooker just let them have it because there was nobody from our side that moved in we just let them walk back in not even with a fight. May be if he had sent in one of our brigades that was in reserve back behind the line James would still be with us and our flag would be over Chancellorsville.

There is a rumer going around that General Hooker got knocked in the head when a rebel artillery ball hit a porch columm that he was leaning agenst.[182] Some of the boys say that they hear he is acting funny like he is dazed but he is still the general in command. I do not know about this and I seldom get close enough to even see him.

Isaac is still well and so am I. Give my boy Luther a hug for me.

Your Freeman

My Dearest Freeman　　　　　　　*May 6, 1863*

I do not know where you are right now and hope this letter finds you safe. Luther has started walking and he keeps me very busy. He took his first steps about a week ago and is now getting around and in to every thing.

There is a letter in the paper[183] about a speech given by one of the Generals about the Emancipation Proclamation. What he said makes a lot of sence and now I think I understand what Father Abraham wants to do. What General Thomas[184] said was that the Union side must keep some men at work growing crops catching fish and making the things that you boys need for fighting. The Rebels have their slaves to do that for them so they can send all of there men to fight but we can not do that. By making the slaves free he has made it so they can not grow there crops or even make gunpowder. General Thomas said he expects to raise may be even twenty regiments of colored soldiers and he wants those not fit to be soldiers to help fight from the rear. It would be interesting to know what would happen if a freed slave meets up with his old master on the battlefield. Any way I thought you would like to know what that General said.

An other letter in the paper come from Lt. Witherell who wrote about the 6 Maine in battle at Fredericksburg. He wrote of the bravery of Co. K I cannot speak too highly. Every man did his duty. The regiment suffered severely, but none faltered. Their cry was "onward." Reading that makes me proud of you but it also makes me fear for you. The paper says Company K had one man killed and twelve wounded and three missing. In the same paper there is a report that says Rebel Gen'l Jackson was injured and his arm was remoofed below the shoulder.

Michael Gaultier has been given a share on Achenar for all four trips to Cape Sable this year he is quite pleased by this.

Please tell Isaac and James that people here are asking about them and hope that they are healthy and well. Katherine showed me his last letter he is still having his dreams. When I told her what you said about the yellow scarf we both broke down crying because we miss our men.

Your Loving Alma and Luther

Richard pulled back on the cue stick, lining up for his shot, more than a little annoyed at the way Dana squawked the chalk across the tip of his own stick. Amanda and Claire sat at the bar, oblivious to the nearby contest, instead chatting about the kind of woman stuff calculated to quickly drive the two men to the sanctity of the green felt. It was obvious that Dana was eager to hustle a few dollars, but this time Richard had a plan of his own.

187

"So you guys are gonna head off to Florida in a week and leave me with the team." The way he said it, maybe it was more by way of breaking Richard's concentration than actual interest. "I can't believe you actually *trust* me with that."

"Three in the corner." Richard pointed across the table then drew back to shoot. "The kids'll take good care of you. It's only two games." The balls clicked and the red ball dutifully disappeared into the pocket.

"Yeah... The *last* two games." Dana chuckled cheerfully, glowering while Richard sank three more, properly calling each shot. "Time for you to go down visit Mama Bellingham."

"Something like that." Richard lined up on the eight ball. "Side pocket," he added, pointing across the table.

"How's Dad-in-law doing with his party boat deal?"

"Albert's having fun." As predicted, the eight ball dropped down and the cue ball retreated to the center. "Rack-em-up, Roscoe," he grinned. "You brought greenbacks, right?"

"About enough to pay for those two." Dana frowned, looking at the drinks with the little umbrellas that Amanda and Claire had just been served. He turned back towards the table to watch Richard break again. "He likes it better'n running a dragger. Is that it?"

"He's swapped working in the cold for swabbing up after seasick New Yorkers."

"Sounds like a good deal to me." Dana chuckled nervously while Richard proceeded to drop more balls than he'd apparently hoped to see. "Pop prob'ly got his bellyfull of ice chasing after scallops."

"No ice in Florida. Seven in the side." A perfect three-ball carom, too. He smirked when he caught a glance of Dana's scowl. "Maybe a few snakes."

When Richard finally missed a call, Dana moved into position to take over. "You guys planning stops on your way down?"

"Nope." Richard went over to stand next to Amanda, sending telepathic messages to Dana to scratch on the eight-ball. "We'll hustle down, take it easy coming back. See something interesting, got time to stop. Can't hang out too long, I gotta hightail it out to Cincinnati. You're looking after Bonkers for us, right?"

"C'mon," Dana replied, sheepishly pulling the cue ball out of the side pocket. "You know he's the only Lawton the kids look forward to seeing." When Richard dropped three more balls off the table, all properly called, Dana stood back with his thumbs hooked in his pants pockets, sporting a glum look. "Hey bro, don't ask me why I thought of this just now."

Richard pointed over at the corner pocket. "Five ball."

Dana leaned forward and looked across the table at Richard. "Something my grandfather told me long time ago," he continued. "His father was wounded in the Civil War. Caught a ball in his leg some place in Virginia called Cold Harbor, left him with a limp. Name was Isaac."

"Yeah?"

"Never read up on it. All I know is, he survived, 'cuz I'm here to tell of it. Sounds like you'll be pretty close to the battlefield. So... You gonna drop in on *Dizzy Miss Lizzie*?"

When the orange ball jumped the bumper and hit the floor just as the cue ball dropped into the corner pocket, Richard glanced up and spotted the innocent smile on Dana's face. "Yeah," he growled. "Gonna stop by and take tea with the Pope, too."

To My Freeman   *May 22, 1863*

I have just received your letter about James. I do not know what to say this is so terrible. After I read it I just hugged Luther and cried and he did not know why but started to cry too. When you boys joined up we never thought maybe you might not come home and now James is gone. Katherine got a letter from the army that said he died a hero but she says even if he is a hero he is still not coming home. All of her friends and family have gathered to help her but she is the one who will be alone after this is all over. Michael is off on Achenar out some where on the Banks so he does not know yet but will be home in may be two weeks.

Her church friends are bringing food over to her every day and just sitting with her and holding her hand. She told me before that she thought that some thing like this might happen but did not want to speak of it. But now her worst fears and mine have come to pass.

Please if you can make sure that James grave is marked so we can take Katherine down after the war is over and she can plant a flower for him. I let her read the letter you sent to me. She asked me to tell you she wants you to keep his Barlow knife until you come home because she is sure he will be watching. Katherine is not the first widow this war has made but so far she is the one I know best.

Luther is growing fast and walking by him self. He makes many sounds and may be soon will speak a real word. I know he misses his Pa and wants him to come home.

Your Loving Alma

My Dearest Alma   *June 11, 1863*

   It pleezes me that so many of Katherines friends have come to be by her side. This is a very hard time for her and for many others too including me and Isaac. Please do for her what ever you think I would be able to do if I were home and be pashunt with Michael because I know James would want him to keep at his fishing so he can learn to be a good provider. Do not let him speke of revenge.

   We have just been involved in a cavaldry fight. They say Jeb Stuart did not expect to find the Union Cavaldry coming at him at Brandy Station so it was a surprise. And for infantry units to cross the Rappahannock with cavaldry to provide support it was even more a surprise when we showed up. We was in the woods watching the cavaldry fight when the First Maine Cavaldry came on the field under Col Douty.[185] We heered later that he promised Gen Kilpatrick that he wud Drive Those Fellows to Hell. His men charged the rebel artillery and captured it but then kept on and the rebels took it back. Twice more they charged the guns and then turned tords where we was in the woods and we come out to stop the rebels from following them.[186] We was right prowd to see the Maine Cavaldry fite like they did sense ever body thot they cud neffer stand up to Stuart.

   It was during the fray I knew James is still with me becuz I was sure I was hit. We was ordered to hold one side of the field so the sesch could not get into the woods to flank our boys but when we come out in the open I was knocked to the ground and felt a seveer hurt in my right leg. I have neffer felt a ball hit before and did not know what it would feel like but right away I seen there was no blood and I could still stand so there was no broken bone.

   It was James Barlow knife that saved me. My right leg has a huge bruise like the time in the yard when I got hit by that dropped timber but that is all. It is hard rite now for me to keep up with the boys but I will be all right. James knife is smashed it will neffer open again but it was James saved me. I will carry his knife with me until I come home to you and then may be James can protect Katherine like he did me.

191

I do not know who won the battle because we withdrew but I do think Genl Pleasontons cavaldry embarrassed the sesech because ever body thought Jeb Stuart could never be beat and we surprised him two times and I know he did not beat us.

We have been ordered to start north towards Pennsylvania. I do not know where we will be going but we will be moving tomorrow. I must end this because all have been ordered to help with the packing. I wish I could be home to help you sellabrate your birthday.

Your Faithful Freeman

My Dearest Freeman   *June 22, 1863*

I write to you on my birthday to give you some news that has nothing to do with the war. Mum and Jake will be married. She told me this yesterday and I told her I was happy for the two of them and I was sure that you would be too. The wedding will take place in September and we all wish you could be here but understand that maybe you will not be able. They will move into a house on Spring Street not far away so she can still help me take care of Luther.

When I told Katherine about how James knife saved you from hurt she said I just knew it that James would not leave his friends side that some how he would still be there to help out. The more she thought about it the more the tears come out and then she put her arms around me and we both just cried like babies. I know Katherine will be all right but she still has some hard days to come.

Michael was quite upset when Katherine told him about James. Zadoc was still putting out dock lines when she went on board Achenar to tell him. She was afraid he would lie about his age and join up to avenge his brother but was able to convince him not to do that as the man of the family he was needed here more than on the battlefield. He came to me to ask about you and I told him that you were doing your best to honor James memory. When I told him about how the knife saved you he got a look that told me he will be all right.

There has been casks of liquor furniture and other things coming ashore along Quoddy Head and Seal Island like from a shipwreck[187] but we have not heard of a lost vessel. May be it came to grief off Grand Manan but all we know is that different vessels have been picking up cargo drifting at sea. I suppose the casks of liquor will find men coming forth to claim them quiet like. Nobody wants to say it but it may be that what ever ship it was had been sunk by the Alabama.[188]

These days I sometimes take your likeness off of the shelf in the parlor and just look in to your eyes like I could may be make you step out of that little box and be by my side. I hope you boys can end this soon before any more have to die and then you can come home to be with Luther and me.

Your Loving Alma

The drive back from Machias didn't take so long, just the usual thirty-five minutes and never any traffic. His order was waiting at the building supply store, and picking up some salad greens from the grocery didn't add to the time that much. Just another boring ride but now he could fix that leaky faucet.

The Historical Society building sported something he hadn't seen in a while: a big "Open" flag. He also spotted Silas Gaultier's Harley parked alongside the building, located just across from one of the town's older cemeteries. Richard could not recall a time when both Silas and his luxurious handlebar moustache weren't fixtures of the town, often just cruising on his motorcycle. There was nothing that had happened in the last fifty years that he couldn't describe in great detail, and the same was true for most everything from the thirty or so years before that time, too.

Why not? He pulled up behind the bike and shut off his engine.

When he shoved open the door and stepped inside, the floor creaked slightly underfoot and the faint musty smell was redolent of childhood visits, but he was struck by the organized appearance that had not been there the last time he'd visited, many years earlier. It was set up to look like the general store it had once been, but there were a few artifacts under the glass that didn't look like merchandise that the store would be selling.

He stood blinking in the dim light, looking about. Silas gave him a wave then continued showing an out-of-town visitor some of the Society's photographs from when Lubec was the Sardine Capital of the World, most of a century earlier.

The tin ceiling hadn't changed and the worn floorboards showed where generations of chairs had surrounded the woodstove. A single light hung down from the center. If he squinted, he could just about make out the men lounging around the stove, whittling big sticks into little ones and trying to outdo each other swapping lies. He smiled, recalling what his grandmother had once told him.

"Women gossip about things *others* probably haven't done," she'd admonished. "Men brag about about things *they've* never done."

High on the wall, right where he'd seen it years before, hung the scrap of wood with the name *Achenar* carved and partly gilt. This story he did recall, how a local schooner was wrecked in the 1869 Saxby Gale, driven onto the rocky ledge just east of Campobello's Lower Duck Pond. That same storm removed the spire from the church everybody knew as "Big White" and laid it almost on the doorstep of the Christian Temple across the street.[189]

The gilt name board was all that remained today of the schooner. It must have been Bennet Rose who put the label below it that said the vessel, apparently named after a navigational star, had been half-owned by a man named Zadoc Dubois but no one had discovered who the other owners were or what kind of cargo the vessel had carried and where.

The screen door creaked closed. Richard looked up just as Silas slid into place behind the counter. "So," he said, "What's new?"

"Not a damn thing." Silas playfully touched Richard on the shoulder with his fist. "You've come to the Historical Society," he laughed. "Nobody comes in *here* for things that're new."

"Okay," grimaced Richard. "You got me."

"Besides," added Silas, a wistful tone creeping into his voice, "since Bennet died, we don't even know what's *old*."

"Bennet? Bennet Rose?"

"We think he's still in here somewhere, hiding in the shadows and enjoying the joke." When Richard didn't respond, Silas continued. "All this stuff here, he knew what it all was. Think someone would take the time to pick his brain and write it down?" He waved his hand around, gesturing at four old boxes that appeared to have been hastily packed years ago and not opened since. "There's a lot more upstairs," he added, pointing at the narrow stairway in the back corner. "We just don't have a friggin' clue."

Richard glanced about the room again. There were so many things cluttering the glass shelves in the cases, some looked usable and some not. Some were completely inscrutable, their original purposes long faded into obscurity. He spotted a knife on the top shelf of the glass-fronted cabinet, or at least what was left of a knife. "There's gotta be a story goes with that."

"That there's a tough one," Silas nodded. "We're quite sure there *is*. We're hoping someone can tell it to us." He reached into the case, gingerly brought out the smashed knife, and carefully laid it in Richard's hand. It was obviously an old pocket knife, of the Barlow style, but had somehow been ruined. What was at one time a man's prized possession was now missing the bone handle from one side, and the liner on that side had been crushed down against the blade with such an impact that he couldn't imagine the blade ever coming out afterwards. When he looked closer he saw that the blade, too, was bent.

"Looks like it got run over by a farm cart. Why would someone hold onto something like this that can't be used?"

"Told you, we don't have a clue." Silas let out a frustrated sigh. "We wish we knew who it was once treasured that, and why it meant so much they held on to it all these years." He carefully took back the damaged knife and returned it to the case. "What we're hoping, someone comes in and recognizes some of these artifacts. Maybe recall something they'd heard from a grandparent or someone like that. Without the memory, it's just junk."

"You've got other things like this?"

"Heaps plenty, kimosabe." He gestured around the cluttered museum. "Up here's something else. Just brought it down yesterday." He pointed up at a wooden sardine crate, perched on an upper shelf, the half-peeled and faded label on the side bearing the Admiral brand. A few yellowed and tattered newspapers lay crumbling on top. "A box of letters and papers. No idea what they are, or how long they've been here."

Richard glanced up at the box and wondered why the name on the label somehow seemed familiar. "Bennet never said?"

"If he did, he never told us." When Silas reached up to bring down the box, a single letter fluttered to the floor, landing between Richard's shoes.

Richard bent over to retrieve it, squinting to read the name on the front. It was in an archaic cursive, with rough letters like it had been written on an uneven surface. "Alma Lawton, Green Street," he read, before tossing it back onto the pile.

"Relative of yours?"

"Never heard of her," Richard shrugged. "Don't think she's one of mine. Anything else in there?"

"No idea. We're looking for someone who can poke through this pile, tell us what it all is." Silas lifted the box back up to the shelf. "Hey, Bro! You busy?"

"Maybe sometime," replied Richard, glancing down at his watch. He'd promised Amanda he'd have the drippy faucet fixed before dinner.

Silas laughed as Richard turned to leave. "Say 'Hi' to Miss Peachy Keen for me!"

My Dearest Freeman   *July 3, 1863*

Elmer Monclef has been hurt bad in a yard accident. The doctor says he might not make it but if he does he will never work again the way his leg got broke. He was helping caulk a schooner and the chocks slipped and the boat rolled partway over in the way. They had to rig tackle pull it upright to get him out but he was trapped for over three hours and was pulled free shortly before the tide come in. I am sure you know what it takes to right a ninety foot schooner even with the ballast out. Men frum the town come over to help but it still was very hard. It happened late in the afternoon and Elmer had been working all day so he was tired but Rodman wanted to finish the job so he was working late when may be he should not have been. He was not able move quick enuff when the boat started to roll. Two other men got away with no hurt but Elmer was the one hurt.

I was in the yard doing what I cud when Rodman told Mister Watkins that it was Jakes fault the boat come over. He told Mister Watkins that Jake made the chock and it split. After they got Elmer out we cud all see the chock it was not split but had slipped so it was Rodmans fault not Jakes becuz it was his job see the chocks was set right. Even I cud see the mark on the planks where the chock slipped but Rodman is telling ever body in town it is Jake to blame. Mister Watkins says that even if the chock had cracked if it was set right it would have held.

So now Elmer may be dying and Rodman is trying to say it was Jake made that heppen. At least they was able fix the cracked frame with a sister did not have to take the boat apart. The owner was not happy but the boat was eleven year old so maybe it did not have many years left.

I am sorry to have to tell you this but I thot you wud want to know. Some how I think Rodman is doing this to Jake to hurt me for finding how his mistakes when he did sums put money in his pocket. That was a year ago and since then he only speaks to me when he must.

The ladies at the church bought a book called Queechy by a woman named Susan Warner[190] for me to read to Luther. I know he does not understand the words yet but laughs and smiles when I read

198

it to him and show him the pictures. I think the only thing would make him smile more wud be for you to read this book to him.

I hope you are not in any big battles becuz Luther and I just want you to come home. Also I want Elmer to get better and I am sure you do too.

Your Faithful Alma

My Darling Alma   *July 4, 1863*

We have been marching constant for so long I do not know when it was I was last able to write to you. On June 27 we got word that Father Abraham has put Genl Meade in charge and that Genl Hooker has been releeved. What is left of 6 Maine is right now in Pennsylvania at a place called Gettysburg after marching all night and most of a day to get here with out taking time even to boil our coffee. They said we did thirty six miles in eighteen hours. One point we saw Genl Sedgwick sitting on his horse watching us go by. Some of the boys put up a cry get a fresh horse Uncle John just try to catch us. Some officers would say that was insubordination but he just tipped his hat stood aside let us pass by.[191]

When we got North of the Potomac some of the people lined up give us water and encouragement not like in Virginia. Even pretty young girls come out to hand us water when we went marching by. One woman said her son was some where in Blue and hoped that some one would give him water too.

We arrived here abowt two in the afternoon and was forthwith sent to support sevral other companies. The sesech had bested our boys sevral times on the first day and we heerd that our losses were bad.

Alma we are not what we once was. Compny K only has thirty four privates and I have heerd that the entire Regiment is down to three hundred fifty.[192] When we first started we was over a

199

thousand strong and Compny K was seventy four.[193] I counted eighty seven men from Pembroke and Perry and Lubec and Eastport and twenty of those are in Compny K.[194] The compny is now under the command of First Lieutenant Charles Witherell[195] who has been with us since the start enlisting as a Sergent. I did see a tent with some nurses I think one was maybe the same woman I seen on a boat at White House Landing a year ago.[196]Old Grizzly is in command of the Regiment and he has got Charlie Clark with him. Capt Furlong is near by with Compny D and his Lieutenents and Sergents are all Calais boys.[197]

Yesterday started with cannonading like I never heerd most was from the Rebel guns. There aim was high[198] and most just went over the ridge and hit no thing. After a while our guns opened up and silenced some of the Rebel guns but still no thing was heppening. The 6 was kept in reserve which meant that they could send us where they needed us but we also kept the sesech from taking where we were with out a fight. I was able to see much of the battle and it was the biggest one I ever saw. At night the campfires both ours and theres spread out as far as a man could see but during the day the smoke made it so we could see very little.

Genl Meade set us on the Taneytown Road on a ridge between a big hill and a bigger hill along with Howes brigade.[199] The 20 Maine fought on the smaller one and they kept both the 15 and 47 Alabama from taking the hill finally stopping there Genl Pickett when Col Chamberlain ordered a downhill bayonet charge. All of us was proud of what our fellow Maine boys was able to do becuz after the Alabama charge got stopped the sesech started to pull back like they knowed they was bested.

After the battle we went out to bring in the wounded and bury the dead and there was a lot of gray uniforms out there. The sesech fought hard to take that hill but they did not get any where I think Genl Meade was able to look into the head of Genl Lee and know what he was going to do. There was a number of wagons with the mark of the Sanitary Commission on the side they was bringing supplies to the surgeons and helping wounded men move to the hospital train.[200]

This is the second time we have come north of the Potomac the first was at Antietam Creek. That time we stopped the sesech from going farther into Maryland and I think that will be the same result this time. I hope the people of Virginia survive this war becuz from what I have seen that is a nice place except for what the war is making it become.

I do not know if the battles that we have fought in are big but so far none were as big as this one. At night as far as we could see there were campfires both ours and theres. There are hundreds of artillery pieces here on both sides and some times the sky is black with smoke. Compny K did not have any casualties but there was one in Compny I. His name is Phineas Bean[201] but I do not know him he was injured not killed.

I do hope to be able to write to you soon. Isaac is helthy and so am I but we are both very tired and there is still no end in sight.

Please give my boy Luther a hug for me.

Your Faithful Freeman

"What's this for again?" Richard followed Amanda up the steps and into the church, past the big Congregational Christian sign, surrounded by the carefully tended bed of blossoming daffodils. He paused to look straight up at the tall spire, the loftiest point in the village and visible far out at sea. It topped the church that had long claimed the highest ground in town. The church seemed to boast of its nickname, "Big White."

"You've been ignoring me about this for a month. It's a benefit for the town's senior fuel fund," she replied, heading off into the big downstairs room. "The church's Ladies' Aid Society does this every year."

"That's a good cause. Can't we just give them some money?"

"What, you would have me miss all this fun?" She shot him an impatient look. "Besides, you forget we write 'em a check every year." Amanda headed off into the rows of tables, looking over the baked goods and knitted scarves and mittens.

Richard wandered off in the opposite direction, heading towards a table laden with used books. It covered one end of the spacious but irregularly shaped room with the wide and worn floorboards, the tin ceiling, the wainscoted walls, and the trimwork encrusted with nearly two hundred years of paint. In the back an oversized stove dominated a large kitchen and on one side of the room an upright piano sat proudly next to the wall with a stack of folding chairs tottering precariously alongside. Several pillars held up the second floor where the sanctuary housed the pews and the large organ, installed in the late nineteenth century thanks to the largess of Andrew Carnegie.[202] The pillars looked like they were tree trunks with white paint.

When his name was called out, he looked up and spotted the leggy blonde teenager Alexa Willett. "Mr. Lawton! You need a few books for your library. I know you do."

"I don't know," he replied, looking where she was pointing. "What'cha got?"

"Wilbur Morris' estate gave us these. They're from his collection," the young woman cheerfully replied. "There's some rare books here."

"Like what?"

She handed over a fragile looking tome. "Interested in the Civil War?"

"I prob'ly should be." He took the book from her hands and looked it over. *Maine at Gettysburg*, he read off the spine. *Commissioner's Report*.

Alexa stood back with a proud smile. "It's dated 1898."

"That was six years before Clancy got here!" He cautiously peeked inside, spotting the regimental histories and black-and-white photographs, the long lists of names.

"Only a bit of foxing, overall in pretty good shape." She smiled up at him. "We've been saving this one just for you."

"Alexa!" He forced a scowl. "I didn't know they taught salesmanship over at University."

"That's a bad thing, right?" Her innocent expression made him laugh.

"So what's my special price?"

"Just for you," she replied, making a show of looking about, dropping her voice and putting her finger across her lips, "we'll let it go for a measly seventy-five bucks."

"You want me to tell your aunt how you sneak up on unsuspecting males?"

She looked up at him with a beaming smile. "I've been working on it."

"So..." Richard reached for his wallet. "You're angling for a career in politics, right?"

"The senior fuel fund thanks you," she replied, carefully wrapping the book in a plastic bag. "Somebody'll be warm this winter and we can all thank you."

"Kids," he muttered, taking the book. "What's this world coming to?" He turned away to see what temptations had snared Amanda.

My Darling Freeman   *July 6, 1863*

We have been heering about the big battle at Gettysburg and how Colonel Chamberlain and the 20 Maine stopped a rebel charge. The Sentinel printed a report about how rebel dead were laid piled in rows like winnowed hay.[203] There was not much in the Eastport paper about the battle so may be that means the 6 Maine was not involved. May be Mister Watkins will get the Boston paper or New York and I can read what they said.

Mum and Jake have been making plans for their wedding they have set the date for September 12. I am real happy for both of them and wish you could be here too. It will be at her church the First Christian and they will move into the house on Spring Street around the corner from our place. Green Street will not be the same when she moves out.

I have herd more about the kegs of rum that was found drifting ashore. A fisherman told Jake that they was not flotsam but was thrown overboard so they would not be taken by a revenue cutter. Who ever did it was ready be cause the kegs was weighted with bags of salt so they would sink but come back up a few days later after the salt dissolved like may be they was lagan cept the other way round. No body knows how many they were able to find later but they did miss a few.

The town had a big parade for July 4. I heared there was lots of fine speeches but I did not go. Some how it does not feel the same after what happened to James and with you gone for so long.

Instead Luther and I went to be with Katherine. She is getting better but I have not heard her laugh like she all ways used to do. I will know she is okay when I hear her laugh agin. She likes it when I read her your letters because you are her friend and she wants to know that you are all right.

The doctor says Elmer is showing signs he may survive but it is too early to know only been three days. He has stopped coughing up blood but has a hard time breathing and has sech a fever he is deeleerius. We are all helping care for him he is at the Staples house in a room close to the kitchen. Mister Watkins says he cannot send off Rodman becuz he is all ready short the number of men he needs to do the work he has.

Luther and I both want you to come home soon. He wants his Pap to read to him and tuck him in bed and tell him that we are all safe.

Your Faithful Alma

They lay together, cooling off, twining their feet, savoring the afterglow and watching the whitecaps on Johnson Bay. "It doesn't get any better than this," he said quietly, listening to the rain drumming overhead. "Making love with the hottest chick in town on a morning like this."

"Mmm hmm," she mumbled. "And who might that be?"

He reached over and gently fondled her left breast. "I remember the first time I was so honored to touch you."

"So do I," she replied. "Leaving the tenth grade dance to go out on the beach was not your idea, it was *our* idea."

He laughed softly. "We already knew we wanted to be together. By that time, I'd felt that way for over a year. Despite Aunt Lizzie's machinations."

"She said something to you that night, right?"

"Lucky me," he said. "She waited until the next day."

"I'm still glad we put off going to the big game until Prom night," she said, nibbling on his ear.

"Me too," he replied, "Although long before *that* night, I had a pretty fair idea how your pieces fit together. You," he added, "were not exactly shy about exploring, either." They fell silent for a couple of minutes.

It was not long after that special evening that they went off to college, he to his and she to hers. Amanda never gloated over her valedictorian status, apparently preferring that Richard feel good about making the Dean's List six semesters out of eight. They looked forward to the times they could both be at home and make themselves scarce. Their friends knew where they were but when asked pretended otherwise

When he started laughing she lifted herself up on one elbow and scowled. "What?"

"Back seat of my father's car. We couldn't come up with something better?"

"I was no less eager than you, got no regrets." She closed her eyes and smiled, as though her recollection was as cherished as his. "Do *you*? Other than being forced to wait for the band to shut down so *Dizzy Miss Lizzie* wouldn't barricade the door?"

"Dana and Claire outdid us. He still laughs about that."

"Neither of us had a lobster boat we could use."

"True 'nuff. Still, they were lucky they weren't found out, at least at first."

Dana had often repeated the story, long after he and Claire were married, about the two of them rowing out late at night to his uncle's boat and tying the skiff to the side that was hidden from the town parking lot. Everybody knew that it was a rare hour when there would be no eyes looking out from that lot, just keeping watch over the town's prize asset: the fishing fleet.

"You don't finish your business before the current turns," Dana'd say, "you won't even *know* you're showing the skiff to the whole damn town. Only one reason why *that'd* be there, that time o'night." Any more, when he'd tell that story, Claire would roll her eyes but then laugh at the conclusion.

Amanda chuckled, thinking about how the story went from there. "They never *did* figure out how many times that skiff was spotted."

"It was the running joke," Richard replied, "at least until they went and got legal."

"Go ahead and say it," she said. "After that they only went out there like that for fun, didn't care *who* saw them."

"Hah!" He rolled onto his back and closed his eyes. "That all changed when Heather came along."

"Humpf," she grumbled, looking aside. They again fell silent. Richard silently chided himself for turning the conversation in that direction.

Amanda sighed. "*Everybody* was happy to see those two get married."

"Yeah," he replied, silently breathing a sigh of relief. "Not like with us."

"Worst part for us was, nobody ever *said* anything. Just those looks, the body language."

"They never said a *damn* thing," he muttered. "It wasn't so many of 'em, for the most part they were all over eighty. Except Lizzie, and she was the worst of 'em. As far as I heard, not one of them *ever* explained why they thought a Lawton and and a

Bellingham couldn't belong together. Like it was any of *their* friggin' business."

"Pretty much that group's all gone now," she replied. "And we still have a great bunch of friends."

"We shove off day after tomorrow. Got your packing under way?"

"It will be." She shrugged. "Plenty of time."

"Speaking of time," he asked, reaching up to stroke the side of her face, "do we have enough for a return engagement?"

"What's this, you getting greedy…?" she whispered, rolling over to face him. "You must think you're the only one on my dance card." The rain continued to pour down outside, and they continued to ignore it.

My Dearest Alma   *July 12, 1863*

We are back in Maryland now after chasing the sesech down from Gettysburg. All along the way we have been seeing there wounded in every farmhouse and church some times more then the building can hold and many are in tents or under trees. A few of there surgeons stayed with there men but most did not.[204]There are many heer from the Christian Commission they take care of the Rebels same as they take care of our men to them it seems all the same.[205]There was also some wagons from the Sanitary Commission in with the Rebel wounded. May be to God the dead are all alike and to the surgeons the wounded are all alike. It made me happy to think that may be your hand was in one of those wagons helping suffering men.

I have seen some rebel dead wearing parts of our uniforms. One had a bullet hole in the back of his shirt but he was not wounded in the back he had been hit in the head. Isaac told me he had seen some of our dead with no clothes stript naked where they fell.[206]

A story we is heering is how a group of wagons from the Sanitary Commission was set upon by Rebel Cavaldry and burned and the surgeons and other men with them captured and sent to Libby. We can take care of there wounded but they still take men prisoner who are here to help and not fight[207]do not effen carry weapons.

We have had a few skirmishes with there rear guard but no thing big they are moving too fast headed south for us to have much of a fight. Besides we are as exhawsted as they are.

We spent one night neer the town of Lewistown[208] on top of a mountain in a potato field. The rain was pouring down a long time and we was all very tired and miserabel one of our worst nights. I do think that if we had been able to catch the sesech we would have defeated them becuz they are as tired as us may be more. One of our officers said that the troops we is chasing is Genl Early the same Genl we bested at Williamsburg.

I want to tell you abowt some thing that Reuel Furlong did today. We was in a skirmish and some were firing on us from a nearby house. Capt Furlong was ordered to take Company D and stop them. He manoovered his twenty four men throogh the sesech picket line then behind the house before they opened fire on the sesech inside. They killed some but captured an entire company of thirty five including two officers then he got his men back along with the prisoners and did not lose a single man.[209] The main body of sesech was abowt to surround his company but he got them away first.

The bugler is playing taps so I must turn in. Tomorrow we will be on the moof again. Please gif my boy Luther a hug for me.

Your Loving Freeman

Neither felt any urgency to get up, preferring to enjoy the drumming on the roof and the opportunity to just lie together. A sudden thought presented itself and Richard got up and headed over to the closet.

"My father thought you'd like to have this." He carefully pried the cover from the antique wooden box. "Right now seems the perfect time to give it to you."

Amanda gasped when he unfolded the yellow scarf. "That's gorgeous," she said, running her fingers along the edge of the fabric. "Where'd it come from?"

"Don't know," he replied. "I think it's pretty old. It was with some things from my grandmother." He put the two medals on the pillow. "He said these came from Luther but didn't think the scarf had any particular significance. This is all that was in this box, first time he opened it."

Richard lifted the scarf and draped it around Amanda's bare neck, ignoring the same static electricity he'd felt before. The silk cascaded across her back and fell down between her breasts, lying supple and smooth as a waterfall. "It's even the right size." He admired the way the bright yellow seemed to illuminate her glowing skin.

Amanda stepped away from the bed to look at her image in the old mirror, turning a bit one way and the other. He admired how the scarf accentuated her glorious nudity, right up to the point he saw her shoulders stiffen.

While he watched, her eyes opened wide and darted back and forth, unblinking, then returned to the old mirror. Her smile had vanished but she held herself proudly, as always. When the silk slithered off of her shoulders, fluttering gracefully into a heap on the floor, it was like an unseen hand had plucked at one corner.

"You don't like it?"

"No," she protested, shaking her head slightly. "I really do." She paused for a half second. "It's very special."

"But what?"

"I don't know." Amanda took a deep breath and looked up at him with pursed lips. "It's just a feeling came over me."

"A feeling?"

"Yeah," she said with a shudder, pulling her robe back on and wrapping her arms across her chest. "It's like somebody says it's not supposed to be mine."

"I see." He carefully folded the scarf and returned it, and the medals, to the box.

She sat down on the edge of the bed and looked his way, still clutching at her chest. "You ready to get on with the day?"

"Sure."

My Dearest Freeman   *July 20, 1863*

I have neffer been in New York City and now I am not sure I want to be. The Sentinel is full of stories about some riots over Father Abrahams order for conscription. Here is what Mr Nutt said.[210]
An extensive riot has prevailed in New York for the last two or three days. Considerable damage has been done and several lives lost. The draft was the occasion of the riot. This is the natural result of the teachings of Vallandingham, Wood, and the peace democracy generally. Vallandingham-counselled opposition to the draft, and

211

law-loving, constitution observing democracy of New York have heeded his advice. Yet the democratic leaders throughout the country are holding up the infernal traitor as a martyr to the cause of free speech.

The Machias Union writes about Clement Vallandingham as a hero and Mister Nutt calls him a traitor. All that I know is that Vallandingham is in Canada West[211] right now and hoping to be elected governor of Ohio and the riots are in New York. Genl Burnside banished him to the rebels but they did not want him either so now he is in the British Colonies.

We have been reading about the big battle in Pennsylvania at Gettysburg. I hope the 6 Maine was not involved in that. The Union Army stopped the sesech from going any farther north but a lot of men died in the fight on both sides. May be I will hear from you soon and will know that you are all right.

Elmer is sitting up now and can swallow reglar food but his leg is in bad condishun. He says he does not know how the accident happen and does not remember laying under the boat. May be that is a good thing. Rodman is still saying that it was the fault of Jake but I do not think Elmer believes him.

Luther and I hope you can come home soon. I worry about you spending another year in this war.

Your Loving Alma

"Be a sweetie and drop this off at the Historical Society for me." Amanda pointed at the big box next to the door.

"What is it?"

"Stuff for their yard sale. A few things we can part with." The box contained a random collection of mismatched lamps, a clock radio, an assortment of mason jars, just the accumulation of life.

"Sure thing." He lifted the box gingerly so the bottom wouldn't fall out, then turned toward the door. "Don't let me forget to tell you about the conversation I had this morning with my father." She nodded in acknowledgement and he carried the box out to the car.

"Richard!" Silas stood blocking the doorway. "Was it you brought this stuff in?" He pointed at a box in the middle of the floor.

"Not me," he replied, surprised at the tone in Silas' voice. He set down the box Amanda had packed and looked at the other box. It was mostly filled with dog-eared copies of *National Geographic*.

"Damn! Another friggin' mystery." Silas carefully picked up a model of a schooner, maybe sixteen inches long. "Here, would'ja take a look at this?" It had been carefully carved and finished, but the scuff marks and broken mast showed that maybe at one time it had been a child's plaything. "Somebody dropped this off, we're trying to figger out *who*."

He eyed the beat-up toy lying in Silas' hands. "Why's it matter?"

"We think this maybe belongs in the collection, not the sale." He pointed to the name painted on the bow, then at the splintered plank high up on the wall. Both read '*Achenar*.' "Somebody in town knows where this has been last few years."

"But you have no idea who?"

Silas stood in the middle of the floor, shaking his head and muttering. "Je déteste ça quand les gens déposent de tells choses sans nous en parler."

"Think it's as old as the original?"

"Don't know. Could be." He placed it on the shelf behind the counter. "Not for sale," he grumbled.

On the way out of the door, Richard glanced up at the shelf behind the glass-topped counter. The sardine crate bearing the Admiral Brand label was still there. No time now, he told himself. They'd be heading off early in the morning on the Florida trip and he had to finish packing up the car.

My Dearest Freeman   *July 31, 1863*

I am glad that the 6 Maine did not get into the fight at Gettysburg. From what I have been reading that was a bad battle and I am just as happy that you did not have to face the sesech like the 20 Maine did. You and your friends have done enough fighting that I think now it is your turn to be in reserve and let some body else lead the charge.

While you were at Gettysburg Gen'l Grant took Vicksburg and now the Union has control of the Mississippi River. The paper printed a story[212] that I will write just as it was printed.

Jeff Davis, in a speech made to the Mississippi legislature, admitted that the fall of Vicksburg would be a fatal blow to the Confederacy. He said "The Confederacy must stand or fall by the defense of the Mississippi River."

The paper says that the south is now cut in half but I do not know if that means the war is nearly over. I do not think it will be over until you boys take Richmond. A report in the paper said artillery threw 25,000 tons of iron at Vicksburg. It would take many barques to move that much iron.

Also in the same paper Mister Nutt said that the Machias Union does not support the war. He wrote that the Machias paper conspired with the enemies of the Republic for its destruction. Some times I am not sure who I can be sure is right. The New Brunswick papers say things that are very different from what the Eastport Sentinel says.

Mum and Jake are spending more time together I am sure there wedding will be the first time they start to relax. Your boy Luther is healthy and very active and wants to see his pap. He likes to play with some of the other children in town.

I am holding your yellow scarf carefully because I know what it is you want. I want the same thing. I love you and want no thing more than to be with you agin.

Your Loving Alma

After several hours on the road it was getting past lunchtime. Departure day had been uneventful, and other than getting stuck in rush hour traffic on the Tappan Zee they'd made good time. Even so, the hotel in Parsippany was welcome and the restaurant was decent. They'd gotten an early start for the second day's push, and the hotel just a few miles north of the Beltway was like plain vanilla. The second day was boring but now they were far enough south maybe they could take it a bit easier,

Long ago they'd decided that stops at highway rest areas were only for gas and the necessaries – that they could do better for meals. The sign up ahead read "Fredericksburg" and the highway was littered by a number of ads for the usual places they'd already passed on.

"Hungry enough for fast-food junk?"

He heard the scoff in her voice. "You can't be *that* desperate."

The off ramp led onto Route 3, passing through town. More of the ubiquitous joints lined the road, all with familiar, over-advertised names, the congestion crowding out any sense of something that was maybe local. In frustration, he took the left onto Lafayette Boulevard and almost immediately spotted the small restaurant.

The sign read "Battlefield Restaurant," and it was located right across from a deeply terraced hillside with well-tended grass. It was a casual place that felt like something from back home, as comfortable as a favorite sweatshirt.

A few glanced up when they went inside but nobody paid them any mind. A collection of high school athletic trophies decorated one wall, a gleaming stainless-topped counter dominated the other, and clusters of patrons engaged in conversation or newspapers sat at scattered tables. In one corner a tall glass case showed off various pies and cakes. A pair of ceiling fans lazily rotated overhead but they were not enough to dispel the aroma of fresh-baked bread.

They picked up menus and headed outdoors to take seats at a big round table shaded from the sun by an even bigger yellow umbrella. For June first, the day was warm, or at least it was warmer than in Lubec.

"Y'all done picked out what'cha want, honey?" The waitress had a number of tables but didn't seem at all hurried. She wrote up their order then returned with two tall glasses of iced tea that soon sat in puddles of condensation. Richard stretched back and gazed at the green hillside.

"What, do you reckon," he mused, "the terraces are for?"

"Unlikely place for grape arbors," replied Amanda, leaning back and wrapping her hands around the cold glass. "Bet they're not for playing croquet."

"Enough time for a stroll," he said a minute later, continuing to look over the hillside with the stairway leading down from above. "We'll go check it out." The kitchen was prompt in sending out his sausage with gravy and her fish hoagie, which were both better than the fast food alternative.

My Dearest Freeman   *August 8, 1863*

This morning Jake come over with a buggy he borrowed from one of his friends. He drove Mum and Luther and me down South Lubec Road and we all visited Loring Leavitt and his wife Wealthy Ellen.[213] You remember her she is part of the Wormell family. Loring took us out to the lighthouse[214] where he is the assistent keeper. I do not know if you come out here since they built it anew but from the tower you can see all most to England the day was clear and sunny. Sail Rock is so close you can all most touch it. The stairway is narrow and round Luther wanted to climb him self but Loring asked me to carry him be cause the steps are too tall for him. We had a grand day. Mum packed a lunch and we ate it on the light house lawn. Luther laffed hard when Mum threw a cromb to a gull and the bird swooped down to get it.

On the way back we stopped at Carrying Place Cove and walked acrost the field to the beach. There were big waves coming in and Luther got to chase them until one caught him. He laughed but it made me sad that you were not here to be with him. Mum and Jake knowed why I was crying but I do not think Luther saw me. We were sorry to come back but it was neerly dark when we got home.

With the election for Governor coming in just a month the papers are getting more nasty then usual. The Eastport Sentinel and Mister Nutt are saying that the Machias Union claims that the Republicans want war with Britain. Here is what the paper just printed.

For ourselves we say that next to a northern copperhead we detest the British government for its bad faith towards us, yet we do not desire a war between the two nations. Not now especially. We must first dispose of southern traitors and northern copperheads.

I am not sure what all this means because there are so many things being printed now you can not believe one with out denying the other. We keep hearing that in New Brunswick and Canada East they are sure we are going to invade and soon. A few days ago a master was in the office he said that if we was to invade British Columbia and Ruperts Land[215] the people there would offer their daughters to our soldiers to be there wives in the hope that our men would stay and settle there. I do not know if that is true but he had recently brought his barque around from Vancouver where he had been commissioned to carry a group of gold miners to the Fraser River.

The next governor will be either Bion Bradbury who is called a Peace Democrat or Samuel Cony who is a Republican. Bradbury says he wants to come to some kind of truce with the sesech and Cony supports the Union effort to win the war. I hope all the men vote for Cony for the sake of our Union and the boys that are fighting to defend what Gen'l Washington gived us. We can not give up what James died for.

Miss Penniman and Mrs Hayden were in Monday last to tell us what good our work has been doing. They showed us a letter from a private in a Pennsylvania company that was written for him by a nurse in the hospital. He said that having the nurses there was the next best thing to having his own sister with him and that if it were not for the bandages we have made he probably would not survive.

Luther and I both miss you and want you to finish this war so we can have you back. I am happy to be helping make things like stockings that may be you will end up using but I would be happier having you right here so I could see you using those things. I pray you never need any of the bandages we make.

Your Loving Alma

The sign identified the walkway along the base of the hill as "Sunken Road." It was a place of peace with trees arching overhead and the smell of freshly mowed grass and cicadas singing in the canopy high above, all set off by the neat stone walls lining both sides. "We have time to stretch," he said. They crossed the road from the restaurant and headed down the path.

Up ahead on the right a small house sat along the road, looking well tended but vacant. "Innis House," a nearby sign proclaimed.

He watched her shade her eyes to get a glimpse through the window, its glass purple and wavy. "Richard..." He heard the surprise in her voice and stepped over to take a peek. Inside, there were wide plank floors but no furniture. The place was completely empty. When he shifted his gaze to the left he saw what had caught her attention. The board wall was covered by splintered holes, large ones. Not the gaping abscesses that an artillery round might make, but rather the ragged penetrations of a large caliber weapon. Or of many such weapons.

When he stood back he saw that the outside of the house also bore such marks, despite numerous layers of paint. It was as if someone had been using the house for target practice with an elephant gun. "Wow," he mumbled. "Something happened here." He glanced at his watch. "We should probably be moving on."

"Those are bullet holes," she said, pointing to one nearby. "If whatever kind of weapon that was could do that to a plank wall, what would it do to a person?"

Just thinking of the hurt made him shiver.

She pointed to a small road leading up the hillside to the left. "Let's just take a look up here." He glanced up the slope, then to the right. Off that way, a road identified as "Mercer Street" led down

219

into a residential neighborhood. Maybe three-quarters of a mile away a river shimmered in the sunlight and children rode bicycles in the quiet neighborhood.

Near the walkway a sign informed any who would read it that the hillside was called "Marye's Heights." He thought for a second about the inscription on the side of Clancy's statue reading "Marie's Heights." *Could it be they're the same?* Maybe there was something in the book Alexa Willett sold him. He made a mental note to check it when they got home.

The upward climb seemed easy enough. The road followed a shallow swale leading through a depression in the hillside. Off to the right a large manor house, beautifully kept and labeled "Private" dominated the hillside. A historical marker said the house was called "Brompton," and was owned by the College of Mary Washington. To the left of the path the steep hillside rose abruptly, climbing maybe fifty feet above the roadway, but the road itself had a gentle slope.

High trees lined both sides and cast the road into a peaceful shade. Scattered shrubbery grew around and Brompton outbuildings lined up against a fence on the right. The delicate scent of dogwood drifted in the balmy air. Overhead a songbird burst into melody and a small child went scampering up ahead of his mother, barely missing Amanda.

Richard spotted the longing look in Amanda's eyes as she looked first at the young woman laughing at her child, and then back at the boy. The woman appeared the very model of tranquility, but her eyes were focused on her young son bouncing ahead of them all, in hot pursuit of a butterfly.

The woman, who appeared to be two or three years younger than they, chuckled when she spotted Amanda's gaze. "Kids," she said. "Gotta love 'em."

Amanda smiled back. "How old is he?"

"Just turned four." Richard turned away so Amanda would not see the look in his eyes.

At the top of the hill the path led off to the left, following the top of the bluff and heading back in the direction of the parking lot. A few cannon with wood-spoked wheels decorated the grassy knoll, pointing off towards the residential neighborhood like they were defending the heights from marauding schoolchildren.

The path led into a large cemetery.

"We should be heading back," Amanda said, pointing over at the stairway leading down the terraced hillside.

Halfway down the stairway, he saw her look closely at one of the markers. Then she dropped to her knees and quickly looked at several more. He followed her, curious as to what had caught her eye.

"There's no names on these stones," she said. "Just numbers." It was true, there were whole rows of markers along the leveled-off stretches of hillside, identified only with a number like '4806' with a single number below, mostly 3's or 4's.[216] One did have a name. It read 'James Davis, ME,'[217] with the number 481 also inscribed. Someone had laid a penny on top of the stone.[218]

"Let's go," he urged, glancing at his watch. "We've got four hours to make Rocky Mount before they give our room away. Can't gamble with rush hour Richmond." He still didn't want to think about what he well knew was on Amanda's mind while she watched the young boy and his mother climbing the shady and peaceful road up the hill. "Tomorrow it's a full day to your parents' place."

My Darling Freeman   *August 20, 1863*

I hope my letter finds you well and in good helth. We are all well here but all is not well here.

Not enough men stepped forward to answer Father Abrahams call like you and your friends did. The newspaper has printed a list of men who are ordered to put on the uniform. There is fifty four names on that list[219] and that is just for Lubec. Pembroke has seventy one more.

I am proud of the way you and James and Isaac knew that you had to defend our country like you have done. I am ashamed of the way more men did not see the need to do that so now they are being required to do what they should have volunteered to do. If we fail at what you are doing then we have failed for Luther and James and we can not stand proud before men.

Do not think I am ashamed of the men who have there names on that list. I am ashamed that more men did not do the right thing simply because it was the right thing. Even the bounty did not make a diffrence.

When you come back home you can put on your uniform and be proud of what you have done. Your grandpap Hiram would be proud too. You are doing honor to the Lawton name and ever body will know that you are a man and your son will know that his pappy did right.

Mister Watkins says he is worried about finding enough men to do the work he has promised to get done. If I could do what you can do I would do it. Michael Gaultier tries but he has only started to learn your trade and he can make more money fishing. It do not look like Elmer will be going back to work at the yard or any where else. His right leg does not work and he says it gives him much pain if he tries to stand. Rodman still says the accident was Jakes fault he will not accept that he has any responsibility.

Luther is starting to talk and sometimes he talks all the time. Mum and me we can pretty much tell what he is trying to say but not all ways. He does not like it when I try to comb his hair and gets mad when I wash it. He is defiant just like his pappy. We want you to come home soon.

Your Loving Alma

My Dearest Freeman   *August 27, 1863*

I aways knowed there was some thing I did not like about Rodman Bellingham and now I know why. His name was on the list of men called to fight but instead of doing his duty like you and James and Isaac he refused to answer the call instead rowed acrost the narrows to Campobello. The paper calls men who run away skedaddlers and now Rodman is one of them. Instead of standing like a man he proved that he is a coward. He is now in British Territory so the provost marshall can not get him long as he stays over there. I heard he rowed over in the middle of the night on the falling tide and dragged his dory ashore in the cove at Mink Point.

Just a few weeks ago we had a parade for the Fourth of July and Rodman cheered as loud as any body. Now he is a traitor. Poor James is dead and you and Isaac is fighting and Rodman is in Campobello pretending to be an American but over here we all know different.

Katherine is still in mourning for James and you are still facing Rebel bullets and Rodman is in Campobello. I hear he found work as a carpenter because they have had so many men go off to fight that he can get work easy enough. I do hope he does not show his face to me because I do not know what I would do. I think I do know what Katherine would do and also Isaacs mother.

Mum tells me I should be a good Christian and find it in my heart to forgive Rodman for being a traitor but I do not think that will ever happen. I hope he rots in those dense woods at Mink Point. May be I will go to Hell for saying that but I am sure that is where Rodman will go and if I see him down there I will spit in his eye.

Luther is a busy boy and has learned to pull things off the shelves. Mum and me have to keep moving things to higher shelves where he can not get to them. This morning I gave him a pot and a spoon and he beat it like a drum until I took it away from him. He knows a barque from a schooner and corrects me if I say them wrong. Everbody says what a smart boy your son is like his daddy.

The list of men ordered to conscription[220] had many names you know like Huckins Leighton McCurdy Ramsdell Tinker Coggins Denbow and Mahar.

Hurry home because we both want to give you a big hug.
Your Loving Alma

223

To My Alma   *September 3, 1863*

   Since the big battle at Gettysburg we have mostly been heading back to Virginia. There has been several skirmishes but no more battles. I think if we could catch the sesech we could best them but they has been moving south faster then we has.
   Our officers told us abowt something that heppened in the 20 Maine. A few days ago they shot five deserters[221] that they had cought trying to get away. The officers ordered the entire regiment to line up and watch the execution. First the five had to dig there own graves then they was shot by a firing squad right in front of ever body. I do not know any thing abowt the five men except that now they are dead.
   I guess I can kind of understand why a man would want to get away from this war speshully after seeing how Genl Hooker let so many good men die and got no thing in return. But if I did some thing like that I do not think I could stand in front of my boy Luther and call my self a man. My grandpappy did not run he stayed right with Genl Washington even at Valley Forge and I will stay right with Father Abraham too. It is our job to finish what Jeff Davis started and we have to do it the right way. No thing but a compleat victory will be good enough come what may. Pleese do what you can to keep Michael Gaultier from getting any ideas abowt putting on a uniform Katherine needs him more then the army.
   This has gone on longer then any body thot it would and we still do not see how it can end. We heer from some of the sesech prisoners that they have no thing but they still keep on fiting. Some times we give them some thing to eat an it is like they have not eaten in a fortnight but in battle they do not gif up ontill they feel our bayonet. The men we capture say they do not own slaves or effen land so they are fighting for some thing else that I do not understand. Ontill they surrender we will keep fighting.
   It made me sad heer abowt Elmer he is a good man and I hop he survives. What do the men think abowt Rodman saying it was Jakes fault. It is the foremans job to make sure that a boat is properly set on the chocks and to make sure the chocks are made right even if they are badly made it is his job to lok them over.
   Please give my boy Luther a big hug for me.
Your Loving Freeman

224

The hotel was quite nice, just four miles out of Rocky Mount and a short distance off the interstate. They weren't late, and best of all it had a beautiful pool. Richard lay back in the water and watched Amanda dive gracefully off the board, secretly hoping the knot on the back of her bikini top was not properly tied. With long, sweeping strokes she surfaced next to where he lounged.

"Feels good," he said, reaching to stroke the side of her face.

"It's been a long day," she replied. "We don't have so many opportunities to talk, just you and I."

He swam a few quick laps, trying to stretch out the kinks of the day behind the wheel. When he climbed out she tossed him a towel and they headed back to the room. He'd made dinner reservations at a five-star, just a ten minute drive away, and time was short.

"I'm told the crab cakes are to die for."

She scanned the menu. "You've been here before?"

"No," he replied, "but remember I've done business in the South."

"Okay." She continued reading the menu. "Should I do them as a dinner or an appetizer?"

"I'll split an appetizer with you." He reached for the wine list. "I'm going for the catfish." He pointed out the bottle and the server left to get it.

The choices were made and they sat back waiting on the kitchen. "Pretty cool joint," he said gesturing around the place. "I hear the father of one of the owners was a legendary sax player."[222]

225

"Richard…" The way she spoke his name, it stopped him cold. "There's something I need to say."

With an opening gambit like that, he knew better than to interrupt.

"We've talked about the hostility that others have exhibited about us being together, not just your grandmother and your aunt…" She paused to take a sip of wine. He'd selected a very good Malbec, and would not ask her to rush it. "We've talked about it, but we don't know what it is. I cannot help but wonder one thing." When he saw the way her eyes sought his he returned the gaze.

"What," he said softly, leaning forward on his elbows to face her straight on, "have you been pondering?"

"You and I have spoken about bringing a child into this world." He'd thought that was where she was going and stifled the urge to respond. "Whatever the source of the ill wind we have felt over just being together, you and I, would not the creation of a child, half Lawton and half Bellingham, be the logical focus of that anmimosity?" She took another sip of wine but her eyes remained locked on his. "Those who opposed us just being together, what would they think about *that*?"

"Mandy…" He poured each another glass. "For starters, I don't think we should *care* what they think. It's not their decision. But…" She was not blinking. "How did *this* thought happen to come to you, just now?"

"It *didn't* just come to me," she sighed. "When we were getting ready to leave, I was dusting the living room and cleaned off the glass on the box with the daguerrotype. Looking at that soldier, it made me think maybe there's more there than we have recognized. And if that is the case, how cavalier was it for me, just plopping down the picture of Nana Bell right in front of him?"

"Sometimes," he said, reaching across to squeeze her arm, "You give me cause..."

"I'm sure I give you plenty reason to worry." She gave him one of those soft smiles that always reminded him why he loved her. "There's times I worry about myself." She took another sip of wine, apparently stalling for the time to compose her next thought. "But," she pressed on, "is it possible those two represent opposite sides in something we don't understand?"

Richard sat back to consider her question. He leaned forward but before he could speak, the house lights dimmed and an electronic "thump" announced that a microphone had been switched on. When the wail of a saxophone flooded the room, he sat back to enjoy the performance, just as their dinner was brought to the table.

To My Freeman   *September 13, 1863*

    Esther Willett is now Mrs. Jake Dubois. The wedding was this morning at the First Christian and it was Deacon Fowler that performed the ceremony. The pews was nearly filled with folks from Lubec and Campobello and Eastport. I think all of Wilsons Beach was over here. Uncle Zeke was here but Grandfather Willett is no longer able to travel. As long as I have knowed Jake I never seen him smile like he did this morning. Luther sat on my lap like he knowed what was happening and he never had so many people want to talk to him. It was all most like they thought talking to Luther was the same as talking to you.
    Mister Watkins gived them a handsome old clock as a wedding present. He said it was given to him by a Master when the yard did some nice work on his ship a year ago. Said it was one of the ships navigation clocks but was getting old and he was replacing them and thought may be he would like to have it for his office. Jake was in charge of that work they replaced some lower spars and he was the one designed the fifty foot lathe and hooked it up to the yard

steam engine. They also did some work that made the Masters cabin look real nice.

After the wedding there was a party in the church downstairs and there was so many people some had to stand on the stair way outside the big front door. It was real nice to see so many people happy. Since the war started there has not been very many times to laugh and be cheerlful and this was a good day.

Jake has been made foreman at the yard. He says he is too old to work like he did when he was twenty but he does a good job hiding that fact. Many of the men work harder for Jake then they did for Rodman. They say that he works hard and they do not want to be bested by an old man even though sevral are older then he is. Mister Watkins says Jake is the best carpenter he has so even tho he owns the yard he pretty much is letting Jake build the vessels and supervise the repairs. Jake never had a chock fail.

Elmer was there too he can move around now. Some of the men made him a chair with wheels two big ones in the back and a small one in the front. They bring him over the yard so he can tell the others how to do their job. They are happy to see him but pay no mind when he gives them instruckshuns. He will be okay except I do not think he will ever walk again says he is looking forward to playing checkers with you tells ever body how he will best you.

Your Col Burnham was in Eastport a few days ago. The paper[223] said he came for the purpose of receiving a flag which the ladies have procured for his regiment. I did not see Col Burnham but I did see the flag Mum and I both gived a little money to help pay for it.

The paper has written that the Machias Union has claimed that reports of Union victories cannot be believed because they promote the success of the Union ticket in their states and that it is in the interest of the anti-war copperheads to denounce these reports as false.[224] I do not read the Machias paper very often but there are a lot of people around here that do and it is becoming more difficult to know what to believe.

Luther and I we want you boys to win this war soon so you can come home. We miss you some thing wicked. I want to wear the yellow scarf for you.

Your Faithful Alma

My Dearest Freeman   *September 17, 1863*

   The election results have been published and I am not sure
what they mean. The Republican Samuel Cony won the election by
18,000 votes statewide but not in Lubec.[225] In Lubec the vote was 203
for the Peace Democrat Bradbury and 181 for Cony. In Eastport it
went opposite with 284 voting for Cony and 203 for Bradbury. I
think this means the men of our state support the Union but the men
of our town do not. Mister Watkins said that the Lubec vote was
close only twenty two apart but I would have been happier if the men
of our town supported what you are doing and what James died for.
Katherine is not happy about this and neither am I. When we met at
the church to work together making supplies for the boys it was all
we talked about. At least the traitor Rodman did not cast a vote he
can freeze to death for all I care in that wretched camp he and the
other skedaddlers have up in Harbor De Lute.

   Over a hundred men from Lubec has answered Father
Abrahams call so far and there will be more speshully when we
count those that signed up for the Navy. We need to win this thing
and bring you boys home but we need to do it the right way.

   Next year the men will be voting for president. May be by
that time they will figure out that our soldiers have the right to vote
too.[226] May be if the men who run our state had to fight like you boys
do they might see some things different.

   Things have been settling down now that the wedding is
over. Mum looks real happy and I think Jake does too. The house is
quiet at night with out her being here but Luther keeps me busy so it
will be okay. Mum is not far away.

   I did not see any thing in the papers what you wrote me
about the 20 Maine. I know how I would feel about a man who did
not do his duty and I am very proud of you for doing it like you are.

   The weather here has been very plesant and good for
bringing in the garden. Luther has been helping me with some of the
crops. I took him out West Lubec a few weeks ago and we brung
home a bucket of black berries for Mum to make pies. There was a
lot of berries but it took me a long time because Luther ate them all
most soon as I picked them. Missus Fowler saw us when we was
coming back thought it quite funny the way your sons face and hands
was all purple from the berries.

229

We hope you will be home soon so we can make you a pie too. I dream of watching you and Luther eat a berry pie together. That is not all I dream of.

Your Faithful Alma

The great dinner and show, excellent bottle of wine, and relaxing evening together failed to bring on a good night's sleep. He forced hmself to lay still, only a quarter asleep, gazing out through the window into the night sky, hoping he'd not disturb Amanda's peaceful slumbers.

A random noise – perhaps another guest closing their door – snapped him into a state of full alert. He needed a few seconds to remind himself where they were before he glanced over at the clock: 3:35. Three hours before they would rise.

Where was she going with that line of questions? He rolled over and tried to block out the nighttime sky. The conversation had been interrupted by the music, then when their dinner arrived further discussion was not possible.

A child, half Lawton and half Bellingham. Besides being the obvious product of a loving marriage, what more *could* it be? Why would it *have* to be more? Was Amanda on to something, wondering about the soldier behind the purpled, wavy glass? Seems there *must* be more.

What would my grandmother say if she knew that's what we're thinking? Damn it all! Why do I care what she would say? Her disapproval of Amanda was never a secret, but she never once said why. Her and Elizabeth. As if there *could* even be a good reason. Was that why neither offered one? Because each knew it would fall short of convincing? Because they knew I'd laugh it off? What was this about a 'curse,' anyway? Is it something like sticking pins in a voodoo doll?

He put his leg over Amanda's, pulled her closer yet, and closed his eyes. Six-thirty could not come soon enough.

Green Street is what? Two, three blocks from Bayview Street. But who was this Alma Lawton? Is there something in those letters I should know?

Chapter 7

Reaping the Storm

I have read a fiery Gospel writ in burnished rows of steel,
"As you deal with My contemners so with you My grace shall deal,"
Let the hero born of woman crush the serpent with his heel,
Since God is marching on.

Julia Ward Howe, 1861
The Battle Hymn of the Republic, third verse

* * * * *

My Freeman   *November 8, 1863*

We have been hearing about how some people in New Brunswick think different about the war and now I have heard it for myself. Captain Gilbert commands the barque Carribean Star and he put in at Mister Watkins yard for some repairs. He told us his ship was carrying shoes and corn from New York to Saint John when he was set upon by the Alabama. He escaped but not before they shot away part of the deckhouse. After he offloaded his cargo he found out that having repairs done in Saint John would be dangerous because he was flying the Union flag so he left in the night to come here.

Captain Gilbert told us there are Confederate officers walking the streets in uniform in Saint John and that he heard that they were trying to lure Union forces into a cross border incident[227] so that may be the British would declare war on the Union. After what you boys did to Gen'l Lee at Antietam and Gettysburg and how Gen'l Grant captured Vicksburg they think that the only way they can win is by getting the British to fight the war for them. There is enough people that think that way in New Brunswick that Captain Gibert thought it best to bring his barque here. So now Jake is working on repairs to the Carribean Star. Captain gave him a fruit like I have never seen called it a Pine Apple. It was some wicked good and Luther got to try it too.

It is a big fruit kind of like a prickly ball with some pointy leaves sticking out of one end. But when you peel it and slice it up it has a sweet juice that is a little tart. Captain Gilbert said that in the Carribbean they have big fields with no thing except Pine Apples and he can sell them for a good price in Boston and New York brings them back as ballast when he takes a cargo of lumber to Port-o-Prince.

Mum and Jake have settled down. He has taken the house up on Spring Street just up the hill from our place. She likes caring for Luther during the day when I am over the yard but she is ready to give him back when I get home. Your little boy is very curious and gets into ever thing that is not locked. Jake has made a fancy wooden case for the clock Mister Watkins gave them and now it sits in there parlor on a little table in the corner. Mum said she never saw a clock to keep such perfect time as this one.

There was a most unfortunate accident in Jonesboro. The paper[228]wrote about three brothers who had careened a schooner on a sand bar to scrape the bottom. The tide come in before they were done and the schooner shifted and killed Kelly Augustus Thompson. He was twenty two and leaves behind a wife and children. I do not know if you knew the brothers but I do think you know the harbor where it happened. He was not as lucky as Elmer the schooner was not in a yard so I do not know how much help they was able to get him before the rising water got him.

Young John Maker of Cutler died the end of September.[229] He was cutting a meadow and come acrost a hornets nest. They swarmed at him and he ran into his scythe and got such a wound he bled to death in two hours. He was fifteen.

Mum will be coming over soon and we are going to go to the Ladies Aid Society and help knit mittens. I do not know where they are going to go the Sanitary Commission takes care of that. But I will knit you a speshull pair. We have been talking a lot about the war and know that there are things we could say if the men would listen.

Luther and I want to see you soon.

Your Loving Alma

My Dearest Alma   *November 9, 1863*

    Two days ago we won a fight at a pontoon bridge the sesech were holding at a place called Rappahannock Stashun right next to a burned rail road bridge. Genl Sedgwick picked the 6 Maine and also the 5 Wisconsin to lead the charge only they had us a little diffrunt then usual. We was in column four wide and attacked with bayonets right at dusk running with a yell they probly heerd in Richmond. Our artillery had been firing for over two hours but at sun down they stopped. The sesech probly thought we was pulling back for the night but that was when we attacked.

    We captured most of a Rebel unit and all most got their Genl Jubal Early who just barely got over there bridge before it was ours. I saw him on his horse galloping acrost but we was not able to hit him with musket fire. This was not the first time he excaped us. The Wisconsin boys were a little late getting into the fray and we was having a hard time of it but when they come in the field was ours.

    I lost many friends in this fight.[230] When we attacked it was hand to hand and we was right at the front. The 6 Maine was the first to raise colors over the battlement but Color Sergeant John Gray who carried the flag up Maryes Heights did not survive. Charley Clark ran a rebel through with his sabre but was injured and Lt Witherell received two injuries.[231]

    We lost more then fifty good men including Capt Furlong. After it was over we found him surrounded by dead rebels. It looked like he had been using a musket for a club after he emptied his revolver. May be the sight of so many of his friends dead waked up a demon and made him become berserk but he was not the only one to get that way. I know you wrote to me abowt him getting married it do not look like he had much time to enjoy wedded bliss.

    I do not know how Isaac and me got through this okay. He was cut on the arm by a rebel bayonet and now my uniform has holes from balls but I did not get a scratch only a burn frum muzzle fire frum a rebel cannon. James Barlow knife was in my pocket so I know he was protecting me.

    After the bridge burned many of the sesech tried to swim the river but mostly they gived up. Some of them threw down there muskets and surrendered. We took many prisoners. Genl Lee was on the other side and he retreated all most right away heading south. We captured many of there flags and guns and even took there adjutants desk with all of the Regiments papers. Some of the guns had our markings that meant the sesech captured them from us and now we have taken them back.

I was part of a group that was ordered to gard some prisoners. We talked and they told us they were running out of ever thing. Coats and blankets either come from home or they had none and several had shoes that looked like they were as good as bare foot and there uniforms was like rags. They told us when they make coffee they have to use acorns along with the beans. They seemed like desent men so we gived them some of our coffee and they thanked us for it like they had not had any in a long time. I do not think they will be getting much coffee where they are going. One of the prisoners sed some thing I thot strange. He sed it was a rich mans war but a poor mans fight. Anuther tole us none of them owned slaves but if a man owned twenty he did not have to be in the war he cud stay home.[232] The same man tole us there officers treated them like they thot they were there own slaves.

Alma I do not no how menny men I have killed in this war but I do not like it one bit speshully if they are like the men we talked to. I know there were a few that felt my bayonet during that charge an they was probly good men. I do not relish the killing like some do I would rather the sesech lay down there arms and go home and we go home too.

Do not get me wrong I know we have a job to do and I will do my part just like my grandpap did and I know we need to win battles to do that. It is just the killing that makes me feel sick. May be if I had not read the letter that Penelope sent to Luke I might not think like this but when I did that I knew that he was just like me and she was just like you.

I have talked with a few negroes and they do seem to be like real people and just want to live like you and I do. I do not know how if there is a just God he would allow such a thing as slavery even if the Bible does say it is okay.

Some things heppen here that tell us that may be some of us are still trying to live a normal life. Early in the day before the battle our pickets saw Charley Clark go with Lt Solomon Russell[233] to the home of a sesech widow that has a young daughter. What we heerd

235

was that Lt Russell was courting the young woman.[234] *The two repaired to camp in good time for the battle and they were both wounded. I know it sounds funny for a Union Officer to be wooing a sesech daughter speshully the same day of a battle but stranger things has heppened.*

Grizzly is back with us after being away. We was told he was partly on furlough and partly doing recruiting but ended up recruiting him self a new wife her name is Seleda.[235] *I hope he does not end up like Reuel Furlong a newly wed and now his wife a new widow.*

Please give my boy Luther a big hug for me and give your self one for me too. I know that better days are going to be here some day and this will all be like a bad dreem. Lukes little boy will never get to know his Pappy but I know Luther will.

Your Faithful Freeman

The hotel had bragged about what they called a Continental Breakfast. Pretty much it filled the empty spot but left the hunger for later. On the way towards the door he tucked a copy of the local paper under his arm and grabbed their bags.

Amanda pulled out onto the interstate and Richard took over the navigation duties, such as they were. "Do we really have to stop at Elizabeth's?"

"We already talked about this." She reached out to pat his knee. "It's the right thing to do."

"You know it prob'ly means we'll end up spending one more night on the road."

"Maybe not, but if so my mother will understand."

When it was clear that the matter was settled and her mind had already gone off on its own journey, he picked up the newspaper and let her be. Out of the corner of his eye, he caught the day's first *South of the Border* billboard as it went sliding by, and wondered how many of Pedro's ads they had already passed since leaving Virginia.

The news was dreary, nothing but murders and burglaries. The Republicans and the Democrats were duking it out and the usual celebrities celebrated being famous. Nothing, of course, about things happening back home. He read the comics twice then set the paper aside so he too could let his mind wander.

Two hours later the sombrero tower, all 165 feet of it, proclaimed Pedro's home turf and the end of the constant parade of signs, at least those seen from the front.

Amanda broke the silence. "Little early for a break, don'cha think?"

"We paid our dues last time," he replied. "I vote we push on." She turned on the radio and scanned through four all-Jesus stations before finding one that at least played music, although it was a far cry from what they'd heard the night before.

"That singer, she was really something," Amanda mused, apparently thinking similar thoughts.

"We'll have to buy some of her stuff," he replied.

Half an hour later the Florence off-ramp flashed by but she continued south. His eyes followed a small cottage with a rusted steel roof sitting in front of what appeared to be a cemetery, all surrounded by unkempt grass.

"You brought up something last night." Richard broke into her reverie as well as his own. "Did we conclude that conversation?"

"I'm not sure that conversation *has* a conclusion." She turned off the radio.

"Prob'ly not." He stared out the window at the South Carolina forests rolling past, interspersed by occasional farmland, dotted with large red clouds pulled toward the horizon by enormous tractors. "But you got me wondering something."

"I can only imagine."

"Mandy…" He turned to look in her direction. "What if there's a whole world out there? One we're not seeing?"

"Go on." He hated it when she said something like that, giving him nothing to know how she might be thinking.

"I don't know," he continued. "What you said last night, what you told me up at Mink Point and about Harbor De Lute, what my grandmother said years ago, none of this stuff adds up. Lizzie probably knows something but I'm sure she's not going to say."

He glanced across at her, saw the way she stared forward, her face a study in stony silence. "Is there someone out there?"

Amanda glanced briefly in his direction, then started laughing. "This is something new."

"Is it?"

"For *you* to be thinking like this?" He hated it when she laughed like that, particularly when he didn't get the joke. "Absolutely."

It struck him that the sound of her laughter was suddenly unfamiliar. It was not her usual cheery mirth. "But how about for you?" he asked.

"Me? I've thought that a long time. That there's something out there trying to get us to listen. Or at least getting me to."

"Some *thing*?" Amanda wasn't laughing any more. "Stop it," he mumbled. "You're scaring me." He swallowed hard and added trepidatiously, "what is it you think they're trying to tell us?"

"If I could answer that, it would no longer scare me."

He stared out of the window at the landscape passing by. "Do you really think we need to stop at Elizabeth's place?"

"Richard…" She took a deep breath and paused for a few seconds. "She's the last one you have from that generation. Think of it as doing it for your mother. She's never been to their place and neither have you. We haven't even really seen them since you helped pack up that truck."

"It still bothers me."

"What's that?"

"She wouldn't even come to our wedding."

"Just because *she's* like that, doesn't mean *you* have to be."

My Darling Freeman   *November 13, 1863*

In just three weeks you will turn twenty four and I will not be able to give you a hug for your birthday. I wish I was able to give you a present but I will save it for when you get back.
The paper has printed a big story about a battle at Rappahannock Station that the 6 Maine was in and I know you must have been part of this. I do hope to hear from you soon so I know you

239

and Isaac are okay. The paper says the 6 Maine had many casualties.

I will write something just as the paper printed it. The Eastport Sentinel wrote *Their works were carried by only 4 regts who on skirmish lines charged the enemy on its line of battle under the protection of its rifle pits.*

Is this possible that you attacked a battle group in formation with only a skirmish line and took the field from them? You have many times told me how they fight but this does not sound like what you have told me.

It has started to get cold at night we had our first frost a couple nights ago. The days are still warm and Luther likes to go outside to play. Your son does not like to stay in the house if there is any way he can go outside. I have read the book Queechy to him more times than I can count but he still asks me to read it again he is starting to say some of the words he heers from the story.

Please write soon so I know you and Isaac are all right.

Your Loving Alma

To My Alma   *November 18, 1863*

We are starting to hear from our officers abowt how we shud re enlist. Most of us in the 6 Maine will have our enlistment end next year in June and they are starting to worry abowt losing us all. We have seen much action and are many times called to lead the charge and we do our best when that heppens. I do not know what will heppen next but I do know that they will be asking us again to lead and when they ask that of us we will do our duty.

Some days I think I shud re enlist because it is my duty to do what I am doing. Other days I tell my self I shud not re enlist because I have done my share and can hold my head high with what I has all ready done. Some nights I just lay awake thinking one way and then the other. When we start losing men lak James and Reuel it meens we are losing the best and for me it means I have to prove that

240

I am worthy of belonging to the 6 Maine. I want this thing to end but to end the right way. No body knows when this thing will end some times it seems like it never will. Them better days can not come fast enough for me. In my dreams I see things like when we climbed Maryes hill and wake up shakin those things do not go away.

May be if I knowed that if I re enlisted it ment that Michael Gauthier did not need to it might make me sign my name on that paper.

Old Grizzly presented our new flag yesterday and it made me very proud to think that you and your Mum were part of it. I teched it and it was all most like I could feel your hand through the cloth. All of the boys are pleased with it but no body more then me becuz you are part of it. I do not no when we will be going into battle next but that flag will be right up in front and devil take any sesech who trys to harm it.

We will be going into winter quarters soon and may be things will be quiet for a while. This war will never end if we do not keep fighting but I do not think Genl Meade wants to do what Genl Burnside did last winter with his mud march. That did not work out too well for us or for him.

It makes me happy to heer that Elmer is getting better even tho he will probly never get well. Please tell him I am hoping soon to play checkers with him but he better not plan on besting me.

I will write soon. Please give my boy Luther a big hug for me.

Your Faithful Freeman

To My Alma   *December 10, 1863*

Ever since the fight at Rappahannock Stashun we has been moofing around a lot and I have not had much chance to write. There was some action at a place called Paynes Farm but the 6 Maine did not get much involved. But we has been moofing anyway.

241

I do not think the sesech has got over what we did to them at the bridge.

We was ordered to start moofing on November 24 but then it started raining just like it did before the Mud March. Finely on the 26 we started but could not moof fast enuff. The night of 29 we slept in the field it was miserabel never so cold as that night. It was like some times it gets in Lubec but then we has a fire and warm things that night we had none of those. By the time we was ready to attack on 30 the sesech had all ready dug in. I think Genl Meade was hoping to surprise them but the rain kept him from that. In stead of attacking their entrenchments we withdrew and I think the sesech were the ones surprised because we were not there.

I do think we will be moofing into winter quarters soon. If you ask me we would be better off chasing Lee and his army because we will not end this thing by sitting in camp playing at checkers. Some of the boys think that is fine and they hope the Cyprians set up there camp too but I am not interested in that.

Some of the boys who get friendly with the Cyprians come back with a burn. One of them from the 7 Maine told me abowt what the surgeon gived him put out the fire. The surgeon gived him an injection with a kind of a long pipe then he had to do it to himself ever three hours for several days. He had to insert the tube into his Thomas way in and then inject medicine he called it nitrate of silver[236] and he had to to do that until he could releef him self with out any burn.

Even if I wanted what a Cyprian had to sell just to know what can heppen is enough that a good family man should stay away. If I comed home with some disease that I gived to you I do not no how I could ever hold my head up agin. You do not need to worry none abowt me. I am happy dreaming abowt you with your yellow scarf.

The bugler is playing taps so it is time for me to blow out my candle.

Your Faithful Freeman

My Dearest Freeman   *November 28, 1863*

    I have read your letter of November 18 many times and do not have an answer to give you. If you do not re enlist the recruiters here will be after you to sign agin and then you do not know what unit you would go into. If you do re enlist then we do not know what will happen but we do know you will still be part of it with your friends and men that you know.

    You do not have to worry about holding your head high. The coward Rodman Bellingham and those other skedaddlers he is hiding with over on Campobello are the ones that need to be worried about that. I do not know when I will see him agin and I hope it is never he can hide over by Bunker Hill with the other traitors but I still know where he is. I all ready told Mister Watkins that I will not work for him if he allows Rodman back in his yard when this thing is over. I do not know how he can be a good foreman if he is not first a good man.

    I do not mean to go on like this about Rodman. Mum has never sed what she thinks abowt the way he blames Elmers accident on Jake but I can tell frum her eyes she is not happy about it. Telling you how I feel will not make you feel any better or help you decide whether you should re enlist. What will Isaac do? He is probly saying the same things to his mother that you are saying to me. I do not talk to Missus Cooper that much not because I do not want to but because she does not talk with any body.

    I told Katherine what you said about Michael. She must have said some thing to him because he came to me to tell me that he was not going to enlist and sense he is only fourteen they can not put his name on the list. Michael says he likes life at sea and hopes to stay on Achenar even after fishing is over.

    The Sentinel printed a story[237] about some former slaves that one of our units gived shelter to. One was a man with his former owners name tattooed on his fore head. There was a woman with deep scars on her back from being flogged. There were also sum fair skinned children who were former slaves. You do not need to tell me where there white skin comed from. Slave owners are so vile they will even make slaves of there own children. The sooner we get rid of

243

them the better. These are the rich men that the rebel prisoner you told me of was complaining about.

There was another story[238] that said that Lord Lyons[239] sent a message late at night to Secretary Seward about a plot of rebel sympathizers from Canada East to burn the cities of Buffalo Columbus Detroit and a few others. Some were saying Vallandigham was behind it but Mr Nutt wrote that he was unwilling to believe him guilty of so base an act and I think he is right.

Luther has started to run and some times I have to chase him. Yesterday he got out and started to run and he was neerly to the church when Mrs Fowler come out. Be fore I got there she had him in her arms and they was both laughing. I all most did not want her to put him back down because they was having such a good time. Your boy likes to run and he can run wicked fast when he wants to.

This morning I told him not to touch the stove told him it is hot. As soon as I stopped looking he put his hand on the top and got a burn. He let out such a howl I do not think he will do that agin.

We both want you to come home soon. May be you can help wheel Elmer around in his speshul chair.

Your Faithful Alma

Amanda followed the Santee off ramp and headed east on Route 6. The mailbox was simply labeled "Willett," but it was right where his mother said it'd be. The home was a modest ranch dwarfed by moss-shrouded trees and surrounded by Magnolia. Out back, Lucas' boat lay to at the dock, rocking to the waves of Lake Marion.

"Richard," Elizabeth gushed, throwing her arms around his neck, "We are so glad you could stop by and see us." Even though it had been nearly twenty years since he'd sat in her fifth-grade classroom, the image of his aunt stalking the aisles in front of the blackboard persisted: tall, upright, and severe - ready to reprove the slightest infraction with a withering stare. "It's good to see you too," she said, addressing Amanda. He wasn't sure whether it was his imagination or what, but he thought a distant chill had suddenly appeared in her voice. She turned back to face him. "You sure you can't stay for the night?"

"I'm sorry, Aunt Elizabeth," he replied, "We really have to be pushing on. But we do want to treat the two of you to lunch."

It was a simple restaurant, not far off the highway, but also not one of the fast food chains. Richard followed Elizabeth through the door with Amanda and Lucas right behind. Fishing gear hung from the open rafters and most of the tables had been fashioned out of wooden hatch covers. The aroma of broiled fish and saffron drifted out of the kitchen.

"So tell me," she asked, "how are things in our old school?"

"Outside of softball season I don't get over there so much, just for town meetings and things like that," he replied. "It's not really the same since the high school got closed. Not even regular basketball games."

"I suppose not," she replied. "How's your mother doing?"

"She's doing fine. They're planning a trip up to Cape Breton this summer." When he looked up he spotted Elizabeth's furrowed brow, and followed her gaze towards Amanda's face. For a split second he thought he was back in the tenth-grade hallway, cowering under *Aunt Lizzie's* gaze, hoping against hope she wasn't aware of his unauthorized excursion onto the beach the previous night with *Miss Bellingham.*

He was relieved to see that Amanda had not spotted Elizabeth's scowl, and instead seemed to be enjoying hearing Lucas expound on the 1992 collapse of the cod fishery. "Back at the time of the Civil War," he grumbled, "I heard tell out on the Banks you

245

could walk t'ween boats like the cod was stepping stones, they'd fight to climb on'ta your hook. Now," he paused for a swig of beer, "ain't enough of 'em out there t'pay for fuel. That's why I got done fishing."

Elizabeth rambled on, speaking of how much she missed Lubec and looked forward to visiting later that summer, about local events in Santee, and of Lucas and his boat. "You do live in a special town," she enthused. "There's more of your ancestors there than you likely know."

When Amanda excused herself for a minute, Elizabeth turned towards Richard. "I don't know what you're thinking," she said, "but I do want you to know one thing." She glanced briefly towards Lucas then continued. "I always figured I had a whole town full of children, maybe that's why we decided not to have any of our own. But you..." She placed her hand on his. "You're my only real kin." She paused for a second and clenched her lips. "I have only ever wanted what's right for you."

Richard took a deep breath and looked into Elizabeth's eyes. "Thank you. I do believe that is what I have."

"I certainly hope so," she replied with a sigh. She pulled her hand back and they both watched Amanda returning to their table, pausing only to admire a large model of a fishing boat.

An hour later they prepared to head down the road. After Elizabeth gave him a big warm hug he watched Amanda's face when his aunt simply reached over to shake her hand. "So happy you stopped by," she said to her. Elizabeth had not spoken Amanda's name, not even once.

Lucas, on the other hand, gave her an enthusiastic hug with a big booming laugh. "Now Amander," he said, "you be taking real good care'o this here lad. One day you and me we get him out on'ta boat see what he can bring in!"

After merging back onto 95, Richard turned her way. "So," he said, "you are very quiet."

"Richard…" She turned to look straight on, unsmiling. "Elizabeth is what she is. She is no different from your grandmother. I do not regret for one minute, us doing the right thing."

My Husband Freeman   *December 10, 1863*

My Grandfather Willett died five days ago the funeral was yesterday. Zeke come down from North Lubec with the carriage to take Mum and Luther and me back up for the wake and we stayed on for the burial. Before he died he told Zeke George Washington gave him his land on Smalls Cove after he fought in the Revolution and he wanted never to leave it so he was buried in a little plot behind the house he built and lived in for seventy years.

By the time we arrived his looking glass was turned to face the wall and his clock had been stopped. You know that glass it is tall and narrow and has a gilded bugle carved on the top of the frame no body else around here has one like it. He was laid out in the downstairs parlor and many people from Lubec and Campobello and Pembroke came to show their respect and even a few from Eastport. There were flowers a plenty and most wept when his coffin was carried out. Jake come by boat to help with sevral others and some of the Gove and Avery familys was there to help carry him out.

Ever body was sorry you could not be here. He had been ill for sevral months and the doctor said the sudden cold was too much. Zeke is well but Mum is still missing Grampa at least she has Jake and she likes being with Luther. They gave Mum his looking glass

247

but she has no place to put it so it will be in our home in the bed room. Mum asked that his clock go to my great-uncle Jasper in Wilsons Beach sense she already has the one Mister Watkins gave them for their wedding.

In two weeks it will be Christmas and again with out you. Deacon Fowler is trying to get me into the spirit but I am having a very hard time doing that with out having you here.

Winter has arrived in Lubec. This morning it was very cold and the sea smoke was blowing acrost the harbor we could hardly see Popes Folly or any of the other islands. I remember the time we went together down to the docks to look at the way the smoke blew acrost the water and how good it was just to be together with you. May be next summer we can row a dory acrost and take our lunch on one of the islands. Thinking about things like that is how I try to stay cheer full with you not being here with Luther and me.

There is some thing interesting in the Sentinel. The steamer Chesapeake was taken at sea by some men who went on board as paying passengers.[240] They murdered the engineer and locked up a few others then took the vessel to Saint John said it was a confederate prize. The paper called it a mutiny but if you ask me it sounds more like piracy. It was from New York bound for Portland and now it is in New Brunswick. I do not know how much coal they have on board but Mister Watkins says there is not much coal to be had in Saint John specially if the authorities know the ship was brought in at gunpoint.

Has Isaac decided to re enlist? This thing has gone on too long all ready but I do know that it will take men like you to end it.

Mum and I will be going to the First Christian this evening to help knit mittens. The Sanitary Commission will send them to units where they are needed the most we do not know where they go but some times we hear back from those who got them. The best part is talking with the other women in town many of them are starting to think we should be working together on other things too. Bernadette Cooper likes to talk about how the town is run by just a few families those that own smoke houses and pay people to do there work she thinks they tell ever body else what to think. Maybe she is right but I do not know if that is a bad thing or how we can change it if it is.

248

I will stay and help until Luther lets me know it is time to go home. Your yellow scarf is in a safe place I want you to come home so I can wear it just for you.

Your Faithful Alma and Luther

My Dearest Alma   *December 24, 1863*

Here it is Christmas Eve and I am in Virginia and you and Luther are at home. Once again we are still apart. I am as comfortable as can be hoped the only thing that would make it better would be for us to be together.

It made me sad to heer of your grandfather but at leest he got a proper funeral. He lived a long and good life still it was sad to lose him. I am glad Luther was part of it.

Our regimental cooks are getting ready to make us a dinner and I am sure it will be fine. We get enough rations we can eat okay but when a cook that knows what he is doing goes to work we can all tell the diffrunce. I am sure that dinner tomorrow night will be some thing fine.

We are in winter quarters now at Brandy Station and will be here until spring weather makes it so we can move with out getting stuck in the mud. Isaac and me and two other boys from the 6 Maine have bilt a cabin. I think you know Henry Denbo and William O'Brien they are both from Lubec.[241] It may not be warm and dry but it is a lot better then the tents we use when we are moving and it stops the wind much better then a tent. We took sum fence rails and sum logs and bilt a frame to make a roof with sum planks we found. Then we covered it with tent cloth to keep out the rain. The chimbley is made of logs with a barrel on top all chinked with this glorious Virginia mud.

Let me tell you abowt the mud it is not like we have in Lubec. When we scoop it up it is like soft butter and it spreads like fine plaster but when it starts to dry just a little becomes hard and you

249

can hardly brake it even with a bayonet. When we light our fire our cabin is as warm as our kitchen in Lubec.

For a bed I have a platform made of planks that I fill with straw and put some canvas acrost. It is a bed that I would be proud to share with you but then I might wish that my cabin mates may be were not here too. I think you know what I mean.

Two nights back I was on picket line when three rebels come out of the woods lade down there muskets said they wanted to surrender. They was part of the rebel picket and the night was verry cold and there cloths were not enuff keep them warm effen on a summer night. One told us he did not mind his army did not gif him enuff to eat but back in Georgia the goverment was letting his children starve and he could not help them effen slaves got more to eat. He said his cousin was cumpelled to trade her vertue for food for her children. Another said that ever week in there regment men who had been cought trying go back to help there familys had to dig there own grave then was shot and he thot if he could not help them then they wud be better off he was prisoner of the federals. He told us they neffer shot a officer only privates.[242] We shared some of our rations then one of our teem took them back to Captain Witherell I do not no what become of them after.

Those newspapers that you sent to me were very welcome. I read them from one end to the other then past them along. Most of the time when we get to see a paper ever body wants to read it and may be it gets past through our entire regiment until the paper falls apart. I have read papers that were four or five months old the paper was so soft it neerly crumbled in my hands but as long as it can be read some body will want to read it. Some times we even get to read a rebel paper. A copy of the Richmond Examiner frum July is in camp it is a source of great levity becawse it reported on how we lost at Gettysburg and the rebels captured forty thousand of our boys.[243] We was there and do not need to be told what that paper is trying to do. It did not egsplain why there big victory ment they had to hurry back acrost the Potomac with their tails held high and there heads hung low and leaf there wounded behind.

My favorite reading is your letters. I no I did lose some at Antietam Creek but only a few and those I have are preshus. I think Isaac and the other boys are tired of heering me read abowt Luther and your Mum but I do not care I will read them again tonight just to feel like you are standing next to me. James used to dream abowt Katherine and I have the same dream of you with the yellow scarf.

Pleese do not be too hard on Rodman. I do not blame any body for not wanting to do what we are doing right now. If it were up to me I would not be doing this but I no there is a job that must get done and if I do not do it my Grandpap would not rest easy. It is not the fear of what heppens to those who run it is the fear of dishonoring his name. We no that we will not win this thing sitting in camp and ever man here wud prefer to be home.

Next Christmas I am sure we will be together. Better days have to be coming this war can not go on forever. Some days it feels like it has all ready gone on forever but I know that is not true. I look forward to being home with you and Luther.

Your Loving Freeman

My Dearest Freeman   *December 29, 1863*

Christmas is over but it was not really like Christmas because you were not here with us. We had a nice tree and Mum and I made sure Luther had nice presents to open. Jake made him a nice toy fishing boat looked just like Achenar all painted nice even had the name on the bow and the Sanitary Ladies knit him a warm sweater. He is old enough to know that things are happening and that this is a special time.

Mum is looking forward to playing Mother Goody for Luther and a few of the other children in town. All her relatives over in Campobello want her to tell them what the children say when she comes in all dressed up to give them nuts and candies and new pencils and she is ankshus to do that. The day after Christmas her sister Agnes rowed over and stayed with Luther and me for the night. We laughed a lot at her stories it was good she came here.

251

Yesterday Mum showed Luther your likeness and asked if he knowed who you is. He told her you are his Pap and you are a soldier in the war. I was never so proud the way he said that. I know he does not understand what that means but some day he will. He does see that some children his age have there Pappy at home but has not yet asked why he does not.

Lately we have been seeing a vessel prowling around Friar Roads and now the Sentinel has written about it.[244] The revenue cutter J. S. Black has been ordered to guard duty here and any vessel entering or leaving at night will be carefully inspected. I do not know how much cargo has come through Saint John that is carried to the sesech but I keep hearing rumors that there are many shipments. Some how I do not believe that the sesech are looking for the rum that some of those vessels bring in. Ever body in the yard knows what is inside those casks they do not make that much salt in Havana and those other islands.

Last week H.W. Carters yard in Pembroke launched a bark of 750 tons[245] for a company out of New York. There is plenty work going on right now for when you come home and I am sure I can find things for you to do at home too. It is cold here now specially at night but we have a good supply of wood and will be warm. I wish you were here to help keep my fire burning.

Your Loving Alma

My Loving Alma   *January 12, 1864*

We remain in winter camp right now and are not going anywhere. It is just one day after another. All there is to look forward to is the mail and the mess. And spring when the roads dry out.

The work that you and your mother is doing with the Sanitary ladies meens much to the boys. Not long ago I saw one of the boys brake down crying because he had been given a pair of mittens that some lady knitted just like you are doing. There was a note inside one[246] from the lady that knitted them said that she hoped he would like the mittens because it was all she could do to help she wanted him to no that some body cared abowt him. He did not know who she was any more then she would know who would get that pair of mittens but to him those mittens was speshul and so was the ladys note. He carried it with him for a week showed it to the entire regiment.

I talked with a boy frum the 5 Wisconsin that had been wounded at Gettysburg. He comed back from the hospital and is now with his unit. He told me that the hospital had several ladies volunteering to work as nurses and he thought that they were more important to his getting better then the surgeons because they cared for him like they was his mother and his sister. He also told me he heard that a few woman nurses have died[247] from disease they caught whilst tending the sick at the hospital. To him they were comrades in war just like members of his company.

Here is a story[248] that is going around the camp. I think may be this is not real but may be it is. They are talking of a soldier of the Irish perswashun frum one of the New York regiments. Pat was asked by another soldier to help him off the field becawse he was shot in the leg. The good harted son of Erin helped him to a horse strapped him so he could sit up straight and forthwith led him toward the rear where the hospital was. Part way back an artillery ball remoofed the poor fellows head but Pat did not see that. When the surgeon asked what he wanted Pat said to him I brought this man here to have his leg dressed. But he has no head said the surgeon. The bloody liar cried out Pat looking back to see. He told me it was just his leg.

So may be we are finding our fun where we can. We have a lot of time to do no thing when we is in winter quarters. Our little cabin is cozy enough. We had snow a few days ago and did not know it until we come out in the morning. So for now we is comfortable enough. Yesterday I beat Isaac four games straight playing checkers.

Some times the smoke here hangs over the camp if the wind is not blowing. Yesterday it lay over the camp like it does in Lubec when the fog comes in with the tide and it is still. Isaac said the smoke was like when the smoke houses are at work and it blows over the town all day long. When he said that it made me sad because I *had all most forgotten what that was like. In Lubec you smell the fish in the smoke but here the smell is just birning wood nothing more but at leest not the smoke of battle.*

Please give my boy Luther a big hug for me and another for yourself.

Your Faithful Freeman

Plans had not included spending that last night on the road, but lunch with Elizabeth and Lucas set them back better than three hours so the choices were few. At Hardeeville the Holiday Inn had a room available and they bragged about the great food available nearby. The next choice would put them in Savannah where prices would be higher and the atmosphere more commercial. They took the room and walked over.

He looked around the tiny restaurant. "Is this Elizabeth's revenge?"

The place had only four tables, the light from the neon "open" sign flickered against the far wall and the restroom appeared to be for both men and women. It did look to be clean. Lynyrd Skynyrd warbled out *Sweet Home Alabama* on an ancient juke box and the sound of clattering pans confirmed that the kitchen was in operation.

"Revenge?" She looked around at the oilcloth covered tables and mismatched chairs. "For …?"

"For me marrying you," he laughed. "If we hadn't stopped we'd be having dinner with your parents tonight."

"Give it a rest, would'ja?" He didn't like the way she raised that one eyebrow. "That story's getting old. Don't you think it's time we tried something different?"

"This's different all right." The pungent hickory smoke from the trailer-mounted cooker had permeated every single item in the place, to the point where it could be scraped off the inside of the windows, although it apparently never had been. He watched the teenaged waitress approaching them with menus in hand.

"Welcome to Hardeeville," she chirped, smiling broadly. "Y'all here for ribs? Y'done come to the raght plice." She seemed authentically cheerful, somehow not part of the establishment. "We'se happy y'all've come hahr." They followed her to the only vacant table and started perusing the menu.

"Mandy..." When she didn't look up he continued. "Earlier today you said something. Auntie Liz and my grandmother. You were making some kind of comparison."

"C'mon," she replied. "Do we really need to go back there? We both know your grandmother held some kind of grudge about me. If she ever told you what it was, you never shared it."

"You think I'd hold back something like *that*?"

"I hope not. But whatever your grandmother's problem was..."

"Got it. Lizzie's infected with the same notion." The menu featured big servings of smoked ribs, bigger servings, and enormous servings, either with or without cole slaw. They both ordered the ribs but opted for iced tea instead of soda.

"I am curious about one thing," Amanda said after the orders were placed. "Elizabeth and Lucas... I never really got to talk much with him before. They seem an odd couple. Does she go by Willett or Lawton?"

"What is it they say?" He looked at Amanda with his eyebrows hiked up. "Something about opposites?"

"She's so proper, and he's so…"

"C'mon, he's a fisherman, used to hard work on the open ocean. But," he added, just as the ribs were served, "they've been together nearly forty years." He paused for a few seconds then started laughing.

She leaned over and speared a rib with her fork. "What?"

"Just thinking," he replied, suppressing a grin. "Remember Dana's story? Late nights in the lobster boat?"

He wasn't sure whether it was a scowl or maybe she got caught up by the mental image. "Sometimes," she said, forcing a deadpan and rolling her eyes, "you can be totally weird."

"Hey! Can't a guy be totally good at *something*?"

"So maybe…" She reached up and wiped a drop of sauce from his chin. "There's still hope for us."

They fell into silence for a few minutes, enjoying the dinner and the ambiance of the modest restaurant. The ribs were better than he'd hoped, with a smoky taste tinged with bourbon and maybe pineapple and brown sugar, served up with rice. He caught himself licking the stickiness off his fingertips.

Outside a cicada launched into song, but otherwise all was quiet including the juke box. Even the aroma of the dinner, and all those that had been served before it, was calming. The "open" sign continued flashing on and off, casting an insistent flickering red glow across the ceiling.

It was Amanda who broke the silence. "Tell me again why you have to go to Cincinnati."

"Maybe Shasta Enterprises will be my next client."

"How'd that come about?"

"Did a bit of direct marketing. Then I found out Adam Shasta was Bruce Johnson's college roommate."

"Johnson?" She looked up in surprise. "From Aladdin? Didn't they drop you?"

"Funny how things sometimes work out for totally weird guys," he said with a smile. "One never knows."

To My Freeman   *Jan 30, 1864*

It is a cold Saturday and we are not able to go outside. Luther wants to go out and may be we will later but only if it warms up a bit.
The ship builders have been busy lately. The paper reports[249] that in the Passamaquoddy district there were fourteen vessels built last year three were schooners and the rest were all bigger. There was one ship it was all most 800 tons but all together they were over 6400 tons. When you come back there will be work for you I am sure. I know that Mister Watkins has to pay more for lumber than he did a year ago it is because they must go farther to find it all of the oak trees around here are all ready part of a vessel.
The paper also says that Col C.H. Smith led the First Maine Cavalry on a raid where they captured many prisoners who told

them how hungry the rebel soldiers are. This was funny because in the same raid Smiths men captured and then ate the Christmas dinner intended for Mosbys[250] men.[251]

People are becoming suspicious of strangers in town. There is a story about a man in Eastport[252] that nobody knew but somebody thought was acting odd. The authorities took him in and asked him a lot of questions but of course there was no thing that he was doing so they let him go on his way. I have not heard of that happening here in Lubec but I have seen the way people look at strangers in town like they think the worst before asking any questions. We have all ways had a very friendly town and now it is like nobody trusts their neighbor any more.

There is not very much else to talk about here with winter on us. The yard keeps busy but there is ice in the river so the vessels do not come in so often. I wish there was some way you could come here to be in winter quarters. Luther thinks so too.

Last night before I went to bed I put on your yellow scarf and stood in front of Grandfathers looking glass like it was you looking at me. Some times when I look into that glass I think it is you that I see. I miss you.

Your loving Alma

My Dearest Alma   *March 11, 1864*

You weel probly read this in the paper before you get this letter but Father Abraham has replaced Genl Meade with Genl Grant as the top General. Genl Grant arrived yesterday during a heavy rain so we was not able to give him a proper welcome.[253] He was the Genl that captured Vicksburg while we was at Gettysburg but he did not face Lee when he did that. I do not know what Genl Grant will do but spring is here soon so we will presently find out if he is the one who will take the fight to the rebels. I do not beleeve any of the other sesech Generals know what they are doing like Lee.

258

We all no that Grant is the fifth general to head the army and that none who went before was able to bring this to an end. Hope fully Father Abraham has made the right choice this time but we will no soon enuff. No body thought this wud go on like it has and at this time we do not beleeve we are any closer to the end then we was all most three years ago.

They are still talking abowt re enlistment and have made a bargain. If I re enlist for the rest of the war they will give me a bonus of $402 and also I get the state bounty. They will also give me a month furlough and train fare home and back and I will stay with my unit. Alma this is enough money to buy you and Luther a nice house and I will get to come home and see my boy and also you. I have not decided what to do yet but if you have some thing to say I want you to say it.

The days are longer now and it is not as cold at night. Hope fully we will soon be on the march so we can finish off the sesech and come home for good. Please give my boy Luther a big hug for me and one for your self too.

Your Loving Freeman

It was a warm evening and the walk back to the hotel was only a mile or so. The bench in the tiny park was inviting and so was the aroma of the nearby pine forest. She readily agreed when he steered her towards taking a break.

Amanda sat back and stretched out her legs. "The other day you were going to tell me about something your father said." She paused, gazing up into the nighttime sky. "We got interrupted. You recall what that was all about?"

"Actually, I do," he replied. "Guess I forgot because he really didn't tell me anything."

"When did you see him?"

259

"Day before we took off. You and Claire'd gone off with the kids, to Machias I think. He was here, needed something at the hardware store. We met for a beer, had the back porch at Annie's all to ourselves. Just talked about stuff."

When Amanda remained silent, he continued. "I asked him why it was, my grandmother held on to the picture of the soldier, the one sitting on our mantle." Richard leaned back on the bench and let out a deep breath. "He said she only spoke to him of it once, back when he was a kid, maybe eight or nine."

"Did she say who it is?"

"If she did, he doesn't remember." He paused for a few seconds. "There was just one thing. She told him the man was very special to the family and he should never do anything to dishonor his name. Apparently, it didn't make much of an impression on Dad because he never thought of telling Mom that part."

Amanda bent forward, pressing her fingers to her forehead. "Dishonor his name..." She fell silent for a minute or so, breathing deeply. "Your grandmother... Did she think that's what *you* did... By taking up with '*one of those Bellinghams*'?"

Her question came at him like a shot, like it was one of those things that should have been considered but never was.

"*No*," he blurted out, maybe a little more forcefully than he intended. Wrapping his arms around her, he continued, now speaking softly. "If you ask me, the Lawton was the winner in that deal."

Heading back to their room, he wondered about Elizabeth's words. How would *she* have answered Mandy's question? Would *she* know who the man behind the glass was?

Today Luther is two years old and I am not there to share the day with my son. I want to tell him some things that may be he will remember when he gets older. If I do not make it out of this thing this is what I want my son to know.

Luther you will be a big strong man some day. You must all ways make sure that you use your strength to do good. Be all ways guided by what is right even if doing the right thing hurts or is dangerous. Some times doing the right thing will make others laff at you but do not pay them any mind some day they will remember that you did right and they will respect you for it.

If you take care of your country it will take care of you. If you take care of your family it will take care of you. All ways stand up for the weak because that is what makes you a man. Having others think that you are a man who tries to do right is more valuable then gold and can not be taken frum you.

Your mother is a good woman and you should follow her example. Also that of your great grandfather Hiram and your great uncle Hosiah they both fought for your country with Genl Washington and helped make it what it is.

Today you are two but it will not seem so long that you are twenty. When you find the woman that you want to make your wife respect her like you do your mother and treat her well and you will both live a happy life. A good woman will be your moral anchor in this sinful world and she will give you her strength just as you give her your own. That is what your mother has done for me.

The measure of a man lies in the constancy of his handshake and in the considerashun he shows those who have no thing to give him.

    Your loving Father
    Private Freeman Lawton
    K Company 6 Maine Volunteer Regiment
    Brandy Station Virginia

My Dearest Freeman   *April 23, 1864*

I have received yours of March 14. I read it to Luther and he smiled like he knew it come from you. After reading it I showed him your likeness and he pointed and said Pa when he seen it. I will put this letter in a speshul place so I can read it to him often until this thing is over and you can say the same thing to him yourself.

Last night I went with Mum to help make bandages and other things for the boys at the front. They say we should not make more mittens because the weather will not be cold and we do not think this thing will continue until next year. Of course that was what we thought last year this time.

We get together in the big downstairs room of the First Christian Church up on top of the hill. Big White is just a short walk but the group usually includes me and Mum also Katherine and Gwyneth and there are a few more including some of the women from the fish houses.

Some times we talk some times we sing but we all work on getting things ready to be sent by the Sanitary Commission down to where it needs to go. Reverend Smith comes pretty regular and he always gifs us some thing to think about. Bernadette talks sometimes about what she heard of the teachings of Lyman Beecher[254] of the problems of drinking and how we might be better off without the demon of rum. Not long ago we had a man come from the Commission to tell us about how our work was helping save wounded men and how much the surgeons and nurses thought we was doing good.[255]

Last week there was a recruiter in town and he was looking close at Michael Gaultier like he did not care that he is only fourteen. I made sure to remind Michael that by going out fishing he is also supporting the men fighting and that James would want him to stay and take care of his mother and Katherine. Even Zadoc is trying to perswade Michael not to put on a uniform and so is Mister Watkins.

We have not had a frost in two weeks so we have been working the garden getting it ready. We know we can not plant any thing for another month but we have all been impatient and want to get going. I am getting impatient about having you come home too. Your loving Alma

262

The ride down from Hardeeville was four and and a half hours but the weather was pleasant and there was no traffic. As usual, the last hour felt like four. They arrived in Steinhatchee mid-afternoon with plenty of time to share a bottle of wine before getting dinner going. Richard followed Albert out onto the deck while Amanda and Julia clattered about in the kitchen. The sun glistened off Deadman Bay like a broad band of silver. An inquisitive pelican cruised past, investigating closely before continuing on his way out towards the ocean, and a crane trumpeted out on the estuary.

"Just like Cutler." Richard looked out at the boats lined up along the banks of the river. "Right?"

"Maybe a little," replied Albert. "Different kind of boats, and…" He pointed out into the nearby stands of longleaf pine. "Here, if it snows, you'll read about it in the paper."

"So how's *your* boat doing?"

"*Marianne* keeps us pretty busy," Albert shrugged. "Summer season's just about kicked off." Amanda appeared on the deck and announced dinner. "Groupers starting to run pretty good right now," he added as they headed in. "Last week, guy brought in a six-foot barracuda. Put up a hell of a fight."

After dinner the four retreated back out to the deck to enjoy the balmy air. The early June evening was warm and humid and the breeze was enough to keep the mosquitoes at bay but not so much to bring out the sweaters. Lightning flickered out of a dark cloud way out over the Gulf of Mexico.

"Last year your team had a great season," Albert said. "You repeat?"

"Last year was pretty special," Richard replied. "This year we did well enough. Won more than we lost."

"What was that kid's name again? Harvey?"

"Herbie," said Richard. "He was a find."

"So what was the deal?"

"Kid needed to feel needed. And," Richard paused for a sip of wine. "He needed to be put in the right position."

"What's that mean?"

"He's left handed. Last time he wanted to play baseball they stuck him at second base. That can't *ever* work, recipe for disaster. I put him on the mound. Kid's got an arm. When his hands grow a bit, he'll have a hell of a knuckleball."

"But then you lost him?"

"By the time I got him he was eighth grade. Now he's in high school." The conversation went silent for a minute or so.

"I am so glad," Julia said, "that you were able to stop by and see Elizabeth and Lucas."

"Thank you," Richard replied. "You have no idea how happy I am we did that." He returned Amanda's glance with a smirk.

Amanda sat back and looked out across the river. "You get many visitors down here?"

"Pretty regular stream," Julia laughed. "Not counting flatlanders who think they have iron stomachs."

"You knew that part before you got into the party boat business," Amanda replied. "At least I *hope* you did."

264

"Chumming is just part of the deal. That's why there's a hose on the boat." Julia passed around the wine bottle. "The Thatchers were here two weeks ago, stayed three days."

"Ernie and Gladys?"

"And their grandkids." Julia looked over at Amanda. "Little Ernie and Kayla."

"That sounds like fun." Richard heard the note in Amanda's voice and immediately found an interesting spot on a nearby tree that needed to be studied.

"Maybe this is a sore point," continued Julia, "but I'll wade in anyway." From the corner of his eye he saw Amanda look up at her mother but she said nothing.

"We were kind of hoping," she continued, "Maybe by now, we'd be spoiling a grandkid or two." She paused and laughed. "It is our job, you know."

"I'm sure you'll get your chance soon enough," replied Amanda. Richard closed his eyes and took a deep breath, waiting for Amanda's next words. "Our stars just haven't lined up yet."

"Probably I never told you this before…" Julia let out a deep sigh and looked towards Albert. "For the longest time, we thought the same thing. Maybe someday."

"That changed," said Albert, touching his wife's knee but looking at Amanda, "the day we lost Mickey."

"Mickey?" The surprise in Amanda's face was obvious. "Do I know that story?"

"Olivia Wilson is my oldest friend," said Julia. "I know you met her but it's been a while. Mickey Olmsted was her husband."

"Olivia... Been a long time since I've heard her name."

"She lives in Los Angeles, we stay in touch," replied Julia. "I remember how much she wanted to have Mickey's baby, but they thought the same thing. Somehow their stars never lined up either."

"So what happened?"

"When the other guy crossed the double-yellow Mickey didn't have a chance." Julia looked up with a grim smile. "For Olivia, before the 'right time' came, it was all of a sudden too late. Wasn't long after that, your father and I decided..."

Richard knew that look in Amanda's eyes. He'd seen it before. "You decided," she said, closing her eyes and exhaling deeply, "I was the right time."

"Gosh! How did we *ever* end up on such a morbid theme?" Julia jumped up and returned with a fresh bottle of wine, topping off glasses all around. "That was so terribly..." Richard caught the exchange of glances between mother and daughter – Julia had a look of triumph while Amanda clearly wore a smirk. "... *Antediluvian* of me to do that."

To My Alma   *May 9, 1864*

I do not haf much time to rite but so much has heppened I must. I am riting on the back of a limber box[256] so pleeze excuse my clumsy words we will moof to a new position soon. Since we left our winter quarters we haf been either marching or fighting all the time so it has been hard to rite. Now we haf just enuff time to boil sum coffee and Isaac is doing it for me so I can rite to you.

266

The 6 Maine is now part of the 6 Corps the Light Division is no more. I do not know what that meens but we did our best and no body but us captured Maryes Heights. Grizzly is now a Brigadier General commanding the 18 Corps under Baldy Smith in the Army of the James so we do not see him. Charley Clark got a discharge for his wound then come back to be with Grizzly.

They is calling this place the Wilderness and I think it is a good name it is all dense forest and you can not see hardly beyond your own muzzle. It is very close to Salem Church where we buried James just a year ago it is like he is still here and looking after us. A unit that set up nearby found remains of members of their own unit frum that battle that had neffer been buried.[257]

Genl Grant ordered the attack on May 6 we could not see the rebels and they could not see us until we was so close we seen their teeth. When they let out a loud yell like they was comin at us we knowed where they was and directed our fire tords the sound. After that neither side durst yell in stead we done our best remain silent.

The forest is thick like up Bassett Creek so neither side could get artillery protection and neither side could make a charge so we just keeped shooting until the woods cought fire. We heered the wounded crying out when the fire took them but we could not do any thing for them. It seemed lik the whole world was burning and we was fighting the sesech in the middle of Hell with the stench of the fire and burning flesh and the cries of the dying. Worst yet is menny of the boys that died was all most reddy to go home be cause there three years was up.

That night there was no moon only the stars and with the fires and the smoke we were not sure but what we had all reddy died. The 5 Virginia was on the other side of the Plank Road and for them it must have been no diffrnt. We all knowed that the tide of battle on the morrow would depend on Longstreet arrivin if we struck first then may be we could hold the field but if he made it heer first then many more wud die. We all waited for the order from Major Fuller.[258] *Sesech under Genl Early was on the other side of the road waiting for us.*

Friday morn we moved out well befor five and attacked. The sesech was on the run when Longstreet come in late morning and changed the battle. Where the rebels had first run they now stood and fought and one regiment even flanked us from the north coming down a old rail bed that our boys had not protected. By the time the day was over ever thing we had won the day before was lost but I think they wud say the same. A rumer is going abowt that Longstreet was wounded by his own men just like heppened to Jackson a year ago at just abowt the same place.[259]

On May 7 it looked lik neether side was going to get the upper hand so Genl Grant pulled us back. We marched west tords the fork with all expecting he would have us turn north again lik all the other Genls did before but when we turned south we knew this Genl was going to fight and set up such a shout I am sure the sesech heered us. This was the Genl who captured Vicksburg and now we no how he done it. Finely we hef a Genl who will let us fight an not just retreat after every battle.

We was so tired boys was falling asleep whilst marching and ever time we stopped we would drop to the ground for as menny minutes we hed. As exhausted as we was the sesech had to be just as bad off they do not know where we will attack them next. But we was happy to be heading south to keep fighting and not north to play checkers. We can not win this thing unless we fight and that is just the way it is. If we stop fighting then it meens they hef bested us.

Alma I fear telling you what it is I hef seen. On the second day we fought on the same ground as the first but now it was covered with boys that were kilt and burnt and sum fires was still smoldring. Menny times we cud not effen tell which uniform they had worn but also we cud not stop to do the right thing. Some probly wud have gone home were it not for the fire. I fear who we haf become what we do to each other what kind of a man you weel haf when I come home. I do not wish to remember this but I can not stop the dreams.

Next we stopped a place called Spotsylvania Court House to set up lines. That was where a rebel sharp shooter kilt Genl Sedgewick.[260] He was at the frunt to help straiten out a line neer one of the batteries and that was where they got him. Uncle John should never have been at the frunt like that. Now the 6 Corps is led by Genl Horatio Wright.

As happy as we was taking the fight to the rebels it made us mad to lose Uncle John. He was the kind of officer we knowed we could trust not to let us get kilt for no thing. We cared abowt him becuz we knowed he cared abowt us. War meens boys getting kilt and there is no way around that but Uncle John made sure it was not needless that we would hurt them at leest as much as they hurt us and now he is gone. Our duty meens we follow there orders and that is how we will win this thing but officers have a duty to us and when they fail in there duty even if it means there getting kilt then they have not done there duty.

So now we wait heer to see what will heppen next. I do not think we will be waiting very long be cuz we kin heer the rebels setting up there lines not far frum ours an thet means the artillery will start soon.

Alma, I have done it. I signed the papers this morning to re enlist. I told them to send all the money strate to you. I weel be coming home for all of the munth of July and I hope you weel be ready. The train weel take me to Portland and then I weel take a steamboat to Eastport. I hop you have your yellow scarf ready becuz I have often dreamed of seeing you wearing that. I weel tell you more abowt my plans when they tell me it is all been ordered.

I must close this now be cuz they are calling for mail. Give my boy Luther a hug and tell him it weel not be to many more days befor I come home to see him and you.

Your Loving Freeman

My Dearest Freeman   *April 27, 1864*

I just read in the paper about what happened at Fort Pillow. Are the rebels such monsters that they would murder women and children? That is what the paper said happened.[261] It said that after the garrison surrendered the rebels commanded by Gen'l Forrest[262] butchered the soldiers negro and white and also some women and children attacked them all with bayonettes. It called the rebel soldiers fiends and that even dead men were attacked and that the unit started out with over six hundred and fewer than two hundred were allowed to live.

Is this really the kind of enemy you are fighting against? You have told me about how you felt about Luke and Penelope. Would

269

Luke have put a bayonet in a soldier that had already thrown down his musket?

I am sorry for allowing myself to get so wrought over this but from here I can not see what you see and when I read about something like this I can not understand how civilized people can be like this. Is this what they mean by chivalry?

May be this Sunday Reverend Smith can say some thing to explain how a just God can allow this to happen but I do not believe he can. I showed the paper to Mister Watkins but all he did was shake his head. Luther and me we just want you to end this as soon as you can.

Your Loving Alma

Dear Alma   *May 11, 1864*

Yesterday we fought neer Spotsylvania Court House at what they are calling the Mule Shoe Salient. We attacked a rebel embankment from woods where they could not see us forming up in ranks but then we crossed a open field in a narrow columm just like at Rappahannock Station. It was only a short distance but it seemed like it was forever and to many of the boys it was forever.

The rebels were surprised when we come at them with a loud yell but they was quick to bring in reinforcements and then the battle was as fierce as anything even like the Heights. Some boys became like they was berserk and climbed the parapets they stood tall and got off maybe five or six shots from muskets passed up to them but then they fell. Others followed them up but the rebels fought like fiends and they lost many men too. I do not know how I survived this but I did the fiting was as bad as any thing I have ever seen. It is like a demon takes over and the fury can not be stopped like no thing they do can hurt you[263] and no thing matters ceptin what you can do to them like I was revenging James and Reuel and Uncle John and all the boys we lost at the Heights an in the Wilderness.

The 6 helped take one of the guns but the gunners took the ramrods when they retreated so we cud not use them. Capt Witherell was hit twice but kept on fiting. Compny F lost there Lt Isaac Campbell[264] frum Pembroke in the fray. The rebels must hef knowed we was coming when our guns stopped firing first it was silent like the dead then Col Upton gived the order and we went in. The 6 was in the second row right behind the 96 Pennsylvania and rite next to our friends the 5 Wisconsin.

Some of the boys broke down crying when the order to withdraw come we pulled back without holding any gains. We was exhausted and most just dropped down and slept in the mud. I do not care becuz we are taking the fight to the rebels and the only way this thing will effer end is if we keep going.

Plees let my boy Luther no I was thinking of him today. Furlough can not come soon enuff for me.

Your Freeman

My Dearest Alma   *May 14, 1864*

This world has gone insane. Two days ago we fought in heffy rain near Spottsylvania at a place we call the Bloody Angle and what a fight it was just each side pouring lead into the other acrost a breastwork of logs for menny hours. The 6 Maine was in the second rank with bayonets fixed and the 5 Maine was in the front along with boys from Pennsylvania and New York. We lost many good men there but did not get any thing in return. And I think the sesech would say the same. Nobody won. I do not no how to describe it other then men passing loaded muskets to the boys at the front and them firing and passing the discharged ones back to be reloaded as fast as could be.

I do not no how menny boys died in this battle but they was piled six deep both ours and theres when we was able to look for the wounded. Some of the wounded was under the dead so we had to look careful. The 6 Maine had thirty seven casualties[265] and that is

271

abowt the worst of it since this war began. I come out with just some minor wounds and so did Isaac Cooper I no we took the fight to the sesech so I do not no why we wuz so lucky when so many others wuz not.

The rebels pulled back but I do not think they was beat. If you ask me this battle was not a victory for either side but they no that Genl Grant will be moving again to the attack but they do not no where.

It makes me feel good that Michael Gaultier is to be a fisherman and it makes me feel even better he is on Achenar becuz that schooner is like a part of our family and he is far safer then he would be if he was here with the 6. Please make sure that Zadoc pays the insurance regular becuz if some thing heppens to me then you will own my fourth of the boat and I want to make sure you receive your due.

I will close this letter while I kin because right now we is being ordered to move again. Genl Grant when he sees we can not take the rebel works has us pull back and then we attack from a diffrunt position keep trying to keep them guessing where we will be next. I think we are going to some place closer to Richmond. We have been marching and fighting for nearly three weeks with out any brake. This time they did give us time to boil coffee.

Those better days can not come soon enuff. Let Katherine no James is still by my side because I have his knife in my pocket. Please give Luther a hug for me and one for you too.

Your Loving Freeman

"Here," she said, "take a look at this collection." Amanda pointed out the family photographs arrayed across the top of the chest in the dining room. "Mom and I went through these when you guys were down at the boat."

Richard scanned across the group of framed images. Most were familiar or easily recognized. There were several that showed Nana Bell as a graceful young woman, and there were the usual shots of Amanda as a toddler or in her graduation gown. Their wedding picture was prominent in the center. Just the typical family assortment.

Towards the back of the collection he spotted a smallish photograph behind a cracked glass, mounted in a tarnished and dented metal frame.

A dour-faced man wearing an overcoat and a Bowler hat peered out as though he were angry about something. He looked to be maybe sixty, rather portly, and stood clutching what appeared to be a Bible. The doorway behind him had the arched top commonly seen in a church entryway. The man's features appeared somewhat reminiscent of Albert's, but the location was unfamiliar. Richard picked it up to take a closer look and found his gaze drawn, as if by a magnet, to the man's eyes.

"You see that too," she said. "Don't you."

"Do we know who this is?"

"There's a name on the back."

Richard turned it over and read the faded pencil inscription. "Rodman Bellingham 1902." He looked up at Amanda. "You know that name?"

"It's Dad's great-grandfather. He told Mom he doesn't know anything more than that, beyond that he once lived in Lubec. Doesn't even know where he's buried."

"So you've never seen this picture before..."

"Aunt Patrice found it buried in an old trunk, sent it along a few months ago. No, I've not seen it before." Something in her voice stopped him short. When he looked up to question the unspoken 'but,' he saw her chewing on her lip.

Amanda took the photograph from his hands, returned it to its spot on the back of the shelf, then glanced up at him. "We're starting to see all these things from the past. Does this mean something?"

"What are you thinking?"

"Do you believe it was coincidental, the yellow scarf was packed in the same box as your grandfather's medals?"

"Never thought of it. What makes you ask?"

"I've tried the scarf on again. Twice."

"I'm thinking that should make me happy."

"Maybe. Don't be too hasty." She paused like she didn't know what to say. "That first time, when we were together... It was like there was a tiny voice, whispering in my ear."

"So..." *She's hearing voices?* "What'd it say?"

"It was a woman's voice, sounded old and frail, from far off. It said '*It is not your right to wear my silk*'."

"The voice didn't say why?"

"No," she shuddered. "It said nothing more. I'm still not convinced any of this is real. But..."

She turned away, eyes closed, pressing her fingertips into her temples.

"The second time I put it on, it was a few days later. You were out. This time I was sure someone was looking out through the mirror."

"The old one, in our bedroom?"

"Your uncle's. The tall narrow one with the gilded bugle on top. But the third time, that was the creepiest. When I pulled it around my shoulders, I felt a cold hand on my throat." She turned to look Richard straight on. "I was the only one in the house." She swallowed hard. "At least I thought I was... The way Bonkers growled, he sensed something too. And..."

"And what?"

"Did you notice what else was in that box, under the scarf?"

"Something that looked like a child's book. Didn't pay it any mind."

"So you didn't see the signature."

"I didn't look inside."

"It was faint, a child's pencilled scrawl, and a date." She paused and looked at Richard, lips drawn tight. "That book belonged to Luther, and the date was March 14, 1871. And there was a child's drawing, looked like a schooner."

"You didn't tell me any of this... Until now." He turned her to look straight on. "Why?"

"You already think me crazy." She turned away and paused, looking down. "Do you really want me to prove it?"

To My Freeman   *May 18, 1864*

    I have received your letter of May 9 and it made all of us very happy that you were not amongst those lost at the Wilderness. Hope fully you will be able to end this soon because too many have died and we do not need to see more gone. It makes me proud that you have done the right thing and re enlisted. The army needs men who have hardened their souls in battle and you are one of those that have done that. Let me know what Isaac has decided to do. I am keeping my yellow scarf safe for when you come home. Jake made me a speshul box with a cedar lining.

    They have set up what they are calling the Coast Guard Infantry and there is a cmpny in Eastport at Fort Sullivan and an other in Machiasport. With the confederates being up in New Brunswick may be it is a good thing but I am still not sure. Men who sign up for this cmpny get to go home when they are not on duty and that makes me think that was why they chose to do that. Waiting for a rebel pirate to sail in by sitting in a back room playing checkers to me is not the same thing as capturing Maryes Heights but to them it may be is.

    Mums sister Agnes told me that Rodman Bellingham is camping with a group on Campobello on the east side of Harbor de Lute near Bunker Hill.[266]*The papers are calling the encampment Skedaddlers Reach.*[267] *I have read there is another camp in New Brunswick and a few more in Canada East. At least the twenty Lubec men who were called up but paid the commutation fee*[268]*were honest about it. You know most of them.*

    Mrs UC Ring has been complaining that First Selectman Samuel Mowry has been holding back part of the pay her husband wanted sent home.[269]*So far this has not happened to me maybe because Jake knows them in the office and they do not want to discuss it with him.*

    There is so much news appearing it is very hard to know what is real. The last issue of the paper said Rebel reports in New York state that Genl Lee has been mortally wounded.[270]*Some how I do not believe that to be true but that is what the paper has reported.*

    I read your letter of March 14 to Luther again last night. He acted like he knew whose words he was hearing but I am sure that when he gets older he will understand them better. I can not read that to him with out breaking down crying and when I do that he starts to cry too.

You are giving him some thing to look up to and I know he will do you prowd. This next winter may be you will be home and we can all go sleighing together. That is one thing I dream about. I also dream about you keeping me warm at night. Most of all I dream about you coming home safe to us and helping me raise Luther to be a fine man like his pap.

Your Faithful Alma and Luther

My Dearest Alma   *May 24, 1864*

We have been moofing fast heading south and right now are waiting to cross the North Anna River. Engineers haf bilt a bridge but heffy rains make it hard and might take the bridge down the river. I hear the rebels have throwed up works downstream lik that is where they expect we weel cross. We had to do some fiting but not like at Spotsylvania.

The last two days we haf been in farm country that has not befor seen the curse of war. Farther north the land has all ben lade to waist and there was no thing to be foraged but down heer there are still crops in the fields and live stock just waiting to be come a hungry boys supper.[271] The provost says we are not supposed to take any thing but after all most three years of army food the devul has set a feast before us and we are dining at his table. I do not think Genl Grant will allow the provost to punish any of his fighting men for finding some thing good to eat. That pig we roasted was some wicked good and there was no thing left. Even the officers had some.

It is time to start moofing agin so I must end this. Please gif my boy Luther a hug for me.

Your Freeman

My Loving Alma   *May 27, 1864*

Since we left Spotsylvania and crossing the North Anna we have been marching every day. Genl Eustis has not told us where we are going but we is heading south and guess it is tords Richmond. Yestiddy they let us stop just long enuff to boil coffee but we have not been able to to that since.

I am healthy and so is most ever body. Isaac never seems to get sick but after we lost James I know he was off. I am sure I was too. That was a cruel blow and not one that I want to think abowt too much.

We have lost so many men I lost count. There has been a steady streem of new men joining us but most of them have not seen the rebels eyes and I fear for them untill they have seen the elephant and know what death looks lik. Sinse Genl Grant took charge things are not the same. With Genl Hooker or Genl Meade after a battle we wud go to camp and rest for a while may be even a few weeks then we would go into an other battle. Now we pull back and start to manoofer and then right away we are attacking the sesech agin with out a brake. To us it is exhawsting but it must be worse for them becuz we have more supplies coming then they do. At least we can eat some times.

Last night in camp Isaac said something curious. He said that the secesh do not have to win this war they just need to make sure we do not win. If Father Abraham agrees to some kind of peace that does not make them surrender then all this will have been for no thing and slavery will not be ended. I for one do not wish that to be the end because then James and menny other men all of them better than me will have died for no thing. If we do not see this through to the finish then we will only be able to say we was whupped and the Negroes will still be slaves. As much as I want peace I do not want that kind of peace because then I would not be able to live with thoughts of what my grandfather Hiram suffered for.

At least when I wear out my shoes my Uncle Samuel gifs me a new pair. The sesech prisoners we talk to do not get new shoes.

278

Some do have new shoes but they do not look like confederate shoes they look like Yankee shoes. I asked one prisoner abowt that he said he got them from a man who did not need them any mor.

Menny of them haf rags for uniforms and most of the soldiers are not wearing gray it is more like a soft brown. Some call it butternut but I do not no except it looks like they would have a very hard time keeping warm in winter quarters and may be cannot even find cloth to make a patch. Only the rebel officers look like they haf proper uniforms.

Give my boy Luther a big hug for me and save one for your self.

Your Faithful Freeman

To My Alma   *June 2, 1864*

We haf arrived at a place cald Cold Harbor may be a days march from Richmond. To get heer we crosd the Pamunkey River where the engineers bilt a pontoon bridge. We heded south but there was a great menny Negroes heded north and a pitiful bunch they was. There was men women children young and old. Most was wearing rags and few had shoes and all were hungry but more then any thing they wanted to keep going north. Some of the men wanted to join us so they cud help free there familys on nearby plantations. I haf heered sesech prisoners call the Negroes lazy but they look desperate to me like they no it is not natural to be held like they was and be forced to work but get no thing for it.

After the Pamunkey we had some action at the North Anna and then the Topopotomy but we kept going to where we are now. We marched all night to get here and are not sure whether we is alive or may be already dead. Any time we stop moofing most of the boys end up on the ground sleeping even if it is only for a minit or so.

I have thought at times that I was tired but never hef I felt like this. Sense befor the Wilderness we has been marching some times over night then fighting during the day and then marching again to some new place. Any time we has to sleep we try to but it is

279

never more then a few minutes. If I was to get a haf hour sleep I wud feel like I sleeped for a week.

Just wen we was coming into where we wud set up camp the 5 Michigan Cavaldry[272] brigade went by led by a most magnificent looking Genl with long yellow hair and a splendid uniform with a big hat an a long feather. One of the boys told me his name was George A. Custer.[273] If luking fancy has enny thing to do with it this man has a promising future in the army.

There was a battle heer yesterday and many men died but the sesech did not carry the day and nether did we. The unit that got the wurst of it was a heavy artillery brigade from Connecticut that had been garding Washington but was orderd to becum infantry. When they arrived heer some of the other units cald them band box soldiers becuz there uniforms were clean and sharp and that got them mad so they went in where others had already pulled back. There Colonel led the way and he was the first one they lost.[274] They akshully took the Rebel works but cud not hold it. An other unit like that was the First Maine Heavy it ackshlly started out as the 18 Maine Infantry but got switched and is now back to infantry even tho there uniforms say Heavy Artillery. That was the unit that Lucius Gibson went into but I do not no what has becum of him. His unit is in the 2 Corps under Genl Hancock and the 6 Maine is in the 6 Corps under Genl Wright there are so many boys here we wud not likely see each other. There haf been several other groups like them thet haf not had any taste of battle and when they go to face the sesech they do not shirk there duty but mostly they end up on the field.

We got here after that part was offer and since that time haf been digging trenches. The sesech is digging too and there is a field may be two hundred yards wide between us with dead and wounded all abowt including ours and theres. We heer the lead flying so if we raise our head we weel become one of them but as long as we keep below the top of the embankment we are safe so there is no thing we can do to except lissen to the wounded calling to us. It is a dredful sound that we heer all night. Some of the poor wretches are just yards away but we can do no thing to help them. We do not effen no if they is our boys or sesech but it do not matter because they is hurt and we is helpless.

280

The sesech are very good at making embankments. If you gif a rebel fifteen minits he has a rifle pit. Gif him an hour he has a trench that you can not shoot into. Gif him three hours an he is standing up in his trench and can command the whole field in frunt. Gif him enny more an he has his artillery dug in too.

We dig with anything we can use like bayonets and our dinner plates. Our artillery and theres trade volleys and sometimes one side or the other akshully hit some thing but most of the time they just throw dirt in the air but in the meen time we are pinned down.

Some times we has to move munitions or rations to men at the frunt trench so we crawl on our belly dragging our burden behind and follow the zigzag through tunnels and behind thrown up dirt walls. We haf sharp shooters and so do they and they are both very good at what they do. Last night there was no moon[275] but some times it looked almost like day with the flashes from the field guns and the musketry. Late at night the field was silent and after the smoke cleared we could see a little by starlight but did not stop bilding trenches and I no they was doing the same.

I no this scene may make you feel like I am in danger but as long as I haf James Barlow knife in my pocket no Minie ball will come my way. Do not worry none abowt me it is Isaac I am worried abowt. I do not like the way he takes chances but so far he is the luckiest man alive.

I hop you can find it in your hart to forgif Rodman Bellingham a man shud not be fawlted for not wanting to do what we is doing heer. Tomorrow is anuther day so I weel finish this and send it off. Give my boy Luther a hug for me and one for you too.

Your Faithful Freeman

It caught him completely by surprise, the way she just sat up in bed, shaking. The last time he had seen her do that was the night Nana Bell suffered her second heart attack. That night, her grandmother was in the nursing home, half a mile away, and Mandy

281

only heard about it later from her mother. But still, she knew that something had happened. Something bad.

The partial moon, lying low near the horizon, glimmered through the window and lit up her face. It wasn't so much a look of fear or surprise that he saw, perhaps it was more like bewilderment.

He rubbed the sleep out of his eyes and reached up to touch her cheek. "You okay?"

"I'm sorry," she said, blinking her eyes and clutching her chest. "Didn't mean to wake you."

"Mandy, I'm your husband." He looked up, into her face. "If you want to talk about something it's okay to wake me. It *is* part of my job."

"Now I remember," she said, lying back down by his side. "The eyes in that photograph. That man, Rodman Bellingham. Where I've seen them before."

"That came to you just now? While you were sleeping?"

"Sounds creepy, doesn't it?" He felt the way she shivered. "But that's what happened."

"Anymore, I'm not sure what that word means." When he caressed the back of her neck, she closed her eyes. "Maybe you can tell me a little more."

"I saw them again," she whispered. "It was all too real, don't think it could have been a dream, I was half-awake. They were back in the trees. That's where I've seen them before."

"The trees?"

"Yeah," she said, still trembling. "At Mink Point."

"Just looking out through the branches, like an owl?"

"Just looking out through the branches... At *me*."

"So now you know who it is..."

"... and it's freaking me out. He's an ancestor I never even heard of until yesterday. How could I see him in the trees on Campobello?" She clutched at him, pulling him close. "It's almost like..." She paused momentarily, still shivering. "Like there's some kind of curse."

"A curse? You don't believe in those things... Do you?"

"Never before. I guess not. But still..."

"Some things are just never explained." He stifled a yawn. "Ready to go back to sleep?"

"Not yet I'm not." She rolled over to face him, pulling him close. "There's something I need from you, right now."

"What?"

"Make love with me."

My Dearest Alma   *June 5, 1864*

I haf seen things that I wish to God you shud neffer see. I haf seen things that I neffer wanted to see and do not beleev a just God would effer allow to heppen. I haf seen things that I most hop I can forget once I cum home to you and neffer see again. I haf seen things that no man shuld effer see and no man shuld effer do. But I haf seen them and done them and will neffer forget them.

283

On June 3 Genl Grant orderd a charge[276] against the sesech position the third one he sent in. We was in reserve for that so did not see much action but the 10 New Hampshire and 98 New York was sent into a trap and lost all most effer thing but gained no thing. Col Wead[277] of the 98 New York made it to the rebel parapet but was kilt there[278] and probly did not see his regiment cut down by canister. Genl Grant is a smart man but to me ordring that charge after the two befor it did not do enny thing except cover the field with blue uniforms it puts me in mind of when we took Maryes Heights only to haf Genl Hooker throw away any advantage we had fougt to gain. I know these are smart men but when they do things like that it makes me think I no why Reuel Furlong went berserk and did what he dun and then I fear for my self. I do not beleeve Genl Grant effer looked at the field him self before making that order and did not bother to see how the sesech was dug in.

Not far away frum where I am is a marshy little thicket with a small crik[279] that runs out tords us. Maybe at one time a boy cud fill his canteen frum that crik but not now becuz the water is flowing dark red. I do not no how menny men alive or dead is in that thicket but I do no I do not want to go in there.

Sence we left winter quarters we hef ben on the move from place to place fiting more battles then I want to remember and losing more good men then I can count. We fite then we moof and then we fite again. I heffent washed my socks in a munth an heffent had a decent meal in menny days. Sence we got here we hef bin digging trenches an bilding brestworks an skirmishing. Any sleep comes fife minits at a time and we are all exhawsted. If I dream I see the hands of the dead reaching up at Maryes Heights like they would stop us but we can not stop we must keep moofing.

Frum where I am rite now I kin heer a man but I kint see him but I no he is in tuf condishun. I dunt effen know what color his uniform be. When I tried to go out to hep him I got a Minie ball through my kepi. Eff I try going out there it will be two of us not jist him.

This war was neffer supposed to go on like this and still there is no end in site. If we gif up then Grandpap Hirams struggles weel be for no thing. And if the Rebels gif up then all they have lost will meen no thing. This weel not stop until one of us destroys the other then I feer whut cums after an who we weel be.

When we was still in winter quarters some times at night I dreamd of seeing you on that pier waving yur yellow scarf when the Eastern City left the dock and we went away frum home. We was sure we wud be back before Christmas. May be we will be together for next Christmas or may be weel not meet agin ontil we both cross thet river. I hop I make it to July so I can cum home on furlough to see you and finely hold my boy Luther and start haffing that dream agin.

Your Loving Freeman

"Was it *really* so important to get on the road this early?" She was not happy. "The sun's not even up, but here *we* are."

The note of irritation in her voice was unmistakable. Richard closed his eyes briefly. "It was you insisted we stop in to see Elizabeth, put us a day behind. Besides, they both have things to get done today. Last thing they need is us hanging out," he mumbled. He hoped his words were convincing. "You know what they say."

When she didn't challenge him he continued. "Dead fish and relatives, after three days…"

"You don't need to make a joke out of it." She crossed her arms over her chest and harrumphed towards the passenger side window. "Go ahead and say it. *You're* tired of my family's hospitality. Mom had rather hoped to make us a nice breakfast." She turned to look down the road, into the dusky dawn. "Good luck finding a decent place open *this* time of day."

"We'll find something." They both fell into silence, driving down the twisting road with the overhanging trees.

"Did you know the story of Olivia and Mickey?"

285

"Before the other day?" She looked over at him. "No." She looked his way for a few seconds. "What brought *that* up just now?"

"I don't know." Just ahead he spotted a restaurant that looked acceptable, particularly since the big red 'open' sign was flashing. "Ready?"

"More than ready." He steered the car into the parking lot.

There's nothing, he thought to himself, like that first mug of hot coffee to make the world seem an okay place. After the waitress took their order he sat back and closed his eyes. When he opened them again he realized Amanda was staring at him.

"What," she asked, "are you thinking about?"

He laughed softly. "This time it's gonna be you think it's *me* gone crazy."

"What do you mean, 'gone'?" At least now she had stopped scowling. Maybe it was the coffee. "You think I would have married you if I thought you were *sane*?" She smiled and closed her eyes. "Maybe the way I woke you up a night ago, now we're even."

"Whatever," he shrugged. That hadn't turned out so bad. "But since you're asking..." He took a sip of coffee. "I was thinking of some old letters."

"Old letters?" She looked back up, now with beetled brows. "What old letters?"

"Silas showed me a box." He paused to look into her eyes. "A box of letters at the Historical Society."

"How many boxes of letters do they have in there?" Amanda chuckled and gestured for a coffee refill. "How many *hundreds* of boxes?"

286

"Probably not so many that were addressed to Alma Lawton."

He caught the fleeting expression in her eyes. "Who?"

"That's just it. A woman on Green Street with my last name…" When he glanced up again he spotted her frown. "*Our* last name." The frown softened a bit. "Probably not so many."

"Alma. You don't know that name?"

"Never heard it before."

"This box… Is it big?"

"A sardine crate."

"With just letters to Alma?"

"That part I don't know."

Amanda sat back with that thoughtful look she got when pieces started to fall together. "So we *are* even. I have Rodman and now you've got Alma. Sounds like when we get home…" The waitress put down two steaming plates of home fries and grits, with big sausages and biscuits slathered with gravy.

"… you and I, we've got some letters to read."

My Dearest Alma   *June 8, 1864*

I do not no why they call this place Cold Harbor. It is hot not cold an there is sure no harbor heer fack there is no harbor for twenty mile.

287

The way we is dug in is a feerful site. We got trenches dug with banks may be two or three feet high and mostly all connected. If you lift yur head abov the level of the trench you becum the target for a Minie ball and it is the same for them. I do beleef if Lee wuz to send the entire Rebel army acrost that field tords us we would be able kill ever last man before they got close to where we are. And if we were to hed there way it would be the same no diffrunt. The way the lead flies over our heads it is like a hale storm cutting young trees and shrubs like Jakes friends has set there scythes to wurk. As long as we keep our heads down we are safe except for artillery balls that drop down on us from the heavens above. Our artillery is dug in just like the rest of us and so is theres and we can heer the balls flying over our heads.

Yesterday evening we hed a two hour truce[280] so we cud bring in our wounded. I do not no why we cud not haf dun it two days ago but by the time we wuz allowd to go out there was no wounded only dead. We knowed that wuz what we were going to find becuz the night befor it was silent front of us not like the nites befor. Two nites ago we heered them moaning and sometimes crying out but then the next nite it was so quiet we knowed what it ment and did not no which was wurst. To no there may be a chance then to no that the chances are gone I do not no which one I wud druther.

I do hop I neffer see a scene like that agin. Our men and theres were all out there right where they fell and all tangled up. Some looked like they had tried to get water from there canteen but they too had ben shot through so they was empty. Many of the Rebels had no shoes and there uniforms was rags falling off at the touch of a hand. We picked up some of there muskets and saw they wuz the same ones like we hed been issued so they probly took them from one of our dead may be in an earlier battle or may be effen a few days ago.

I saw two of ours who tried to survive by piling dead men up to make a barrier that the sesech could not shoot through. The dead were both ours and theres but once they are dead all stand alike befor God. The two survived the musket fire for a while but did not survive the heat and their wounds.

The sun during the day is wicked fierce so the faces of the dead wuz all black like they wuz Negroes. All we cud do wuz bring them back and put them into shallow graves. A few had pinnd there

288

name inside there jacket but most weel neffer be known agin. The way they looked effen there friends cud not recugnize them.

I am lying in a little shallow spot just below where they kin shoot and waiting for my chance to moof. I heer the bullets whissling over my head but here I am all right. There is not much of a moon and it will set soon but the night will still be verry long. The smoke luks like fog but the flashing of the cannon lites up the field. Not very far frum where I am is a dead mule. We hed to lissen to the pitiful cries of the beast before it died but now it haf been silent three days and haf put up such a stench but there is no thing we can do abowt it.

We haf lost so many gud men not just James but menny more and each one hed some body waiting for them to get home. Some times I do not feel worthy of being in sech compny as these men who haf lost all but I must keep going. My hart ackes to see you and Luther and walk wif you in the morning sunshine wearing cleen cloths and not duckin Minie balls an I dreams abowt doing thet with you in only a few weeks.

God must hef a plan for me to let me

June 9, 1864

Alma: This is Isaac writing now. It is with a heavy hart I tell you that Freeman died a hero. The Johnnies must have known he was here because the shell that exploded over his head fell short of where its fellows was aimed. It was me thet found him and I wish to God it were not so. He died instantly and did not suffer like I know many others have. He is now with God and living where there are no more bullets only peace.

He spoke often about how eager he was to go home on furlow next month to see you and Luther. Many others who will be going home held back from going into this battle but not Freeman. He was a credit to his uniform and his name and this battle was no different he fought to win and all ways said James was fighting right next to him.

Freeman kept all your letters. He got very upset when he lost one and that did not happen very often. I will send them back to you. He loved to sit by the fire when we was in camp and read them all over again. I think I know most of them and can recite your words from memry. Anyway maybe Luther might like to read them some day so I will send them right away.

Please let Katherine know that I have James knife the one she gave him. It is not much good after it saved Freeman but she might still like to have it back. Freeman was sure it saved him sevral times after that time it got smashed at Brandy Station. He liked to say no Minie ball would ever get him long as he had James Barlow knife and no Minie ball did. It was artillery got him.

I wish it were not me to be the one to have to tell you this but if it were me I would want Freeman to tell my mother instead of it being some one else to let her know. If I survive this I will let you know where your husband and Luthers father is laid to rest.

> *Your Friend, Isaac Cooper*
> *Private, 6 Maine Volunteer Regiment, Company K*
> *Cold Harbor, Virginia*

My Dearest Freeman   *June 8, 1864*

I have been reading about this battle you are in and it makes my heart ache with fear that some thing might happen to you. Your letter of June 2 did not make me feel any better. Yesterday evening I took Luther out to show him the moon before it set I told him you were looking at the same moon and wishing you was here. Some day he will know what that meens.

When I went to bed all was well but just now I woke up shivering like it was very cold and sweating like it was very hot but it was neither. It was some kind of horrid fear that come over and waked me and I do not know what it was.

At first I thought the best thing to do was go hold and hug your son Luther and show him your likeness but that did not make me feel any better only scared for him. When he asked me what was wrong I had no answer.

That was when I decided I would write this letter to you asking you to be careful. I do not want you to feel like things are not good here at home. Mum and Jake are happy and just a short walk away and we see them ever day. Luther and me is comfy and ever thing is well just this fear that you are not safe. But still I have this fear it makes me feel scared for you.

If some thing has happened to you and Rodman comes back I will curse his name to his face and his children too. Mum would not approve of me doing that she would say it is not Christian but I will do it any way even if I burn in Hell for it. That is not some thing I would be proud of doing but if I were him I think there is very little I would be proud of. You have ever thing to be proud of.

Today is a work day and Mister Watkins expects me to be at work like usual so I will go back to bed and try to get some sleep. I do hope to hear from you soon and we all dream of welcoming you home in just a few weeks. I will wear your yellow scarf when I sleep until I hear from you.

Your Loving Alma

June 16, 1864

Alma. This is Isaac writing agin. By the time you get this I am sure you have got my message to you frum a week ago and may be even one frum the War Department. When Genl Eustis heard your letter had come in he had Captain Witherell give it to me to send back to you.

Right now we are on a steamship headed down the James River to Bermuda Hundred. Out of all of us on that ship from Eastport that waved good bye to you there is only may be two hundred left including those who joined later. They say we is to be disbanded and moved into a Maine veteran unit because there is not enuff left of the 6 Maine to be effective even if we are one of the scrappiest units in the Army of the Potomac.

It is not easy for me to set on the deck of this ship and write this letter I would much rather be playing checkers and losing to Freeman. For me it will never be the same with out him and I know that is double so for you and Luther. He was always the one who would talk to people like Rebels and Negroes and not menny of us can do like he did. We will miss him but not like you and Luther will.

Freeman always found the good in what everybody else thought was only bad.

> *My injuries are not so much it was just my leg and no broken bone. Surgeon says I will be back in action soon maybe just a few weeks. I was one of the lucky ones.*
>
> *I too signed up again and they set me to go on furlow in September. Married men with children were set to go first. If it is Gods will I will soon be able to tell Luther my self what a fine man his father was.*

Isaac Cooper

Richard spotted the sign on the freeway; it read 'Cold Harbor Battlefield.' "Dana mentioned something about this place."

"You want to stop and look?"

"Been a long day," he said, steering for the ramp. "The room's paid up, no need to rush."

"Sounds good to me." She stretched her legs out and yawned. "What's today? Eighth of June? We don't need to be home for another four days." Amanda turned to gaze out at the rolling fields with the tidy rows of tomatoes and the wispy evening fog drifting across the land. "You know anything of the story here?"

He followed Creighton Road past the Fairmount Christian Church to the intersection with Cold Harbor Road. "Think I slept through that lecture. All I know's Dana said somebody back in his family tree was wounded here."

"Wounded?"

"Think he said his name was Isaac. Apparently he survived."

The visitor center had closed hours earlier and the parking lot was deserted, but under the gibbous moon the signs were all clearly visible, despite the wisps of fog slowly snaking out of the woods, hovering just above the ground. They headed off towards the stand of trees.

It wasn't a big monument. It stood in a small clearing, maybe five minutes in from the parking lot.

She got down on her knees to read the inscription, partially obscured in the inky shadows. "Second Connecticut Heavy Artillery." A nearby sign described how the unit had been trained to use siege weapons and spent much of the war guarding Washington, but had been pressed into infantry service by manpower demands. Stung by taunts of 'band-box soldiers' by veteran infantrymen, their wounded pride drove them to take chances that others shunned, with disastrous results.

"Three hundred and twenty three casualties," he read, shuddering in disbelief at what the carnage must have been. "Sounds like they got butchered." They continued their way down the silent trail, threading between the parallel rows of trenches lining each side.

Despite the gloom of the nightime forest, the farther in the trail led them, the more obvious the trenches became. They meandered across the landscape, past embankments two or three feet high connected by shallow zig-zag furrows maybe a foot deep.

Richard and Amanda strolled down the trail into a wide open field where there were no trenches. The battlements were arrayed on two sides of the moonswept opening and were obviously constructed in opposition; mute testimony to two armies doggedly contesting the field.

When he squinted, the wispy fog almost looked like groups of men surging back and forth across the field. He held her hand and kissed her while they stood in the center of what had once been a no-man's land dividing bitter foes, each honoring a sacred pledge to the other's annihilation, separated in places by scant yards.

He turned her way. "Your dream, two nights ago..."

She stood with her eyes closed. "Yes?"

"You used the word 'curse.' Remember what my grandmother said about you being 'one of *those* Bellinghams'?"

"I remember how proud *my* grandmother was that a Lawton had *married* a Bellingham."

"All but Elizabeth know the Lawton was the winner in that deal." He brushed the hair back from her face. "But do you think..." He raised her hand to his lips. "*Rodman* Bellingham would be able to explain what both of them meant?"

"It's like you said," she replied. "Maybe there's some memories that *never* get explained."

"Maybe those letters..." They walked on in silence.

Moonlight filtered through the fog and the gravel crunching underfoot echoed like the tramp of a host of ancient footsteps. Crickets chirped in a nearby marshy thicket and a small creek trickled out across the field, the burbling water running slow and clear and glistening in the dim light. He reached down, brought a fingertip to his tongue, and found the water sweet and pure.

They wandered, hand in hand, across the open space. The day had been long, the June evening was warm, and their dinner had been good. The nearby trench invited, new-grass green and gently sloped. When she dropped down and stretched out, he joined her. They fell into silence for a few minutes.

Richard again broke the stillness. "I've been thinking…"

"That's a good thing to do," she said, after he retreated inwards for perhaps half a minute. "We should all do that once in a while."

"Your mother is right."

"Amazing how sometimes *that* can happen." Amanda chucked softly, perhaps at the incongruity of his comment. "What was it she was right about?"

"That we *have* waited long enough, *too* long." Amanda made no reply, just cuddled up next to him, kissed him on the cheek, and reached over to take his hand. "I think the time has come," he said, returning her kiss. "You and I will wait no more." He reached his arm around and held her tight.

When he heard her soft, steady breathing he closed his eyes. Didn't matter if it meant they would get to the hotel late – he was happy just being with her, alone in the darkness, enveloped by the fecundity of the hallowed earth.

The noise didn't start up right away, instead it built gradually, almost imperceptibly, but for Richard time had morphed into a swirling purple mist and the shapes in the fog continued to move about. A flash of light from the distant trenches lit up the sky out in front and then a roar cascaded across the field. Back behind he heard an explosion and men shouting, but somehow it all seemed normal, as though it had gone on yesterday and would likely continue tomorrow and maybe the day after that too. The light from several flashes, coming from well behind where they lay sheltered below the edge of the embankment, reflected off the forest and an answering roar followed immediately, then a pair of explosions far out in front flickered against the tongues of fog.

A low whistling sound started up overhead, like the buzzing of a multitude of bees swarming in both directions at once, and a chorus of moans was heard from just beyond the parapet, coming from somewhere out on the open space, maybe just a few yards away. One whimpered like a hurt animal, and several more cried for water or called out names he didn't know. The stench of decomposing flesh fouled his nostrils; it was mingled with the sulfurous smell of gunpowder.

From behind, it sounded like a series of explosions and the dancing light was nearly continuous, then came a sound like rolling thunder. The guns out in front returned the volley and for a couple of minutes the bedlam was complete with men shouting, flashes from a multitude of muzzles, and the explosions of incoming shells. Deep-throated shrieks passed overhead going in both directions, each followed by a detonation that flickered light across the surrounding forest. Clouds of acrid smoke drifted across the field and for a while the cries of the wounded were muffled by the cannonading.

A single shell fell directly in front, maybe twenty yards or so off, producing a deafening roar and shaking the ground, followed by a rain of dirt and stone. Almost as by signal the guns quieted, first those in front then those to the rear, answered now only by the rattle of musketry.

He spotted two men heading his way, striding unconcerned across the open space, both standing erect and walking confidently despite the angry tumult. They were the only ones to be seen and he puzzled at how they moved the way they did. The bullets whizzed across between the two opposing lines but the men appeared oblivious to the hurricane of lead. A cloud of smoke drifted across the field, momentarily obscuring the pair.

A minute later they materialized out of the swirling blue haze, now just a few yards off. One was very tall and both wore dusty blue uniforms with bright brass buttons gleaming in the moonlight. Each cradled a long musket with a fixed bayonet. The needle-sharp points sparkled ghastly, as if they were the personal tool of the Angel of Death, but the men seemed unconcerned. Neither man pointed their weapon his way but as they drew near the tall one reached out, pointing with his finger, stretching and trembling slightly. Richard did not feel threatened, somehow he knew that they had come in peace.

The tall soldier had a gaunt face, plainly visible in the moonlight. It was blackened with soot and smeared with dirt but his eyes were clear and bright and his expression glowed with a confidence that did not entirely conceal a deep concern. His demeanor suggested that he knew who it was he was approaching, and that his motions were as deliberate as his intent. There was something about the man; he appeared to be burdened with a deep sorrow, a profound regret that only he had the power to cure. A sudden chill came over Richard when he realized he was looking into the very same eyes as those back home in Lubec, peering out from within the antique wooden case on their mantle.

The shorter of the two said something but his words were swallowed by a sudden squall of musketry. Despite the roaring noise, Richard was sure he heard a fragment, the name "Freeman."

The tall man nodded in response and stretched his arm out to touch Richard.

It wasn't so much the soldier's light touch that startled him, it was the sudden absence of a heavy burden, a cruel weight in his breast that had always been there but had never been recognized. Realizing the touch belonged to Amanda, he caught his breath.

"The man…" When he gulped his eyes open they darted left and right in confusion. The fog continued to creep across the serenity of the sacred field and the moonlight lit up a few strands of grass waving to an unfelt zephyr. Peace lay across the open space – the silence like the snowdrift that remains after the blizzard departs.

"A man?" Amanda shook her head slightly and clutched at his arm. "There was a man?"

"*Two* men." He rubbed his eyes. "You… You didn't see them? You didn't see… *Freeman?*"

"No," she whispered. "I saw no one."

Richard lay back, holding her right hand tight like he was afraid that if he were to close his eyes again, she too would disappear into the smoke and chaos of the battle, following the two men back out into the gloom and the labyrinthine trenches.

"It's okay," she said softly, putting her left hand on his. Waves of relief rolled through his heart when heard her add, "You are right here with me."

Inhaling deeply, he found the air fresh and clean with a piney scent, the tranquil evening washed by the soft moonlight, and the sinuous tendrils of fog creeping across the open field. Crickets in the marshy thicket continued their symphony, and the little creek flowed sweet.

Author's Comments

Setting a novel during the Civil War, I have come to appreciate, is not something that ought to be undertaken casually, if the author will avoid catcalls and ridicule from the army of historians, both professional and amateur, who have studied the American Cataclysm in excruciating detail. Many carry long knives in the hope of catching hapless authors committing careless errors. I have written many novels, but this is the first to include citations and a bibliography. I have not documented every factual detail because there are some things that are readily available and listing them would serve only to clutter the page; the reader is cautioned not to take a historical detail as fiction merely because it lacks an endnote. A few readers have objected to the citations, terming them a "distraction," but I have elected to leave them in place to establish that these details are *not* fictional.

Simply the term "Civil War" raises regional hackles, with preferred titles according to the geographic origin of the questioner. My intent is not to offend, but to describe – at least in part – the experience as seen through the eyes of ordinary people. In this case, the chosen descriptor is understood even by those who would prefer another.

An example of this prejudice is seen in the name commonly given the world's first battle between ironclad warships: "The Monitor and the Merrimack." Following the fall of Fort Sumter, the US Navy abandoned the USS Merrimack at its dock in the Norfolk Navy Yard, burning it to the waterline. In an act of inspired genius the Confederacy wrested the hulk from the mud, created the ironclad, and renamed it the CSS Virginia. It is often remarked that history is written by the victor, but it has been long acknowledged that there was no victor in that epochal battle. Is the refusal to refer to the ship by the name she bore during her only action – Virginia – simply a matter of Union hubris?

The reader should understand that in the historical context, I am less interested in the facts that have been confirmed subsequent to the war than I am in what was understood by the common man at the time these events were still unfolding. A few details in this narrative may be disputed as far as historicity is concerned, but they are documented entries from contemporaneous sources (primarily the *Eastport Sentinel*, the closest newspaper to the community where the story centers). Whether the reader regards these as propaganda, disinformation, or gospel they were what the wartime public read.

The only unverified historical narrative in this work deals with the women of Lubec, Maine, gathering to produce relief supplies to be sent to the front and to the hospitals. While such circles have been clearly documented in hundreds if not thousands of communities throughout the Union, historical disruptions within the church congregations of Lubec have left records of the Civil War era missing or inaccessible. Given that close to 200 men from Lubec fought in this war, out of a total "White Male" population of 1,290 of all ages (according to the United States Census of 1860), I believe it likely that the women of Lubec would be motivated to contribute in a manner similar to that of their sisters elsewhere. In this particular case I urge the reader to accept the characterization of the Lubec group as stand-in for these groups as a whole since all had the same charitable intent: to ease suffering. In that regard, these relief supplies were commonly used indiscriminately to the benefit of those Confederate wounded who found themselves in Union hands, as well as the husbands, brothers, and sons of the women congregated in church basements.

Today we enjoy the ability to look backwards through the eyes of professional historians, but the information sources that were available in the mid-19th century were paltry compared to the twenty-four hour news cycle to which we have grown accustomed. Uncounted hours of research were expended to learn what a woman living in a small town in Downeast Maine during the 1860's could have actually seen, heard, and experienced. The conflict spawned two private relief organizations, the *United States Sanitary Commission* and the *United States Christian Commission*. Sometimes competitors but more often collaborators, both are seldom heard of today except in one by their successor, and the other by their parent: the Red Cross and the YMCA.

Some source material remains unfound, such as the official records of the Town of Lubec. Original hand-written documents are available dating to the town's 1814 incorporation, but those from 1861 to roughly 1885 are missing. I had rather hoped that those records might have given insight into the town's 1863 gubernatorial vote for the "Peace Democrat" Bion Bradbury over the Republican Samuel Cony, running counter to the state and also to the nearby town of Eastport.

One source that I would be remiss in not mentioning is that of my own ancestor, Capt. Shepherd Pryor, CSA, whose name both my mother and grand-daughter bear. In an ironic but factual episode Capt. Pryor, then of the Twelfth Georgia Regiment, faced down the Sixth Maine in an inconclusive nighttime firefight in a wheatfield at Garnett's Farm. In this case – an unexpected but fortuitous discovery – my ancestor and one of my lead characters engaged in mortal combat. Fortunately, both survived. Pryor and his unit were present during the battle of Chancellorsville, the Confederate victory in which General Thomas "Stonewall" Jackson received a mortal wound from his own men. The Sixth Maine was also there.

I am deeply indebted to each of the authors listed in the bibliography. Some wrote during the Civil War, some wrote during the years of the Grand Army of the Republic (the era's equivalent of the American Legion, dissolved when the last Union veteran died in

1956), and some have written in more recent years. Research today, thanks to the Internet, is a very different thing than it was fifty years ago when Robin Winks wrote his monumental doctoral dissertation about American and Canadian relations during the Civil War.

JD Rule
Lubec, Maine
March, 2017

Endnotes and References

[1] Mundy

[2] Matthews, page 139

[3] Mundy, page 265

[4] Charles Tripler Witherell. B 10/11/1836, D 12/31/1928, Detroit MI. Enlisted in the 6th Maine at Eastport on 7/15/1861 as Sergeant, promoted to Second Lieutenant 3/10/1862 and to Lieutenant 2/13/1863 and Captain 9/13/1863. Brevet Major 10/19/1864. According to one writer, "He has been in 60 battles, was wounded eleven times, and five times consigned to the hospital."

[5] O'Leary. As part owner of the vessel, Freeman would be entitled to a portion of the boat's share. If he worked on-board as a crewman, he would be entitled to an additional, negotiated share.

[6] *Eastport Sentinel*, published in Eastport Maine; the closest newspaper to Lubec and the city from which the 6th Maine, Company K mustered. Frequent references will be made to this paper.

[7] United States Census Bureau. The 1860 Census counts one "free colored" male in Lubec, no females. The 1870 Census has the same count, but without the "free" label.

[8] Local oral tradition; not verified

[9] According to the roster provided by Mundy, three Lubecers were included in the original Company K of the Sixth Maine Volunteer Infantry, and one more joined later. The plaque in Lubec's Monument Lot lists a total of 187 men from Lubec who served in the Civil War.

[10] United States Census Bureau, 1860 Census. Also shows 1258 female residents.

[11] Clark

[12] Reuel Williams Furlong. B 11/23/1835 Calais ME, D 11/7/1863, Rappahannock Station, Fauquier County VA. Schoolteacher. Joined Maine 6th, Company D, elected Lieutenant on July 1, 1861. While on furlough, married Fannie B. Higgins of Eastport, on 3/7/1863. Reportedly, when his remains were returned to Calais the ships in the St. Croix River flew flags at half-staff.

[13] Hiram Burnham, B 1814 Machias, ME. D 9/29/1864, Chapin's Farm VA. (Alt spelling: Chaffins Farm). As a young child, witnessed his mother's murder by his father, was raised by relatives. Held office as County Commissioner, Coroner, organized militia regiment in Aroostook War (1839). Lumberman. Joined 6th Maine as Lt. Col on 7/15/1861, promoted to Col 12/12/1861. Brigadier General 4/1864.

[14] Mundy

[15] Stanley & Hall, page 338

[16] Clark

[17] *Hardee's Rifle And Light Infantry Tactics*, Brevet Lieut. W.J. Hardee, J.O. Kane, New York, 1862

[18] Mundy; Witherell mustered with Company K in Eastport.

[19] Mundy provides much of this information in the company roster.

[20] Mundy

[21] Hardees

[22] Ambler, Isaac W. *Truth is Stranger Than Fiction*, pub 1873. Mundy dismisses Ambler's claims as having been involved in combat with the 6 Maine as 'self serving' but accepts that he may have been hired in Portland to teach weapons skills. Ambler was a deserter from the British Army who had been stationed in the British Territories.

[23] According to Malcolm, Smith replaced Garrity on July 11, 1861

[24] Hardees, page 73

[25] Hardees

[26] Mundy, page 39

[27] Mundy, page 40

[28] Mundy

[29] Wright, page 213

[30] Clark, Page 7

[31] "Corner Stone" Speech given as the inaugural address by Confederate Vice President Alexander H. Stephens on March 21, 1861 in Savannah, GA. Available through multiple sources.

[32] Today known as the Christian Temple. The current building was constructed in 1892, according to Two Hundred Years of Lubec History and confirmed by Malcolm.

[33] Temperance Hall is shown on the 1861 map of Lubec, directly opposite Big White. Ownership and condition of this structure are described by McGregor. Per Malcolm, the building was later moved and the current Christian Temple was constructed nearby. According to *200 Years of Lubec History*, the present Temple was constructed in 1890. Comstock does not describe the heresy charge leveled on Garrity by Fowler; this appears only in Malcolm. Malcolm describes an ironic event, wherein the Big White steeple fell during the 1869 Saxby Gale, landing on the doorstep of the Temple.

[34] Malcolm

[35] Inaugural speech by Confederate Vice President Alexander H. Stephens, given at Savannah Georgia on March 21, 1861.

[36] *Eastport Sentinel*, July 24, 1861

[37] Located directly across from Big White, according to the 1861 Lubec Business Map, from the collection of Davis Pike. Malcolm terms it "Sons of Temperance" but no record has been located placing that organization in

Lubec.

[38] McGregor termed the Mason's investment "a waste of money."

[39] Wright

[40] Leech

[41] Boatner

[42] Long, p14

[43] Authorized vendors who would follow the army to sell the men necessities. Many would accept credit between visits by the paymaster.

[44] *Eastport Sentinel*, August 7, 1861

[45] Nutt was the publisher of the *Eastport Sentinel*

[46] Martha Ballard was a midwife in rural Maine during the eighteenth century. She left a remarkable diary but died in 1812, well before the Civil War. Her name was used to honor the profession. None of the story draws from her diaries.

[47] Mundy

[48] Boatner

[49] Wright

[50] O'Leary, appendix 3 & 10. A Quintal is 112 lbs of dried salt cod, prepared at sea.

[51] Pryor

[52] Eastport Sentinel, *Vital Records*

[53] Colby Atlas

[54] Mundy, page 41

[55] *Eastport Sentinel*, September 4, 1861

[56] Clark, page 8

[57] Mundy, quoting Clark. Page 42

[58] Clark, p 9

[59] Secessionists. There were many names given to Confederate soldiers however few letter writers – at least of those reviewed for this story – termed them 'enemy,' at least before encountering battlefield losses.

[60] Mundy

[61] Uncertain. Neither Clark nor Mundy specify what company he began with. Prior to leaving the regiment (following Burnham's death) he was Adjutant.

[62] Charles A. Clark. B 1/26/1841, Sangerville ME. D 12/22/1913, Iowa, Age 72. One of 9 children, Clark was a student at Foxcroft Academy when the war started. Awarded the Medal of Honor for assuming command and leading regiment to safety at Brooks Ford (Fredericksburg). Left service in 1864 after conducting the remains of Hiram Burnham to funeral in Cherryfield. Breveted Lt. Col.

[63] Clark

[64] Pryor. Although Shepard Pryor's viewpoint is Confederate, since his

camp was plagued by measles and was in the same climate, it is likely that the disease would be present on both sides of the line.

[65] Boatner

[66] According to Boatner, this was Robert E. Lee's first action as a commanding general.

[67] Long, p24

[68] As described by Long

[69] Courtesty Lost Fishermen's Memorial Association of Lubec.

[70] Lewinsville, in modern-day McLean, Virginia.

[71] William Farrar "Baldy" Smith, (B 2/17/1824, St. Albans VT D 2/28/1903, Philadelphia)

[72] *Bangor Daily News*; Pembroke Iron Works Flourished During Era of the Square Riggers; Val Atwood, May 27, 1991, page 37

[73] See Richard for a complete description of the United States Sanitary Commission and their efforts to improve morale and health.

[74] Thanksgiving Day was recognized as a National Holiday in 1863.

[75] Winks and others

[76] Cougle and also Winks

[77] privateers

[78] This incident is fictional. The mermaid superstition was commonly held by sailors; they were considered a harbinger of disaster.

[79] Mundy, P 45

[80] Described by both Clark and Mundy

[81] Ursula Martha Penniman. (B 12/10/1809, Machias; D 3/3/1893, Machias. Age 83.) Daughter of Polly Burnham and Jacob Penniman, one of six children. Member of family of Jeremiah O'Brien, of Margaretta fame (Revolutionary War). Miss Penniman is listed as the Associate Manager for the New England Women's Auxiliary Association, Machias office, in the Association's *Annual Report*, serving in that capacity from 1862 until 1865. The Association was a component of the United States Sanitary Commission. She later was the first Board President for the Porter Library in Machias. Never married, was the namesake for the Women's Club established in Machias.

[82] Mundy, Clark both

[83] According to Boatner, William Farrar "Baldy" Smith was promoted to Brigadier General in August of 1861. Mundy has Smith as a Colonel at the time of this incident.

[84] *Easport Sentinel*, December 4, 1861 reports this gift to Company K, adding "evidence they are not forgotten at home."

[85] United States Christian Commission. This group was formed by the Young Men's Christian Association (YMCA) and during the early years of the war concentrated on serving the spiritual and religious needs of the

soldiers. The Sanitary Commission was a separate group, affiliated with the government but not funded by it, and worked to fill material and hospital needs.

[86] According to Richard this was a common concern and recognized by many in and out of religious communities.

[87] Clark. According to his personal account, the time period was "about two weeks."

[88] Cougle, p 19, and also Winks. According to Cougle, "winter of 62 was a very bad winter."

[89] Pinkham

[90] *Eastport Sentinel*, December 18, 1861. 'Lincoln Cavalry' was the popular name given to the First New York Cavalry Regiment.

[91] *Eastport Sentinel*, December 11, 1861

[92] Winks

[93] *Eastport Sentinel,* December 18, 1861

[94] Winks

[95] ibid

[96] Winks

[97] *The Eastport Sentinel,* January 16, 1862

[98] Mundy, P 50

[99] According to Mundy, Chandler was regarded as a martinet

[100] Shepherd Green Pryor is an ancestor of the author, on my mother's side. My mother and also my grand-daughter bear his name. He was born in 1830 and died 5/2/1911 in Sumter, GA. A planter and slave-owner, he served as Sergeant in Company A of the 12th Georgia Infantry, rising to Captain before being wounded at Culpepper Court House in September 1863. Pryor owned fewer than twenty slaves, thus did not qualify for exemption from military service.

[101] MaineMemory.net

[102] As reported by *Eastport Sentinel*, Jan 22, 1862

[103] *Eastport Sentinel*, January 29, 1862

[104] Quoted verbatim from the Eastport Sentinel, March 5, 1862

[105] Also known as the Aroostook War. This was the last armed confrontation between the United States and Britain, and led to the 1842 Ashburton-Webster Treaty that established the border between Maine and New Brunswick, and placed Campobello Island in the British Colony. The matter was triggered by a dispute over logging rights.

[106] *Eastport Sentinel*, February 19, 1862. The *Encyclopedia Virginia* describes the Confederate Congress' suspension of habeas corpus on February 27, 1862, and Jefferson Davis' declaration of martial law on March 1, 1862. There is no mention of civil unrest and further research has failed to find evidence to support this. Food riots occurred in Richmond in

1863 triggered by the high price of bread.

[107] *Eastport Sentinel*, February 19, 1862

[108] Quoted verbatim from the *Eastport Sentinel*, March 5, 1862

[109] Mundy, P51

[110] From the report by Monitor Chief Engineer Allan C. Stimers, quoted by the *Eastport Sentinel* on March 19, 1862. Stimers also claimed the Monitor was "the finest sea boat I was ever in."

[111] *Eastport Sentinel*, March 19. 1862, mentions a two-day storm that left the roads closed.

[112] Mundy, Brigade Roster P 224. Little has been published about Rev. Zenos Thompson. According to Mundy, he resigned his commission 7/15/1862.

[113] Mundy quotes Sgt. William West describing the USS Monitor, page 56

[114] Mundy, P58

[115] Reported by Mundy, Page 58, and also *Eastport Sentinel* April 30, 1862

[116] Mundy, p 59

[117] Mundy

[118] This story is related by a news correspondent and published by the *Eastport Sentinel* on April 30. Mundy lists a man by the same name, home, and date of death, as having joined from Eastport

[119] Mundy, P 75

[120] Mundy, P 80. Refers to a range of illnesses including diphtheria, typhoid, cholera, and others.

[121] This story is related by Mundy, pages 64-70.

[122] Stephen Crane describes one such conversation in *The Red Badge of Courage*.

[123] The correct spelling is Marye's Heights, however this alternate spelling is seen in some cases. The site was named after the Marye family, which owned a large property at the battlefield location in Fredericksburg.

[124] Garrison. These were the nurses of the United States Sanitary Commision, and Frederick Law Olmsted was present for that organization. Georgeanna Woolsey was assigned to the *Wilson Small* during this period. Woolsey later worked as a nurse at Gettysburg.

[125] *Eastport Sentinel*, June 4, 1862

[126] *Vital Statistics, Eastport Sentinel*

[127] Per O'Leary, the US Government subsidized the Cod fishery from 1792 until 1890, with just a short break during the 1810-20 period.

[128] *Eastport Sentinel*, June 11, 1862. This is a reference to the Battle of Puebla, celebrated in Mexico and elsewhere as 'Cinco de Mayo.' As the battle took place on May 5, this delay illustrates the lag in news from outside the United States. It was first fully reported by the *New York Times* on June 27, after the receipt of official dispatches.

[129] Multiple sources describe Stuarts attack on White House Landing. On departing, Union forces set fire to the remaining stores.

[130] Shepherd Pryor, Capt. CSA, from the 12th Georgia Rifle Company, describes this battle in the compendium of his letters *A Post of Honor*. Pryor is the author's ancestor, on his mother's side. From the author's viewpoint, it was a strange feeling being in the position of having his real life ancestor facing, across the field of battle, one of his principal fictional protagonists as a member of a real fighting unit.

[131] Mundy, page 84

[132] *Vital Statistics, Eastport Sentinel*

[133] *Eastport Sentinel*, July 19, 1862. Letter from Governor Israel Washburn Jr. (B 6/6/1813, Livermore ME. D 5/12/1883, Philadelphia.)

[134] Clark, page 25

[135] Hatch, Page 512. The author mentions the incident but did not provide a date. It is likely that this was not an isolated incident.

[136] Municipal Correspondence, Maine State Archives, July 21, 1862

[137] *Eastport Sentinel*, July 30, 1862

[138] *Eastport Sentinel*, August 6, 1862

[139] *Eastport Sentinel*, December 16, 1863, reports that cordwood in Eastport is $6.00 per cord but in Augusta the price is $8.00 per cord.

[140] Pryor, page 260

[141] Smith describes this incident as "the Humiston children" on page 175. The children in the photograph were later identified through the efforts of the United States Christian Commission and became the impetus for the establishment of a war-orphan's home. The soldier was identified as Sgt. Amos Humiston from Portville NY, of the 154 New York Volunteer Infantry. According to Smith, it was only after the children were identified their mother learned she was a widow.

[142] Major General Israel Richardson, (b 12/26/1815, Fairfax VT. d 11/3/1862, Sharpsburg MD.) Richardson was credited with seizing the high ground that led to taking "Bloody Lane." He was at the front directing artillery fire when hit by a shell fragment. At first he was expected to survive, but infection then pneumonia set in. Richardson died nearly two months after the Battle of Antietam.

[143] Mundy, Page 95

[144] Frederic W Morong of Lubec enlisted in the 6th Maine on 8/3/62 at the age of 21. He served as lightkeeper at the Sparkplug 1890 before transferring first to Libby Island then Little River. He died in Lubec in 1920 at the age of 77. Several Morongs, including Frederic, are listed on the plaque in Lubec.

[145] Trescott was incorporated at that time. The town disincorporated in 1945 and became part of the Unorganized Territories governed by the county.

[146] *Eastport Sentinel*, Sept 10, 1862

[147] *Eastport Sentinel*, Sept 3, 1862

[148] *Eastport Sentinel*, August 6, 1862

[149] Known today as Reversing Falls, in Pembroke.

[150] The incident is mentioned in the October 8 edition of the *Eastport Sentinel*, but without first names. The entire article is 5 lines long and includes no details. Isaac's name was provided by Bonnie Healy of the Trescott Historical Society.

[151] Eastport Sentinel, Sept 24, 1861

[152] See Winks.

[153] *Eastport Sentinel*, November 19, 1862

[154] First played July 5, 1862. *Mel Bay Presents Infantry Bugle Calls of the American Civil War*, page 20

[155] There are multiple reports of this sighting including in the Park Service video shown at the battlefield visitor center.

[156] *Eastport Sentinel* December 24, 1862

[157] O'Leary

[158] *Eastport Sentinel* December 24, 1862

[159] Ibid

[160] Albion K.P Avery, also MI 'T.C.' B 11/20/1840. Avery has been listed by Ross and McGregor as part of the US 17th Infantry, but not by the US Park Service. Per Ross, he enlisted 4/17/62, served as a sergeant. The 17th was part of the regular US Army and not a state-sponsored unit such as the 6th. McGregor includes a photograph. Avery had four brothers, one sister, and a half-brother. Cemetery records at Fredericksburg include only one Avery – Sgt. James T., from Michigan. It is highly probable that Albion Avery lies in an unmarked grave, possibly sharing it with others.

[161] Mundy describes the "Whiskey Riot" that followed the "Mud March," page 101

[162] Multiple records have described this incident but none have provided a list of casualties.

[163] Winks

[164] The details were published in the March 11, 1863 *Eastport Sentinel,* and by many other sources.

[165] *Eastport Sentinel*, February 25, 1863

[166] *Vital Statistics, Eastport Sentinel.*

[167] *Eastport Sentinel*, April 1, 1863. The paper did not name the Captain.

[168] Mundy, page 107

[169] *Eastport Sentinel*, April 8, 1863

[170] ibid

[171] Mrs. Aaron Hayden, aka Jane Thomas [Briggs] Hayden, B 12/15/1825, Robbinston, ME, D 5/8/1909, Robbinston ME. As was customary, married

women were known by their husband's name. Little can be confirmed about the life of Mrs. Hayden, beyond her participation in the Women's Auxiliary Association.

[172] Maine Geneaology Archives

[173] The depicted relationship between Penniman and Hayden is not supported by documented evidence and is disputed by some. For the purposes of this narration it is assumed as both had similar objectives and were geographically separated to the point where they would not likely see themselves as competitors. No colleague located in Lubec has been identified. Hayden was born Dec 15, 1825; Penniman is known to have lived beyond 1890. Both are listed as Associate Managers of the Women's Auxiliary Association of the United States Sanitary Commission in 1864 and 1865. Penniman is also listed in 1862.

[174] Mundy describes this scene but others have questioned whether it is accurate.

[175] Major Joel A. Haycock, (B 1/11/1836 in Calais), per Stanley & Hall, page 365.

[176] Color Sergeant John Gray, Maine 6th, K Company. Gray died at Rappahannock Station on 11/7/1863. By trade, a cooper.

[177] Mackowski *et al*

[178] Letter in *Eastport Sentinel*, May 23 1863. According to Mundy, the Sixth captured the Washington Artillery, from Louisiana.

[179] Clark. Charles Clark was awarded the Congressional Medal of Honor for his role in this action.

[180] Clark describes this event in detail.

[181] Mundy, p 134. Reports said Burnham "cried like a baby" with relief to see the Sixth come back across the lines.

[182] Described by Mackowski *et al*

[183] *Eastport Sentinel*, May 6, 1863

[184] United States Adjutant General Lorenzo Thomas (B 10/26/1804, D 3/2.1875), speaking at Lake Providence, Louisiana.

[185] Col. Calvin Sanger Douty (B 1815, D 6/17/1863 in action, Battle of Aldie).

[186] Stanley & Hall describe this action, page 263.

[187] Pinkham

[188] CSS Alabama. Screw sloop-of-war built in England for the Confederacy in 1862. Served as commerce raider in US and foreign waters, was sunk by the USS Kearsarge in 1864 in the Battle of Cherbourg.

[189] Malcolm

[190] Susan Bogert Warner (popular author of 30 titles, b 7/11/1819, d 3/17/1885, sometimes wrote as Elizabeth Wetherell)

[191] Mundy describes this scene during the forced march to Gettysburg.

[192] *Commissioner's Report*, page 396

[193] Mundy. Includes only original muster roll.

[194] *Commissioner's Report*

[195] *Commissioner's Report*, page 405

[196] Garrison describes Georgeanna Woolsey's (B 11/3/1833 in Brooklyn NY, D 1/27/1906 in New Haven CT) work at White House Landing in 1862; several other sources place her at Gettysburg.

[197] *Commissioner's Report*, page 400

[198] Account of Isaac R. Pennypacker

[199] Wikipedia states that the names Little Round Top and Big Round Top were not used until well after the battle, and that there were several other names in common usage. The earlier names are not used here, to avoid confusion.

[200] Stillé

[201] *Commissoner's Report*, page 397

[202] Malcolm

[203] *Eastport Sentinel*, July 1, 1863

[204] Mundy, page 153

[205] Smith

[206] Williams describes the privations of Confederate soldiers, particularly following the collapse of southern industry.

[207] Stillé describes this incident in detail.

[208] Letter from Charles Clark, included in *Commissioner's Report.*

[209] There are numerous references to this raid but Mundy (page 154) provides the best description I have found. Furlong was commended for this action.

[210] *Eastport Sentinel*, July 15, 1863

[211] Now known as Ontario, the western and English speaking territory that joined with French speaking Canada East in 1867 to form Canada.

[212] *Eastport Sentinel*, July 29, 1863

[213] Maine Memory Nework

[214] Loring A. Leavitt was the Assisant Lightkeeper at the West Quoddy Head Light from 1861 to 1867, per the West Quoddy Lightkeeper's Association. The Keeper at that time was George A. Case. The lighthouse was first built in 1806, and was rebuilt in 1857.

[215] Now the prairie provinces; this was the name used before the Canadian Confederation of 1867. The name refers to the land owned by the Hudson Bay Company, which held a Royal Charter from 1670 granting ownership of all lands that drained into the Hudson Bay.

[216] According to multiple sources, the second number states the number of unidentified remains interred beneath the stone.

[217] Park Service records list 25 soldiers by this name who served in Maine

units. Further research might reveal which were lost at Fredericksburg.

[218] According to multiple sources, a penny means someone visited the grave. A nickle means the visitor went to boot camp with the deceased and a dime means they served together. A quarter means the visitor was there at the time the deceased was killed. Traditionally, these coins are collected on Memorial Day and used for cemetery maintenance.

[219] *Eastport Sentinel*, August 19, 1863

[220] Ibid. These names are still common in Lubec.

[221] Hezekiah Long relates this story in *Hard Times, Hard Bread, and Harder Coffee.*

[222] R&B Saxophonist Ed Wiley Jr. (1930-2010) was the father of Ed Wiley III, Managing Partner of Rocky Mount's Prime Smokehouse.

[223] *Eastport Serntinel*, Sept 2, 1863

[224] *Eastport Sentinel*, Sept 9, 1863

[225] *Eastport Sentinel*, September 16, 1863

[226] *Absentee Soldier Voting in Civil War Law and Politics*, dissertation by David A. Collins, Ph.D., Wayne State University, Detroit MI, 2014. Lincoln's reelection was the first time Maine soldiers were permitted to vote, supported by Gov. Samuel Cony.

[227] Winks describes this in extensive detail.

[228] *Eastport Sentinel*, October 14, 1863

[229] As related by Pinkham

[230] Fox sets the losses for the 6th Maine at Raphannock Station at 56 killed and wounded – the highest casualty rate for any action for the regiment. Losses at Fredericksburg totaled 38, according to Fox.

[231] This includes details from the account by Brev. Major Charles T. Witherell, believed penned in 1913.

[232] Williams

[233] Per the NY Times, Solomon Wright Russell Jr., 1836-1917.

[234] This episode is described by Clark and also by others. According to Clark, after the war Russell married the woman, Anna Dixon (Anna Ashton Dixon, 1848-19120, and had a long and fruitful marriage.

[235] Per the Cherryfield Public Library, Burnham's first wife, Elizabeth, bore him 8 children, few of whom lived beyond 10 years. Elizabeth was born "about March" 1815 in Nova Scotia and died 8/15/1860. Second wife Seleda Sproul was born 2/23/1826.

[236] *Venereal Diseases*, Dr. Freeman J. Bumstead, in a publication distributed by the United States Sanitary Commission.

[237] *Eastport Sentinel*, November 18, 1863

[238] Ibid

[239] Viscount Richard Bickerton Pernell Lyons, British envoy to Washington, 1858-1864 (B 4/6/1817, D 12/5/1887)

[240] Winks describes the Chesapeake incident in great detail. This was the first mention in the local press; *Eastport Sentinel* Dec 9, 1863.

[241] Both are listed in *Commissioner* and also on the Lubec Historical Society plaque; Denbo has no 'w' in *Commissioner*.

[242] Williams describes this situation in detail.

[243] *Encyclopedia Virginia*

[244] *Eastport Sentinel*, Dec 19, 1863

[245] ibid

[246] Richard describes several such actions in *Busy Hands*

[247] ibid

[248] This story appears in Stanley, page 108

[249] *Eastport Sentinel*, January 28, 1864

[250] Col. John Singleton Mosby (B 12/6/1833, D 5/30/1916) commanded the 43rd Battalion, 1st Virginia Cavalry. He was known as "The Grey Ghost" for his quick raids and ability to vanish.

[251] Eastport Sentinel, January 6, 1864

[252] ibid

[253] Cannan describes Grant's arrival and observed that in the Western Campaigns he faced "mediocre" commanders like Bragg and Pemberton

[254] Lyman Beecher (B 10/12/1775 D 1/10/1863) was co-founder of the American Temperance Society and the father of Harriet Beecher Stowe, among others.

[255] Stillé describes these traveling lecturers. It has not been established that they visited Lubec.

[256] An enclosed wagon used to transport artillery munitions.

[257] This is reported by Cannan. The discovery was made by members of the 11th New Jersey Infantry; they found the skull and cap of their Sgt. Daniel Bender of Company H, lost a year earlier at Chancellorsville.

[258] Major George B. Fuller from Corinth. Per Mundy, mustered in 5/22/1863, resigned 7/28/1864. Identified by Cannana as commanding 6 Maine during Wilderness.

[259] Cannan describes this. Longstreet survived but was out of action for several months. Two of his staff members were not so lucky. Thomas Jonathan "Stonewall" Jackson was shot by his own men a year earlier, losing an arm then dying of complications.

[260] Major General John Sedgewick (B 9/13/1813) was the highest ranking Union officer killed during the Civil War. Dunkerly *et al* includes an eyewitness account, beginning on page 38. His last words: "They couldn't hit an elephant at this distance."

[261] *Eastport Sentinel*, April 27, 1864. The incident is well documented elsewhere, although some descriptions may be biased.

[262] Major General Nathan Bedford Forrest (b 7/13/1821, d 10/29/1877)

following the war was the first Grand Wizard of the Ku Klux Klan.

[263] Shay, a psychiatrist, describes this state of mind, which he termed the "berserk state" entered by warriors under extreme duress. He wrote about a different war but very similar circumstances.

[264] Isaac C. Campbell, B 1841. Maine Post 1 of the Grand Army of the Republic, established in Pembroke, was named in honor of Campbell, who joined at age 20. Prior to the war Campbell worked as a carpenter. The GAR building was originally the home of the Sons of Temperance, Pembroke Chapter, and is currently occupied by Masonic Lodge, Crescent #78.

[265] Fox

[266] Not yet confirmed. This spot was suggested by Sandra Bourque.

[267] Winks and others

[268] McGregor lists the Lubec residents who chose to pay the fee.

[269] Maine State Archives. Letter from Wm H. Chase to State Adjutant General John L. Hodson, Dec 7, 1865.

[270] *Eastport Sentinel*, May 11, 1864

[271] Dunkerly *et al* describes this and confirms that Grant refused to allow the provost – Brig Gen. Marsena Patrick – to enforce the 'no foraging' rule.

[272] Rhea

[273] Boatner places Custer at the Battle of Yellow Church, a cavalry engagement at the start of the battle of Cold Harbor.

[274] Second Connecticut Heavy Artillery, commanded by Col. Elisha S. Kellog (B 11/27/1824, Glastonbury CT, a machinist by trade.)

[275] The New Moon occurred on June 4. During the evening of June 1 the moon set two hours before the sun.

[276] Rhea discusses Grant's deliberations prior to ordering this attack, suggesting that political reasons and information that the Confederate morale was low justified the decision, but that neither Grant nor Meade viewed the terrain beforehand.

[277] Colonel Frederick Fuller Wead (B 1/26/1835, Malone NY, D 6/3/1864, Cold Harbor) Col. Wead was wounded during the first day of the battle and returned, against surgeon's orders, to lead his men in the third charge.

[278] Rhea, pp 352

[279] Park Service signs show this as "Bloody Run."

[280] Rhea describes the truce and the negotiations that preceded it.

Bibliography

Beattie, Donald W. et al; *A Distant War Comes Home: Maine in the Civil War Era*; Down East Books, Camden ME, 1996

Boatner, Mark M III.; *The Civil War Dictionary*; Vintage Books, 1988 (first published 1959)

Cannan, John; *The Wilderness Campaign*; Combined Books; Comshocken PA; 1993

Chowning, Larry S; *Soldiers At The Doorstep : Civil War Lore*; Tidewater Publishers, 1999

Clark, Charles A, *Campaigning with the Sixth Maine*; University of California Libraries, reprint of original 1897

Colby, George N, *Atlas of Washington County*, 1881

Comstock, Edith; *History of the Christian Church Disciples of Christ, Lubec Maine*; private publication, 2006

Cougle, Jim; *Canadian Blood American Soil*; The Civil War Heritage Society of Canada, Fredericton 1994

Dunkerly, Robert M.; Pfanz, Donald C.; Ruth, David R.; *No Turning Back,* Savas Beatie 2014

Eastport Sentinel, *Vital Records,* from the collection of the Lubec Memorial Library

Fox, William F., *Regimental Losses In The American Civil War,* Forgotten Books, reprint of original 1898

Garrison, Nancy Scripture; *With Courage And Delicacy: Civil War*

On The Peninsula; Savas Publishing, 1999

Hardee's; *Rifle and Light Infantry Tactics*, J.O. Kane, New York; reprint of original 1862

Hatch Ph.D., Louis Clinton; *Maine: A History, Volume II*; The American Historical Society, New York 1919

Hutchinson, Vernal; *A Maine Town in The Civil War;* The Bond Wheelwright Company, Freeport ME, 1957

Kallgren, Beverly Hayes and Crouthamel, James L, editors; *Dear Friend Anna*; University of Maine Press, 1992

Leech, Margaret; *Reveille in Washington*; Harper and Brothers Publishing, New York, 1941

Long, Hezekiah; *Hard Times, Hard Bread, and Harder Coffee: The Civil War Correspondence of Hezekiah Long, Company F, 20th Maine Infantry*; Edited by Richardson's Civil War Round Table, Northport ME, 2008

Lowry MD, Thomas P., *The Story The Soldiers Wouldn't Tell: Sex in the Civil War,* Stackpole Books, Mechanicsburg PA 1994

Maine at Gettysburg: Report of Maine Commissioners; Maine Gettysburg Commission; 1898

Mackowski, Chris & White, Kristopher D.; *Chancellorsville's Forgotten Front: The Battles of Second Fredericksburg and Salem Church*; Savas Beatie, 2013

Malcolm, Dr. Alan S; *The Spire at Flaggs's Point*; Collection of Lubec Memorial Library, 1995

Matthews, Frederick C., *American Merchant Ships*, 1850-1900, Dover Publications, New York; reprint of original 1930 issue

Mundy, James H.; *No Rich Men's Sons*; Harp Publications, Cape Elizabeth ME 1994

Oates, Stephen B., *To Purge This Land With Blood,* Harper & Rowe, New York, 1970

O'Leary, Wayne M., *Maine Sea Fisheries*, Northeastern University Press, 1996

Pinkham, Marjorie Sprague; *Shipwrecked From the Sea of Time*; undated from the collection of the Lubec Memorial Library

Pryor, Shepherd G.; *A Post of Honor: The Pryor Letters 1861-63*; Garrett Publications, 1989

R.H. Stanley & Geo. G. Hall; *Eastern Maine and The Rebellion*; 1887 reprint by Higginson Book Company

Rhea, Gordon C.; *Cold Harbor: Grant and Lee*; Louisiana State University Press, 2002

Rhodes, Robert Hunt; *All For The Union*; Andrew Mowbray Inc., 1985

Richard, Patricia L; *Busy Hands: Images of the Family in the Northern Civil War Effort*; Fordham University Press, 2003

Ross, Ken; Washington County, *Maine in the Civil War, 1861-66.* Pub by St. Croix Historical Society, 2011 private printing.

Shay, Jonathan M.D., Ph.D.; *Achilles in Vietnam: Combat Trauma And The Undoing Of Character;* Scribner, 1994

Smith, Rev. Edward Parmelee; *Incidents of the United States Christian Commission*; first published by Lippincot, 1871

Sneden, Robert Knox, *Images from the Storm*, The Free Press, New York 2001

Stanley, R.H.and Hall, Geo. O.; *Eastern Maine and The Rebellion*; re-issue by Higginson Book Company of Salem, Mass, of original 1887 publication.

Stillé, Charles J; *History of the United States Sanitary Commission, Being The General Report Of Its Work During The War Of The Rebellion*, 1866. Reprinted by HardPress Publishing

United States Census Bureau, *Ninth Census of the United States, 1870: Vital Statistics*; United States Printing Office, 1872. While not directly cited, this source provides a listing, including geographic distribution, of fatal diseases of the time including the contemporaneous names of those ailments.

Wilkinson, Warren; *Mother May You Never See The Sights I Have Seen*, HarperCollins, New York, 1990

Winks, Robin W., *The Civil War Years: Canada and the United States*, McGill-Queens University Press, Montreal 1998 (First published 1960)

Williams, David, *Rich Man's War*, The University of Georgia Press, Athens GA, 1998

Wright, Mike *What They Didn't Teach You About the Civil War*, Presidio Press, Novato CA 1996